The
GhostNet
Intrusion

TOR SVANOE

Dec 11, 2012.

Merry Christmas Mitch!!

Tor.

This book has a literary copyright registered with the
Canadian Intellectual Property Office

ISBN-13: 978-1468012392

ISBN-10: 1468012398

This novel is dedicated to my late partner Susan,
the nicest person I've ever known.

Her inspiration helped me to start this project,
and her constant interest in the book kept it moving forward.
I owe her so much, including this book.
I only wish I could have finished reading it to her.

****

I want to thank my family members and close friends
who continued to read these chapters as they were completed.
Their comments and support really helped
to keep new chapters coming along,
and provided the motivation to finally complete this novel.

****

A special thanks to the talented proof-readers for their
discoveries, thoughtful comments and helpful suggestions.

****

I would also like to thank Gerald M. Chicalo
for his experience, guidance and help
in preparing this book for publication.

****

Thanks as well to Skip Robinson
for the permitted use of his photo on the cover.

www.TheGhostNetIntrusion.com

The
GhostNet
Intrusion

TOR SVANOE

Chapter 1

Jen's inexplicable, automatic cerebral alarm lifted her eyelids seconds before the audio assault of the electric alarm clock was set to begin. As usual. What the hell was up with that anyway, she wondered again? For as long as she could remember, waking up just before the alarm was set to go off was always the norm. After locating and flipping the kill switch like a striking cobra, she settled back into bed to allow the normal transitions, from the fleeting details she could remember of her dream state, to the slow percolation of clues beginning to form a picture of today's reality.

Did everyone go through this morning mental phase, or was it just her? It was like that elusive instant when we enter the invisible door to the dream world. No matter how slowly we walk down our conscious halls towards the door of dreams, we never get to see that damned door at the entrance to our sub-conscious thoughts.

Maybe I've missed the 'Please drop all your conscious realities before approaching this door' sign-post all along. Doesn't mean I won't stop looking. Like a lemming at the ocean...she thought.

Things had been different since returning from her second tour in Iraq. Setting out from Buffalo, New York, she'd made it out west to Portland in thirteen days and was determined to start a 'normal' life, whatever that was. Her interview at 11:00 a.m. this morning was her first real chance at any employment prospects despite the strange ad in the paper.

It had started as a joke when she'd launched a dart at a map on the wall. Two weeks ago, that dart had hit a bull's eye as it struck Portland. Maybe if she had thrown it a little harder she'd be lounging in a beach chair by the ocean. Now that she'd dropped the damage deposit, plus the first and last month's rent, this place was her new home. She had a distant view of the Columbia River from her second-floor bathroom window. A-standing-on-the-seat-view, that is. It was only a partially furnished one bedroom, older and in need of some updates, but at least it was her place. It felt like the Paradise Hilton after living in tents on the desert with thirty people roasting inside a fabric sauna.

FORGET IRAQ! FORGET IRAQ!

Twelve kills isn't easy to forget when you're twenty-three and you were the shooter.

Seven combatants and five innocents were in the wrong place at the wrong time. Did they see that door on the way out, she wondered? Or is that a different door at the end of the 'One Way Only' hall, with the, 'Sorry, No Returns' sign? What really goes through someone's head when they watch and feel the results of a close-range AK-47 shredding their physical universe and soul? Knowing they've just received their return ticket from a calm and deadly serious young American girl.

Watching five friends blown apart when an RPG hit their position, just as she stepped away for three minutes of privacy, wasn't an easy thing to forget. Jen had grown up fast in Iraq; too fast.

She'd started helicopter training at the Fort Wainscot Training Facility right after her first tour and had over a hundred hours of dual and forty-five hours solo time.

"We need you to complete one more tour with Special Operations, due to the current specialist shortage," the Staff Sergeant had said.

Jen had grabbed any chance she could for extra flight training in Iraq, but realised she still had a long way to go to before becoming operational. Landing a large helicopter in a blinding sand storm created by the main rotors was not something you could master during a friendly chat in a small cafe. 8:00 a.m., coffee time—instant coffee time.

Jen had unloaded her dark grey Ford Explorer the night before and managed to cram three boxes of clothes into the two dresser drawers that came with the place. One small closet with four hangers held her coats and one jacket, and would also store a small stack of locked black metal totes. A wooden box of kitchenware was put up in the mostly-empty kitchen cabinets and drawers. The four-piece, assorted color dish set with an extra mug and a few small pots, pans, and utensils would serve her needs for the time being. She could definitely survive in a jungle with her training and a standard issue military knife if need be. Rushing out to start decorating the kitchen wasn't even on the outside edges of her radar screen. One hardboiled egg, an orange, and a cup of instant black would do for breakfast this morning.

The shower pressure was a slow drizzle at best. One of her boxes had a good selection of tools, and within minutes she'd removed the shower head, fished out the water-saving device and drilled out the shower head. A decent cordless driver was her idea of a good kitchen utensil. The shower was now flowing like Niagara Falls and she was happy with that. Something about a strong shower always seemed to bring on a relaxing, meditation-like state, at times ending when she drained the tank dry. Must be some form of payback for all the water deprivation in Iraq.

She, unfortunately, was not a member of any group fighting the regional water shortage problem. She wondered about how many people had lived through their days, unaware or unable to complete a five minute plumbing fix in their own homes. And then of course, how many people would feel they must have dreamed their way into a Five Star Resort to be standing under this shiny metal wonder, with warm clean water raining down luxuriously on their heads. Something millions of people will never know.

Dressing in the only clean khakis and top she had left from her trip, she easily made herself very presentable. Jen was a couple of inches shy of six feet and very fit. She had a great complexion, with medium length dark blond hair and unusually striking cobalt-blue eyes. Anyone who knew her family knew she had acquired them from her mother's side. Her mother's father had been working for the US Embassy in Damascus years ago when he'd married his beautiful young assistant from Syria. That distant family history had given Jen a unique and slightly exotic look. That, combined with great teeth and a warm, disarming smile, had kept her feeling confident in any country. She had heard many interesting stories from her mother about her grandfather's assignments in the Middle East. The historical roots of US dealings in the region had been growing for many years behind many closed doors, and they were unlikely to stop anytime soon.

Nine-thirty—Jen got her jacket, wallet, and cell phone and checked the place over quickly before locking it up. Heading down one flight of stairs and out the door, she was glad to see the Explorer still parked across the street. That truck really needed a wash and she needed a city map. With a little luck she could find a gas station with a car wash and still have time to make the interview by 11:00 a.m. with Doctor James Clayton, 1765 West Cedar Drive, Northern Estates, Portland.

The sky had a stratocumulus ceiling this morning, maybe fifteen hundred feet above sea level with a few low clouds and showers. It had taken ten minutes to find a gas station and now the truck was filled and the fluids checked. No luck finding a car wash, but that could wait with this weather. Studying her new map she realised there was still a considerable drive ahead, but felt she could still make it on time.

The traffic was reasonably light at this hour, and the worst of the winter driving conditions had passed. It was early April, and some signs of spring were showing as the industrial areas gave way to the rural landscape, rolling by her windows. Two more exits and then off the I-5 to the northwest.

The lack of information regarding this job was strange, and she hoped to learn more today. Private Security Assignment; excellent remuneration; resumes only to Box 3412, Portland Herald.

It was ten-thirty when she reached her exit off the I-5. She watched as the higher elevations with tall forested areas gradually became more and more prevalent. She was on a beautiful back-country highway, winding up through the hills towards the Northern Estates area, which was completely devoid of traffic. A spectacular stone and timber structure marked the entrance to the Northern Estates.

West Cedar Drive, according to her map, was the lower route of an upcoming fork in the road. Now and then an occasional opening in the forest would reveal itself, but after a mile or two on the low road things started to open up. Nowhere in her life had she ever seen places like this! These were not just million dollar homes, but massive multimillion dollar estates.

Almost all the driveways where gated and some were guarded with modern surveillance systems. Most of the estates appeared to be about half a mile apart, and she was now starting to get the occasional glimpse of impressive stone and timber mansions set deep in tall stands of mature conifers. Her sense of curiosity was now on full alert as she closed in on the address etched in her mind: 1765 West Cedar Drive. Next left.

Chapter 2

Box 3412 had received 118 resumes. This Doctor James Clayton had no intention of hiring any fools or idiots for this unique and potentially dangerous assignment.

Resumes with any spelling or grammatical errors quickly appeased the insatiable appetite of his new office shredder. No second thoughts. Chronological timeframe gaps, weak grades, lack of references, unsuitable skills, or people just obviously in love with themselves were making a true glutton of his faithful shredder. He wasn't looking for any grade nine dropouts with short careers as nightclub doormen or bouncers likely demoted by their subsequent injuries.

Fourteen resumes had been sent to a leading employment screening company and James was conducting every single inquiry option available from this well-known firm. Dessert was served up to the shredder once the results of the screening had returned. He certainly knew how people could fabricate the truth in their pursuit of self-enrichment. Fortunately he could easily afford the screening fees and didn't want any more hiring regrets.

Three candidates had enough potential to be granted preliminary interviews. Two interviews had been carried out yesterday; one had potential and the other didn't. This wasn't exactly a straight forward task as he had no intention of discussing any details of this assignment. It was simply too confidential to share with someone he might never hire. This position would involve lots of travel and certainly wasn't any normal nine-to-five job with weekends off. At one thousand US a day, plus expenses, he had the right to his own personal selection.

He needed someone with extreme loyalty who was totally committed to the task, available anytime, and paramount of course, was their ability to protect Kyle. The last candidate, Jennifer Lamar, was scheduled for 11:00 a.m., not long from now.

Inevitably, whoever he hired would find out that a bullet had created the new vacant position. It had been almost two years since the shooting on the outskirts of the university grounds. Alexia Clayton and her son Kyle had been escorted to their own personal vehicle by campus security. They were being driven back to the Northern Estates by Kyle's personal guard, Ivan, a trusted Russian friend. It was late in the afternoon with darkening skies and sleet blowing sideways as they approached the intersection. The light had just changed to green about one hundred yards before the crosswalk.

As they drove through the intersection the first shot disintegrated the driver's window and struck Ivan above the ear. He fell forward, slumping over the steering wheel in the last seconds of his life. The next shot struck Alexia in the top of the throat and shattered several vertebrae in her neck as she turned toward Ivan.

Without slowing down, the car suddenly jumped the slushy curb and flew across a small parking lot before crashing through two plate-glass windows and destroying a large display-stand inside a popular video outlet. For a few lucky customers, looking at other films had likely just spared their lives.

Thanks to the immediate assistance and phone calls from the people in the store the emergency response crews had arrived within minutes and Alexia was rushed to the nearest emergency department. The police had picked up Kyle and put him in the back seat of their cruiser for questioning. Ivan, now officially DOA, was being transported by a second ambulance to the university morgue.

Kyle, being strapped in the back seat, was uninjured, but he remembered every second of that event as clearly as he remembered virtually anything that entered his field of vision. This memory clearly included the face of a man with silver eyeglasses and wearing a dark winter coat, as he fired two shots in rapid succession from a small revolver in his outstretched hand. They were overtaking Ivan on his left side and driving a dark blue sedan without plates. What Kyle knew, and what he'd disclose, was any one's guess. What the shooter didn't know was that every detail of his face had been permanently locked into Kyle's mind after only a split second glance.

Doctor James Clayton was a well-respected trauma surgeon throughout the city of Portland. When he got the call about Alexia he simply couldn't leave his team. Patients were still coming in from a bad accident on the I-5, including three very young, critically injured children. He knew the people working at the university hospital were doing everything possible for Alexia. She'd worked for the university as a professor in the Quantum Mechanics Department, primarily in the engineering research labs, for almost five years. At thirty-eight years of age, her life would certainly never be the same again.

When James finally made it to the University Hospital Emergency Center, the prognosis wasn't good. Alexia appeared to be almost completely paralyzed from the spinal cord damage she had sustained and remained in a coma inside the ICU. He was devastated.

After consulting with the attending physicians and studying the images from the CT scan, Doctor Clayton knew his wife Alexia would unfortunately be in the ICU for a long, long time. Ivan's body was being held for an almost certain autopsy. A police investigation was already underway with a small group of senior homicide investigators.

Five months after the shooting Alexia was still in the hospital; her future as a quadriplegic was all but certain. The destruction of her larynx and the spinal area below her brain stem was just too complex to expect any further improvements. A team of top US neurosurgeons had met for three days of collaborations and had been unable to find any further options or surgical procedures that would improve her condition. She'd been finally upgraded to stable, but would continue to require full-time care for years.

The police investigation had also dragged on for months. After wasting hundreds of thousands of dollars they continued to call the case a 'random drive-by shooting'.

An autopsy was performed on Ivan that concluded that the gunshot to his brain was the primary contributing factor in his fatality and all the subsequent secondary crash injuries likely occurred after death. No measurable quantities of illegal drugs or alcohol were detected in his blood.

Although Kyle could have offered additional information, he was curious to see just how proficient a city's police force really was. There was obviously no way he could undo the shooting or change the fate of Ivan or Alexia caused by this unforeseen event. Yes, this was just a simple evaluation of their collective crime solving skills; a test. Something he was continually required to do. Besides, if they failed the test he would simply revisit the relevant case details and solve that problem later on in life. He already knew, from listening to his father's vocalized telephone discussions with a certain detective, that an explanation of a 'random drive-by shooting' would not be considered a 'passing grade.'

Six years ago James and Alexia had suspected from very early on that something was different about Kyle. As a baby his huge blue-grey eyes had an intensity to them that was difficult not to notice. His concentrated, unblinking gaze had triggered various optometry tests in his first few months. All results clearly supported the conclusion that everything concerning his vision and optic structures appeared normal. Although the optometrist had agreed with the fact that Kyle's overly intensive focus and lack of blinking were unusual, he couldn't detect any physical abnormalities.

Still, James and Alexia were now convinced that Kyle was not developing in a way anyone would consider 'normal'. As he physically learned to pronounce sounds he began pronouncing any words he heard in context. They soon realized that he was actually remembering all the words he'd heard. He had a good appetite, but slept very little. His crying was virtually nonexistent as long as he was listening to people talking or watching educational DVDs.

By the age of two it was confirmed that he was not only reading, but had an extreme hunger for new information. Kyle would tell you immediately if he had seen that DVD before or even if you'd told him something for a second time. In the absence of DVDs, James had purchased educational CD sets that were kept running overnight at a low volume. Any questions concerning information played during the previous night were calmly and correctly answered the following day. Kyle was actually able to learn and retain information from simply listening during his sleep.

By the age of three, James and Alexia had decided to hire a part-time elementary school tutor. Later, and on her recommendation, arrangements were proceeding for Kyle to officially challenge the knowledge requirements needed to pass grades one through seven. They would take place in four months and he would be allowed to challenge them sequentially until he was unable to pass a grade. The examinations occurred over a four-day period and he easily passed all seven grades. His marks were comparable with those of the top percentile of regular students in the public school system. One of the most interesting observations in the analyses of the test results was that the few topics left unanswered were on material the tutor had failed to cover. People were becoming very interested in Kyle, and at four years of age he was a confirmed member in Mensa. The upper limit of his IQ was not yet known, but the fact he was 'in the club' was beyond dispute.

Several new tutors where hired over the next two years in preparation for another sequential challenge. This was to include most high school courses, including math and the sciences. Once again his results were astonishing; he completed all the exams with marks between ninety-six and one hundred percent. At the time of his sixth birthday he was officially the youngest known high school graduate with near perfect grades.

Kyle simply did not forget things and the scope of his abilities and potential continued to generate extreme interest, both locally and worldwide. James and Alexia were having difficulty separating Kyle from his continuing thirst for knowledge. As an interim solution they'd agreed to let him tag along with Alexia to her university lab, and shortly afterwards the shooting had occurred.

Interest in Kyle from universities and companies around the world was now intense. James had agreed to a secret US Government proposal that would involve Kyle attending six different universities in the United States and Canada. It would be a custom, two year master's degree program with a highly specialized curriculum.

The university curriculum would be designed specifically to help determine the exact area of Kyle's most gifted abilities. Following the two years of university a specialized two year program involving rotational short term collaborations at leading scientific research facilities would commence. When Doctor Clayton and Kyle had agreed to this quiet arrangement it was not without reward. This was, in fact, a secret scholarship, designed and structured by upper levels of the US Government. Direct escalating deposits to Doctor Clayton, and an additional trust fund established for Kyle, would begin at two million US per year.

James again reflected on the current candidates applying for this position. He liked the man he had interviewed the day before, but he was also still anxious to meet Jennifer Lamar. That fact that she had shot some non-combatants was troubling, but as with any report of this nature, there's always two sides to every story.

His wife was now living her life in a wheelchair inside the new ground floor addition. This was a specialized addition, built to accommodate her needs and attached to the west side of the main house. Alexia had never regained her brain or speech functions and two full-time nurses now resided in attendant's quarters, built as part of the new addition.

James was still busy working as a trauma surgeon and he needed someone here soon. Kyle was preparing to defend his master's thesis on particle physics at the University of Western British Columbia and was expected back here next week. He would be escorted home by US Government security agents, and after that, his new candidate would take over. James had never believed the 'random drive-by' theory in connection with the shooting and continued to be very concerned for his son's safety.

Checking his watch, he realized the intriguing Ms. Lamar should be arriving any minute.

Chapter 3

Driving alongside a tall stone wall for almost a mile was shifting Jen's senses into overdrive. She started slowing down when she saw the opening up ahead and turned the Explorer into the driveway entrance, easing it up to the large wrought iron gates.

Most of the rockwork was gradually losing the battle with the ivy cascading over the top of the wall. A small bronze intercom faceplate was set in the granite stonework about ten feet before the gate. On top of the adjacent wall she noticed a pair of motion sensors, as well as a remote camera system, also mounted on the wall. She rolled down the window, reached out and pushed the call buzzer.

"Yes," said the voice over the speaker.

"Is this Doctor Clayton?" asked Jen while pressing the call button.

"No. Is he expecting you?" replied the voice.

"Yes, my name is Jennifer Lamar and I have an appointment with him at eleven this morning."

"Just a moment please," replied the voice from the wall.

Several minutes passed before she heard "please wait until the gate is completely open and then park in the second parking area on the right. Someone will meet you and escort you to the front door of the main house. Please remain in your vehicle once it's parked."

The iron gates separated in the center; each half rolling slowly out to the sides. The driveway was laid with rustic terracotta pavers and meandered up the hill through the spacious mature forest surrounding fantastic lawns and rock gardens. A few small ponds were visible around the property, in this stellar example of natural landscape design.

Flowering cherry trees and dwarf Japanese maples complimented each other as they revealed themselves throughout the garden's trees and ponds. The diversity of colors and the many different types of plants made her feel like she should've paid an 'admission' just to enter this place.

Several buildings were now coming into view. They all had a stunning stone and timber frame design with a huge two-story main house further up the drive. Off to the right appeared to be a residential work shop or a similar type of a structure. It was apparent there was more than one boy mowing lawns around here as it would take a small army of various landscaping personnel to maintain a property as large and beautiful as this one.

After driving past the first parking area she was now approaching the main building. This was a huge two-story structure with four stone chimneys. The majestic design of the building must have been created by a gifted architect, with this address being another prize in his portfolio.

It had a massive timber frame drive-through entrance area with four huge iron and glass hanging lights suspended from above. Stained glass set amongst giant timbers climbed high up the walls around the two massive hand-carved doors of the main entrance. Turning into what appeared to be the second parking area—Jen parked her car and regretted not getting a car-wash this morning.

As she sat in the truck she was suddenly startled by the appearance of three silent visitors. She hadn't seen any animals on the estate, but in this instant, and from out of nowhere, she was now surrounded by three, tall black dogs of a breed she had never seen before. They were completely silent and studied her intently as she sat inside the truck. Even with all of her training, the fact that anything could get that close to her without her knowing about it was a shock in itself. Then, as if by some silent command, this mysterious pack of dogs instantly resumed their patrol and vanished into the trees without a sound. She glanced at the house and noticed a lady in a window waving her over to the main doors.

Walking up to the main entrance, she felt as if she was about to start her dream ski vacation.

From the variety of stone on the walkways and on the sides of the building it was clear they must have come from many different locations. The doors had an intricate relief carving depicting an old growth forest scene carved out of huge dimensional cedar slabs. The obvious skill and talent of the carver, with his choice of wood and stains, was further complimented by the impressive bronze door fittings selected for this home. As she was about to try the door chime one door began to slowly open.

"Ms. Lamar, please come in. Doctor Clayton is expecting you," said the lady who answered the door. The height of the ceilings, and artistry of the timber work, just about took her breath away.

"Thank you so much," replied Jen in the sweetest tone she could. A fire was burning in a large fireplace across the room, in yet another beautiful example of a stone mason's skill.

"It's a pleasure to meet you, Ms. Lamar. My name's Lisa."

"Hi Lisa, please, just call me Jen."

"May I take your coat, Jen?"

"Sure. Thanks. This is quite a place here," Jen replied.

"It most certainly is. Shall I introduce you to Doctor Clayton?"

"Yes, thank you," she replied as she felt the butterflies in her stomach preparing to take flight.

They walked together down a church-like hallway with cathedral-style timber frame arches and impressive stone floors. Lisa stopped at the first set of doors, knocked twice, and they both heard a distant "Come in."

"Ms. Lamar is here for her interview Doctor Clayton. Shall I send her in?"

"Yes, please do. Thanks Lisa," said the doctor.

Jen walked into the spacious office and saw Doctor Clayton writing at his desk. She approached the desk as he stood up with an outstretched hand.

"Pleased to meet you Ms. Lamar, so glad you could make it."

"Please, just call me Jen," she said as they shook hands. At that instant a wall clock made its eleven o'clock chime.

"Punctual. I like that," said the doctor. "Have a seat."

Jen sat down in one of the two very comfortable dark leather chairs facing his desk.

"Any trouble finding my place?" asked the doctor.

"No, not after I bought a city map," Jen replied. "It's such an impressive place you have here!"

James was already mentally sizing up this Ms. Lamar. As they say; you only have one chance to make a first impression. She truly was a beautiful and fit looking woman and he already liked her easy going confident nature.

"We think so. My wife and I have been developing this property for about twelve years now."

"Well Doctor Clayton, can you give me any more information about this employment position? The ad in the paper was a little vague."

"Intentionally so," said the doctor. "I suppose I can tell you it involves keeping an eye out for my son." James liked the continuing contact with those dark blue eyes.

"Keeping an eye out for him in what sense?" she asked.

"In a security sense—he'll require an escort for some traveling during the next couple of years."

"Is your son in some type of danger?"

"Details of that nature will be discussed with the successful applicant," replied the doctor.

"May I ask how old your son is Doctor Clayton?"

"Yes. He's eight years old," replied the doctor.

"Well, that's certainly a little young to be travelling on your own," she said.

"It is," agreed the doctor.

"Where will he be travelling?" asked Jen.

"It should be mostly in the United States. Those details will be discussed with the successful applicant," said the doctor once more.

"So it sounds like you're really looking for a full-time, long-term commitment for this position," she said.

"Yes, sometimes more so than others, but you'll need complete availability and a willingness to travel anywhere at any time," replied the doctor.

"Would I continue to live in the city?" she asked.

"You could keep your place if you wanted, but you would also have a place here on the estate."

"I'm not sure I could afford that," she said.

"Any and all expenses of the successful applicant will be covered, as well as an excellent remuneration package," said the doctor.

Jen was becoming more interested by the second. She definitely wanted this job. Right now she wanted this job maybe even more than a flying job.

"From what I've heard so far, Dr. Clayton, I can say that I'm extremely interested in this position," trying to sound her professional best.

"Tell me about how you ended up killing some non-combatants in Iraq," he asked from out of nowhere. Jen could feel her life-blood falling from her face. How the hell could he know about that? Those were sealed, confidential military files.

Without a flinch, she said, "My partner and I had just entered a small warehouse looking for the source of recent persistent gunfire during the day. It was poorly lit and filled with various equipment and barrels. During our search an insurgent rolled out from behind a machine firing his weapon. After the ensuing gun battle we regrettably discovered that we had also killed several other people who were living in the warehouse."

James considered the scenario and knew that stories like that probably happened every day somewhere in this world, and especially now in Iraq. "War is never what you expect," he said.

Jen didn't dare ask how he knew this. "I've heard you've done some helicopter training with the military," said the doctor.

"Yes, I've completed all my basic training here, and then I was asked to return for another tour," she said.

"How did you like learning to fly?" asked the doctor.

"It was the best thing that ever happened to me in the forces. Just sorry I wasn't able to fly over there."

"That can have its dangers as well," he replied, as if speaking from experience.

"That's true," she said.

Jen was impressed by Dr. Clayton's cool, intelligent demeanour. He seemed about fifty, tall, and looked like a runner. He was wearing a casual grey sweater over a light blue cotton shirt with a closely trimmed salt and pepper beard. A short moment of silence followed and she wondered if he was about to offer her a job.

"Is your son here?" she regretted asking.

"No, he's out of the country right now."

James then rose from his chair. "It was a pleasure talking with you, Ms. Lamar. Jen—I expect to reach a decision in the next day or two. I'll let you know as soon as possible."

Relieved, and with her most confident smile she said, "Thank you so much Doctor Clayton. The pleasure was all mine," as they shook hands once again.

James was surprised by the strength of her grip. "I have to go out Jen, but I insist you allow Lisa to prepare you some lunch before you leave," said the doctor as they both walked out to the hall.

"That's very kind of you. Thank you very much!"

Jen was starving and didn't want to leave this place one minute sooner than she had to. James walked Jen through the main living area and over to the main kitchen entrance. Opening the door and smiling at Lisa he said, "I hope you don't mind, I have a surprise lunch guest for you Lisa," and waved them both good bye.

"Of course not, have a great day," Lisa replied.

One look around this kitchen told Jen it was built like the rest of the house; a walk-in freezer, a walk-in cooler, several dishwashers, and a towering stainless steel hood mounted over two gas ranges, for starters. A maple prep island was located in the center of the room and a large selection of pots and utensils hanging above the counters gave it a very professional look. "Would you like something to drink?" Lisa asked.

"Sure, coffee would nice, thanks." Lisa poured her a large mug of fresh coffee and Jen fixed it up with flavoured creams and sugar.

"What would you like for lunch—how about a soup and sandwich maybe?"

"Sounds great," she replied.

"Make yourself comfortable out in the main room, or up in the loft if you like. I'll bring you out a tray shortly."

"Okay. Thanks Lisa."

Jen hadn't really noticed the carved curving staircase and its details before. After climbing the stairs she entered a large upper room with several leather couches and comfortable chairs. Most of the perimeter of the room was covered in book cases filled with enough books to stock a small library. Several carved coffee tables were set down on throw carpets on the stained wooden floors. Relaxing into a soft leather chair with her coffee she thought about her morning and all the missing parts of Doctor Clayton's story.

Lisa came up the stairs and placed the lunch tray on the table. "Let me know if you there's anything else you need."

That's unlikely, she thought, as she glanced at the tray. "Thanks, this looks great!"

"Come and see me when you're done, and I'll let you out the main door."

"Okay I will. Thanks again Lisa."

James thought about the interview as he drove into town. Maybe he shouldn't have asked her about shooting the non-combatants. He wanted to see her reaction to what would have been a bombshell question to most. Was she the type to question his authority? Really, she had handled it well. There was no doubt she would've been shocked by the fact that he had that information, but it hardly showed when he watched her response.

James had a dossier on her almost two inches thick with every shred of information the U.S. government, CIA, or the military had ever acquired concerning Ms. Lamar. He knew her educational grades, college marks, and flight training results. Details of all weapons, survival, first aid, search and rescue and martial arts training were also included. Scores of comments and recommendations written inside that dossier was why she was still on his list. He knew that acquiring this dossier was most certainly facilitated by the government's very keen interest in Kyle.

Should it be him or her—he wondered to himself.

The 'him' was a slightly older ex operative from Blackerwater, a group of private military contractors that hire themselves out to various governments, the CIA in this case. He had spent several years in Iraq providing personal security for civilian contractors working on telecommunication facilities. Not exactly high profile targets, but with the recent escalation of foreign contractors disappearing in Iraq every foreigner was a potential target. He had been involved in three abduction attempts in four years, successfully protecting his men in two roadside shoot outs, with three insurgents killed.

During the third and last abduction attempt he had been shot twice. While he was escorting three male clients home, a roadside bomb had flipped their vehicle: one man was killed instantly and the other two were abducted. He had taken a grazing shot to the head and a direct hit in his upper arm. Left for dead, he was hanging upside down by his seat belt pressed up against the dead front seat passenger. After a week of unsuccessful negotiations with their captors, the other two men disappeared, fates unknown.

In some ways, the 'him' definitely had more experience in direct ambush situations, but then again, so had Ivan. Rest in Peace.

Jen needed that lunch more than she realized. She had sensed Doctor Clayton's reluctance to provide information during the interview, but maybe that was normal. Maybe she was one of ten applicants. How was she to know?

Had Lisa been serving other applicants lunch for the last two weeks? How did they afford this place? Where was his wife? How could he have known anything about her military history?

She had enough questions to write a book. With another glance around she thought: who has two thousand books in their loft? The Clayton family certainly did. Really, she had only slightly more information now than before she arrived.

Despite the unknowns she did like the doctor. He appeared very intelligent and must have had his reasons for keeping things so confidential. "Details will be discussed with the successful applicant," again replayed in her mind.

Not wanting to overstay her welcome she picked up her tray and went down to the kitchen.

"Thanks, Jen. Just drop the tray anywhere and I'll get your jacket for you," said Lisa.

"Lunch was great. I wasn't expecting that." Jen thought about quizzing Lisa, but decided against it.

As Lisa opened the main door she instructed Jen, "Please stay on the pavers and walk directly to your truck, and remember to stay inside your vehicle at all times until you're outside the gates."

"Okay, I will," Jen replied, and waved goodbye.

As she walked down toward her truck she noticed an addition off the main building. Although it was some distance away, it looked like a lady in a wheelchair, wearing some form of neck brace, was sitting right up against the window. She seemed to be staring directly at her and watching her every move.

Expecting the trio of dogs to appear any instant, she quickly started the Explorer and drove towards the gate. The sensors had calculated her arrival and the gates began to open as she approached. They started closing immediately after she drove through and she turned right on to West Cedar Drive for her trip back to Portland.

Later on, if she happened to find an Internet cafe, she would try to put a name to those mysterious dogs. They looked like a breed of giant black Dobermans on steroids.

Chapter 4

Thermonuclear fusion power is to modern man as fire was to our stone-age ancestors. Back then the use and control of fire separated animals from mankind. These days the fusion race has been running, worldwide, for decades. The definition of limitless energy is when a controlled fusion reaction creates more energy than is required to start it, the 'Holy Grail.'

Our Sun will generate one-hundred-million times as much energy in one second as the entire planet uses in one year. Conversely, harnessing all the energy produced by the sun for ten seconds would meet the energy requirements of planet Earth for the next billion years.

Professor Kavi Akkaim knew this and so did his team. Being the first to successfully exploit this 'Holy Grail' would separate them from the rest of mankind. Professor Akkaim had been recruited years ago from India to lead and direct the complex development efforts of RA-9. This was a group of nine countries, spurned in their efforts to be included in the international fusion project known as Frontier International Thermo Experimental Reactor.

The sun god 'Ra' was chosen as the spiritual deity to guide the combined efforts of all nine countries and led to the present name of their group, RA-9. A secret underground facility close to the Iranian border had remained undetected throughout the invasion of Iraq. Modifications of existing reinforced bomb shelters had provided an ideal location for the fusion facility, as well as a state-of-the-art underground cyber espionage center. Further expansion into depleted oil caverns was continually ongoing using a mobile material extraction system that converted waste into a sediment slurry that could be pumped to other locations by converted underground pipelines.

A small underground concrete facility, utilizing emission sequestration technology, supplied most of the daily construction requirements. Vehicle entrance points for both access tunnels were well-hidden in two separate locations; both within ten miles of the facility. The entrance points were concealed within two large warehouses and utilised modified carrier-style lifts. These had the ability to lower construction vehicles into the staging areas of the subterranean road system.

An older tunnel boring machine was being used in the construction of a small-scale underground rail system that had been under construction for the last four years. That system would eventually have three access points; two built within the basements of different office buildings, and the third; underneath a modern manufacturing plant. Several small electric trains were beginning to service some of the underground requirements involving the movement of personnel and supplies. The facility also included a network of vertical emergency evacuation tubes however they mainly functioned as primary air induction inlets for the sophisticated underground air purification and conditioning systems.

Lessons learned from the deployment of U.S. bunker busting bombs during the Iraq invasion had fundamentally changed the ongoing design plans for the RA-9 facility. The initial lateral expansion plans had evolved into a new descending, vertical development. Three separate, but interconnected, levels now existed and construction of the largest and deepest fourth level was well underway. Level one contained the cyber espionage labs. Level two was the self-contained personnel accommodation area capable of housing over two hundred people.

Various isolated chambers, as well as the original fusion reaction chamber and containment blankets, were located on the third level adjacent to constantly-developing physics labs. Design and construction of the large Tokomak, a huge toroidal magnetic containment device, had been facilitated by the continuing success of a dedicated team of cyber intrusion experts. The methodical advancements in backdoor system exploitation via phone and Internet lines deployed a break-through sleeping nano virus that continued to remain undetected in all the various infected computer systems worldwide.

The current Tokomak mirrored the early Russian designs that became available after Professor Akkaim's cyber espionage team successfully penetrated the Russian Tokomak computer systems. A Tokomak design was chosen over other designs, such as the Stellarator that used external magnetic fields for plasma containment. Although useful in research, many problems continued to plague these designs for use in power generation. They had temperature limitations that require the use of lighter atoms for fusion reactions. The problem of containing fusion waste continued to undermine these designs. If higher temperatures could be achieved, heavier atoms could be used, which produced less waste.

The K-Z5 machine at Skandonia International Laboratories has produced temperatures up to 6.6 billion degrees Fahrenheit, but has no means to contain the plasma of a fusion reaction for power generation.

In 2008, the National Petawatt Laser fired up and became the most powerful laser ever built in the U.S. Both of these facilities were of intense interest to RA-9, but by far the most important of all was the Central Fusion Research Complex 8 (CFRC-8) currently under construction in the Frontier National Laboratories, located in Livermore, California.

The computer espionage teams of RA-9 constantly focused their activities to further infiltrate these and other facilities, with sophisticated computer-generated spyware probes. The largest cyber success so far involved deflecting host spyware detection systems to ghost IP addresses throughout China. The existing deflection effort code named 'GhostNet' had been working beyond all expectations.

Infiltration of the Frontier International Thermo Experimental Reactor (FITER) project's mainframe computer system four years ago had been a celebrated victory. This consortium of five participating countries; China, France, Japan, Russia and the US, had after many years, reached a decision to build an experimental reactor in France. After six months of studying the FITER plan in great detail, a decision had been made; Professor Akkaim and his group would follow a different path.

Level four of this facility was being built to almost exactly the same specifications as the laser ignition facility; CFRC-8 in the US. This design required a huge area with hundreds of amplified lasers focused on a single point. Calculations have shown that targeting a tiny gold hohlraum containing a fusion fuel pellet the size of a pencil eraser could replicate the fusion conditions at the center of a star. Each and every amplified laser in the facility was precisely aimed at the hohlraum, and together they would fire a massive computer-controlled, split-second burst of energy directed at the target. The resulting fusion reaction caused by the X- Ray burst from the two isotopes within the gold target conditions would allow detailed thermonuclear fusion studies to be conducted within the confines of the laboratory.

Problems concerning the conversion of a fusion reaction to electricity remained, but undeterred, the RA-9 facility was now well under construction. At this stage ongoing cyber penetration was critical to the success of RA-9's laser fusion program. During the last two years cyber security had been increasing in sophistication. Private companies and most university labs continued to be easy targets, but the ramped-up security of US defence research labs was causing unacceptable delays. Fortunately the 'GhostNet' was still diverting all system intrusion investigations back to China.

The RA-9 computer labs had remained undetected, thanks mostly to the many brilliant minds working there. Professor Akkaim had acquired an admirable team of dedicated engineers and scientists supplied from within the nine countries of RA-9. The procurement division of RA-9 had well-established connections throughout various manufacturing and transportation sectors of its member countries. One dedicated manufacturing plant had been built nearby to grow and cut the large KDP crystals needed for the fusion project. Passing infrared lasers through the KDP crystals converted the infrared light to ultraviolet light and created much more favourable results when striking the fusion fuel target.

The manufacture and procurement of complex parts and materials required by the new level-four development was unfortunately grinding to a halt. Everything depended on the cyber espionage superiority of the RA-9 computer team. They had to continually provide the classified design information needed to build and manufacture all the various components required for the RA-9 laser fusion program.

The human resource procurement division had proved to be a vital component of the RA-9 complex. The back channel recruitment routes of member countries had produced some promising talent from various universities and research labs. These were paid contract positions within the RA-9 complex and these personnel comprised about sixty percent of the working research staff. The main problem was that this was the first facility of its kind ever built in the region, and being classified curtailed the use of all normal and worldwide recruitment campaigns. Cyber espionage delays often mandated the call for direct action procurement of required specialists.

Professor Akkaim was expecting a call on today's date from Sinzar Bakkir; head of the RA-9 human resource procurement division. Nothing would be said. The time of the call was the code. Sinzar Bakkir would pick up the professor's 'wish list' from different pre-set global locations every four weeks like clockwork. The 'wish list' would include the names and relevant information on who RA-9 required, and their level of priority. Rewards and reporting dates, along with information regarding associated motivation targets, was also included.

RA-9 would always double Sinzar Bakkir's financial reward whenever a motivation target was taken along with the required scientist or engineer. Motivation targets where generally children or direct family members of the new recruits, but not always. It was most certainly known that the efficiency of new RA-9 recruits almost doubled when a motivation target was taken as well.

The people abducted for motivational purposes were required to produce a vast array of pre-recorded messages that RA-9 kept on file to help motivate the new recruits. The new workers would generally be allowed one phone call every six months to their loved ones. The technicians monitoring the call could quickly select and play the appropriate response from hundreds of pre-recorded options. Calls were kept brief and could be terminated at any time by RA-9 technicians. The motivation program was simple but effective, as the loyalty of newly kidnapped scientists was never assured. Fates of the motivators varied once the required response recordings had been completed. Often it wasn't even necessary to ship them to the facility, as long as the response recordings had taken place and there wasn't any doubt in the minds of new recruits about exactly who was caring for their loved ones.

Sinzar Bakkir rubbed the sleep from his eyes as the slow motion of the boat kept pulling him back to his dreams. The hypnotic pull towards the fading dream state was difficult to resist as the boat crested each wave with the steady time of a metronome. Enticing thoughts were pulling his mind to somewhere nice, and he was slipping—slipping away—gone. Sometime later on and for no reason in particular—he forced his eyes open a second time, shook his head and snapped out of it.

It was time to wake the hired help and pull up the anchor. Today was reporting day. The time code reporting system was working well. Conversations of this nature simply could not take place over normal phone or satellite links. This was simply a progress report for Professor Akkaim's sake, and he could always send or request details during the next 'wish list' pick-ups.

Professor Akkaim had requested several new electrical engineers to assist in the electrical upgrades necessary for the laser fusion project. Sinzar Bakkir was grateful for the RA-9 document division and the vast amount of resources at his disposal. This certainly enhanced his freedom and ability to move around the globe while conducting various RA-9 affairs.

It had taken him almost three weeks to track down this renowned electrical engineer who was vacationing in a tiny village on the western coast of Mexico. Fortunately his wife, who was on the motivator list, was also with him. Working with two young assistants, and a tried and proven knock out drug, they were both quickly extracted from the grass thatch beach hut.

Tranquilizer cocktails fired from a powerful dart pistol made quick work of incapacitating the pair. Shooting them through the open windows as they slept was usually safer than risking any defensive fire from a direct entry. Under the cover of darkness they were quickly loaded in the small life boat which glided quietly through the water on its way back to the anchored cabin cruiser.

Sinzar Bakkir and his assistants tightly wrapped and immobilized the two new guests with rolls of industrial shrink-wrap while they were still unconscious. Each captive had several flex tubes, and a modified face mask and mounted snorkel, placed in their face; all securely held in place with multiple layers of shrink-wrap and duct tape.

It was mandatory that the new engineer saw his motivator in captivity before he could be shipped to RA-9. Sinzar Bakkir was using newly recruited local help on this job and would retain them for most of the voyage. They still had an all-day boat trip further down the coast where he would hand over his new bounty. The engineer would be crated and flown back to RA-9 and his wife was destined for a recording studio in Mexico City. "Does it get any easier than this?" he caught himself saying out loud.

The new guests awoke four hours after their abduction. Water bottles taped securely to the upper body should keep the two plastic cocoons alive. Thin plastic tubing with one way check valves were routed through the shrink-wrap and in to their mouths. After seeing they had taken a few drinks from the tube, Sinzar decided to inject them again, knocking them out for the next stage of the voyage.

A beautiful sunrise was unfolding as they started the trip south. Sinzar Bakkir had an easy day ahead and planned to arrive at the small marina two hours after sunset. Fortunately the tanks were full and the boat was running well. The size of the waves increased as they moved offshore, but his two assistants were handling the boat like skilled sea captains. Sinzar Bakkir went down below and reloaded both tranquilizer pistols and his favourite small-calibre handgun.

Memorizing the phone time codes had taken him several days when RA-9 initially started the program. He would place the call this afternoon, between fifteen and twenty minutes after two p.m. P.S.T. Professor Akkaim would know from the time of the call that the new recruit was being shipping by air freight on the following day, and also that the motivator would be remaining in the country.

Sinzar Bakkir made sure the phones where charged and the cocoons where still breathing. His contact tonight was a trusted police officer with long-term ties to the local drug cartels. The cocoons would be crated and loaded onto trucks for shipping. Sinzar Bakkir could start to relax knowing he had used this connection before without any problems.

Taking his satellite phones and the last three Corona's topside, he offered each of the locals a beer and made himself comfortable. This job was as good as done. He'd picked up both his targets as well as the motivators on the last 'wish list.' Watching the time carefully, Sinzar Bakkir made his call at sixteen minutes after two p.m. P.S.T. Once the third ring had been confirmed, that was all he needed to know; the message had been received.

Later in the afternoon he decided to give both cocoons another injection before they woke up. He heated up some soup for the three of them and promised his helpers dinner at the marina. Five miles from the marina, just after a beautiful sunset—Sinzar Bakkir shot both unsuspecting helpers at close range with tranquilizer darts. A pistol in each hand, he fired simultaneously into their backs as darkness fell. He had carefully mixed a fast-acting drug that caused them both to drop immediately. Sinzar went down below and pulled out the two large cinder blocks supporting the lowest shelf in the galley. Lugging them topside, he wired one block to each helper, tight at the neck, and slipped them overboard. As he was watching them sink head first below the waves he reflected on the loss of small pawns in this ongoing chess game. Security precautions for the success of RA-9 were constantly required.

Sinzar Bakkir now had the marina in sight and slowly manoeuvred the boat towards the small pier. One large slip was vacant and he could see the small truck parked alongside as he slowly guided the old cruiser into the berth. His overweight contact, standing on the dimly lit pier, helped him secure the mooring lines.

They waited for a short time to confirm all was quiet before they moved the cocoons up and into the back of the truck. The water bottles were refilled and the flex tubing re-inserted into each snorkel mouthpiece. Several new layers of shrink-wrap were wound tightly around the heads to hold the air and water tubes in place. As long as they were immobile, silent, and hydrated, they would live for some time, provided the temperatures weren't too extreme.

Sinzar Bakkir's connection had brought both shipping crates and the appropriate documentation so the loading was quickly completed. The girl would likely be transferred to a reefer truck and shipped only at night, and the engineer would be on a plane within hours. The cartel associates and other RA-9 transport agents all knew that bonus funds were never paid for DOA shipments.

Satisfied, Sinzar Bakkir untied the boat and pushed it back off the pier. Starting up the inboard he pulled away from the dock and set a slow course back up the coast. After several hours he killed the engine and dropped anchor. Sleep was calling from the bottom of the boat. Ten days from now his new instructions would be waiting in Santa Monica, California.

Chapter 5

Doctor Clayton didn't like the mayhem going on in the ER department tonight. They were almost always short of staff, but tonight's additional shortages were going to be costly; likely resulting in additional lives lost. Five ambulances had just arrived within the last ten minutes. A faulty train signal had caused a direct collision between a loaded van and a fast moving freight train. Paramedics using the Jaws of Life worked feverishly to extract the dead and those clinging to life. A total of nine people had finally been pried from the mangled remnants of the van and wrecked metal destroyed by the train.

He had privately developed his own five second assessment. First impressions do matter, especially to trauma surgeons; survivable or non-survivable. It's always tough to go through the motions when your patient has failed the trauma surgeon's five second assessment.

Doctor Clayton felt like the final gatekeeper, the 'Sorry, no returns' man. He had pronounced four people DOA and three others had failed his five second assessment. One of them had lasted almost twenty minutes. Seven new bodies for the morgue and two girls listed as 'critical' in the Intensive Care Unit. After two hours of surgery and close to three hundred stitches, as well as the extensive removal of embedded metal and glass, they were now on the edge; the edge of life and death.

"Dr. Clayton, call waiting on line two if you're available," echoed through the operating room. He pulled off his blood-soaked coat, mask and gloves and sat down in the adjacent office.

Tapping the line two selector—he picked up the phone and said, "Doctor Clayton here. How can I help you?"

"I can think of lots of ways, Dad."

"Kyle! Where are you?"

"Do you want specific terms?" Kyle replied.

"No, general terms are fine."

"Okay then. I'm beside an imitation stone counter in the northwest corner of the UWBC library on the third floor."

"Do you have an escort?" asked James.

"Yes, two at the moment," Kyle replied while casually studying the armed guards at his table.

"Did you get your master's degree?"

"Is it 'silly question time'?"

"Congratulations! When are you coming home?"

"I'll be home in about eighty-six hours."

"That's great!" said James as he made a note of the time. "How was your night?"

"Are you asking in specific or general terms?"

"General terms are fine," Kyle replied.

"Busy. Not the greatest."

"LDR?" asked Kyle.

"Two over seven," said James.

Kyle knew that it must be hard for his father to lose seven out of nine patients in one shift.

"Sorry to hear that Dad."

James didn't like exposing Kyle to all the details of his work, and the Life-Death-Ratio had become their abbreviated form of the father-to-son trauma center report.

"Have you received my internship schedule yet?"

"Not yet Kyle, I got a call last week and we've agreed to meet soon and finalize your schedule for the year."

"So, do I have any time off then?"

"He mentioned two or three weeks anyway."

"Why so long?" asked Kyle.

"It's what people do Kyle. We'll find something for you to do."

"Dad, have you hired my personal escort yet?"

"I'm in the process of making that decision," James replied.

"What's to decide? Just hire Jen."

"How do you know about her?" asked James, shocked.

"Sorry Dad, you know how much I like hacking when I'm bored."

"So, you've hacked into my computer system? Kyle, are you still there?"

"Yes twice. Do you know why she's the best candidate?"

James was aware that Kyle could have hacked into his system as easily as any kid could take cookies from a jar. Not only that, but by now he'd most likely read and memorized both dossiers and effortlessly subjected them to the highest level of logical comparative analysis.

"No Kyle. Why should I hire Jen?"

"It's simple—she has a helicopter license and you have a helicopter."

"I don't need a personal pilot. I usually fly myself."

"That's true, but it's what tips the scale in her favour. You might not need a full time pilot, but with her you'll get protection for me and a potential pilot for your machine."

"Well, that's a good point. There may well be medevac or other occasions when it may be beneficial. I'll sleep on it and make a decision before you get back."

"Don't burn your bridges with the other guy when you let him down."

"I won't," he said without thinking. "Look Kyle, just how long did it take you to hack in to my computer system?"

"Forty-four seconds," Kyle replied.

"I don't know what to tell you about that. We'll discuss it further when you get back home."

"Sorry, it's an addiction. You know I can't resist the challenge."

"So you've hacked into other systems?"

"Is it silly question time again?"

"Okay, as I said, we'll talk about this some more after you get back," said James as he checked the time.

"Sure Dad, one more thing."

"Yes."

"I'm not the first one to infiltrate your computer system."

"What are you talking about?" asked James.

"I'm not sure yet. One of my diagnostic programs detected an unusual, possibly dormant nano virus."

"What exactly is a dormant nano virus?"

"I'm still researching that. It's definitely the result of some form of infiltration or assault on your system. I'll let you know when I find any new information."

"That's a little hard to believe Kyle."

"Believe it Dad. See you in less than eighty-six hours. I've got to go."

"Okay Kyle, see you then." James hung up the phone and went to check on the girls in the ICU.

Doctor Clayton conferred with the attending ICU physician and they decided not much more could be done tonight. He had finished his shift and would be driving home after his replacement had arrived.

It was unfortunate to have reported such a poor LDR to Kyle, especially after not speaking with him for so long. He had to admit Kyle had a good point about Jen and the flying. He had mostly dismissed the idea of her actually flying due to her limited hours, but knew it wouldn't take long to check her out in his machine.

After a brief talk with his replacement he picked up his car from the underground parking lot and started driving back to the estate.

James had served one tour in Vietnam prior to entering medical school. His main duties revolved around flying medevac helicopters throughout his six month tour of duty. He had about fourteen hundred hours, mostly on the UH-1 Iroquois (Huey) and had never flown commercially after returning to the United States.

Five years ago he and Alexia had been in a position to purchase a Bell 407 for private use. He often flew to various hospitals in Portland for emergencies. Occasionally he'd be asked to cover on back-up medevac flights if the local ambulance helicopters were unavailable. He had a small hanger with an automatic landing pad built farther up the hill on the top of his estate. His Bell 407 was purchased new with all the bells and whistles. It was on low skid gear with a pop-out float kit and was certified for instrument flight. The machine had a black factory paint job and was equipped with full medevac provisions. With the quick disconnect pedals, installing dual controls for any training was a quick and easy task. Although too young to obtain a FAA license, Kyle had memorized the aircraft flight manual and was becoming a proficient pilot, despite his minimal time at the controls. If James ever had a heart attack while flying and Kyle was on the dual controls, he was confident Kyle could safely land the helicopter with ease.

Kyle's discovery of a dormant nano virus was troubling. Who would be interested in a surgeon's computer? In any case, he decided he could curtail the use of his system, at least until Kyle gave the computer a clean bill of health. He also hoped Kyle could determine how long the system had been compromised. He certainly wasn't happy about Kyle hacking into his system in the first place, but as always, justifying any punishment for Kyle was generally a futile effort.

The estate gate opened as it detected the electronic ID code from his vehicle. Although it was late and very dark his peripheral vision could sense the three dogs; one running on each side of his car and one just behind. Demonstrating their herding traits, they could keep up with most any vehicle on the driveway to the house. James never regretted all the initial difficulties they had in finally locating and bringing these dogs here from France. Although a full-time trainer had been required for the first two years, they were now very independent and required only part-time maintenance and tactical training.

James parked his car and walked towards the main house. Lisa was opening the huge doors as he approached, "Good evening, Doctor Clayton, may I take your coat?"

"Hi Lisa, sure that would be great, thanks," he replied.

"Would you like anything to eat or drink tonight?"

"Thanks Lisa. A mug of coffee would be nice. I'll be on the outer deck, upstairs," he replied.

He never had much of an appetite after a two-over-seven LDR. James wanted to call his 'other' applicant, who he suspected had now returned to the Middle East. Calling this late at night might work well with the time difference. Originally he'd planned to send an e-mail, but decided against it after Kyle's discovery of the nano virus. He reached for his phone and checked his directory as Lisa set a coffee and a small plate of coffee cakes down on the outdoor table. "Thanks Lisa," he said as he pressed the numbers into his cell.

"Hello," he heard over the poor connection.

"Bill? Is this Bill Riker?" asked James.

"Yes. Who's calling?"

"It's James. We spoke the other day."

"James, do you have any good news for me?"

"I'm sorry Bill, but pending a confirmation, I've decided to hire another candidate."

"When will you know for sure?"

"I'll know within the next twenty four hours and I wanted you to know that you're my first choice if the deal falls through."

"Okay, that's fair enough. I can give you another twenty four hours, although I sure was hoping for some work in the States for a change."

"I know you were Bill," James replied in his most sympathetic voice. "If anything changes, I'll be calling you. By the way, can I call you if I have any other requirements in the future?" asked James.

"Sure. I don't know if I'll be available, but you're always welcome to try."

"Okay, thanks Bill. Good luck with whatever you're doing over in that part of the world if I don't need you this time."

"I can always use some good luck over here. Take care."

James had no idea why Bill had left the country so quickly after the interview, but he'd asked James to let him know where he stood as soon as possible. That's done, he thought as he relaxed into his comfortable deck chair, savouring his fresh coffee. He spent the next several minutes contemplating the best future arrangements for Kyle and Jen.

In the morning he would arrange for Chalet Number Five to be prepared for Kyle and Jen. It was a spacious two-story timber frame set further up the slope, above the main house. Jen would have the ground floor and Kyle could take the top floor. The only access to the top floor was through the suite on the ground floor. Each level was nicely furnished and mostly self-contained. Any maid or room services would be available through the estate staff.

He would need to make arrangements for a substantial electronics upgrade including high speed Internet and a new computer system. He wasn't sure if Jen would be moving in, but knew it was likely once she'd seen the chalet.

James finished his coffee and took a walk downstairs through the living room. The main fire was now just a glowing bed of embers as he passed by. Walking quietly he proceeded down the spacious hallway towards the newly renovated area designed for Alexia. After opening the doorway he walked over to her bedside for their nightly visit. It was clear that the two assisted-living nurses were now retired for the night. Alexia was asleep on her adjustable medical bed with a small lamp turned on by her bedside.

James took her hand and sat beside her as he often does. No words were ever spoken. Alexia lay on her back in the same position each night, always wearing her cumbersome neck brace. Although he should be used to it by now, it was still disconcerting to watch her sleep with her mouth and both eyes wide open. Placing her hand back on the bed, James made his way back to the master bedroom in the main estate. Getting ready for bed he was grateful he hadn't received any messages from the emergency department. That meant two young girls in the ICU were still clinging to life.

Jen checked her phone for the twenty-fifth time; no messages, no calls. The battery still had a decent charge, but it was also starting to get late. She'd managed to find an Internet cafe and was on her fourth coffee, so far. The search for the mysterious dogs had taken almost two hours. They were a breed from France, known as Beaucerons. From her Internet research she'd learned they were a rare, very protective and highly intelligent breed. The dogs were occasionally also used for herding because of their speed and protective traits. They were large, powerful and very dominating dogs whose mere appearance demanded respect.

James considered phoning Jen, but decided it would be best to call her in the morning. He needed to make sure that he had a valid pair of scentlets to give her before she came back to the estate. New scentlets were issued monthly to anyone living or working on the estate. Any person not wearing them had to remain in their vehicle or in the designated safe areas near the main house.

The Beaucerons were a highly tactical guard dog unit, trained to rapidly interrogate any visitors on the property. A valid pair of scentlets worn around your ankles would assure your safe passage. Anyone discovered without them would be lucky to walk again, or even survive, if the inevitable canine attack wasn't called off in time.

James rolled over and flipped on the bedside lamp. Reaching for his cell he prepared a brief text message for Jen. "Meet me for lunch, 12:00 @ Angry Horse Cafe, Doctor Clayton." He pressed the send button then shut off his phone and night light. His alarm was set early and he needed all the sleep he could get.

Jen jumped when she felt the vibration and muted ring tone of her phone. Flipping the phone open, she retrieved and read the new text message. She had the job—she didn't have the job—she didn't know. The agonizing suspense continued. It felt promising; why would you bother with a face-to-face if you weren't going to hire someone? Jen typed, "The Angry Horse Cafe plus map," in the search engine. It looked like a popular place. With her city map and this information she knew she could find it. She desperately wanted to text a response, but was unable to retrieve his number from the call display. She knew that James knew it was unlikely she wouldn't be checking her phone messages. Jen logged off the computer, grabbed her coffee, and went over to pay the attendant.

"Four coffee's and three and a half hours online is twenty-six dollars and fifty-five cents," said the attendant. Jen gave him thirty in cash and told him to keep the change as she walked out the door.

The Explorer was still parked about half a block down the street. She passed two small groups of people huddled in alcoves under makeshift piles of blankets before she reached the Explorer. The Internet cafe had good coffee, but next-to-nothing for food. It dawned on her that she was starving. It had been a long time since she had eaten and she'd need to find somewhere to eat or buy groceries tonight.

Driving towards home she pulled into a twenty four hour
Denny's. She was now so full of caffeine it was pointless
to try and sleep. Jen parked close to the front window and
found an empty booth where she could watch the Explorer.
It was late and the place was starting to fill up with the
after-hours nightclub crowd.

"Would you like a coffee or a menu, Miss?" asked the
older waitress.

"Just a menu for now thanks."

After filling up on a full dinner and a large dessert she
remembered that she still needed to pick up a few things
for the morning. She left a tip for the waitress and paid her
bill. Hopefully some funds will be rolling in soon, she
thought. On the way home she picked up some juice and a
few things for the apartment. It was close to three a.m. by
the time she got home.

Things appeared as she'd left them and her three black
totes were still in the closet. Most of these contained
various small arms and munitions that she probably
shouldn't be packing around in public. Jen pulled out one
tote and slid it under her bed, then set the alarm for six
thirty a.m. She was sure the alarm wouldn't be required,
but sleeping in and missing her lunch meeting was not a
possibility she could risk. She also needed some clean
clothes and would have to do a laundry first thing in the
morning.

Waking up automatically at six twenty-eight, she went
through her normal routines and finished off her laundry
using the coin machines in the building.

Finding the Angry Horse Cafe was easy with the help of
last night's research. After the thirty minute drive she
pulled into the large parking lot at eleven forty-five.

It was an upscale place that was just getting busy. The
hostess asked if she had a reservation and she mentioned
Doctor Clayton's name. After being told there was a
reservation she took a seat in the well-furnished entrance

area. Ten minutes later Doctor Clayton walked in and they were escorted to their table.

"Well I see you got my text message last night," said Doctor Clayton.

"Yes, I did thanks."

The waiter appeared with a pitcher of ice water and two menus.

"Good afternoon Doctor. Would you or your guest care for anything to drink?"

"What would you like Jen?" asked Doctor Clayton.

"Coffee's fine, thanks."

"Coffee and a green tea, please," Doctor Clayton told the waiter.

"Right away Doctor," he replied.

"So Jen, are you still interested in the position?"

"Yes, very much so Doctor Clayton," she replied.

"And you still don't have any restrictions in regards to your availability if I hire you?"

"No. None at all."

The waiter dropped off the beverages and took their lunch orders. By now almost every seat in the house was taken and this was obviously a very popular establishment.

"You do realize that this position will often require long days, as well as traveling with my son Kyle when required?"

"Yes, you'd mentioned that in the interview," Jen replied. "Where exactly does Kyle travel?" she asked.

"I'm expecting to receive a detailed list of travel dates and locations within the next few days," said the doctor.

"What does he do when he's away traveling?"

"He will be doing various scientific internships at selected research labs and universities."

"Who makes up his schedule?"

"The US Government," replied the doctor.

"That's absolutely incredible. And you said Kyle was only eight years old?"

"Yes I did. A very gifted eight-year-old," replied the doctor.

"In what way?" she asked.

"In the intellectual way—He is one of the smartest eight year old kids in the U.S. today, and quite possibly the smartest. They have yet to determine the upper limit of his IQ."

The waiter arrived and set down their meals, "May I get you anything else?" he asked with a slight bow, his hands together.

"No, that's great for now. Thank you," said the doctor.

"I find all of this, so fascinating," Jen replied. "Is he in any sort of danger?" she asked.

"We can't say for sure. Kyle and his mother were in a vehicle that was hit by gunfire a couple of years ago. The police have called it a 'random shooting'."

"Was Mrs. Clayton driving?" she asked.

"No. We had a different driver at the time, and unfortunately he received fatal injuries."

"I'm sorry to hear that," she replied. "Did you feel it was a random shooting?"

"Really, I don't know for sure. I am just continuing to take any and all precautions concerning my son."

"Yes, I can see now why you would. Was it your wife in the wheelchair, back on your estate?"

"Yes, it was. Her name is Alexia. She was rendered a brain damaged quadriplegic after the shooting."

"That's such a tragic story."

"Yes, it certainly is. Alexia was a gifted physics professor at the university."

The waiter returned to pick up their plates, "Can I offer you any desserts or refills?" he asked.

"Anything for you Jen?" asked the doctor.

"Maybe some more coffee, thanks."

"One more green tea, and another coffee please," said the doctor to the waiter.

"Well if I were to get this job, when would I be starting?" she asked.

"Oh pardon me. I've decided you've got the job and you've already started."

"Wow! That's fantastic news," she replied with a wide smile.

"I've deposited two weeks' salary in your chequing account early this morning."

"I don't know what to say," said Jen, still in a state of disbelief.

"Keep track of any and all of your expenses, including meals and rent. Also keep track of your day-to-day costs and you'll be paid on the next deposit."

"Thanks again. What a wonderful surprise."

The waiter approached the table and dropped off the beverages.

"You mentioned I've already started working. Is Kyle home now?"

"No. He should be home in a few days. In the meantime I'm having some renovations done to Chalet Number Five and that will be exclusively for you and Kyle."

"Will you want me to move up to the estate?"

"I'll leave that up to you. Your primary task will be to ensure Kyle's safety and well-being, in any way you see fit. There are also various vehicles on the estate that will be available for your use. While we're on the topic I'd like you to stop by and visit my mechanic, at M & U Motors. He's expecting you at two-thirty and he'll install a gate transmitter in your vehicle. I have an envelope for you, and the address of his shop is written on the back. It shouldn't take more than an hour, and after that the estate gate will automatically open whenever it senses your vehicle approaching. I want you to consider the estate your home and feel free to come and go as you please."

"That sounds great, Doctor Clayton. I'll be looking forward to that," Jen replied, still smiling.

"Anything else for you today?" asked the waiter.

"No, just the bill please," replied the doctor.

"Doctor Clayton—"

"Yes Jen."

"What about the Beaucerons?"

"I'm impressed that you happen to know the breed of those dogs."

"Well, I did a little research last night, to ease my curiosity."

The waiter smiled and dropped off the bill, in a dark leather folder.

"I was getting to the Beaucerons, as they also concern the envelope I've brought for you. It contains two valid scentlets that you must, I repeat must, be wearing anytime you're on the property. These dogs have a fantastic sense of smell and they're trained to attack anyone without a valid scentlet. They attach like bracelets around your ankles and have to be cut off when removed. It's imperative to monitor the validity periods of the scentlets as it's your only ticket to safe passage with these Beaucerons. These are not a hop-in-your-lap-and-lick-your-face type of dog."

"Thanks Doctor Clayton. I'll definitely make sure I'm wearing them before I come over."

Doctor Clayton glanced at the bill and then slid sixty dollars into the jacket of the folder as they got up to leave. Doctor Clayton followed Jen outside the cafe and over to the Explorer. "Here's the envelope Jen, I've also included a few contact numbers for the estate, and myself as well. Along with the scentlets you'll find keys for the main building, and also keys for Chalet Number Five. Later on I'll show you the main key locker at the estate. It contains the keys for anything with a lock on the estate."

"Okay, that's great. Thanks again for everything, including the nice lunch."

"You're welcome, it was my pleasure. I have to go to work and check on a couple of patients. See you soon."

"Bye then. Call me if there is anything you want me to do."

"I will. Don't forget the appointment this afternoon, or the scentlets."

"Not a chance," she replied, as she shook his hand.

The doctor walked over to his car, started it up, and waved goodbye as he drove off the lot.

Jen got in and locked the front door of her Explorer. She needed a few minutes to finally relax and contemplate the events of the last hour. She was still ecstatic about landing this interesting assignment, but was already starting to worry about her new responsibilities. The boy's last driver had been killed. She still hadn't even met Kyle, or his mother who was now a quadriplegic after being very nearly killed herself. She was definitely hoping that she wasn't getting in over her head.

He said he'd made a deposit of two weeks' salary. How could the doctor possibly have known her private banking information? Then again he obviously had some type of access to her personal information judging by the questions at the interview. This job was already keeping her mind filled with questions. Jen reached over and pulled out her city map from the glove compartment. She didn't want to be late this afternoon, even if it was just an appointment at the garage. It didn't take long to get her directions planned out with the address and her city map.

She decided she may as well drive over to M & U Motors and arrive a little early. After twenty minutes she pulled up to the shop and parked the truck outside an empty garage bay. Walking into the office a man looked over and said, "You must be Ms. Lamar. I'm Mike, pleased to meet you."

"Hi Mike," she replied.

"I'll need your keys and it'll be about an hour and a half until I'm finished. There's some magazines and coffee on the counter if you like, or a mall across the street."

"That's great Mike, I'll see you in an hour and a half." Jen preferred the mall option and walked across the street.

She needed some cash and noticed a bank outlet with an ATM. She was down to twelve hundred in cash after paying her rent. Landing this job was a huge stroke of luck. After typing in her PIN and checking the balance she was stunned to the core. Fifteen thousand, two hundred and eighteen dollars! How could that be possible? Did she really just get a fourteen thousand dollar deposit for two weeks? It was either a simple mistake or an extremely 'generous remuneration', as stated in the ad. Sensing a small line forming behind her, she made a hundred dollar withdrawal. It was a perfect time for a little window shopping, or maybe a visit to the local drug store.

Dr. Clayton was checking on the two girls in the ICU. One was still listed as critical, but the other was stabilizing nicely. He didn't want to report any LDR changes to Kyle if that topic came up again. James felt his cell phone vibrating in his jacket pocket and thought it must be Jen. Normally his personal phone was turned off when he was at work, but she wouldn't know that.

Jen found a washroom in the mall and locked herself in a cubicle. Opening the envelope she carefully examined the scentlets. The validity period was stamped into the side of each one. This set expired at the end of the month. She could smell a faint unusual scent, but they certainly weren't overpowering. They had the appearance of medium sized drinking straws constructed from a tough blue plastic with a latching mechanism similar to those used on handcuffs. This place was as good as any to put them on. Lifting her right foot onto her left knee, she fastened the first one on her right ankle. It felt comfortable enough, so she attached the other scentlet to her left ankle.

"Hello, Dr. Clayton here. How may I help you?"

"James, this is Mike, from M & U Motors. Hope I'm not interrupting anything important, if you're at work, that is."

"No, not at all, how can I help you?"

"Well, Ms. Lamar just dropped off her Ford Explorer for the gate transmitter installation."

"Yes, I know. I just gave her your address."

"Well, are you currently tracking her?"

"No. What do you mean?"

"Well when I lifted her truck up on the hoist I found a small GPS tracking unit magnetically attached to the right side of her gas tank."

Jen glanced at the time and started back over to Mike's to check on her truck.

"James? James? Are you there?"

"Okay thanks Mike. Listen—just leave it there for now and please don't tell anyone you've found it. I'll need to investigate this further."

"Okay, will do. See you later."

"Thanks Mike."

Jen opened the door and walking into Mike's shop.

"Your truck's ready for you, Ms. Lamar. I've checked all the fluids and every thing's good."

"Thanks. I tend to keep an eye on things like that. Do you have a bill for me?"

"Not today. It's all been taken care of."

"That's great. Thanks again," said Jen.

Driving home she was suddenly becoming aware of an unknown and invisible enemy. Just simply being on the payroll seemed to elevate the risk factor. Jen could feel the new scentlets riding on her ankles. Unfortunately she knew they'd be tested soon.

Chapter 6

Professor Kavi Akkaim hadn't arrived where he was by not acting on information. The sleeping nano virus had been lying dormant in Doctor Clayton's computer for almost a year. The RA-9 facility had been closely monitoring Kyle Clayton and his intellectual progress by any means possible. The computer engineers at RA-9 had activated the spyware several weeks ago as Kyle would be finished university shortly. The timing of the spyware activation couldn't have been better. They successfully downloaded all the latest information on Kyle and also the dossiers of Bill Riker and Jennifer Lamar. After studying the information he was surprised at the weak credentials of Kyle's potential body guards. One was a young female, and the other a wounded Blackerwater operative. This would certainly make any future abductions of the boy, that much easier.

The professor had several teams working in the north western US, but due to recent developments most of their plans were constantly changing. Some teams were studying potential abduction targets and others were collecting information on the recent installation of several hundred lasers in the fusion facility in California. The critical problem now, was the sudden termination to the free flow of stolen information from the super computer at the Central Fusion Research Complex 8 (CFRC-8). The RA-9 project was designed to duplicate this installation in every way possible. Having detected the 'Ghostnet' intrusions, senior management and CFRC-8 project security personnel had decided to sever all connections to outside phone lines as well as the Internet.

It was now imperative that Kyle was allowed to attend his internship at CFRC-8 prior to his abduction. His unequalled ability to memorize information and his demonstrated photographic memory would ultimately make him a prize asset for the RA-9 project. Plans were still being formulated concerning potential motivator targets however any details concerning the methods or locations of future abductions would be handled by Sinzar, as always. He still had one week remaining until he was scheduled to surface in Santa Monica.

Professor Akkaim was hoping Kyle's internship schedule would be arriving soon by e-mail before anyone discovered the spyware installed in Doctor Clayton's computer. If not, general surveillance would be required to monitor and track all his activities. Professor Akkaim could only hope that Kyle would be scheduled to visit CFRC-8 sooner rather than later. It seemed plausible that the inexperienced Ms. Lamar might be hired as Kyle's escort. That development, if it did happen, would certainly please the well-trained surveillance operatives currently working in the U.S.

Two RA-9 agents had been recently dispatched to monitor Bill Riker's whereabouts and activities. With great difficulty they'd finally managed to track him back to Iraq, where once again it appeared he was somehow becoming involved in the murky covert affairs of Blackerwater operations.

Both agents, although considered competent, had only limited experience with surveillance work in this part of the world. Although communications were generally good, both men were now overdue for their check-ins.

The location of Doctor Clayton's estate was known to local RA-9 operatives, although no one had ever entered the property. Ms. Lamar's activities would be of increasing interest, if in fact she was hired to guard Kyle Clayton. For now she was considered a low priority target after the recent installation of a GPS tracking unit on her vehicle. That would always keep the local agents informed of her current location or activities. The installation had gone unexpectedly well after she'd parked so far away from an Internet cafe she was visiting.

Plans relating to the location of other operatives would be delayed until the details of Kyle's schedule became known. The importance of his schedule was growing daily. Sinzar Bakkir, although an intelligent and logical man, was not a patient man. He definitely wouldn't be happy to be kept waiting for months until Kyle was ready for transport. In the back of his mind Professor Akkaim was developing an alternate plan for Sinzar Bakkir.

He'd performed his Mexican assignment satisfactorily and the electrical engineer was still alive when he arrived at the RA-9 facility. His wife had lost almost fifteen pounds during the two day trip, being tightly wound in shrink wrap. The required transcripts were eventually recorded prior to her disposal, her body stitched inside a mattress and dumped at the city landfill.

Those minor details were out of Sinzar's hands, but as in almost every other case, Sinzar always delivered his targets.

Throughout the history of the Human Resource Procurement Division only two targets ever evaded procurement and only four were dead on arrival. The most common cause of death was asphyxiation. Shrink-wrap was typically inhaled to the point that it managed to cut off the airflow through the snorkel inlet. Cheap construction of the coffin sized crates often resulted in hot windy conditions within the crates. These conditions were at their worst while travelling along long desert highways, strapped to the timbers of flat deck trucks.

This problem had now been greatly reduced with new modified taping techniques, and also by denying payments for DOA shipments. There were times Professor Akkaim wished for better communications with Sinzar, but this method of prearranged locations and telephone time code reporting had remained secure since its inception. He knew Sinzar was a dedicated and loyal member of the RA-9 team, but would never welcome change to his methods of operation.

Communications with field agents involved in various support activities were less classified than with direct abduction staff. Professor Akkaim would take any information from wherever he could, provided it wasn't compromising the RA-9 project. He was beginning to get the feeling that this upcoming acquisition might require some additional leverage; possibly someone working the inside of the estate.

Professor Akkaim put out a request for information concerning any available records on past and present employees of Doctor Clayton. He was also seeking any known information on immediate family members and relatives of people with access to Doctor Clayton's estate. Unlimited financial incentives were always available in exchange for inside services, however; that method was usually more costly and often less reliable. RA-9 had a proven system in place that ensured the productive motivation of most new recruits.

Jen decided to park in the alley behind her building. Everything had changed today. She would no longer travel anywhere unarmed or unprepared. With darkness approaching she'd found a somewhat secluded parking spot down below her apartment.

One of the many things ingrained into Jen's mind was to know the current condition of any aircraft she was flying. Detailed, meticulous inspections were carried out daily and even more so after any maintenance had been performed. This philosophy was easily transferred to vehicles or weapons. Jen removed her police flashlight from the glove compartment and pulled the hood release. After taking a good look around her immediate surroundings she got out and lifted the front hood. She was very familiar with this vehicle and had spent many hours studying and working in the engine compartment. It took about five minutes to discover the location of the new gate transmitter. It was professionally mounted on the engine firewall and the power source was connected to the main ignition circuit.

She took her time, rechecking all the fluid levels, and also checking the tire pressures with her pocket gauge. The truck wasn't jacked up, but the clearance was high enough for leak checks with her flashlight. Be slow and meticulous, without any distractions, is how she had been taught to inspect her aircraft. While carefully examining the gas tank her flashlight scan stopped suddenly on the right side of the tank.

She lay there, frozen on her back, studying the small metal box within the beam of light. Her mind replayed images of any type of explosive or detonation device she'd ever seen during her training or assignments in Iraq. This unit had no wires leading to a power source, nor a visible timer. That didn't rule out a C-4 charge with a remote detonation system. Her nerves were now so tense she couldn't have moved if she'd wanted to.

Subconscious thoughts reminded her that this was exactly the last type of image numerous bomb experts had witnessed just prior to their obliteration; the calm before the storm. A tiny green LED flashing on the far side of the unit confirmed an internal battery as a power source. Using her stopwatch she timed the flash intervals; it was constant and not increasing. There was no evidence of any mounting hardware or adhesive residue so she concluded it was likely a magnetic bond.

She was ninety five percent sure this wasn't an explosive device. The other five percent was telling her it could be one, a very small one, because it was attached to a gas tank. Reaching up she took a firm hold of the box and rolled her wrist. It snapped clear of the tank, and on closer inspection she knew she had a GPS tracking transmitter in her hand. Raising the unit into position it jumped from her hand, back home to the side of the tank.

Jen locked her truck and went inside to consider her options. Once again the apartment was as she'd left it. Certain things were becoming clear; the invisible enemy had now made an introduction, and she was going to require more equipment.

Putting on some water for coffee, she laid her three totes on the floor and opened them for inspection. She needed to select various items to carry on her person and also in her vehicle. She'd keep her other two totes for back up. She strapped on her chest holster and holstered her street-silenced Glock 17. Her gun holster had a small custom knife sheath on her back-strap that held a thin stiletto in the inverted position. She strapped a separate slim-line knife sheath on the inside of her calf, just above the left scentlet. Her munitions belt was well concealed under her jacket and contained three spare magazine clips, a set of lock picks and also a small set of jeweller's tools. A pair of two small mace charges, designed as decorative pendants, hung from her casual silver necklace.

She'd keep one ex-police issue Stun Gun under her dash on the driver's side and also hide an additional knife in the rear of the Explorer. A tiny small-calibre pistol fitted in a metal magnetic box would be attached to the underside of the vehicle. Her favourite multipurpose knife would stay in her front pocket. What she did need was a communications upgrade and also some personal GPS locators once Kyle returned. Jen poured some instant coffee in her mug and filled it with boiling water.

She needed to know if she was being tracked by satellite or actually being followed. After coffee she locked up her place and went for a drive. Starting out on the main roads she gradually moved into residential areas. After an hour of driving she was fairly sure she wasn't being followed. After checking that her fuel was okay she returned to the main highway.

After driving past a twenty four hour truck stop she turned around and drove back towards it. It was well after dinner time, but this place was still doing a good business judging by the amount of semi-trailers, buses and vehicles in the lot.

Jen took her time, deciding exactly where to park. The semi-trailers were generally lined up on the east side of the lot and the buses and vehicles were parked in front. A lighted gas bar was close to the building and a diesel card lock was off to the side. Jen parked close to the semi-trailer area and went in for dinner.

After deconstructing the largest knife and fork burger she'd ever laid eyes on she kept on drinking more coffee than she knew she should. She still had a reasonable view of the lot, but needed a better feel for the movements of the local people and their vehicles.

Two hours later this truck stop wasn't showing any sign of ever slowing down. Leaving a tip, she went over to pay her bill and bought a six pack of cola cans. When she got inside the Explorer she grabbed a few old coffee cups and walked across the lot to the garbage bin by the side of the diner. Jen picked out an old lunch bag and brought it with her to the truck. Sitting inside the Explorer she pulled most of the cans from their plastic retainer and placed them in the paper bag. After her walk across the lot she had a better picture of which trucks had which plates.

Ten minutes passed and a spot opened up between a rig with Texas plates and one with Florida plates. She started her truck, moved over and backed it into the open slot, with her right side tight against the Florida rig. Walking to the rear of her truck with her paper bag, she opened the hatch as she inverted the bag. With a little help from her foot the cans rolled beneath her truck and the adjacent trailer. Dropping down to retrieve the cans she removed the transmitter and attached it to the underside the of the Florida trailer. The units would be sensitive but unlikely to detect a thirty inch transfer from her tank to the trailer.

That should buy her some time if the apartment wasn't being watched. After close to forty minutes both drivers had returned and the tractor's diesel engines finally belched to life. Jen watched as the semi-trailer slowly rolled out of the lot and turned to the southeast.

There was an undeniable instant feeling of freedom driving without the tracking unit.

That feeling however didn't last long. She wanted out of her apartment, and soon. Whoever had planted the tracking unit knew her vehicle and most likely also knew her address. She needed another vehicle and a new place soon, if she were to remain in this city. Her truck would have to disappear and she would as well. Jen remembered Doctor Clayton's offer about vehicles at the estate. Hopefully she could travel tonight under the cover of darkness.

Driving a good twenty miles, she found an open Super-Mart and began shopping for a few miscellaneous items. After returning to the apartment she parked in the alley at the rear of the building and walked slowly up the stairs. Turning the door knob silently it stopped early and felt locked. She wasn't leaving anything to chance. Quietly, she inserted a loaded magazine clip in the handle of her silenced Glock 17. Memories of Iraq instantly streamed to the forefront of her mind. Unlocking the door, she conducted a quick tactical search of her small place. The apartment was empty and exactly as she'd left it; her black metal totes untouched.

Repacking the original boxes, she began loading up the Explorer with all her possessions. She opened a new package of curtains purchased at Super-Mart. One window was dressed with nothing but glass. Stepping on a sturdy box she nailed the oversize fabric straight to the wall, well above the window. Placing a new lamp in the bedroom, she closed all the drapes, and left only two lights turned on.

Soon, after several trips, the truck was loaded and she was ready to travel. Locking the only door to her suite she squeezed a quarter tube of instant super-strong glue deep inside the keyhole and wiped the excess clean. She then taped a small note on the door: Back in Two Weeks, then left. When she got to the truck she had one last look around before starting up and driving away.

She kept driving until she'd found an ATM located in the downtown core. Jen withdrew the maximum daily cash limit and then drove towards the residential section on the other side of town. Tomorrow, she could try and make another withdrawal in person. She couldn't risk leaving electronic footprints everywhere she went.

Jen wanted her own secret hiding place, known only to her. She needed something with a garage or underground parking. After two hours of searching she found a low-rise apartment with a small 'Furnished Suite for Rent' sign staked in the front lawn of the building. She slowed down and parked, then walked over and jumped the stairs of the front entrance.

The manager eventually answered the intercom and, despite the late hour, agreed to show her the suite. It was a one bedroom, third floor corner suite, with underground parking included. One storage locker was provided and the building had a common laundry room for tenants only. It was sparsely furnished with a few basic necessities including a single bed. Paint was needed everywhere inside this building and flyers, litter and newspapers lay scattered along the halls. This place was definitely located in a lower class section of town and almost completely surrounded by low-rise rental housing.

After completing the rental paperwork she handed over most of her cash with the balance due in twenty four hours. Keys in hand, she drove the truck underground and parked out of sight. Luckily the building had a service elevator with access to the underground parking area. After three trips in the slow speed elevator she locked the apartment door from the inside and studied her noisy new place.

Doctor Clayton was nearing the end of his shift; an unusually quiet night in the trauma center. The second of the two girls from the train accident had also been downgraded to a 'stable' condition. Soon she'd be released from his care and transferred back to her regular GP.

He'd tried twice to contact his government liaison concerning Kyle's schedule. It was very unusual not to hear back from him and he'd already left two messages. He needed answers about the tracking unit and details about their plans for Kyle. If they hadn't installed the tracking unit Jen could well be in danger on the first day of her new job. With each passing minute he wished more than ever that he'd just told Mike to remove the tracking unit. So what if it was a government unit? They should have asked his permission in the first place. Above all, he should have at least told Jen about it.

It was two days until Kyle was due to return. James still hadn't heard anything from Kyle regarding the computer, or anything from Jen, for that matter. He pulled out his cell phone and called Lisa at home. "Hi Lisa, have you heard anything from Kyle?"

"No, I haven't heard anything yet Doctor Clayton."

"Did Jennifer Lamar come over and visit the estate tonight?"

"Not that I know of."

"How about the contractors, were they working on the Chalet Number Five?"

"Yes, they'd been working all day."

"Okay, thanks Lisa. I'll be home in a couple of hours. Please make sure my computer stays off."

"Yes, will do. See you soon."

"Thanks Lisa, bye for now."

While he still had the phone out, he dialled his government contact Al Anderson one last time.

"Hi. You've reached Al Anderson. Sorry I can't take your call right now. Please leave your name and number and I'll get back to you as soon as possible."

James snapped the phone shut as he'd already left two messages and wasn't planning to leave a third.

Sixty minutes later the intake nurse tapped him on the shoulder, "James, there's a man by the admitting desk to see you. His name's Al Anderson."

"Oh that's great, thanks a lot," he replied. James walked into the admitting area and found the man by the desk.

"Good evening Doctor Clayton. Al Anderson. Do you have a few minutes?" he asked, smiling and extending his hand.

"Sure. Let's sit over there Al," gestured James with a nod of his head while they quickly shook hands and walked towards an empty row of seats.

"I've been trying to reach you all day."

"Yes I know. Can I call you James?"

"Sure, of course you can."

"My apologies for not returning your calls, but I've received an alert from our security division informing me that unfortunately your phone lines have been compromised. I'd like you to discontinue using your cell phone as a precaution. We'd also like to install some auxiliary diagnostic equipment on your home phone tomorrow."

"That shouldn't be a problem, I'll be home all day. Are you positive about my cell phone?" asked James.

"Yes, they don't issue those alerts without a good reason."

"So, who's tapping my phone lines?"

"As of yet we don't know, but we're trying to find out. Cell phone security is notoriously poor so it could be anyone."

"Do you have Kyle's internship schedule yet?"

"Yes, I have it with me in an envelope for you. It's becoming very confidential classified information, and I wanted to deliver it personally."

Al Anderson removed a sealed envelope marked, 'Classified Documents: U.S. Security Level Four,' from his jacket pocket and passed it to James.

"Thanks Al, I appreciate that. I'll study it carefully once I'm home."

"Does Kyle have any time off before he leaves?"

"Yes, about two weeks."

"That's great. How can I contact you if I have to?"

"Leave a message on my voicemail and use a land line if possible. I'll meet you in person at the hospital."

"I'm not always at this hospital."

"Don't worry, I'll know where you are."

"Okay, thanks for the phone warning, and the schedule."

"My pleasure, we'll keep in touch."

"Al, one more thing—are you currently following me or any of my staff with any sort of GPS tracking units?"

"No. That may be a possibility once Kyle's back, but nothing's happened yet. I'll let you know if we do."

"Okay, thanks again. I'll talk to you soon."

"Bye for now, take care," said Al as he departed the admitting area towards the emergency entrance doors.

James noticed an uneasy awareness of the classified envelope just placed in his possession.

As far as James was concerned the temperature of this situation was rising faster than a rampant fever. There was a very real possibility that Jen could be in trouble, and the fact that he hadn't heard a thing from her was becoming even more troubling. It was now obvious that someone was tracking her movements. He'd expected Al to tell him that 'yes', they'd been following her. And unless he was lying, then someone else was following her.

He found an empty hospital office and called Jen's cell number on the hospital phone.

"The customer you have dialled is either temporarily away from the phone or out of the cellular coverage area."

James hung up and considered driving to her Portland address after his shift. He realised her address was still in his home office and he didn't want Lisa relaying that information over an unsecured phone. He'd have to go home first and personally find her address.

He called Mike from M & U Motors and got his recorded message. In the message Mike listed his cell number 'for emergencies only' and James decided to give him a call.

"Hello, Mike speaking?"

"Hi Mike. It's Doctor Clayton calling."

"Hi, this is a late call. What can I do for you?"

"Mike, I'd like to arrange for an inspection of my vehicle. I'd like you to search for any tracking hardware on my vehicle as well."

"Sure Doctor Clayton. Shall I book you an appointment tomorrow?"

"Mike, it's very important to me that I get it done as soon as possible."

"When could you make it to my shop? I'll need to raise your vehicle," said Mike.

"How does an hour from now sound?" asked James.

"Sure, I can make that. I'll see you there."

"Great! Thanks Mike. I'll make it worth your while."

After forty five minutes in the shop Mike gave Doctor Clayton's car a clean bill of health. James told Mike to send him the bill and gave him an extra two hundred in cash for his troubles. James decided to drive home and check if there was any new information regarding Jen. He felt reassured that at least he wasn't being tracked, but still needed Jen's address if he decided on driving back in to town.

Jen was still uneasy and found it difficult to shake that 'hunted' sensation. Her phone had been shut off for hours as she'd recently become aware of all the latest developments in cell phone tracking technology. She equipped herself with her standard list of weapons, locked the suite and left on foot. She'd micro-marked the door and windows with ultra-thin slivers of clear scotch tape and she'd know if any of them had been opened. After two blocks of passing shady pedestrians on this poorly lit sidewalk, she wished she'd brought her Stun Gun as well. This was not any upscale part of town.

From what she could remember, she had about a ten block walk to get to a small twenty-four hour gas station. There was some sidewalk lighting, but limited. Really she was more worried about being stopped by police than panhandlers or slow moving cars looking for working girls.

It was nearing midnight and she'd planned to call a cab from the next gas station. The streets were very quiet and she hadn't seen any cabs at all. A group of three men, all smoking, were approaching her from the opposite direction. All three were wearing dark kangaroo jackets with the hoods pulled up over their heads. Crossing her arms, she kept her right hand on the reassuring grip of her loaded Glock 17. With the street silencer she was ready to use it if she had to, but hoped that wouldn't be necessary. The tallest of the three let out a loud whistle as they passed by each other. She kept walking, stone faced with her head down, ignoring the group completely while the fortunate trio continued down the road.

When she arrived at the station she could see a phone booth on the far edge of the lot. She had no coins for a payphone and would need some change and the telephone number of a cab company. Jen had managed to keep one hundred dollars away from the hungry hands of her new landlord. An older man was working in the small gas station office that was equipped with a cash window only.

"May I have some change for the phone, please," she said as she slipped a twenty through the tiny window.

"How much do you need Miss?"

"Five dollars in change should be fine, thanks."

"It's a little late to be out walking alone in this part of town," said the attendant.

"Thanks, I just needed to use the phone. Is there a phone book in the booth?"

"Yes I think so, but I'm not sure if they've replaced the receiver yet."

"It's missing?" she asked.

"It was a couple of days ago. Repairing payphones isn't really a high priority in this part of town." The old man slid her change out through the small metal gate.

"Thanks, I'll go take a look." Jen walked across the lot to an old phone booth with two broken windows and no door. The phone line hung down to where the receiver should have been. Coloured copper-tipped wires protruded from the coiled nickel shielding. A partial phone book was hanging in the booth, tattered and covered in old scribbled phone numbers. The incomplete yellow pages still listed two taxi companies whose numbers were easy to memorize.

She could've asked the attendant for the number or had him call a cab, but decided against it. She had to keep hiding her tracks. Passing by the office, the man waved her over. "Did they fix the phone?"

"No, not by the looks of it," she replied.

"Well you can't come inside this office. It's a time lock system here and nobody uses this phone. There are a few payphones outside the stadium, about seven blocks to the north."

"Thanks for your help," said Jen as she started walking north.

Her surroundings where gradually changing from low income residential to industrial. After ten minutes she could see the stadium in the distance. The blocks were getting longer, but at least it was a dry evening. Fifteen minutes later the stadium was dominating the skyline and she could see a line of wall mounted payphones. As she approached the stadium two younger ladies wearing short neon skirts were talking by the farthest phone. Jen picked up the nearest phone and called for a taxi.

"Myline Taxi," said the man on the phone.

"Yes, I'd like a taxi please."

"Where are you going to this evening?"

"I'm going to West Cedar Drive, in the Northern Estates."

"That's a long fare. Where are you calling from?"

Instantly realising she didn't really know, she said, "Outside a large stadium across from a truck depot' this phone number has a six-three-five prefix."

"Okay, I think I know where you are. Will you be paying with cash or a credit card?"

"I'll be paying with cash."

"We should have a taxi there within ten minutes. What's your name?"

"Susan," she lied.

The two girls at the other end of the phones had been joined by several other women. The talkative group was studying her from the short distance away. Realising she might be stepping on their turf, she started walking away towards the street.

"Must be a really rich John you have up there in them Northern Estates," called out one of the girls.

"Better not show your face down here again," yelled another.

Jen ignored the women and their cat calls while calmly walking further away. She didn't need any unnecessary violence with this group of hookers, especially in such an open location.

She could see a taxi driving in her direction from a half block away. Moments later, the taxi slowed down as she waved and walked towards the cab. The driver lowered the power window and said "Susan?"

"Yes, that's me."

"Hop in Susan. Front or back, whichever you prefer."

"Thanks," she said, as she opened the back door and jumped in.

"West Cedar Drive, in the Northern Estates please. Do you know how to get there?"

"Yes, I think I can find it. Do you have a residential address?" asked the driver.

"No, sorry I don't. I'll know when I see it."

"Okay, that's fine," said the driver as he drove off.

They both watched as a spinning bottle flew across the hood of the cab and exploded on the road. "Friends of yours?" asked the driver with a grin.

"Not really," she replied while sinking into her seat.

The driver was a middle aged man who often admired Jen in his rear-view mirror. After putting the chill to his small talk she settled into the back seat and concentrated on the dollar amount displayed on his meter. This would be close, very close. Forty minutes later the meter read eighty nine dollars as they started driving uphill towards the Northern Estates. When they reached the large rock and timber Northern Estates sign, just before the fork in the road, it read ninety eight dollars.

"Right here is perfect," she said.

"Are you sure? There's nothing here," said the driver as he pulled off the road.

"Yes, I'm absolutely sure. I'm meeting a friend here."

"Do you want me to stay until he arrives?" asked the driver.

"No Thanks, I'll be fine."

"That's ninety-eight dollars please," said the driver as he turned around.

Jen gave him everything she had left, knowing he'd made next to nothing for a tip.

"Sorry I didn't have any more cash today. Thanks again for the ride."

"You're welcome. Don't worry about the tip Susan, it's still a good fare for this time of night. Bye."

Jen watched as the cab turned around and stared as the tail lights disappeared down the hill. It was pitch dark and the stars were free from their hazy veil of city lights. Tonight, of all nights, the moon was nowhere to be seen.

She remembered just how quiet this place was the last time she was here. She followed the road by watching the notch of missing trees in the skyline above. At the fork in the road she took West Cedar Drive and was soon walking alongside the old granite wall of the Claytons' estate. She had no way of opening the gate and didn't dare use the intercom at this hour. Finally, after noticing what looked like a shallow dip in the top of wall, she jumped across the small drainage ditch flowing next to the road. It didn't take long with her agility to reach the top of the wall. The wall was about eight feet high in most places, and walking on top was easy with these large granite capstones.

The only thing visible on the other side was the dark vertical voids of passing tree trunks. She would soon have a few additions for her equipment list, a flashlight among others. After walking the capstones for several minutes Jen began to see an occasional faint light flickering through the dark tree trunks. Jen removed her Glock 17, checked the safety switch, and strapped it back in the holster. She slowly sat down on the very edge of the cold granite wall. With both hands close to her sides, and twisted slightly for a better grip, she pushed herself blindly into the black night air.

Chapter 7

The large bright red circle flashed repeatedly on his screen. "Go and find Professor Akkaim," the technician told his assistant.

"Is it important?" asked the assistant.

"I'm not sure! Go and find the Professor—Now!"

Professor Akkaim was led along the line of operators working in the cyber espionage labs. "What's going on?" asked the professor.

"The three hundred mile perimeter alarm was just activated on Miss Lamar's vehicle."

"Is she still traveling?" asked Professor Akkaim.

"Yes, she's currently driving southeast," replied the computer technician.

"Are the local agent's aware of her current movements?" asked the professor.

"I'm not sure. I don't think so."

"Tell me why the local agents responsible for her movements wouldn't know if she'd left the city," the professor demanded in a frustrated, rising tone of voice.

"Well, she's been listed as a low priority, at least until Kyle Clayton returns. The local agents usually transfer monitoring back over to us at nine p.m., P.S.T."

"So you're telling me that she's traveling at night and no one knows where," barked the professor. "Do you even know for certain that Kyle Clayton is still in Canada?" demanded the professor, not even trying to hide his anger.

"According to our data stream from the US Customs computers, he hasn't cleared customs yet."

"Is that the only assurance you're relying on—Kyle Clayton clearing US Customs?"

"We also have agents working at the Vancouver Airport. They're watching a small unmarked grey jet that we know belongs to the CIA. They always use that jet to fly Kyle Clayton and his guards. They've been parked for a day and a half at the south terminal and we'll know as soon as it departs."

"Listen to me! Pick up your phone and call our sleeping beauties in Portland. Tell them to check Lamar's place and start following her signal from the transmitter. If we lose her and she's transporting Kyle somewhere I'm putting their names on Sinzar's 'to do' list! They'll know exactly what that means."

"Right away Professor—I'll call them straight away." replied the computer technician.

"What about the two agents following Bill Riker. Have they checked in yet?" asked the professor.

"No, we haven't heard anything. They're still overdue."

"I want to be informed as soon as you have any new developments, in the US or Iraq."

"Yes Professor Akkaim. I'll notify you immediately."

The technician used a mobile satellite uplink routed through a deflection processor to call the agents in Portland. The call would be placed under routine 'GhostNet' protective protocol. Any trace actions would display a partial number only, originating from the crowded suburbs of China.

It was becoming a late night for James. He hadn't known if he was going to be able to get an appointment with Mike so late in the evening, but he had known he wanted his car searched right away. The thought of being followed was bad enough, but being followed with Kyle's schedule in his pocket was even worse.

He drove straight home from M & U Motors and found Lisa still awake. "Any news from Kyle or Jen?" he asked.

"No Doctor Clayton, nothing at all. Is everything okay?"

"Oh yes probably. I just thought they might have called, that's all. I'm sure there is nothing to worry about," said the doctor. "Is my computer still turned off?"

"Yes it is," Lisa replied.

"I'm going to be unplugging all the phones in the house, and if you have a cell phone I'd like you to leave it turned off. Make sure you tell Alexia's staff as well. I don't want any calls made from the estate until the telephone company has finished their work here tomorrow."

"Okay, I understand. Do you want anything from the kitchen before you go to bed?"

"No I'm fine. I may go back and check on someone at the hospital tonight. If I do, I'll let myself in when I get home."

"Okay then Doctor Clayton. I'll go and tell the nurses about the phones. Goodnight. I'll see you in the morning."

"Thanks. Good night."

James walked back down the hall to his office. Opening the door and turning on the lights, he could see the computer was still off. He unplugged every line going to the computer and also the desk phone. There were six phones on the estate and James walked through the house methodically disconnecting every phone he could find.

As a surgeon, being away from a phone was very rare. He knew the radio and satellite phone in the helicopter would work from the top of this hill if he had to make a call. After he'd finished with the phones he went back to his office and opened his file cabinet. His paper file on Jen was still very thin, but it contained her original résumé and her address in Portland. James jotted down her address and put it in his wallet. Walking over to the office wall, he took hold of the frame of a beautiful eighteen by twenty-four painting of Alexia in her twenties and pulled on the right side. The magnetic cabinet catch released its grip and the painting opened quietly to reveal an antique Murphy wall safe mounted in the wall above a row of shoulder-level, solid brass coat hooks. He slowly turned the dial knob of the older wall-safe as he entered the combination, and then opened the safe.

It was equipped with a dim internal light that illuminated his Colt 45, cash, and assorted documents. He took the classified envelope from Al Anderson and placed it in the safe. He'd open and study it later when he had more time. James thought about taking his Colt 45, but decided against it. As far as he could remember he had to notify the police before transporting his handgun and was only licensed to use it at the shooting range.

He locked the safe and closed the frame of Alexia's painting against the wall. James checked his scentlets, put on a warm leather jacket and locked the house. He started up his car and drove towards the gate. He hadn't seen any sign at all of any of the Beaucerons tonight although he'd only been walking in designated safe zones. Pulling through the gate, James had a general idea of where Jen lived and estimated it would be about a forty minute drive. He enjoyed driving these high-end cars and turned the music up, higher than usual.

The loud ring of the phone jolted the two agents in the hotel. No one ever called this room. Most nights they were out enjoying the city, but the good life was catching up to them. Tonight they were both in a deep REM sleep and the phone nearly wasn't answered.

"Hello," whispered the half asleep agent closest to the phone.

The RA-9 computer operator quickly relayed the message from Professor Akkaim. Sinzar's reputation was well known throughout this organization and no one in their right mind ever wanted their name on any list of his.

Both men quickly dressed and left the hotel. They had no idea why she'd leave Portland, unless maybe she hadn't got the job. That was definitely a possibility if she was leaving before Kyle had returned. Maybe she had another job offer or a long distance romance. Whatever the reason, they needed to find out. Turning on the laptop they could once again trace the signal from the Explorer. She was now just leaving southeast Oregon and entering northwest Nevada.

"We better check her place before we leave town," said the older agent to his younger partner.

"Do you remember how to get there?" said the younger agent.

"Not exactly—look up the trip log on the tracking program. It'll show all her movements, including the coordinates of where she parked last night."

"Good idea," said the younger agent. "We're not that far away now, another six blocks down this road."

Finding her place was confusing as the address was a storefront and her second floor unit was fronting the back of the building. They pulled slowly up the alley and parked a half block back. Casing the building, they found the stairs leading up to her flat.

"The lights are on, but I don't see her truck. There's something on the door. Can you see it?"

"Yes, let's have a look."

Both agents walked quietly towards her door, hands gripping their concealed handguns.

'Back In Two Weeks,' read the note on the door.

"It looks like she's left town alright," said the youngest agent.

"It also looks like she could still be inside her place," said the older, more experienced of the two. "Be quiet— let's move back down to the alley."

"Okay" said the younger agent.

Both agents returned to their vehicle in the lane.

"Check the laptop and tell me if she's still moving. I'm getting a couple of things from the trunk," said the older agent.

"Okay. I'll let you know in a few minutes, once I'm up and running."

He opened the large trunk which was stocked with a wide variety of equipment. After a few minutes he removed a Crossman .177 millimetre 8-shot semi-automatic air pistol and inserted a new CO_2 cylinder inside the handgun. The gun had been modified with a short, noise-suppressing barrel extension and would fire as fast as he could pull the trigger. He also slid a charged battery pack in a small cordless drill and pocketed a new inch and a half high-speed boring bit.

Closing the lid of the trunk, he walked up to the front of the car to see how his assistant was doing.

"I've got her signal. She's still moving southeast and she's now in northwest Nevada. She's got almost four hundred miles on us," said the young agent.

"Relax, we'll catch her. We can drive twenty four hours a day and she will have to stop sometime because she'll need sleep eventually. Come with me. I have to know if she's in there."

They turned off the laptop and walked past her building and further down the alley. The long barrel of the CO_2 pistol made it a very quiet weapon with a wide variety of uses. Although it was under powered and only lethal in certain close range head shots, it also worked well for knocking on doors from a safe distance.

About a hundred yards past her apartment they concealed themselves behind a parked van with an open view to her door at the top of the stairs. Using the far side mirror of the van as a rest, the older agent aimed and fired a rapid burst of four lead pellets at the center of her door. Ta-ta-ta-tat!

"If she's home she should be answering the door soon," said the older agent in a confident manner.

While they waited several minutes, he put the Crossman CO_2 pistol in his pocket and inserted the new drill bit in the chuck of the cordless driver. Although the area was not especially quiet, it wasn't noisy enough to be out breaking windows or knocking down doors. They both had some training in picking locks, but the difference between a novice locksmith and an expert was time. In this situation that commodity was in short supply.

"Follow me and keep your gun ready, safety off," said the older agent.

Together they walked quietly up the stairs and towards the door. They exchanged a silent look of acknowledgment at the tight cluster of hits in the center of the door.

"Keep a good lookout. This won't take long," said the older agent. He pulled the drill from his jacket pocket and quickly bored two large holes straight through the soft wooden door.

The holes where positioned one inch apart, exactly at the agent's eye level. Placing his eyes next to this pair of holes was like looking through an open door.

"Let's get moving. The place is empty," said the older agent as they walked back to their car.

The younger agent started up the laptop as his partner put away the equipment. "Do you want to drive?" asked the younger agent.

"Yes, I'll take the first shift. We've got lots of ground to cover," he said as they started the car and sped off.

James was now on the correct street and closing in on the address. Her building ended in an odd number and those were now on his left side. This was almost more of a commercial area than residential. He was now in the correct block and slowed his car down while he looked for any visible address numbers. After a couple of minutes James pulled over and parked. He'd find the building on foot as most of these address numbers weren't even lit at this hour.

After walking along the sidewalk, he found her numbers posted on the wall beside the entrance to a used furniture store. A small sign read 'Apartments around the Back'.

Walking back out on the sidewalk he could see several windows above the worn out store canopy and no obvious pathway to the rear of the building. One window was lit even though the curtains were pulled. James had to walk to the end of the block, up the side street and back down the poorly lit alley.

Approaching the building he could see a wooden staircase leading up to an exterior hotel-style covered walkway. An old wooden handrail ran the length of the walkway and he could see three doors; two along the wall and one at the very end. Climbing the dark set of stairs, James could see that Jen's Unit 3 was the last door at the end of the walkway. Units 1 and 2 were either unoccupied or empty and Unit 3 was the only one with a light on. He had been looking for her truck, but as of yet hadn't seen it anywhere.

Walking along the walkway it was obvious from fifty feet away something wasn't right.

The two large holes bored in the door looked like a large pair of eyes peering through the door. A pile of fresh wood shavings lay at the foot of the door and James could now see a group of tiny holes in the front of the door.

A sick feeling was moving quickly into his stomach as he neared the door.

"Jen—Jen—are you in there? Is everything okay? Jen, are you there? Jen, please answer. It's me—James. James Clayton," he yelled as he pounded on the door.

James stood on his toes and cautiously brought his eyes against the pair of holes in the door. There was a small lamp on, but from what he could tell the place was empty except for a few pieces of old furniture. Looking down he noticed a small square of paper with a boot mark on it. He crouched down, reached over and picked it up.

'Back in two Weeks' was written with a black felt pen and two pieces of tape were still attached to the paper. James folded the note and put it in his pocket.

Now he was really feeling sick; sick from guilt and worry. What had just happened here and where was Jen? If she didn't want this job she could have let him know. He could probably still get Bill Riker, but something was wrong here; very wrong. James hated himself for not telling Jen about the tracking unit. She could be dead for all he knew and it was all because of him. James spent the next hour carefully searching for her vehicle.

After checking every street within three blocks on foot he dropped to his knees and vomited in a small rock garden. Nothing was left to do here. James returned to his car for the drive home. Who was responsible for this—for Alexia?

Tomorrow James would have to contact Al Anderson and give him a full report on everything that's happened. He could have told him about Jen and the tracker the last time they spoke and now he desperately wished he had.

The Beaucerons had not been sleeping. Although things may have looked dark from the top of the wall the view from the forest floor was crystal clear. On a calm dark night any potential intruder formed a clearly silhouetted target while walking the top of the perimeter wall. As in the hierarchy of a wolf pack, each one knew its position.

Jen could feel the heightened tension due to darkness, but was confident she'd 'land on all fours', even if she couldn't see the landing.

Her release from the wall signalled the Beaucerons like the green light on a 'Christmas Tree' signals a Top-Fuel dragster. They had started the coordinated intercept run simultaneously. One tight to wall behind her, one tight to the wall ahead of her and the third on a direct intercept course from the forest.

Jen could feel the thick ivy cushion her landing, but wasn't prepared for the slope. She caught her left foot in the vines and tumbled forward as she landed in the thick sloping ivy.

She could feel herself instinctively curl up into the foetal position. The unmistakable sound of animals crashing through in the ivy was growing with each passing millisecond. The knowledge she was at its epicentre was certain. The two intercepting Beaucerons tracking the wall flew over her downed body at full speed in opposite directions as the third jumped her and seemed to run straight up the wall. She desperately fumbled with the snap lock on her Glock 17 while her hands shook uncontrollably.

At that instant she could feel the cool wet nose of one dog probing her neck and face. The sensation of each blast of hot breath hitting her face made her freeze solid as the Beaucerons hovered inches over her face. The other two keenly interrogated her lower body, one dog on each leg with their heads held low. She could feel the heat from every breath as they collectively formed a tighter circle while sounding their guttural growls over her trembling neck and face.

Time had slowed to an eternal pace as the heads of the interrogating Beaucerons blocked out the light from the evening stars. An unstoppable fear began to overwhelm her as she lay beneath the dripping hot saliva and hot blasts of breath. This growling canine judge and jury was intently deliberating her fate. She was sharing the same last view as seen by many animals' last seconds before leaving this world; staring at the face of death and knowing you are about to be eaten alive.

Moments later, after reaching their collective verdict, they lifted their heads and departed through the ivy. The stars returned to illuminate the night sky.

Physically she'd never heard her own heart beating so loudly. It was as if an invisible stethoscope connected her heart directly to her ears. Jen lay motionless, stargazing from the ivy as she was simply shaking too severely to stand. She pressed the snap shut on her Glock 17 retaining strap. Now she definitely knew the meaning of 'frozen with fear.'

The testing of her scentlets had been much more traumatic than expected. She wondered if this would happen every time, and then slowly came to realise they hadn't harmed her in any way. One thing was sure, wearing the correct scentlets on this property was a deadly serious business.

Close to twenty minutes later Jen stood up on her feet and began fumbling through the darkness towards the distant lights. The growth of the undercover thinned out as she got closer to the lights. Jen could already see the vague outline of the house forming in the distance. As she got closer a line of low-profile amber landscape pathway lights delineated the driveway and main walkway extending from the parking area and service buildings up towards the main entrance doors.

This was the first real view of the main house during darkness and she could notice the driveway and path continued up the hill past the house. Exterior lighting majestically showcased the main house with obvious careful planning as to their exact placement and the desired lighting effects. The main house and Alexia's addition were mostly dark at this hour and Jen also noticed Doctor Clayton's car wasn't in its usual spot. From this vantage point it certainly looked like everyone in the house was now asleep.

She knew she was probably in a designated 'canine safety zone', but hadn't seen a trace of the Beaucerons since the attack in the forest. Jen walked past the house and followed the road further up the hill. Several hundred yards ahead the road widened slightly and was soon flanked by two long single-story buildings. Each building looked like a five car garage; five white doors, side by side, facing its own identical twin building. Jen wondered how many small families really needed a ten car garage.

After walking through the garage door gauntlet the driveway faded out into a meandering pathway bordered by lower-output ground lighting. Once again she was surrounded in the forest darkness as she kept moving uphill along the pathway. The walkway looked like it was constructed with reclaimed cobblestone. The forest wasn't completely silent; every now and then she could hear the snap of a nearby branch. If the sounds were caused by the Beaucerons, they certainly knew exactly where she was. After several gradual sets of stairs a new path, branching off to the right, was coming into view. A low level stone planter displayed an impressive rustic metal sign. This set amongst the stones and read; 'Chalet Number Five' with an underlying heavy-set arrow that pointed up the path.

Jen continued up the walkway, guided by the ground lighting. A short distance later the path opened into a large clearing in the tall forest. The interior lights were off, but the silhouette of the building stood out. This building was designed in a style similar to the main house. It was an obvious two-story structure with a full balcony on the front of the second floor and a high forward-facing 'A' frame. The building was constructed with even more logs than the main house, almost like a large European style ski chalet.

Jen searched her pockets and found the key James had left in the envelope. Walking up to the heavy doors she inserted the key and turned it clockwise. She pushed the heavy door open and stepped inside. The chalet was completely dark and she slid her right hand along the interior wall, feeling for a light switch. Her hand stopped on a large double bank of switches. After experimenting with most of the switches, she selected a nice combination of interior lights and studied her new surroundings.

This place was almost as breathtaking as the main house. It had a somewhat open floor plan with another majestic rock fireplace dominating the room. A first floor bedroom with an en-suite washroom, laundry machines, kitchenette and nook were located on the back side and a large living room and office combination on the front.

After a quick search she could see that the kitchen and fridge were well stocked and the pillow-top beds were made up with clean thick eiderdown duvets. Except for the ongoing renovations, it looked as if there was also a regular maid service. A heavy log staircase led up to the second floor. It was obvious something was going on here as cardboard boxes were scattered throughout the chalet. Some had been opened, but many were still in original, unopened packing. Unfinished wire and cable hung from junction boxes opened in various locations in the walls and ceiling. Jen checked the cardboard boxes and could see that most of them contained new computers and related accessories. 'Why so many?' she wondered.

Jen climbed the staircase and had a look around on the second floor. There was one private bedroom, a washroom and an office undergoing renovations complete with still another well stocked library. She walked outside on to the huge covered balcony, comfortably furnished with a couch and lounge chairs sitting below the deep extended soffits. Through the trees she could just make out a few tiny lights from the main house located further down the hill.

Jen locked the front door and turned out all non-essential lights. The washroom connected to the first floor bedroom was laid out with a luxurious walk-in shower and top-of-the-line plumbing fixtures. The shower room had beautiful tiles laid on the ceiling, walls and floor. Twelve inch rain-style shower heads were mounted on all four walls with one central control. The towel racks were full of fresh clean towels expertly matching the tile work, and a fresh bathrobe hung on the wall. Nothing was missing or needed anywhere in this Chalet Number Five. A generous selection of hotel-style soaps, shampoos and conditioners were there for the taking. Jen finally gave in to temptation and had the best shower of her life and soon buried herself under the luxurious thick eiderdowns. Tomorrow she'd definitely try to move a few things from her suite over to Chalet Number Five.

James still wasn't feeling any better after his trip to town. The drive home seemed like it had taken twice the normal time. After passing through the gates and parking his car he remembered that he still hadn't seen the Beaucerons anywhere.

He went inside and walked down the hall to his office. Once again he pulled on the frame of Alexia's painting and opened his antique Murphy wall-safe. He found a freezer bag and carefully removed the note from his pocket and placed it in the plastic bag. It could be future evidence and it clearly had a visible tread mark on the paper. Where could Jen possibly have gone for two weeks? He placed the bag in the safe and locked up his office. He needed sleep and knew the telephone crews would be here soon. First thing in the morning he'd call Al Anderson, and if he didn't have any satisfactory answers he was calling Bill Riker.

The RA-9 operator in charge of monitoring the Clayton surveillance file was having difficulty staying awake. The equipment used for recording the cellular phone calls of James Clayton and the land lines to the estate had been quiet for too long. Disconnect verification had arrived on the central feed program currently monitoring his personal computer. The duration of the zero-activity window had prompted an RA-9 investigation advisory. Why such an extended period of silence? The operator monitoring the situation followed standard RA-9 operating procedures and was subsequently required to notify Professor Akkaim.

"Did you say the computer is disconnected as well as all the phone lines?" asked the professor.

"Yes, that's the way it looks—all but one line."

"Find me a staff member who speaks perfect English. We'll place a call through the deflection processor."

"Yes, right away Professor Akkaim."

Ten minutes later a young man arrived and they were ready to make the call.

"What do you want me to say Professor Akkaim?"

"I want you to say, 'Congratulations! The person answering this call has just won fifty-thousand dollars US in the National Telephone Call Lottery! And who's the lucky winner I'm speaking with?'"

James tossed and turned in bed as the remaining minutes of his sleeping time slipped away. Unable to sleep he got up and went downstairs to the kitchen. It was still dark and even Lisa was still asleep. He brewed himself a large mug of coffee and while he drank it he reflected on all the events of the last twenty-four hours. Sitting on a kitchen stool, he thought about Jen's disappearance, the computer virus, Kyle's new schedule, and the phones being tapped. In his mind he once again counted through the six lines to the estate.

James jolted to attention and accidentally splashed hot coffee on his cotton pyjamas. He had forgotten about one phone line; the line to Chalet Number Five. After a five minute search of the kitchen James managed to find a small working flashlight. He took his remaining coffee down the hall to the small electrical service room in the far end of the house.

Jen was, without a doubt, having the best sleep in her life. This mattress and blanket combination lulled her off to dream land in record time. Something was ringing, over and over, distantly in her dream. The tired mind has a way of gently trying to fit certain sounds into the logical context of your dreams. Suddenly her eyes shot open. A phone was ringing. Ringing, right here in the dark! She jumped off the lofty pillow-top mattress and honed in on the sound. The phone was ringing from somewhere in the downstairs living room or office.

James had always known the location of the main phone junction panel. He had insisted it was installed during construction to simplify and centralize phone hook-ups throughout the estate. Opening the blue-grey cabinet door he could immediately see a small green LED flashing on line six.

Someone was either calling the estate or placing a call from the vacant Chalet Number Five.

Both scenarios were very unusual, and especially so considering the present time of day.

As Chalet Number Five was unoccupied it must be an incoming call and he'd have the phone crews attempt to trace it as soon as they arrived.

Jen could see the phone on the cluttered counter-top. She leaped over the back of a couch, desperately trying to reach the phone in time; a response developed early in life.

"Hello" Jen gasped, happy that she'd managed to beat the ringer.

"Congratulations, the person answering this call has just won fifty thousand dollars US in the National Telephone Call Lottery! And who's the lucky winner I'm speaking with?"

"My name's Lisa" said Jen, as the line went dead.

Chapter 8

It only lasted a split second but James had seen it. The flashing green light over line six in the junction box had changed to a steady green. The call was somehow completed just before he disconnected the line. James went back to the kitchen and refilled his coffee. After contemplating the possibilities of what could've caused the completion of the call, he knew he'd have to investigate the vacant Chalet Number Five. This time he would be packing his loaded Colt 45.

That was certainly one of the strangest calls Jen had ever received. Winning fifty thousand US dollars one hour after secretly arriving at the chalet? It just didn't add up. Maybe someone was looking for her here? Probing, looking for names. She couldn't let her guard down, ever.

Jen quickly found a piece of Stacrofoam from the computer box packaging. Using her multi-tool knife she cut a couple of three inch strips with a groove removed from the top. She still had almost half a tube of instant super-strong glue in the plastic canister and used just enough to affix the strips on the inside top of the front door. After a quick look in the kitchen cabinets she found two ceramic dinner plates and balanced them both on the Stacrofoam strips, leaning against the top of the door trim. They wouldn't survive a fall to the slate tiles if the door was ever opened. Satisfied she'd have some notice if any uninvited guests showed up she climbed back into bed and tried to remember her last dream.

Both agents had seen the highway sign, 'Welcome to Nevada.'

"How far ahead is she now?" asked the older agent.

"It looks like she's just west of Salt Lake City, Utah," replied the younger agent.

"She will have to stop for fuel soon. She's been driving almost ten hours."

"That's right. Maybe she's going to Salt Lake City, or spending the night there," said the younger agent. "We have to close the gap on her. I can't tell Professor Akkaim that we need help."

"He's too angry for that," said the older agent.

"Do you want me drive for a while?" asked the younger agent.

"No. Turn off the tracker and try to get some sleep. I'll drive until the next fuel stop. If there's a store we'll stock up on food and you can drive after that. If she does spend the night in Salt Lake City we'll be there in the morning."

"Okay, sounds good," said the younger agent.

James hated nothing more than missing an opportunity to sleep. Going without sleep and taking quick impromptu naps were facts of life for a trauma surgeon. He selected some clothes and took a shower in his en-suite washroom. Two mugs of coffee and a hot shower was his best chance of feeling better.

Lisa should be awake soon and he could get her to make him a proper breakfast later on. Luckily he wasn't scheduled to work this morning. It was still dark after he finished his shower and James dressed for the cooler weather. He used the flashlight to double check the expiry date on his scentlets and walked down to check on Alexia.

It seemed as if he spent more time with her when she was asleep than when she was awake. Unfortunately it wouldn't make any difference to her. The visits were becoming more of a symbolic ritual than anything else. James sat on the edge of her bed as she slept in her comatose state. He would often manually close her eyelids, but they would just roll back up to reveal her blank comatose stare. Her pulse was steady and her breathing was sporadic as usual. He laid her hand back down, stood up and walked over to his office.

James opened the safe and removed a box of 45 calibre bullets. He carefully filled two clips and inserted one in his Colt 45 and made sure the safety was on. The main key locker was located in his office up on the wall behind his desk. James opened the locker and removed the key for Chalet Number Five. He placed the Colt 45 and the flashlight in his coat pockets and left through the side door.

Usually Lisa set the food out for the Beaucerons first thing in the morning and they could often be found outside the kitchen just at dawn. It was still completely dark as James started walking up the cobble stone pathway. They had removed most of the motion sensor lights around both garages, and also from several other locations, as the Beaucerons were continually activating them during the night. It was about a ten minute walk from the house to Chalet Number Five.

As he approached the three-way junction he was immediately surrounded by all three Beaucerons. It's as if they're challenging you to try and make a run for it. They always closed in from three different directions at the same time, converging on the target. Their stalking tactics were continually improving and they were well aware that night time movement on the cobble stone paths was much quieter than running through the trees. After a ten second interrogation all three dogs resumed their patrol. Even though the lights were off James approached Chalet Number Five quietly and with extra caution.

There was no doubt in his mind that a telephone call had taken place, here, this evening.

James kept his flashlight turned off and removed the door key from his pocket. He slowly unlocked the door and pocketed the key. Preparing himself, he put the flashlight in his left hand and the Colt 45 in his right hand, safety off.

The faint sound of a key sliding slowly into a lock tripped an alarm deep in Jen's cerebral cortex. In an instant fluid motion she rolled out of bed, snatched her Glock 17 and flew up the heavy wooden stairs. She positioned herself flat on the floor at the top of the stairs with the Glock 17 resting on the top rise of the staircase. Her view of the main door and the two balancing plates was marginal at best with so little ambient light. The mix of tactical advantage and personal cover was excellent considering the limited warning she had. That tiny head start could mean the difference between life and death. Jen shuddered at the thought of not having her natural ability to wake up before the alarm. To think she had planned to be sound asleep while waiting for just a ten second warning was troubling. Now, at least, she was ready for anything coming through that door.

James tried to remember the location of the interior light switch. Was it inside on the right wall with a double bank of switches? With his flashlight he'd find them quick enough. He turned his flashlight on and pushed hard on the main door. His senses told him something wasn't right. The stereo-like impact of something hard hitting him on the head and shoulders occurred first. In the time it took the plates to drop and shatter on the floor his eyes detected three rapid muzzle flashes from above. The muzzle flashes from the Glock 17 lit the dark room like an automatic flash camera, followed by the deafening noise a split second later.

"Freeze! Drop your weapon, now! Now!" yelled Jen from her darkened, offset, second floor position.

His Colt 45 and flashlight hit the floor before he could remember dropping them. He had never been shot at in his life and especially from close range.

"Place your right hand on your head and slowly, slowly raise your left hand and turn on the lights!"

James was unable to speak; the symptoms of involuntary shock were setting in even though he couldn't feel any pain. Slowly he fumbled around in the dark, walking on the broken plates until his shaking hand found the light switch.

"Oh no—Doctor Clayton, I'm so sorry," said Jen, visibly shaken.

"Jen, it's you! I'm so happy you're okay! I've been worried sick about you. Can I put my hands down?" said James as the feelings of extreme fear and shock gave way to a new sense of relief.

"Of course you can. So many things have happened since our lunch yesterday," said Jen as she walked down the stairs.

"Yes, I don't know all the details, but somehow things went very wrong yesterday. Listen, we can discuss it later over breakfast. There's an alarm here in the downstairs bedroom. Let's meet at nine-thirty in the main house for breakfast. Lisa will fix us something nice. I'll make sure that no contractors arrive here before then."

"Okay, thanks Doctor Clayton. I'll see you then. Good night."

"Good night Jen. I'll let myself out. Bye."

"Bye. See you for breakfast."

James picked up his flashlight and Colt 45 from the broken porcelain beneath his feet. Switching the safety on, he ejected the clip and placed it in his pocket. As he pulled the door closed the holes of Jen's bullets were clearly visible in the front of the door. One hole was about four inches above his head and the other two had struck on each side of his face. They'd hit at an angle and all three were stopped due to the angular trajectory into the thick wooden door. James closed the door and suddenly realized just exactly how close those shots had been.

Jen would've been trained to be the first to gain control in any confined hostile situation and she had clearly just demonstrated that ability. Still, his head was just framed with lead, and if any bullet had missed its mark he might have just died in Chalet Number Five.

Jen cleaned up the broken plates and balanced two new plates on the Stacrofoam blocks. Luckily James had pointed the flashlight down when he entered and the silhouette of his head and shoulders had been visible in the doorway. She was confident in her close range shooting skills and even more so with a good gun rest.

In the morning she would discuss cash and vehicles with Doctor Clayton. She still needed to pay the rest of the rent and hopefully secure a different vehicle. Jen set the alarm and climbed back underneath the thick eiderdown duvet.

James reached the main house and walked in through the kitchen door. Everyone was still asleep as he went to the office and locked up his Colt 45. He would have to tell Jen about the tracker this morning and possibly have Mike remove it at the shop. He considered turning it over to Al Anderson as his experts might be able to determine its origin. Her truck—where was her truck? He just realised he hadn't seen it anywhere this evening. That could wait until the morning. James went upstairs and tried to squeeze in a few more hours of much needed sleep.

"She's stopped in Salt Lake City," said the younger agent.

"Excellent. Can you pinpoint her location?"

"Well, yes. I have the coordinates, but I don't know what's there."

"How long has she been stopped?" asked the older agent.

"It looks like she's been there for about five minutes."

"Okay, I saw a sign indicating fuel available on the next exit. We'll pick up some snacks and fill the tank. You can do a shift of driving and I'm going to try and get some sleep."

"Okay, should I leave the tracker on?" asked the younger agent.

"Yes, leave it running. How far ahead is she now?"

"She's about three hundred and sixty miles."

"Well, she's travelling slower than us, but not by much. Make sure you don't get stopped for speeding. We won't be able to explain all the equipment in the trunk," said the older agent.

"Yes, I'll be careful. Hopefully she's stopped at a hotel for the night."

"Yes, let's hope so. We're not gaining much ground on her."

Kyle's mind had drifted from his usual scientific studies and the never-ending challenges of leading-edge computer hacking. Certain characteristics of the nano virus in his father's computer were unlike anything he'd seen before. He'd adjusted his dad's requisition list earlier on, his list concerning his preferred selections of the additional new computers that were being purchased for Chalet Number Five. Something about this new virus prevented normal reciprocal tracking programs from revealing the true destination of the stolen data. This new type of cyber shield was facilitating an effective barrier that currently protected these unknown Internet intruders. Nothing occupied Kyle's mind more intensively than an unsolved mystery. He was already devising further tests and diagnostics for his father's hard drive as soon as he returned home.

He didn't know for sure yet, but was reasonably certain his dad would've hired Jen, and Kyle hoped that was exactly what had happened. Arrangements were proceeding for his return to Portland and now he was looking forward to getting home.

Sometimes the pilots on the grey CIA jet would let him fly during the cruise portion of the flight, but he always kept asking them if he could fly an approach or take-off. He knew they couldn't let him, but he still enjoyed trying. In his own mind he was confident he could perform a precision landing or take-off in that jet with ease. Sometimes he'd be transported to the estate with an armed escort and occasionally he'd be flown in a helicopter. On several previous occasions his father had flown out and picked him up, but that was an exception.

James wasn't always available and they preferred to have guards on board during any trips to and from the estate. It always took a fair amount of imagination to picture someone hijacking a helicopter, but he knew they had valid reasons for their concerns. Kyle would get to review his internship schedule soon and was hoping to visit several leading-edge physics facilities. The Central Fusion Research Complex 8 was on the top of his list. CFRC-8 was currently the most advanced laser fusion facility in the United States.

The two agents pulled up to the pumps and stopped the car.

"I'll fill the tank and you can buy some food, pick up a few road maps if you can," said the older agent.

Ten minutes later, they switched positions and pulled out of the station.

"Is she still stopped in Salt Lake City?" asked the younger agent.

"It looks that way. She's not showing any motion and the coordinates are still the same as before."

"Good. We'll start closing the gap now," said the younger agent.

"Remember, watch your speed."

"I will," said the younger agent, happy to be driving for a change.

It hadn't taken long for Bill Riker to secure a protection contract after his return to Iraq. Men with his skills were highly sought after in this part of the world. This new job involved operations in several different areas and also in what was left of Baghdad.

A group of individuals were involved in the offshore procurement of various prohibited materials. These were required for a private venture that involved growing highly specialized crystals for some unknown purpose. Whatever his clients did wasn't particularly important, just as long as they weren't killed doing it. Twice he'd suspected that he or his clients were being followed, but because the streets were always so crowded it was difficult to prove.

He had to know; that was part of his job. He intentionally started moving throughout the city to confirm if he was, or wasn't, being followed. After several sightings of the same two individuals he had seen four miles away he knew he definitely had a problem. Once, or twice maybe, but three sightings in such a short time span was highly unlikely.

It didn't take long until Bill was following the two men who were now searching for him. It was getting late in the day and with some luck they'd return to a hotel or where ever they were holed up. Although most crimes were relatively easy to commit in this area, daylight shootings still attracted some attention. After almost two hours of futile searching both men had made their way back to the compound where they knew Bill was currently staying.

They were parked in a vehicle that had a distant view of compound entrance gates. With their binoculars they could keep the entrance gates under surveillance from their off-road position. Bill called a close friend with excellent logistical connections. An hour later he met up with the driver of a flat deck truck covered with an olive green canvas. A small choice of arms was laid out in the back including a battle worn RPG launcher.

He showed the driver which vehicle he wanted and climbed in the back. A vertical tear in the fabric would serve his purpose well. The driver waited for the local traffic to die down before he started up and slowly drove alongside the target vehicle.

Both men turned towards the truck and stared wide-eyed as the launcher tube emerged from the canvas.

Bill only needed one close range, direct hit from the RPG to completely destroy the vehicle. To his well-trained eye their chances of surviving that destruction were zero. He still had no idea who had been following him or why, only that they weren't following him anymore. If possible, an effort would be made to locate any fragments of identification from the body parts, provided the local police hadn't yet responded. Unfortunately it would almost certainly require the services of a forensics lab to reconstruct any remaining remnants from their personal identification.

"Something's happening with her vehicle. It's starting to move," said the older agent.

"Check the trip log. How long was she parked?" asked the younger agent.

"Twenty seven minutes, according to the trip log data. She's probably stopped for a meal or gas. It doesn't look like a hotel stop," said the older agent, yawning as he spoke.

"Well, what about Kyle? Any chance that he could be with her?" asked the younger agent, keeping his speed up.

"Anything's possible. I'm sure he knows how to drive from what I've heard about him, but I doubt the kid has a driver's license."

"Still no information on exactly where they stopped?"

"No, I've just got the coordinates."

"Try entering the coordinates in Google Map."

"Okay, that's a good idea. I'll try it."

"Have you used it before?" asked the younger agent, knowing he had the edge concerning computer skills.

"Okay, I've entered them—now what?"

"You have to pan and zoom in on the coordinates. See if you can tell where they've stopped."

Several minutes later he said, "It looks like a large truck stop or truck transfer yard. It's hard to tell for sure with this much zoom."

"Okay. And she's still moving now?"

"Yes, she's back up to highway speed, still heading southeast."

"You may as well shut the laptop off and try to get some rest. We can check it again the next time we switch seats."

"Okay, drive carefully."

"I will," said the younger agent, pressing just a little harder on the accelerator.

If Lisa had been a light sleeper she wouldn't have slept through the noise from Chalet Number Five. She had her alarm set earlier than usual because the contractors and telephone crews were scheduled to work today. Although it wasn't required, she always set up an impressive table of coffee and snacks during the day and prepared a quality sit-down lunch for anyone interested. Mornings were the busiest time for Lisa with the household breakfast orders and lunch and dinner preparations. Fortunately the kitchen was so well designed she could place large food orders as the walk-in fridge and freezer provided ample restaurant-style storage.

After her shower she went down to the kitchen and started brewing the morning coffee. Looking outside she could see the sun creeping over the trees as she started preparing the three meals for the Beaucerons.

A section of their kennel had three private stalls within the enclosure located off the side of the kitchen that were equipped with safety dispensing doors for feeding. A manual lever operated the feed gates, and after she placed the dishes out, the lever would open the chain link doors to allow the dogs into their own private feeding stalls.

It also provided an ideal time to lock the Beaucerons inside their individual kennels as they had to walk to the back of each stall to reach their meals. She could see all three dogs waiting this morning and decided to lock them in their feeding stalls for now. Each kennel had an electric sliding entrance door and the control panel offered several different boarding configurations.

Selecting the confinement option activated an invisible motion sensor beam. When a dog passed a pre-set point two thirds of the way into the stall the tripped beam opened the food door as the containment door closed. Doctor Clayton would occasionally issue temporary scentlets when people were required to work outside of designated canine safety areas. If Lisa wasn't sure she always tried to confine the Beaucerons until she checked with James.

The dogs appeared extra hungry today and were easily confined in their kennels. As Lisa went to pick up her coffee mug she noticed a note from Doctor Clayton on the kitchen cork-board; 'Good Morning Lisa. Jen is staying in Chalet Number Five. Can you arrange a breakfast for the two of us at nine-thirty, preferably upstairs in the loft if you don't mind? Thanks.'

Lisa was surprised and happy at the same time, to hear Jen had returned to the estate. That would be a little extra work, but nothing she couldn't handle.

Lisa helped on occasion with Alexia's nutritional needs, but for the most part the nurses looked after her dietary requirements. She was long past the point of attending scheduled sit down meals and would often require various intravenous feeding solutions.

James's dream had warped into a movie scene resembling life at the center of a thunderstorm. The light from the gunshots had lit the dark Chalet like bolts of lightning and the gunshot blasts felt like nearby thunder. Opening up his eyes and blinking a few times confirmed that he'd finally managed to get some sleep. After checking his clock he again rolled out of bed and went for another hot shower. The contractors were due to finish the work at Chalet Number Five tonight and they would certainly be wondering about the new bullet holes in the door. James hoped a believable explanation for the bullet holes might come to him after his morning coffee.

He picked out some clean clothes, dressed and went downstairs.

"Good Morning Doctor Clayton, would you like some coffee?"

"Yes please. The biggest mug you've got."

"I've got just what the doctor ordered," she said as she fixed him a grossly over-sized mug of fresh coffee.

"Thanks, that's perfect. I see you've got the dogs confined this morning."

"Yes. Shall I leave them in today?"

"Yes, that's probably a good idea. I'll let you know when it's safe to release them."

"Very well Doctor Clayton. Nice to hear Miss Lamar is back. Will she be working with Kyle?"

"Yes, she started yesterday. Please try to accommodate any requests she may have. I've given her lots of latitude in her new role and plan to assist her with any requirements she may have."

"Yes of course. I'll do my best."

"I know you will Lisa, thanks. We'll see you at breakfast."

Jen opened her eyes well before the alarm was set. It was getting light and she realised there was a problem to be addressed. Jumping out of bed she dressed in the only clothes she had and went to make some coffee. Smiling to herself, she realised there wasn't any instant coffee to be found. She poured some fresh coffee beans into the grinder and started a pot of coffee. As the coffee brewed Jen took a careful look at last night's damage. The broken plates had been swept up after the shooting and so far there wasn't any trace of the bullet holes. She removed the two dinner plates and cut the Stacrofoam blocks off the top of the door. Opening the front door, the location of the holes was now obvious. The bullets had entered at a downward forty-five degree angle. James was standing in front of the door as he pushed it open which had given Jen a split second profile shot from her position. The holes were located at eye level and would be seen by anyone entering the front door.

Using her knife she trimmed any splinters around the holes flush to the door and almost filled the holes with Stacrofoam. She kept the wooden splinters and carved more from the bottom edges of the door. Jen returned to the kitchen and cleaned out the electric coffee grinder. Filling it with all her wood shavings, she pressed the top down and ground them to fine sawdust. Jen poured the sawdust in a tin can and mixed in the last of her glue. She now had matching, workable wood filler that nicely filled the top portion of the bullet holes. With a few passes from the file on her multi knife, and scuffs from an old furniture rag, the holes were now virtually invisible. Happy with the repairs she locked the front door and filled a large mug with fresh coffee.

Jen settled into a comfortable couch with her coffee and admired the beautiful Chalet Number Five in the morning light. It certainly appeared much larger during the daylight than it had last night. It had such a grand majestic style that just being here and watching the sunrise uplifted her spirits.

The younger agent was making good time now that his partner had fallen asleep. The country was starting to open up nicely west of Salt Lake City. The long straight stretches of open highway made speeding effortless. Doing the limit in the mountain highways seemed appropriate, but not out here in this vehicle. No expenses had been spared during the custom modifications and equipment installations in any dedicated RA-9 vehicles. It could easily travel at one hundred and thirty five miles an hour with good stability and handling on roads like this. The faint flashing light in his mirror remained unnoticed.

Seeing the city limits signage the younger agent started reducing his speed.

"Wake up! We're getting close to Salt Lake City. Try to get the tracker up and running," said the younger agent.

"Are the rear RPG launchers armed?" asked the older agent.

"Yes. Why do you ask?"

"There's a police car behind us and he has his flashing lights on. I told you five times already to watch your speed," cursed the older agent.

"Should we take him out? It's before sunrise and there isn't much traffic," said the younger agent, clearly agitated.

"I don't think we have any other options. He's probably got us on camera by now and with all the equipment in this vehicle we'll be arrested for sure," said the older agent, frantically studying his surroundings. "Pick up your speed and hold your lead. I don't want him coming up on us until we're closer to the lake up ahead. We need a stretch of road next to deep water, and as close as possible."

"I understand," said the younger agent as he pressed his foot down hard.

Jen made her bed and cleaned up any trace of her stay. She wanted to be out before anyone arrived and she left nothing behind in the chalet. Locking the front door she admired her repairs. Even in the direct morning sunlight it would take a searching eye to find them.

Her scentlets were still valid and she now felt reasonably comfortable walking on the grounds. After walking along the cobblestone pathway from the chalet she came to the main pathway to the house. A left turn would take her downhill to the main house and a right turn continued up through the trees. She still had no idea where the other chalets were located, but she was looking forward to doing some more exploring just as soon as she could.

Walking down to the house she once again passed between the two garage buildings. All ten garage doors were closed and she was tempted to try and open one. After a quick look around the sides and back she didn't notice any windows, just a single door at each end.

Jen also scanned the adjacent trees, but couldn't see any sign of surveillance cameras. Not wanting to trip any silent alarms she continued on her walk to the house.

Further down the road she heard the dogs barking occasionally. It dawned on her that it was the first time she'd ever heard them bark. As the house came into view she could see the fenced-in kennel enclosure next to the kitchen. Even though she couldn't see the dogs it was apparent they were inside this private kennel enclosure. Jen walked up to the side kitchen door and could see Lisa setting up a large table. She tapped on the window and waved as Lisa came over and opened the side door.

"Good morning Jen. I heard you were back on the estate. Please come in," said Lisa with a welcoming smile.

"Thanks Lisa, it's nice to be back."

"Come and sit down. Would you like some fresh coffee?"

"Sure, I'd love some. Thanks," said Jen as she hopped on a stool in the kitchen.

"You look like you've got the busiest job around here. Do you work alone here in the kitchen?"

"Is half and half okay Jen?"

"Sure that's great."

"Well yes, it's mostly just me. I occasionally bring in extra help if there's something special going on, but that doesn't happen too often. Sugar?"

"Yes please. Thanks."

"I hear you and James are having breakfast at nine thirty in the loft. I've started setting things up for both of you. He should be along soon. He's still in his office with the contractors talking about the upgrades to Chalet Number Five. You can wait upstairs in the loft or out on the balcony, which ever you prefer."

"Okay, thanks Lisa," said Jen as she hopped off the stool and departed the kitchen. Jen walked upstairs and settled into a comfortable chair on the covered balcony. She could get used to this.

"Why do you need so many computers set up in that chalet Doctor Clayton?" asked the foreman of the installation crew.

"The question of 'why' is not really relevant. I want all the hook-ups wired in close proximity to the stations on the first floor, but mostly on the second floor. You can set up the primary double computer system upstairs and a single backup system downstairs. Leave eight additional computers in the original unopened boxes upstairs and a single spare downstairs. Please make adequate provisions for multiple computers at both the upstairs and downstairs computer stations. Also check the available power from the main electrical panel in the chalet and upgrade it if you have to.

The phone lines are all down on the estate for security reasons and please tell your crews that I want all cell phones turned off and kept that way. If you need to bring in an electrician have someone drive well clear of the estate before calling them. Make sure they get the message about the phones as well. I'll remind you again that I don't want the system powered up or connected in any way."

"Thanks for the clarification. I'll do some electrical load calculations. These are about the most powerful computer models available in this city and I'll make sure you have the electrical provisions to run all twelve."

"That's great news and for your information I'll be having another crew working on the phone equipment today. Hopefully they won't be in your way. We'll keep the kitchen open all day, so feel free to come and help yourself anytime you like."

"Okay, that's great. I'll let you know when we're done. Talk to you later."

"Thanks. You can find me around here today if you have any additional questions," said James as he escorted them from his office and out through the kitchen.

"Hi Lisa, any sign of the telephone crews?"

"No. I haven't heard anyone call on the main gate intercom, but I'll let you know if I do."

"What about Jen? Has she made an appearance this morning?"

"Yes. She's having a coffee on the upstairs balcony."

"Oh, that's great. I'll go and have a word with her."

"Shall I bring you a coffee before breakfast?" asked Lisa.

"No, that's fine. I'll find a mug and fill it myself."

"Sure. It's all in the usual place."

James poured himself a cup from the kitchen and went upstairs to talk with Jen.

The installation of RPG launchers in RA-9 vehicles had a few variations, but not many. They were almost always mounted beneath a false floor in the large rear trunk. Sometimes they were positioned to fire directly aft, but the preferred installation was a fifteen degree angle towards the center. If fired simultaneously the converging impact point of both grenades would be forty yards behind the vehicle. A pair of false back-up lights at the rear of the car concealed the ends of the recessed launching tubes. The lights had an automatic latch that flipped open the hinged lens covers the instant the launchers were armed. The covers still had to be closed manually after use and each launching tube was only preloaded with a single rocket propelled grenade. It was a highly effective, dual-shot system designed exactly for this type of requirement; the requirement to totally destroy any vehicle in pursuit of RA-9 agents.

"We're going to have to act soon. This lake can't be more than two miles long. Should I slow down and let him get closer?" said the younger agent.

"Yes, the lake along here looks deep. Try to keep him about two hundred yards behind you."

"Where do you want to take him? On a corner or a straight stretch?" said the younger agent while trying to gauge his speed to maintain the desired lead.

"A left curve would've been best except for the guard rails. I want the vehicle cleared off the highway after the hit. It would take time to unbolt guard rails and we might be seen."

"Good point. You want a straight stretch then?" asked the visibly nervous younger agent.

"Yes, with a good drop off the right side of the road and deep water. No beaches."

"Okay, he's still got his lights and siren on. Let's take him out soon."

"It looks like a good long section next to the lake is coming up," said the younger agent.

"That might work. Get ready to start slowing down. Put your right signal on. Better arm the RPG's before he gets too close," said the older agent.

"Are we going for a dual shot? Or singles?" asked the younger agent.

"A single outside shot on a highway curve will almost always cause the car to leave the road. In this case we'll take him on a straight stretch with both launchers. I want to hit him at the convergence point, forty yards to the rear. We'll definitely need to destroy his forward camera and a dual converging hit will cause the most damage. If we're lucky the car will reach the lake anyway."

"Okay, I've armed both launchers. I'll slow down as if I'm pulling over," said the younger agent.

"Good, can you see any other traffic?" asked the older agent.

"No. Just the cop closing in from behind."

"Okay, this stretch looks good. Slow right down and fire on my mark."

"Okay, he's getting close now," said the younger agent.

"I'm watching behind us. Keep driving farther up this hill. It's a better drop off."

"Okay okay, just tell me what you want," said the younger agent.

"Get ready, start accelerating slowly. That's good. I want him exactly forty yards behind us. Hold it, hold it. Fire!"

Chapter 9

Professor Akkaim dialled the shift supervisor working in the computer cyber labs.

"Hello," said the supervisor.

"It's Professor Akkaim and I want to see you in my office."

"Okay. How about an hour from now?" asked the supervisor.

"How about right away?" said the professor as he slammed the receiver down. Sometimes the personnel performance of abducted recruits was better than those hired through normal channels.

The supervisor stopped what he was doing and made his way to the professor's office.

"You wanted to see me Professor?" asked the supervisor.

"Yes, I want a current update on the situation in Portland and I want to know if you've heard anything from the agents sent to shadow Bill Riker?"

"No, they are both still overdue on their check-in and we've had no other information as of yet."

"Have you been monitoring financial transactions from the agents in Iraq?" asked the professor.

"We've been trying, but cash is the preferred currency these days in Baghdad, and we haven't received any recent transaction notifications."

"When was the last transaction that you know about?"

"They withdrew four thousand dollars US and converted it to local currency about two hours after arriving in Iraq."

"So they haven't even acknowledged finding Bill Riker at this point."

"That's correct Professor, we haven't heard anything from them," answered the supervisor.

"What about the two agents following Ms. Lamar's truck? Have they checked in since they left Portland?"

"No, I expect that it won't be too long until they make contact. They probably want to locate her first and then give us an update."

"What's her location?"

"The last time I checked she was just over one hundred miles southeast of Salt Lake City."

"Has she been traveling the whole time?"

"Yes," replied the supervisor.

"Well then it's possible she's not alone."

"It's possible, although some people can drive for very long periods. We'll know more as time goes on."

"As time goes on," repeated the professor. "I want information now. Do you understand that?"

"Yes of course Professor, we're doing what we can."

"Have you been able to access information about the current financial affairs of the Clayton family or Ms. Lamar?" asked the professor.

"That's always a challenge with the latest security installed on all the banking systems. We have basic access to credit card transaction data, but not to any personal accounts. We came close with our link to the doctor's home computer, but as you know that connection has been recently terminated."

"Any contact from our friends in Vancouver, Canada?"

"No, they'll call if they notice any activity around the CIA jet."

"Do we have twenty-four hour surveillance at the airport?"

"Yes, around the clock. If anything happens they'll contact us immediately."

"You haven't intercepted any new telephone communications from the estate?"

"No, nothing at all. The landlines and cell phones have all been quiet except for our direct call last night."

"Who's the 'Lisa' that answered the phone?" asked the professor.

"I believe she's an employee, a cook maybe."

"I've requested information on all current and former employees and expect to receive that soon."

"Why was the call cut off?" asked the professor.

"I don't know for sure, but it was somehow terminated from the estate," replied the supervisor.

"We seem to be losing control of everything concerning this case. I want you and your computer team to find a way of accessing the current financial details of the Clayton family and Ms. Lamar. This isn't a suggestion, it's a direct order and I want it followed! I've transferred additional personnel from Seattle and Sinzar Bakkir will be arriving in California later next week."

"Okay Professor, I'll get our best personnel working to find a way into the banking system. We might not be able to transfer funds, but I'm optimistic we can at least view statements."

"That's a start. Keep me informed of any new developments, no matter how small."

"Yes Professor," said the supervisor, as he stood up and walked out of the office. He was already worried about the problems of hacking into any American financial institution.

"Good morning Jen, nice to see you up so early. Oh please, don't get up," said James as he sat down next to her in one of the comfortable balcony chairs.

"Good morning Doctor," said Jen with a smile and a handshake. "You have such a beautiful view from here."

"Yes, I like it too. I often sit out here," said James as he set his coffee down on the small table between them.

"Sorry about last night. I'd received a strange call earlier at the chalet and I wasn't taking any chances regarding security," said Jen with a sincere look at the doctor she'd nearly killed.

"That's perfectly understandable. Frankly I was impressed with how quickly you secured the situation," replied the doctor. "I'm sure today's contractors will be curious about what exactly transpired last night up in Chalet Number Five."

"Are you referring to the bullet holes in the front door?" asked Jen.

"Yes, they can't help but notice them when they enter this morning," said the doctor.

"I repaired them this morning," said Jen.

"Really—that's fantastic! How did you manage to do that?" asked the doctor, visibly impressed.

"Oh, I just used a little of this and that. I'm sure they won't be noticed."

"Well, that's a nice surprise. Who called last night?"

"A representative from the National Telephone Call Lottery claiming I'd won fifty thousand dollars US. Then they asked me for my name."

"Did you give it to them?" asked the doctor.

"I used Lisa's name and then the line went dead," said Jen.

"Why did you use her name?" asked the doctor.

"As I said, lots of things happened yesterday. I discovered a tracking device attached to my gas tank."

"How could you have found that?" asked the stunned doctor.

"I was just doing a routine personal inspection after the installation work at M & U Motors. I was wondering if maybe you were following me?" asked Jen.

"Jen, I'll be honest with you. Mike notified me about the tracking device and I didn't know anything about it. I was going to tell you after I spoke with the government agent that deals with Kyle's affairs."

"And you've spoken with him concerning the tracking device?" asked Jen, intently curious.

"Yes, they said they didn't know anything about it."

"That's strange. Could this have anything to do with Kyle?" asked Jen.

"Of course that's certainly a possibility, but we don't have any idea who's responsible. I've just been informed of recent telephone and computer surveillance attempts and we are taking all the necessary measures to address those issues," replied the doctor.

"Good morning, breakfast is ready over in the loft," said Lisa with her normal cheery voice.

"Thanks Lisa," replied the doctor. "Let's move to the loft and we'll continue our conversation over breakfast."

"Sounds good," said Jen as they rose from the comfortable balcony chairs.

James led Jen through an interior second floor walkway overlooking the main living area and connecting with the loft. Jen felt a sudden shiver when she noticed Alexia's wheelchair down below. Her head was cocked back in her neck brace as she stared straight up at the two of them.

Lisa had set out a large selection of light foods and open face sandwiches almost like a Scandinavian-style breakfast with fresh juice and a new pot of coffee. The breakfast was set out on a low table between two couches and they both settled into the comfortable cushions, facing each other.

"It looks beautiful. Lisa certainly knows what she's doing," said Jen admiring Lisa's obvious talent.

"Yes, we were lucky to find her. She's very skilled at what she does."

"I can see that," said Jen reaching down for a side plate.

"I tried to call you last night but I couldn't get through," said the doctor.

"Sorry. After I found the tracking device I started taking additional precautions."

"So you turned your phone off?"

"Yes I did. New methods of reverse cell phone tracking are becoming quite common."

"After I couldn't reach you on the phone I tried to visit you at your apartment to warn you about the tracking device," said the doctor.

"I appreciate that. I know that was well out of your way," said Jen impressed by his concern.

"And I wasn't there obviously," said Jen, wishing she hadn't.

"No, you weren't. But someone else was," said the doctor, watching the sudden surprise in her expression.

"Someone was at my apartment?" she asked with genuine shock at the news.

"Yes. I don't know if they were *in* your apartment, but they were definitely *at* your apartment. Did you have any holes in your front door?"

"Did I have holes in my front door? No, absolutely not. What kind of holes? Did somebody kick the door in?"

"No, it was from a large drill. Someone drilled two large holes, right at eye level, side by side, in your front door," said the doctor with the seriousness of delivering a cancer diagnosis.

"No. That definitely happened after I left," said Jen, visibly disturbed at the news. "So someone really is looking for me."

"That's the way it appears, but unfortunately I don't have any other information to give you."

"I'm going to need a replacement vehicle and some cash today if that's possible," said Jen, utilising her best strategic timing to raise the question.

"Of course, we have lots of vehicles available here. I'll give you a master key for our two garage buildings and you can help yourself. Check the plates for insurance, but I think most of them are still valid. As for cash, I have about five thousand if you need it. You can take it as an advance on expenses. That's fine with me."

"That's excellent. Thanks. I'll take you up on that. I'd prefer using cash when possible rather than leaving a financial trail of my whereabouts."

"I agree. I don't think you can be too cautious at this point," said the doctor.

"Where were you last night, if you don't mind me asking?"

"Not at all, I installed the tracker on a decoy target and found a new place to live and hide my truck. I made my way back over here late in the evening hoping to get another vehicle in the morning and possibly some working cash."

"Well, you did have a busy night. How did you get back inside the estate?" asked the doctor.

"I climbed the wall."

"Then you obviously remembered to put on your scentlets," said the doctor.

"Yes, fortunately for me I did. That's a very impressive group of dogs. They were definitely 'on duty' last night."

"Yes, they usually are," said the doctor while holding her gaze.

"Excuse me Doctor Clayton. There's a van at the front gate. They said Al Anderson sent them to work on the phones," said Lisa.

"Thanks. Let them through and have them come up to the main house. Thanks for the nice breakfast."

"My pleasure, I'll let you know when they're here."

"Thanks Lisa, we'll be in the office."

"Have you had enough to eat Jen?" asked the doctor.

"Oh yes, that was excellent, thanks."

"Let's go down to my office and I'll show you the key locker and find you some operating capital."

Jen followed the doctor downstairs and over to his office. She never mentioned seeing Alexia to the doctor, but felt strangely relieved that she'd vanished from the living room.

"Have a seat Jen," said the doctor as he walked over to Alexia's painting. He opened his antique wall-safe and removed a master key and five one thousand dollar bundles of US currency.

"Here you are Jen. This master key will open the key locker over on the wall. Here, let me show you. The contents are clearly delineated, as you can see. You'll find keys inside for everything on the estate. Take this garage master key with you and help yourself to whatever you need. All the vehicles have main gate transmitters and you'll find keys in the ignition and insurance and gas cards in the glove compartments. We don't usually lock them up once they've been returned to the storage garage.

"Here's a five-thousand dollar advance for expenses. Are you going back to your new place today?" asked the doctor.

"Yes, I have a few things to take care of. Do you know when Kyle is expected to return?" Jen asked.

"He should be home soon, within a day or two."

"That's great. I'm keeping the location of my new place confidential and I'll probably start moving a few things over to Chalet Number Five if that's okay with you?"

"Absolutely, let me know if there's anything you need. We'll all get together and discuss Kyle's new internship schedule after he returns."

"Okay, see you later then. I'm looking forward to finally meeting Kyle. Thanks for everything," Jen replied as she got up to leave and noticed Lisa at the door.

"Excuse me Doctor Clayton. The men from the phone company are at the front door. Should I send them in?" asked Lisa.

"No Lisa. I'll meet them out front in a few minutes."

"Okay. I'll let them know," said Lisa as she spun around and walked down the hall.

"I have to run Jen. You can slip out through the kitchen if you like. Perhaps you'd like to walk up to the garage buildings and examine your choice of vehicles."

"Sure, that sounds like a great idea. Thanks again."

"You're welcome. Have a good day," said the doctor as he locked up the safe. He noticed Jen's note with the boot print on it and realised he'd forgotten to mention it to her.

"Excellent shot! Hurry, stop the car and back up now! We have to confirm the forward camera was destroyed," yelled the older agent as he removed two pairs of gloves from the glove compartment.

The sheer force of dual RPG's striking an oncoming vehicle peeled the front hood and roof open like a sardine can. The failure of the forward engine mounts rotated the engine up and through what was the windshield. The remains of the partially decapitated officer were nearly invisible behind the rear of the deformed and twisted engine block, lodged in the back of what was the front seat compartment.

"Put these on and bring me the sawed off shotgun from under the front seat!" demanded the older agent as he jumped out of the car.

"Okay. What do you want for ammo?" asked the younger agent as he ejected a shell from the breech with the pump action.

"What's in there now?" asked the older agent.

"Bear slugs."

"That will work fine. Come on, we need to locate the camera recording hardware," said the older agent as he began scouring through the wreckage.

"I've found the camera body and I'm trying to trace out the wires. I've got a red, yellow and black, but they just disappear into the console debris," said the older agent.

"Have you tried the trunk?" asked the younger agent.

"No. Go take a look and shoot it open if it's locked. Hurry, we have to get out of here," yelled the older agent while still frantically looking for the correct color combination of wires.

"It's leaking gas everywhere back here," yelled the younger agent.

"Then kneel down and shoot up. We have to destroy the recording equipment."

"Okay, stand back," said the younger agent as he walked further to the rear. He slowly crouched down and then blasted a slug through the lock.

"Did you get it open?" yelled the older agent.

"Yes. Hey, there might be something here on the right side."

"Have you got wires running out of it?"

"Yes."

"How many?" yelled the older agent.

"Three, a black, red and yellow," said the younger agent as he leaned forward into the rear trunk.

"Let me have a look. That might be it," said the older agent as he ran to the back of the patrol car. "I think that's it. Go up to the front and put a couple of slugs through the camera body then come back and do the same here. Be careful where you aim, it's unusual the main gas tank didn't explode and I don't want to be standing beside this wreck if it does. I'm going back to the car. Are the keys still in the ignition?" asked the older agent.

"No I've got them. Here they are," said the younger agent as he tossed him the keys.

Almost anything hit at close range with a twelve gauge bear slug is never the same again. The forward camera body was completely destroyed by the first two rounds and the young agent eagerly put three more slugs through the recording box bolted in the trunk of the patrol car.

The force of the initial blast had brought the patrol car close to the edge of the road, but it still needed help.

"Get in," said the older agent after he'd positioned their front bumper against the back of the patrol car.

"Should I shoot the gas tank first?" asked the younger agent.

"No, take a stick of dynamite from the trunk and crimp a ten second fuse into a blasting cap. Punch a hole in the stick with a screwdriver and push the cap about halfway in at a forty five degree angle. Let me know when you're ready," said the older agent.

The younger agent was never comfortable working with dynamite and it always made him nervous.

"Okay—now what?" he said with trembling fingers.

"Just keep it ready. Get back in the car and roll your window down. Have you got a lighter?" asked the older agent correcting his alignment with the bumper of the patrol car.

"Yes, I think so," replied the younger agent.

"Get ready to light the fuse. Lean out the window and toss it into the open trunk. Okay?"

"When?"

"When I say so," said the older agent applying some power to see how easily he could push the patrol car. "Do you see any cars coming?" asked the older agent.

"No, it's all clear."

"Good," said the older agent as he slowly pushed the wrecked patrol car closer to the edge of the steep embankment. "Light the fuse and toss it in the trunk. Don't miss."

"I won't," replied the younger agent as he stretched unnaturally out through the passenger window and tossed it in the trunk.

With one strong rev of the engine the wreck was over the edge and accelerating towards the lake. The blast from the dynamite immediately detonated the fuel tank as it rolled down the steep embankment. The height of the flames and cloud of black smoke was followed by a vertical plume of steam as the hot metal disappeared below the murky surface.

"Good throw," said the older agent. "Let's toss the rest of the debris over the edge and get going. Close the lens covers on the launch tubes while you're out there. We'll change our license plates at the next suitable pull-out," said the older agent.

Together they lifted the mangled vehicle hood and cart wheeled it down the hill and into the lake. The destroyed front bumper and one door were almost fifty yards from the wreck and luckily they also disappeared beneath the water due to the steep grade of the hill. Nothing could be done about all the broken glass on the highway. Hopefully it wouldn't be detected by anyone passing by at highway speeds.

"Okay that's good enough, let's go. Get out the laptop and start up the tracker," said the older agent.

"What about the RPG's? Should we reload them?" asked the younger agent.

"No. That takes too long. We'll do it later, maybe, when we're changing the plates."

"Okay. I'll let you know when I'm receiving her signal," said the younger agent.

"Good. Get her current speed and distance from of us as well."

"Okay, this shouldn't take too long—I'm picking up her signal now. She's one hundred and ten miles ahead and traveling at sixty-five miles an hour."

"Any routing changes?" asked the older agent.

"No, she's still heading southeast."

The pair of telephone technicians knocking at James Clayton's door had no idea they were lucky to be alive. Only the last minute news of a possible visit by Al Anderson to the Claytons' estate had averted their substitution with two RA-9 agents. Al Anderson was the only one who probably knew the technicians personally and would surely have recognised any impostors.

The new agents just flown in from Seattle had worked with lightning speed and extreme efficiency to plan all the necessary ground work. The fake road maintenance scene on lower West Cedar Drive included a carefully laid out traffic diversion marked with the standard tall orange cones. The RA-9 agents were professionally attired in reflective vests and hardhats and each was equipped with professional-looking handheld stop signs. The quick and efficient two person switch planned at the roadblock would have occurred with relative ease. These two unsuspecting phone technicians were almost certainly not even carrying weapons.

Opportunities to enter the Claytons' estate and service the entire telephone system were extremely rare. Professor Akkaim had been informed of the scheduled service call from recent wiretap information and had directed his supervisors to act immediately. News of the sudden precautionary cancellation had not yet reached the professor and would definitely be a disappointing setback.

"Good morning Doctor Clayton. I trust Al Anderson told you we were stopping by today," said the telephone technician.

"Yes he did. Please come in. Where would you like to start working?" asked the doctor.

"If you could show us the main telephone control panel first, that will be a good place to start. We'll be installing several new pieces of equipment, designed to detect the source of any system intrusions."

"Great, follow me and I'll show you the electrical room. The tables over there behind me have coffee and snacks available if you like, and the door to the contractor's washroom is to the left of the main kitchen entrance."

"Thanks. We'll do our best to restore the privacy of your phone service."

"I appreciate that. Let me know if I can be of any further assistance," said the doctor.

"This should keep us busy for the morning. Thanks Doctor Clayton."

James showed the technicians to the electrical room and returned to the kitchen. He certainly missed being without secure phone communications and was anxious to see them restored.

"Hello again Lisa, are the Beaucerons still locked up?"

"Yes of course," Lisa replied.

"Just double checking, there's lots of people around today and I wouldn't want any accidents."

"Yes Doctor Clayton. Should I prepare a hot lunch for the contractors?"

"Just something light is fine, use your discretion. I'll be over in my office if you need anything."

"Okay, thanks," said Lisa as she continued with her preparations.

Jen had never walked anywhere with five thousand US dollars crammed in her pockets. The variety of denominations created a sizable fold of cash along with the inescapable awareness of its presence. After thanking Lisa again for breakfast she started walking back up the path to Chalet Number Five. The weather was cool and sunny with a light breeze from the northwest. She knew it would be a great day to do some exploring around the estate, but decided that could wait. She had to pick a vehicle and make the trip to her new apartment.

She had everything with her that she'd brought over the night before and wouldn't need to return to the Chalet this morning. Carrying this much cash around felt unusual, but it was something she could probably get used to. Hiding excess cash in Chalet Number Five today wasn't an ideal option with all of the current renovations underway.

The discussions this morning with Doctor Clayton had really opened her eyes to the seriousness of her current position. It was one thing to *suspect* someone was following you, and quite another to *know* they were following you. She was going through a steep learning curve with all of the constantly changing developments and security issues around the estate. She could sense the growing realization that maybe Kyle was the target of all this attempted surveillance. Still, she was looking forward to meeting him and wondered just what their future had in store.

As Jen approached the two garage buildings she could see each one had a white south-facing metal door. Although she still couldn't detect any alarms systems on the garage buildings she knew the Beaucerons were certainly an effective alternative. With her master key she opened the door to the dark interior of the garage.

The building had no windows or skylights, and the five garage doors were all built with hinged, solid panels. The interior light switches were easily located just inside the door. Turning the lights on revealed a single long room with a concrete floor and fairly low ceilings.

Jen locked the entrance door and proceeded to explore the building. Each garage bay door had a different vehicle parked behind it. A long metal service counter ran the length of the building with shelves mounted above and cabinets installed below. The garage itself had an impressive assortment of tools and equipment as well as a large air compressor with ample hoses installed by the end of the counter. A large vice and bench grinder were mounted to the counter and a heavy duty drill press stood in a corner.

In the first bay was a black, late-model Chevy four by four truck with a solid canopy. The next was a rare dark blue 2010 Ford Mustang GT-500 with tinted windows and a Shelby 725hp Super Snake package. In the center bay was a silver Dodge utility van with several seats removed and piled on the counter in front of the van. The fourth was a late model, black AMX that looked more like a stock dragster with the size of tires installed on the vehicle. The last car was a slightly older, dark green Range Rover with roof racks, a spare tire and a spare fuel container mounted on the rear.

With such an impressive selection of vehicles it was hard to imagine needing another garage. The overall condition of the building appeared well maintained. The counters were clean and organized with low level fluorescent light fixtures and ample room lighting installed throughout.

Jen tried the door on the Range Rover and found it unlocked. The keys were in the ignition and she turned them to the accessory position to check the fuel quantity. The tank was almost full and the interior was spotless. Jen released the hood latch, opened it up and checked the oil. It read 'full' on the engine dipstick and the oil was in near-new condition. After closing the hood she checked the papers in the glove compartment and found the Range Rover was built in 2005 and insurance was valid for another ten months. A quick glance at the odometer showed there was only seven thousand miles on the vehicle and it was easy to see the near mint condition.

Climbing inside the Range Rover she noticed the garage door control box and a radar detector were both installed above the dash along with a mobile phone, mounted between the seats. Each vehicle had its own bay and the remote door controls matched the motors mounted on each door. According to the placard on her control box she was now in Garage 1, Bay 5. Flipping the open switch on the control box the door behind her rolled smoothly open. She started the Range Rover and backed out of the building. Once clear of the doorway she flipped the switch to the close position and watched the metal door roll back down.

This was a large enough vehicle selection for the time being and a Range Rover would more than accommodate her needs today. She could look forward to exploring Garage 2 at a later time. Jen started driving slowly down the driveway and out towards the main gate. True to the doctor's word, the main gate rolled open as she approached and closed after she'd passed through.

Jen turned the radar detector on and checked the mobile phone for a dial tone. Wishing she'd brought her street maps with her, she started driving down West Cedar Drive knowing it may take time to locate her new apartment again during daylight hours. After driving for about a mile or so she came upon a couple of road construction workers retrieving their orange traffic cones. Fortunately she had just missed the road maintenance work and could drive right past without being stopped by the flagmen. Jen gave them a nod with her head as she flew past the two men wearing their reflective vests and hardhats.

On the outskirts of Salt Lake City they pulled the RA-9 vehicle into a deserted highway rest stop. A small cinder block building with a metal roof housed the most basic washroom facilities.

"Let's change the license plates now before we get into the city," said the older agent as he pulled into a parking stall.

"What do you want to put on?" asked the younger agent.

"Put some California plates on this time, they're still common around here."

"Sure, I think we still have a set or two of those in the trunk. I'll find them in a minute," said the younger agent as he got out and walked over to the washroom.

The older agent hopped out and pulled a small tool box from the trunk. One open-end wrench and a short wide-tip standard would be all he needed to change the plates. The younger agent returned from the rest stop washroom facilities.

"Are you sure you don't want to reload the RPG's here?"

"No, it's too risky, we would have to remove everything from the trunk and then unscrew the false bottom floor. I'm not starting on that until we've found a safer location to work."

After switching the plates and using the washroom they were quickly back out on the highway. The tracker was now less than a mile away from the GPS coordinates in Salt Lake City where they'd detected her last half hour stop. Currently they were now driving on a city bypass with four lanes and surrounded by a mix of mostly commercial and industrial properties. Up ahead both agents could see a large paved parking lot with a card lock with self-serve fuel service available. Two semi-trailers were taking on fuel and another was waiting in line. The facility was designated as 'diesel fuel only' and had no other amenities available, not even a store or cafe.

"Why would she have stopped here for so long? There isn't even a restaurant here," asked the younger agent.

"It's hard to say. Maybe there was a line-up? There's one truck waiting right now," said the older agent.

"Well, I guess that's possible. Still, it seems like a long fuel stop for a small truck," said the younger agent.

"Do you still have her signal? How far ahead is she now?" asked the older agent.

"Yes I've still got her. She must be slowing down because I'm only reading an eighty mile spread," said the younger agent.

"That's great. We're definitely closing the gap now. I'll keep driving until our next stop," said the older agent as he took a good look around and accelerated away from the fuelling station.

Professor Akkaim picked up his secure line from the shift supervisor who had been in his office earlier. "Yes."

"You said you wanted to be informed of any new developments, so I'm letting you know we had to cancel your plan to replace the two telephone technicians with our own men from Seattle."

"Why was that? People went to great lengths to have these men in place by this morning," said the professor, unable to hide his disappointment.

"We picked up a cellular phone conversation between Al Anderson and the telephone technicians. They asked him if he could come over to the estate this afternoon and check the new monitoring equipment," said the shift supervisor.

"Well I can see how that would changes things. Have you had any contact from the other agents following Ms. Lamar's truck?" asked the professor.

"No, still nothing," replied the shift supervisor.

"What about our work on accessing Ms. Lamar's financial records, or anyone else from the Clayton family?" asked the professor.

"As a matter of fact, we've been able to open a new temporary account under Ms. Lamar's name and have successfully linked it to her current chequing account."

"That's excellent," said the professor, happy to see some progress. "What have you learned so far and has there been any recent financial activity?" he asked.

"Only three transactions have occurred with this account since her arrival in Oregon," said the supervisor.

"What type of transactions?" inquired the professor with growing interest.

"Early yesterday morning there was a fourteen thousand dollar direct deposit to her chequing account. The second one happened during the afternoon, a one hundred dollar withdrawal from an ATM in a small mall. The last one happened later in the evening, her daily cash limit was withdrawn from a downtown ATM."

"Well done, that could prove to be very useful information. Have you cross referenced the ATM times with the trip log data from her tracker signal?" asked the professor.

"No, not yet—we've just recently acquired the ability to access to her financial statements."

"Well get someone working on that immediately and report back when it's completed," demanded the professor.

"Yes right away Professor. I'll call you soon," said the supervisor as he hung up the phone.

Professor Akkaim suspected a deposit of that size likely indicated the confirmation of Ms. Lamar's employment by Doctor Clayton. It was becoming apparent that the Claytons' child, Kyle, would require someone to accompany him personally to the various scientific facilities. If Kyle was now on the road with Ms. Lamar, and not in Canada, someone would be held accountable. It was still imperative that Kyle be allowed to attend the CFRC-8 laser fusion center prior to his abduction. If Ms. Lamar had somehow managed to get him out of Canada she was now travelling to a new destination and not towards California. It didn't matter, the priority now was to always know exactly where Kyle Clayton was at all times and then have a fail-safe plan to acquire him once he'd completed his internship at the Central Fusion Research Complex 8. The success of the RA-9 project might well depend on it and no expense would be spared.

The ring from the phone disrupted the professor's train of thought. "Yes, Professor Akkaim here."

"Professor, we've cross referenced the banking statements of Ms. Lamar with the tracker data information as you asked," said the supervisor.

"Yes, and?" asked the professor.

"Yes, and it looks like we have a problem," said the supervisor.

"What kind of problem?" asked the professor, tiring of these linguistic games.

"Ms. Lamar's four-hundred dollar withdrawal from an ATM in downtown Portland took place at the same time her vehicle was one hundred and thirty miles, southeast of Portland."

Chapter 10

Both of the new agents from Seattle were disappointed about the last minute cancellation of their plans. After packing up all the equipment needed to stage the construction roadblock they proceeded back towards the city where a small warehouse space had been rented to assist with the additional RA-9 activities in Portland. They were told to expect an updated file complete with the latest information on everyone involved in the Portland case.

They both fully expected details of another new assignment would be included as well following the sudden cancellation of plans due to Al Anderson's visit. The beautiful young woman in the Range Rover had caught both men's attention as she drove by. Soon they'd be too busy with other assignments to have time for observations of that nature. Both field agents were highly trained with diverse backgrounds and a wide range of expertise.

An additional two person support team had also arrived in Portland that would serve to compliment the two field agents. Skills such as graphic design and vehicle painting become invaluable when a vehicle required a specific look for a given assignment. Together they had quickly converted a late model white truck into an identical replica of a local municipal engineering service truck. Complete vehicle transformations were often needed depending on the specific requirements of a particular assignment. Everyone had pulled out all the stops to be ready to go this morning and they would do so again as soon as their new operational instructions arrived.

Jen had easily adapted to driving the Range Rover. The smooth synchronization of the gears and strong pull from the engine made it a pleasure to drive. Fortunately she wasn't delayed by the work crews finishing up on West Cedar Drive this morning and was now getting close to her new apartment. She had promised to pay the landlord today and would probably pay for an extra month while she had so much cash on hand.

There was virtually nothing but lower class apartments throughout this area and luckily she'd remembered the address from last night. As she pulled up to the front of the building she could see the vacancy sign had been removed. Jen parked the Range Rover on the street and let herself in the front door. She could feel the countless silent stares from the windows of the adjacent buildings when she walked from her truck up to the front door. People just didn't drive Range Rovers in these neighbourhoods and she stood out like a white limo in Harlem.

The Range Rover was definitely the wrong choice for any future daylight trips to this apartment. In hindsight she should have taken the silver Dodge van rather than a near-new safari-ready four wheel drive.

After letting herself in the front door she glanced in her mailbox slot and confirmed it was empty. Sprinting up the stairs of this dilapidated building she found and knocked on the manager's door.

"Who's there?" was the response from a man's voice behind the locked door.

"It's Jennifer Lamar. I rented the third floor apartment from you last night."

"What do you want?" replied the man's voice.

"I'm stopping by to pay the rest of the rent," she said and glad she was still carrying her loaded Glock 17. After the sound of two deadbolts and several barrel bolts the manager opened the door. He was a frail looking man, dressed in a dark red terri-cloth robe. His face was gaunt with thinning white hair and he smelled like a dirty ashtray.

"Come inside. Hurry," said the manager as he whisked her in and glanced up and down the hall. After locking two deadbolts he invited her to sit down at his small overcrowded kitchen table. The table was cluttered with assorted papers, various old picnic condiments and a large overflowing ashtray sat in the center.

"Is everything alright? Jen asked, surprised at his level of security and state of paranoia.

"Yes, it's just that cash is such a valuable commodity in these parts and lots of people in this part of town will do just about anything for it," he said.

Jen had seen his worn baseball bat propped against the door frame when she walked in. Around here going to jail is seen as a vacation from the hardships of life. Free heated rooms with beds and blankets with meals included isn't much of a deterrent against crime in these parts.

"You owe me another five hundred and twenty-five dollars. With the three hundred from last night that covers one month's rent at five hundred and fifty, and the two hundred and seventy-five dollar damage deposit," said the manager, looking much older in the single overhead fluorescent kitchen light.

"I'll give you that plus another two month's rent. However, if you promise never to disclose any information about when I use, or don't use, my place I'll tip you an extra two hundred in cash."

"Is someone after you? Never mind, just forget I asked you that. Sure. I'll keep your secrets for two hundred in cash if anyone asks."

"It's a deal. If anyone does inquire about me I want you to tell me about it. Try to remember all the details you can about the person."

"Okay, I will. I hope you're not bringing a lot of extra trouble over to my building."

"I don't think so. I'm just taking some basic precautions like you and one more thing. Never give my name out to anyone. Do you understand? Not under any circumstances."

"I understand. Fair enough then, you owe me eighteen hundred and twenty-five and you're good for three months."

"May I use your washroom?" asked Jen not wanting to show him all of her cash.

"It's the first door on the right, just down the hall. It won't be the cleanest one you've ever seen" said the manager.

"Thanks, I'm sure it won't be the worst either," said Jen reflecting on her memories of the 'sand box' in Iraq.

Jen flipped the lid down, took a seat and pulled the thick pile of bills from the inner pocket of her cargo khakis. In an assorted mix of denominations she counted out the cash for the manager. She was tempted to round it out to two thousand, but didn't want to be returning to the doctor's office with her hand out anytime soon. She slipped the cash for the manager into a separate pocket and walked back out to the kitchen.

"Here you are, eighteen-hundred and twenty-five dollars," she said as she passed the folded stack of bills to the wide eyed and unshaven manager.

He got up, walked over and cautiously closed the venetian blinds in his kitchen window. He sat down again and slowly and methodically counted out the cash on the kitchen table, one bill at a time.

"Would you like a receipt?" he asked after close to ten minutes.

"No thanks. No receipt please. Have I paid you enough to use a fictitious name in your records?"

"I'm sorry, that will cost you another two-hundred."

"Okay fine but I don't want my name on any paperwork in your office," said Jen as she turned and removed another two hundred from her bill fold.

"I'll make sure that nothing here has your name on it, including last night's rental agreement. Do you want me to use any name in particular?" he asked.

"Use whatever name you like, just not my name," said Jen as she handed him another two hundred.

"Okay, I'll think of something, and thanks for the cash. Anything else I can do for you?" asked the manager, rising to his feet.

"No, that's good for now. Let me know if you have any inquiries," said Jen as she waited for the manager to walk ahead of her down the cramped hallway.

"I'll let you know if anybody starts asking about you," said the manager as he unlocked both deadbolts.

Jen couldn't help but notice six different locks installed on his door including several security chains.

"Thanks again, see you later," said Jen as she walked out the door and back to the concrete staircase, sprinting up to the next floor. The next time she spoke privately with Doctor Clayton she'd ask him if he knew how to acquire any false identification papers. Maybe his government connection that handled Kyle's affairs might be able to help. It was certainly worth a try. Professionally-made false ID was worth its weight in gold in many situations around the world. Even just renting an apartment would have been far easier and safer with good quality false ID. The whole issue was becoming crystal clear; the more choices she had available for her personal paperwork the safer she'd be.

"She's slowing down. It looks like she may be coming to a stop," said the younger agent.

"Excellent!" replied the older agent. "How far away is she now?" asked the older agent.

"Fifty-eight miles ahead of us and she has definitely come to a stop," said the younger agent.

"Well let's hope she stays that way for a while. I'm having trouble staying awake."

"Do you want me to drive for a while?" asked the younger agent.

"No. Remember what happened last time you drove? I'll keep on driving myself," said the older agent increasing his speed ever so slightly. "Do we still have some caffeine pills in the glove compartment?"

"Yes I think so," said the younger agent.

"Pass them over here when you find them."

"Okay, I've got them, here you are," said the younger agent as he passed them over to his partner.

"Thanks, I'll keep them in my pocket for now," said the older agent after tossing a small handful back in his mouth.

"Sure, no problem," said the younger agent looking down at the laptop screen.

"Have you entered her new coordinates in Google Map?" asked the older agent.

"Not yet, I'll try that now," he said as he waited for an image to appear.

"Okay, it looks like another large card lock or a truck stop. It's at the junction of two rural highways."

"Good, is she still parked?"

"Yes, still parked," replied the younger agent.

"What's our distance from her now?"

"Forty-seven miles," replied the younger agent.

"We'll catch up with her in about forty minutes if she stays put," said the older agent, feeling the onset of a shuddering kick start from his excessive dose of caffeine.

Jen walked slowly up to her apartment, relieved not to find any holes drilled through this door. So far she hadn't seen anyone at all in the building and preferred it to stay that way. She pulled out her keys and dropped them by the edge of the door. Kneeling down she could see her tiny slivers of tape were still intact and the odds were good that no one had entered her apartment since she left last night. Even so she could be dealing with highly trained professionals. Instinctively her right hand slid into the left side of her jacket and removed her Glock 17. Switching the safety off, she turned the key, opened the door and quietly entered her suite, safely behind her outstretched Glock 17.

After a quick and deliberate search she was sure her place was empty. Checking the slivers of tapes on the windows also confirmed that her apartment had remained empty since her last visit. Satisfied, she secured her gun in its holster and locked the front door. This place wouldn't be set up with anything other than just the bare necessities. In all probability it would serve more as a confidential storage area as well as her private sanctuary away from the estate if she ever needed it.

Today she was planning to transfer some of her equipment and belongings over to Chalet Number Five. Walking back and forth to the Range Rover with boxes or totes wasn't a great option so she'd have to drive it underground and load it down there. It would take two trips to load the Range Rover and she didn't want to leave anything unattended.

This time a Stun Gun would be leaving with her. The need for quiet, non-lethal stopping power was always greater in developed countries. Jen proceeded to organize several smaller duffel bags with her personal belongings and carefully selected a few additional pieces of equipment from her black totes. She would leave a few basic personal items here if she ever needed to stay overnight.

Soon she had all of her possessions divided into two piles. One was going with her and the other was staying behind. As she had some extra time today she set out a few things around the furnished apartment and once again stocked the dresser and closet with a few spare garments, then left a toothbrush and a few basic items in the washroom. The kitchen cupboards and drawers were mostly bare and the dirty fridge was unplugged with an old box of open baking soda in the back. She plugged in the fridge and set the thermostat as the noisy compressor roared to life. This place could use a few survival rations and she'd try to keep that in mind for the next time she was coming over.

After stacking her remaining boxes in the closet and rechecking her slivers of tape on the windows she locked up and walked out to the Range Rover. There weren't too many pedestrians walking around, but she could see right away that someone had just keyed the Range Rover.

Several deep scratches ran from the rear bumper down the full length of the truck and on the roof above the passenger side doors. Jen couldn't see anyone near the vehicle and would probably just have to ignore it. It simply wasn't worth pursuing under these circumstances. She started up the Range Rover and drove it down to the gate, opened it and then drove further underground towards the service elevator.

As she pulled up and parked by the elevator she noticed her Ford Explorer parked several spots away. It was sitting on four orange milk crates with all her mag wheels and tires missing. Jen turned on her cell phone and snapped a few pictures of the scene. Walking over to examine her truck, she could see it was still locked. It was an older truck and not equipped with alarms or locking wheel lugs.

Jen unlocked the Explorer and transferred all her paperwork and the few weapons she had concealed in the vehicle. After looking around in the Range Rover she found a surprisingly well equipped tool pouch and used a couple of them to remove the plates from her Explorer. This crime also wasn't worth pursuing with any local authorities and she was fairly sure Doctor Clayton would consider this loss an expense. She'd simply have to leave it here and see what remained of her Explorer the next time she came over.

Jen locked the Range Rover and took the service elevator up to the third floor. Opening her apartment she closed the blinds and turned off the lights. Piling both loads outside her door, she bent down and reinstalled her sliver of tape at the base of the door. The service elevator was being held in place with the 'off' switch while she shuttled both loads of gear from her apartment and loaded them into the service elevator.

Jen pressed 'P1' and waited for what seemed like an eternity for the elevator to descend four floors. As the doors opened she could hear the sounds of people running away from somewhere inside the parking area, but couldn't actually see anyone. She unloaded the elevator and loaded up the Range Rover.

She wondered if the manager had known about her Explorer when she talked with him this morning. If not he'd know soon enough she thought as she started the truck and drove away. The contractors were probably still working at the estate and she could take her time returning to Chalet Number Five.

"What's our distance from her now?" asked the older agent still reeling from the overdose of caffeine pills.

"She was twelve miles away, five minutes ago," said the younger agent studying the laptop intently.

"I don't care about five minutes ago! How far away is she now?" barked the older agent, clearly tiring of this chase.

"I think we've got a problem, I'm not receiving her signal any anymore," said the younger agent still working with the laptop.

"What do you mean you're not getting her signal," yelled the older agent.

"I mean just what I said, I'm not getting her signal," repeated the younger agent.

"Sorry for yelling, I took too many of those caffeine pills and my nerves are shot. Do you still have her last coordinates?"

"Yes, we were receiving her signal clearly for almost an hour. She was stopped in the same location and then we just lost her signal. I don't know if it's a problem with the transmitter on her truck or something with our tracking program. I'll re-boot the laptop and see if that helps," said the younger agent.

"Well there's really nothing else we can do right now that I can think of. She was stopped for an hour and now you say we've just lost her signal. That seems very strange to me."

"Okay, I've re-booted the laptop. Wait a second while I bring up the tracking program. I've got it here now. No, there's still no signal. We should be arriving at the location of her last stop very soon," said the younger agent.

"Yes, I can see by the road signs that there's a highway junction up ahead. Can you create a waypoint from her last position on our GPS that we can use to home in on," asked the older agent.

"Yes, I'll make a user waypoint from her last position and we can use the 'go to' function for an accurate distance between us to the waypoint," said the younger agent while trying to remember how to create a user waypoint.

"Good, there's something up ahead. It looks like another diesel card lock fuelling station and a truck wash. Have you got the way-point entered yet?" asked the older agent.

"Yes, I'm just switching to the navigation mode. Okay, I've got the pointer function working. It's pointing to the station up ahead. The distance is in feet. Nineteen hundred and forty feet away," said the younger agent, holding the handheld GPS up on the dash so they both could see the GPS display.

"So is the arrow pointing towards her last position then?" said the older agent.

"Yes, just keep driving in the direction the arrow is pointing," said the younger agent.

"Okay, I've got it figured out now," said the older agent, watching the arrow pointing towards the car wash as he took the highway exit.

As they pulled off the highway they turned into the card lock fuelling station. Over on the side of the lot was an automated BriteCo, High Pressure Truck and Chassis Wash facility. Payment was with cards only and it was an open-bay drive-through design, equipped with high pressure water nozzles throughout the enclosure and recovery tanks below the steel grate floors. Only one other semi-trailer was on the lot and he was fuelling up at the moment.

"What's our distance now?" asked the older agent.

"One hundred and thirty feet," said the younger agent as they both realised the arrow was pointing to the BriteCo facility.

"I'm going to drive up to the entrance," said the older agent. "What's our distance?"

"Thirty feet," replied the younger agent.

"Let's go and take a look around," said the older agent as he stopped and got out of the car. They started walking through the open facility with its still dripping walls and steel grate floors.

"Over here!" yelled the younger agent as he sprinted up ahead. "This is why we weren't getting her signal," he said as he picked up the crushed tracking unit from the steel grate floor. "Something heavy has driven right over this thing, maybe more than once," said the younger agent.

"I think you're right. It must have been blown off during a chassis wash and crushed by the next truck going through here. We'd better take the unit with us. I still don't know why she'd take her truck inside such a powerful truck wash. Let's go, we don't even know which highway she took and the chances of finding her now without a signal are almost zero. There's nothing more we can do now." said the older agent.

"Back to Portland?" asked the younger agent.

"No, let's get a meal and find a hotel. I need some sleep. I'm sure they've already been expecting a report from us for some time and Professor Akkaim definitely won't be happy when he hears about this.

"You drive," said the older agent as he walked around, opened the front passenger door and collapsed on the seat.

"Talk about bad luck. We were so close and we almost had her," said the older agent as his eyelids sealed tightly together and he nodded off to sleep.

"Don't worry, we'll get them yet. It's just a matter of time," said the younger agent as he started the car and accelerated back towards the freeway, happy to be driving this car again.

"Watch your speed," said the older agent, suddenly opening his left eye and looking over.

"I will, I will, don't worry," said the younger agent as he levelled off at the posted highway speed.

"Lisa isn't it?" asked the contractor as he opened the kitchen door.

"Yes, that's right," said Lisa.

"Is Doctor Clayton still here?"

"Yes he is. I'll get him for you," said Lisa pulling off her apron and walking out of the kitchen and over to his office. "Doctor Clayton, the contractors from Chalet Number Five are waiting for you outside the kitchen."

"Okay. Thanks Lisa, I'll be right there," said the doctor, getting up from his desk and following Lisa down the hall.

"Well, how did you guys make out? Did you finish everything up today?"

"Yes, we have all the computers set up as you asked and ample power supplies and Internet connections have been installed at both stations."

"Excellent. And everything is still disconnected?"

"That's right. Nothing has been connected, but everything is ready to go when you want it."

"Thanks for all your work in the chalet. I appreciate you coming all the way out here."

"My pleasure, just give me a call if there's anything else you need."

"Thanks I will. I'll make sure Lisa opens the front gate for you when you're ready to leave."

"Great. Bye for now Doctor Clayton."

"Bye, take care," said the doctor as he smiled and closed the door.

"Lisa, did you hear anything from Al Anderson?"

"No, I haven't. Are the phones working now?"

"You know, I'm not sure. I'll go and find out," said the doctor as he turned to leave. James walked down the hall past his office and found both men still working in the electrical room.

"How's it going? Any trouble hooking up your new monitoring equipment?"

"No, there are just a lot of tests and connections with all the lines installed around here. Sorry to tell you Doctor Clayton, but it does look like we'll have to change your home number."

"That's unfortunate. Are there no other options?"

"I'm afraid not. This will give us a clean slate when we're monitoring any phone calls in and out of the estate."

"Out of the estate—what do you mean?" asked the doctor.

"Oh nothing really, it's all the same thing. If someone is trying to tap into your lines this equipment is the best chance we have of trying to trace its origin. We should be done fairly soon and I'll give you your new number before we leave."

"Okay then, I'll talk to you soon," said the doctor as he walked back to the kitchen to give Lisa an update.

The phone on Professor Akkaim's desk continued ringing. He was busy studying the new file he had received an hour ago. It was the file containing all the available information on every past and present employee who worked at the Claytons' estate.

"Yes," he said as he lifted up the phone.

"We've received a report from the agents tracking Ms. Lamar's truck."

"Excellent. How far did she get and where is she now? Is the boy with her?"

"We don't know," said the supervisor.

"You mean they still haven't caught up with her? Are they driving one of our vehicles?"

"Yes, they are. They had some trouble west of Salt Lake City and managed to take care of that."

"What kind of trouble?" asked the professor.

"They were being chased by a patrol car and had to dispose of it."

"Who was driving?"

"I think it was the newer guy, the young guy."

"What about Ms. Lamar? Did they find her truck?"

"No, but they got the transmitter back. Apparently it had been blown off at a truck wash and then crushed under a tire."

"Where are they now?"

"They're in a hotel in Salt Lake City."

"Have them stay there for now. I may have a new assignment for them soon."

"What do you want to do with the men in Portland?"

"Ask them to study the possibility of installing a remote surveillance camera with a view of the main gate at the Claytons' estate. They have tall trees and forests in that part of the world. Maybe they can install a remote control camera with a view of the main gate. It'll be useful to record exactly who is coming and going from there, and when."

"If it can be done, I'm sure they will manage to find a way how to do it," said the supervisor.

"Do you have access to the ABM photo log from the night Ms. Lamar withdrew her cash in downtown Portland?"

"No, just banking statement information so far."

"Well the truth of the matter is that we still don't even know if Ms. Lamar ever left Portland. She could have been here the whole time or else another person could have her bank card. Maybe she was robbed and forced to give up her personal identification number."

"That's also a possibility. Do you want a report back from our agents in Portland or just ask them to install a camera if they can?"

"Have them install the camera—as long as they can do it without getting caught."

"Very well Professor. I'll let you know if they're unable to do it."

"Still no word from the agents in Iraq?"

"No, we haven't heard a word. I'll let you know if we do."

"Okay" said the professor as he hung up the phone, now fairly certain they wouldn't be hearing anything from the men in Iraq.

"Lisa, did you see what vehicle Jen took this morning?" asked James as he went for a snack in the kitchen.

"Yes, I saw her leaving in the green Range Rover," replied Lisa.

"Oh good, she'll like that truck, it's still quite new. Alexia used to like driving that one before the shooting."

"Yes, I remember that. It was her favourite," said Lisa with downcast eyes. "This morning, I saw Alexia sitting in her wheelchair on the patio watching Jen drive away in the Range Rover," said Lisa.

"I don't think she was actually watching her. She must have just been left out there facing the driveway by one of her nurses. That's all," said the doctor.

"No, I watched her head turning slowly and following Jen as she drove down the driveway. She was watching her," said Lisa.

"Well that must have been some sort of coincidence, maybe a spinal spasm or involuntary muscle contraction," replied the doctor defensively.

"Are you planning to do any tests on this equipment from here?" asked one of the telephone technicians.

"No. There's not much we can do until we get some incoming calls. Everything looks good to me and they now have clean Internet and phone connections up here. I'll call Al Anderson and see if he's coming over. Other than that, I think we're done. We'll pack up, go and find the doctor and give him the new number."

"Okay, sounds good," replied the other telephone technician. "We still have remote access to all this equipment from downtown. It'll be easier to monitor calls from there anyway. Are you ready?"

"Yes, let's go and find the doctor."

Both technicians packed up their tools and equipment while the final checks were made on the new line.

"Are you going to give Al Anderson a call?" asked one of the technicians.

"Sure, I'll try him on his cell. He may not be comfortable using it yet and he won't recognize this new number."

"You're probably right, but we should give him a try."

The technician that was finished packing called Al Anderson's cell number. "The cellular customer you have dialled is currently busy or away from the phone. If you would like to leave a call back number press five."

"Hi Al, just letting you know we've just finished up here at the estate. The number on your call display is the new number for the Claytons' estate and I'll be giving it to the doctor before we leave. Give me a call or I'll see you later back at the office."

"He's not answering his cell. Let's go and find Doctor Clayton."

"Okay, I'm ready," said the other technician as they had a final look around and closed the door to the electrical room.

Both men walked down the hall towards the kitchen and saw Doctor Clayton coming out of the kitchen. "There you are. Have you finished everything you came here to do?" asked the doctor.

"Yes, we're all done for now. I've written your new number down for you and I'm recommending everyone here at the estate acquires a new cell phone for their personal use. I'll discuss that with Al Anderson and maybe we can supply them for you. He may want us to personally inspect them first, but I'll let you know after we've spoken with him."

"I thought he was coming over today. Have you heard from him?" asked the doctor.

"No, I did call him, but he wasn't answering. I left a message on his voicemail."

"So he has the new number then?" asked the doctor.

"Yes, I left it on his voice mail so you could hear from him anytime."

"Well, thanks for everything. Make sure you both help yourselves to some coffee or lunch before you go if you're hungry," offered the doctor.

"Thanks, we might just take you up on that," drawn to Lisa's irresistible selection of choices laid out on the main dining table.

"Well thanks again for coming over. Lisa will let you out when you're ready to leave and she'll also open the main gate for you," said the doctor as he started walking to his office.

"Great, see you next time Doctor Clayton. Thanks again for lunch."

"You're welcome. Bye," said the doctor.

James returned to his office and plugged in his office line. He needed to place calls to several hospitals and give them his new number as soon as possible. It was imperative that trauma surgeons were available around the clock and he had been unavailable for too long. Turning on his personal computer would have to wait until Kyle was back. James knew his son wanted this 'sleeping nano-virus' quarantined in the disconnected hard drive until he returned back home.

Jen was having second thoughts about having spent so much money on her new part time suite. Even though it was nice to have a private space it could very well be ransacked the next time she returned. A refund from the old manager with the baseball bat was highly unlikely at this point.

It might have been a better idea just to keep the cash and use hotels when needed. As of yet she didn't even know where she might be during the next three months. Hopefully the doctor would understand her need to hide the truck and get out of her last place as soon as possible. As for the Explorer, it was probably best to just leave it where it was. It would have to be covered with a tarp and towed as is, or new wheels and tires would have to be purchased. Sitting underground without license plates was probably just as safe as having it locked up in a compound somewhere.

Fortunately she had taken some good pictures of her truck in the parking lot which would make explaining it to the doctor that much easier. Between the money for the manager, the value or her wheels and tires, and the damage to the Range Rover, she had cost the doctor almost five thousand dollars in less than an hour. It was important to Jen that the doctor had complete confidence in her actions and it was unfortunate she went through so much money that quickly. Jen slowed down and pulled into a small strip mall just off the main street.

Doctor Clayton had reconnected all the phones in the estate except Chalet Number Five.

The nurses and Lisa now had the new number and everyone was told about the cell phone replacement plan recommended by the telephone technicians. The doctor heard a tap at his partially open office door.

"Should I let the Beaucerons out Doctor? The two telephone men just left through the main gate."

"Sure, I think that's safe enough now. I don't imagine Al Anderson will be stopping by if we haven't heard from him yet. Do you know if Kyle has a valid pair of scentlets?"

"No, I'm not sure about that. I doubt it because he's been gone for a long time now," said Lisa.

"Yes, I think you're right. We still have a supply in the office filing cabinet. Do you remember how to open everything around here?"

"Of course, I never forget things like that," said Lisa, somewhat surprised that he even asked.

"Let's make sure we remember to keep a new set out for him. He could be here at any time. I'll get a pair out right now that you can keep in the kitchen if you like."

"Sure. I have a good hiding place in the kitchen," said Lisa.

James found a key and opened the deep drawer in the metal cabinet. He checked the expiration dates on a new pair and handed them to Lisa.

"Thanks. I'll give these to Kyle the first chance I get," said Lisa as she put the scentlets in her apron pocket.

"I'm getting a little concerned that we haven't heard anything from Al Anderson. He usually keeps us up to date on any travel arrangements for Kyle."

"Yes that's true. Well, he could still call any minute," said Lisa with her optimistic tone of voice. "Will Jen be joining us for dinner this evening?" asked Lisa.

"We didn't discuss that this morning, but I would think she should be home soon. It's probably a good idea to stock up the chalet with a grocery order today or tomorrow so Kyle and Jen will have some additional flexibility with regard to their meals."

"Sure, I'll start packing that right away," said Lisa while spinning around and walking back to the kitchen. Lisa stopped at the automated kennel console and released the Beaucerons before starting to compile a grocery list for Chalet Number Five. She hadn't forgotten any of Kyle's favourite items and really didn't know anything about Jen's preferences. She'd have a few cases of supplies ready to go in no time at all.

Kyle didn't have any details yet, but he was packed and on a standby travel alert. From past experience, things never stayed that way for long. He could appreciate the logistical details of his cross border travel arrangements and knew that the wheels were now in motion.

Both pilots in Vancouver were also on yellow standby alert meaning they needed to be able to lift off within two hours-notice. Generally most flights were conducted at night, but not always. The strict security surrounding Kyle's travel arrangements meant that even the pilots didn't know where they were going until the last possible minute. The jet was already full of fuel and both pilots were staying at a hotel on the airport grounds. A change in alert status to green was likely at any time. Any time Kyle was preparing to travel was a busy time for Al Anderson. Endless small details and the coordinated movements of people, vehicles and aircraft was a task managed by a large team within the US Government, directed by Al Anderson.

The latest plan was a night jet flight to a private strip in central Oregon and a night VFR (Visual Flight Rules) helicopter flight from there to the estate. Weather forecasts for southern Washington and central Oregon were a current concern and nothing would start moving until conditions improved. The private strip had an approved GPS instrument approach that would allow an IFR (Instrument Flight Rules) approach for the jet in poor weather conditions. The helicopter waiting at the strip needed better weather for a night flight in VFR conditions to the estate. Mixing bad weather and night VFR flying was always a recipe for disaster.

Jen had picked up a few personal and security items at the mall and was just pulling into the estate. The doors split and rolled open as she approached the iron gates. The sudden appearance of a pair of Beaucerons flanking the range Rover and one racing up from behind was a formidable sight. They seemed to be challenging the Range Rover to a race and knew the finish line was close at hand.

As she neared the house Jen slowed down and parked by the kitchen to talk with Lisa. She knew she was still in a canine safety zone and the Beaucerons had given up the chase as she slowed to park. Walking inside she met Lisa and got caught up on all the day's events.

"Are you sure you don't want to join us for dinner tonight Jen?" Lisa asked.

"Yes, thanks Lisa. I had a late lunch at the mall and I want to start getting a few things unpacked up at Chalet Number Five," said Jen.

"Sure, that's fine. You know how to find the kitchen if there's anything you need. I'll help you load a few boxes of groceries in the Range Rover if you like."

"Sure, thanks Lisa."

"Did you find the quads yet?" asked Lisa.

"No, I haven't seen any quads at all," Jen replied.

"There's several in Garage 2, Bay 6. The road only goes up to the garage and the quads are great vehicles for running around the estate."

"Thanks Lisa, I haven't opened Garage 2 yet. I'll get one when I park the Range Rover."

"You're welcome. They're fun to drive and that will get your gear up to the chalet in a hurry. I'm not sure if anyone has told you, but make sure you don't connect any computers until Kyle returns. He should be home soon," said Lisa.

"I won't connect anything until he gets back. When will he be here?" asked Jen.

"We don't exactly know, soon I think."

"Well thanks for helping with the groceries and the information about the quads. See you later Lisa."

"Bye Jen, stop by any time you like," said Lisa as she closed the kitchen door.

"I will thanks," said Jen as she hopped in and started the Range Rover. As she approached Garage 1 she touched the automatic door control and the white door opened smoothly.

Jen walked over and used her master key to open Garage 2. It was almost a replica of Garage 1 except for three new and interesting vehicles. Bay 6 had two quads and Bay 7 had three motorcycles. The three vehicles would receive a closer inspection the next time she was here.

The four wheel quads all looked similar and she sat on the one closest the garage door and opened the door to Bay 6. Turning the key she shifted the gears until she had the neutral light indication, and then hit the starter button. It fired almost instantly and she drove it out and over to the back of the Range Rover. After checking the fuel she locked up Garage 2 and loaded some gear on the back of the quad. Strapping it down with two bungee cords she took off up the cobblestone path to Chalet Number Five.

Rain was possible by the look of the dark clouds moving in, but hopefully she could get everything moved before the weather turned worse. Darkness was starting to set in as well and she estimated she would need about four trips on the quad.

As she approached the junction with the right turn for the chalet the Beaucerons intercepted her with astonishing speed and a calculated choice of location. One had charged up the path from Chalet Number Five on the right and another jumped from the undergrowth on the left. The third had charged down the path from above the junction with such speed it was now standing with its front paws on the handlebars of the quad with its head inches from hers. Never had she experienced such a determined, close range, eye-to-eye stare-down.

The first night time attack was different. The intensity from such a close proximity glare during daylight really made her wonder about the mental abilities on the other side of those eyes. Jen killed the engine and sat frozen in a totally submissive position as the other two dogs interrogated her scentlets. Ten seconds later they broke up and resumed their patrol.

It had taken close to an hour to shuttle everything up to Chalet Number Five and lock up the Range Rover. The winds were picking up and she was glad to be finished her move just as darkness set in. Jen was starting to feel like she finally had some time to herself to organize her equipment and settle in for the night.

The amount of computer equipment set up on both floors was a shock. She had counted at least a dozen large computers and several monitors and keypads. She would likely know the reason for such a complex installation soon enough.

As well as a main fireplace the chalet also had a Tulikivi; a small wood stove built from soapstone. The ability of soapstone to retain heat has made them famous worldwide for their heating efficiency. It didn't take long to light a fire in the Tulikivi and find her way back to the chalet's deluxe rain room for another long hot shower. When she finally turned the shower off, she could hear the loud knocking on the main entrance door. She wasn't nearly as prepared as she was last night and quickly found her Glock 17 and a Stun Gun and then wrapped herself in a bathrobe.

"Just a minute, I'll be right there," she yelled.

"It's me, Doctor Clayton. Please, don't start shooting." Jen knew that very second that she should have purchased a spyglass for the front door. That would be first on her list the next time she went to town.

"Doctor Clayton? Is that you?" said Jen with a Stun Gun in her robe pocket and the loaded Glock 17 in her right hand.

"Yes—Jen it's me, Doctor James Clayton. We met here at the door last night," said the doctor, feeling relieved she knew it was him at the door.

Jen opened the door a crack and saw the doctor standing outside in the dark. The wind was blowing the tree branches around and rain drops were just starting to fall.

"Sorry Jen, Lisa said she didn't tell you the phones have been repaired. You can plug the chalet phone back in when you want and here's the new number for the estate. I've written it down for you. I forgot to reconnect this phone or I could have called you with the news."

"What news?" she asked as water dripped on the floor.

"We may have to pick up Kyle tonight," said the doctor.

"Oh excellent, he's coming home tonight? Are we taking the Range Rover to pick him up?" asked Jen.

"No, if we get the call you and I will be taking my helicopter," said the doctor.

"Your helicopter—you have a helicopter?" said Jen in a shocked, state of disbelief.

"Did I forget to mention that? It's just up the pathway at the top of the hill. It's a black, well equipped Bell 407. I've just finished installing the dual controls and if they send us out later tonight, you'll be doing the flying."

Chapter 11

Despite weeks of careful planning, current events were starting to form a logistical logjam in Al Anderson's office. The pilots in Vancouver had been on a continual two hour standby for nine days and would have to be replaced if they weren't dispatched soon. Everything was acceptable for a Vancouver departure except the weather in south-central Oregon.

Al Anderson's options ranged from postponing the departure or choosing an alternate destination for the Vancouver aircraft, as well as various ground-based options. Kyle's presence wasn't immediately required, but he knew from discussions with the armed guards at UWBC that he was also becoming very anxious to leave.

The option of flying to Portland and taking a helicopter flight to the Claytons' estate was a possibility, but weather conditions around Portland were still showing low ceilings, gusting winds, and heavy rain was being forecast over the next six hours. Low flights around the city might be possible, but the elevation up at the Claytons' estate made conditions risky for a night flight.

Most of the higher elevation areas were obscured in cloud. After a final check on the current weather conditions, Al Anderson decided to call the pilots in Vancouver. This would start a long sequence of calls that would at least get Kyle repositioned to the main airport in Portland. If the weather continued to deteriorate an escorted armoured vehicle would be waiting for a ground-based transfer.

The captain was somewhat surprised to receive a dispatch from Al Anderson this late in the evening. He was only told to expect the arrival of three passengers arriving at the aircraft in less than two hours. Al Anderson arranged for a dedicated airport service van with tinted windows to be waiting for the pilots. The van was black and marked with a Customs Services logo on the side doors. The captain and his co-pilot managed to depart their hotel room in less than five minutes. Details such as the room payments and false identities were handled through Al Anderson's office. After descending seven floors, they both crossed the lavish hotel lobby and entered the waiting van. Both men wore civilian clothing and nothing that resembled the usual flight crew's attire of captain's hats and suit jackets with gold epaulets.

The captain's map case had remained in the cockpit and any required flight planning would take place onboard the aircraft. Both men carried small-calibre weapons and their open customs clearance had remained in effect throughout their stay in Vancouver. In general, there was certainly far more cross-border co-operation on security issues than most people ever realised.

The drive to the south terminal had taken about ten minutes and the driver slowed down and swiped a level three security pass to open the vehicle-access gate. After a short distance both pilots were dropped off close to the wing on the right side of the grey Learjet 35.

Their luggage and gear were quickly stowed and the co-pilot started the walk-around inspection of the aircraft. The captain was reviewing the current weather data and began to prepare a flight plan. His destination had only just been revealed by a text data link in the cockpit. They had ample fuel for this flight, including enough reserve fuel to reach a variety of alternate airports. The driver of the van had arranged for a portable Auxiliary Power Unit (APU) that would soon be brought up alongside the aircraft to assist in the engine start.

Kyle jumped off the couch when he heard the knock on his door. Hopping up on his box, he checked the spyglass in the door and recognized the distorted images of the two guards in the hall. "Finally it was time to leave," he thought as he opened the door. Both men were dressed in dark coloured rain gear and seemed to be in good spirits.

"Okay Kyle, we're going for a drive. We'll help you with your luggage as soon as you're ready."

"Thanks, I'm just about packed and I'll be ready in a couple of minutes," said Kyle as he spun around to get his things, obviously excited at the news they were leaving.

"Are we off to the airport?"

"Sorry Kyle, you know the procedures. We can't tell you, we don't know."

"Do I have the same two pilots as the pilots flying on the second to the last time you landed with me on the third time we all went flying?"

"Kyle I know what you're trying to do. You've been writing too many IQ tests. I'm not sure who the pilots are."

"I love flying," said Kyle with a grin.

"Are you ready to leave? I'll take that bag for you."

"Thanks, I'm ready, let's go," said Kyle as he walked off between the two guards.

The elevator was only a short walk from Kyle's door and all three of them would soon be travelling in an additional armoured Customs Services van to the south terminal. The van had a solid bullet proof wall professionally installed between the two front seats and the rear passenger compartment. Kyle was dwarfed as he sat in the center of his two guards in the back of the van. The travel arrangements from UWBC to the airport were just another small detail smoothly coordinated by Al Anderson's team. The rain continued coming down in typical Vancouver-style, as they departed the university through the UWBC Endowment Lands.

A quick call from the night-shift wildlife control officer was placed shortly after the unknown vehicle arrived at the Learjet. Being parked on the other side of the active runway was just about the worst possible location for this surveillance and he needed a closer vantage point to be effective. Although he was equipped with an excellent pair of binoculars the rain, darkness and distance continued to hamper his observations. Crossing the active runway might take time, but it was his only real option.

"I need to know if a small boy is boarding that aircraft. Do you understand?"

"Yes, I'm going to try and reposition. I can't say for sure from here."

"Call me immediately if you have any new information."

"Alright—will do," said the wildlife control officer as he started slowly driving forward. He had more privileges than most when it came to driving around this airport, but as always a high level of ground control remained in effect. Radio clearances were required for most movements around the infield and mandatory for any runway crossings.

The RA-9 agent had spent several days in a rented camper van, sitting in the long term parking area. He quickly relayed his new information using a satellite up-link and a remote deflection processor temporarily installed inside the van. With this news the cyber surveillance supervisor would immediately step up in house monitoring of any available US Customs data pertaining to travel clearances issued for Kyle Clayton. If he *was* travelling, they needed to know where.

Efforts to penetrate the FAA air traffic control computer system had been ongoing for years, but so far all intrusion attempts had been successfully prevented.

"Vancouver Ground this is Wildlife Control 12 requesting permission to cross Runway 08 at Bravo 2 crossing."

"Stand by Wildlife Control 12."

The grey Learjet was almost out of sight after his drive along the runway to the nearest crossing.

"Wildlife Control 12, you are cleared to cross Runway 08 at Bravo 2 crossing southbound after the West Jet, now on final, passes your position."

"Understood—Wildlife Control 12."

No one would notice, or care, as he moved to a closer surveillance position.

Al Anderson called the military helicopter crew waiting in eastern Oregon. The weather was still well below VFR limits and they were informed of the flight cancellation for safety reasons. The crew had been brought in from a military base in Montana and were now free to return at their discretion. The Learjet would be arriving in Portland later this evening and the method of transportation to the estate was yet to be determined.

Ground or air, the risks were deemed to be about equal. Arrangements were being made to keep a US Customs Special Services van on standby. A flight using James Clayton's helicopter was still possible, but the weather remained an issue. The flight time from the estate was only about 20 minutes, so a decision wasn't urgent. Al Anderson's conversation with James Clayton earlier in the evening had gone well, and he knew he was prepared to go if asked.

The wildlife control officer again pressed the 'send' button on his cell phone

"Yes?"

"Someone is definitely in the cockpit. It's very dimly lit, but I've seen at least one person inside."

"That's it? I have people waiting for information right now."

"Wait, there's a small truck pulling up alongside with its lights off. It looks like an APU vehicle. That's used for starting the jet?"

"Yes. Two people are getting out."

"Do you see a boy?"

"Not yet. I can only see two men. It looks like they're connecting a cable from the truck to the jet."

"They're departing without the boy?"

"I don't know, they haven't left yet," replied the wildlife control officer.

"Keep watching and call me immediately if something changes."

The wildlife control officer would make more tax-free money in his last four shifts than he did in six months on the job. Employer loyalties were out the window at five thousand dollars a day.

Jen dressed quickly after the doctor's surprise visit. It was almost unbelievable that she hadn't been informed about his helicopter, or the fact that he was a pilot. That night of rest and relaxation she'd been looking forward to, had been instantly changed into a night of stress and anxiety. It had been months since she'd been flying, and she couldn't even imagine lifting off in this weather. If James Clayton was comfortable flying in these conditions he was either a very experienced pilot or worse—a very inexperienced pilot. She'd know soon enough.

Kyle always had a habit of mentally timing his trips. "If we are going where I think we are going, we should be there in fourteen minutes."

Both guards glanced across at each other, but neither one spoke a word. Although they had never personally defended an abduction attempt, they were constantly on edge when travelling with Kyle. They were both fully aware that anything could happen at any moment and it showed in the seriousness of their demeanour.

"Twelve minutes," said Kyle without looking at his watch. He would often mentally visualize the second hand of a clock as it moved around the clock face and had the ability to effortlessly count seconds with astonishing accuracy.

The co-pilot had almost finished his walk around inspection of the Learjet and ran up the short set of stairs into the cockpit. "We've got the APU hooked up whenever you're ready to start," said the co-pilot.

"Alright—sounds good. Any problems with the walk around?" asked the captain.

"So far everything seems okay."

"Try to minimize using your flashlight if possible, we'll be doing a dark start and I want to keep this departure as low key as possible. Have you done the fuel drains or obtained any fuel samples?" asked the Captain.

"I did the drains, but I didn't get any fuel samples."

"It's probably okay. I hate leaving the jet parked outside for days in this weather," said the Captain.

"Me too, it's too bad we couldn't keep her in the hanger. It's really coming down out there."

"Yes I can see that. Keep your eye open for our passengers. They should be showing up soon."

"Okay, I'll see you in a while," said the co-pilot as he flipped the hood up on his rain jacket and walked down the stairs.

"Ten minutes" said Kyle without the slightest shift in his position or expression.

The wildlife control officer was now on the south service road of the infield and slowed to a stop. As a bird clearance specialist he could be stopped virtually anywhere on the airport at night without attracting any attention. With his lights out, he drove slowly eastward on the edge of the south service road, searching for the best surveillance position.

"Eight minutes" said Kyle, going for an extended check of his clock visualization abilities. His personal record was three hours and he was off by one minute. He called three hours, at two hours and fifty-nine minutes—still plenty of room for improvement in his mind.

"Hey Kyle, what time do you have?" asked one guard, somewhat aware of Kyle's two minute countdown.

Kyle closed his eyes and tilted his head back, making sure not to look at his watch. "It's 9:38 p.m.," said Kyle without moving.

"He's right!" said the other guard who was staring at his watch. "Do you think they'll even let him in the casinos when he gets older?" asked the guard.

"I doubt it. He's probably already hacked into their mainframes," said the other guard as they both watched Kyle, starting to grin.

"What do you think Captain? Are you ready for a start?" asked the co-pilot as he reached the cockpit. "The APU is still hooked up and ready to go."

"Yes, I see that. Okay let's start up the engines. Any sign of our passengers?"

"Nothing yet—I'll stay outside and load them when they arrive."

"Okay, make sure all the covers are removed."

"That's all done Captain. I'll make sure everything's clear before we start the engines."

"Good, I'll be winding up the first engine shortly."

"Okay, give me a few minutes," said the co-pilot as he went back outside.

Jen had done a lot of training in the military version of a Bell JetRanger and only two flights on a Bell 407 as a passenger. The latter was a stretch version that had seven seats instead of five and four rotor blades instead of two. She would have to study the aircraft flight manual to learn the new aircraft limitations and emergency procedures and the automated engine control system. She could be doing that right now if the computers were online.

The butterflies in her stomach had no intention of settling down. All she could do was try to remember as many details as possible from the two flights she had taken. Right now it seemed as though they'd happened years ago. Although the possibility of flying with this job was fantastic news, just thinking about a flight in tonight's storm was terrifying. In some ways it seemed Doctor Clayton was continually trying to test her abilities.

The cross-border movement of certain approved people was more of a formality than any serious obstacle. Kyle maintained a 'steady green' status and a simple notification was all that was required for cross border movements in either direction. Al Anderson currently had Kyle's customs forms displayed on his monitor and only needed to hit the 'send' icon to complete his notification. Generally, he preferred knowing Kyle was onboard an aircraft prior to submitting the required notification. The weather in the Portland area wasn't showing any signs of improving and he'd have to monitor the situation continually.

James Clayton was seated in his office reviewing his aviation maps of the Portland area. Most major cities had certain arrival and departure corridors for helicopter traffic along with altitude restrictions for noise abatement procedures. James had flown in and out of the airport many times in the past, but mostly during daylight hours. Rain always reduced the visibility substantially, and gusting winds made flying that much more challenging.

He was carefully checking for any new 'Notams' and advisories pertaining to his potential flight to pick up Kyle. If they were dispatched, the two guards would accompany Kyle on the flight back to the estate. Ground-based return transportation would then be arranged for the guards once Kyle had arrived home safely.

James would also review all the radio frequencies he'd be using throughout the flight. It would be unfair to expect Jen to handle all the communications, as well as the flying, on her first flight in months. James continued to be concerned about the possibility of low ceilings. Clouds could easily blend into the tree tops in the hills surrounding the estate. It was imperative that they always kept good visual references with the ground—especially at night. The small hanger on top of the hill was equipped with raised halogen lighting that illuminated the pad and the small field around the hanger.

Most of the hazardous trees surrounding the hanger had been topped in recent years, but a steeper approach was still required due to the height of the trees and the small size of the clearing. James opened his office window and studied the trees swaying in the wind. He could already hear his inner voice objecting to any helicopter departures tonight.

"Four minutes" said Kyle, with head back, eyes closed and his small hands folded on his lap.

This time the wildlife control officer hit the 'redial' key. "Yes? Has the boy arrived?"

"No—I haven't seen anyone arrive, but they've started the engines."

"You can hear that from your position?"

"Not really, but I can tell by the way the exhaust is blowing the water on the ground. I can see that clearly with my binoculars and the APU truck is disconnecting the cable right now."

"What about the other pilot?"

"He's still outside with the APU truck," said the wildlife control officer.

"Then they're leaving without the boy?"

"I don't know. They haven't moved yet."

"Okay, I have to update my superiors. Call me if anything changes."

"Okay, I'll be watching."

The captain was in the process of filing his flight plan for the trip Portland; Vancouver to Portland with three passengers. The jet was fully equipped with instrument approach plates and maps for any destination in the world. Soon he'd receive a departure clearance and a time slot valid only for a short period of time. So far the start-up had been routine and all temperatures and pressures were indicating normal.

Kyle opened his eyes and looked outside the van. "Well, we're obviously at Vancouver Airport and I'll guess we'll be arriving at our aircraft within the next minute."

The APU driver had left the vehicle gate open and the second Special Services van also shut their headlights off as they drove through the gate.

The sound of the running engines were easily heard as the driver pulled up near the front of the Learjet. Greeted by the co-pilot, Kyle and both guards quickly unloaded themselves from the van and boarded the waiting jet. The co-pilot escorted his passengers into a first class area at the front of the plane and assisted them in stowing their luggage before giving them the usual safety briefing. He then went outside for a final look around and verified all the vehicles had cleared the ramp. Once everything was clear he entered the aircraft, secured the main door and took his seat in the cockpit.

The wildlife control officer hit the 'redial' one more time.

"Do you have any new information to report?" asked the agent with an agitated voice.

"Yes, another Customs van just pulled up beside the jet. It was only there for twenty seconds and then drove off."

"The boy—did you see him get on the plane?"

"I can't say for sure, it looked like several people may have been dropped off. It's impossible to get a good view of the front door from where I'm parked. Wait, the Learjet is starting to roll. It's taxiing with its position lights off."

Al Anderson's flight-following equipment was indicating the Learjet was starting to move. That's all he needed to know. They wouldn't be going anywhere if Kyle wasn't on-board the aircraft. He changed his computer screen back to the US Customs notification page and hit 'enter'. Kyle was now officially on his way to Portland with an estimated time en-route of ninety minutes. The weather at the Portland airport was showing a slight improvement, but low ceilings were persisting throughout the region and gusting winds could also pose a problem.

The on-shift supervisor at the underground RA-9 facility had just received the latest report from their agent in Vancouver. It was unfortunate that no visual verification of Kyle's presence was obtained however, confirming of the departure of the Learjet was definitely worthwhile news.

If a US Customs notification had been filed, as in previous cross border flights, they'd soon be able to cross check new data from the US Customs computers. At that very moment he heard a quick tap on his door.

"We've just got a copy of the US Customs notification. Kyle Clayton has departed Vancouver, Canada for Portland, Oregon."

"Excellent, notify our team in Portland."

"Yes, right away sir."

"What about the two agents in Salt Lake City?"

"What about them?"

"Do you have any notification or instructions for them?"

"Not yet, their status is currently under review by Professor Akkaim."

Jen couldn't stop pacing around inside Chalet Number Five. Were they actually planning a flight in this weather? It seemed unbelievable. Why hadn't James called to cancel yet? The least he could do was keep her informed about any new developments. Maybe he was waiting for information as well, going through the same nervous anticipation. Jen finally sat down and placed the phone on her lap. She was dressed for the foul weather outside and was wondering how far away the helicopter was located. Would they be walking or driving the quads? If it wasn't for the storm and the darkness, she'd love to go for a flight. The chances of her landing a civilian flying job with her experience were remote. Maybe Doctor Clayton was planning to upgrade her skills. If this flight did take place it wouldn't be a steep learning curve; it would be a vertical ascent.

Al Anderson continued to scour through the latest available weather data. He was well aware a decision was required very soon. The ground-based transportation would take substantially longer, but the weather was just not co-operating this evening. He knew that Doctor Clayton's helicopter was equipped for instrument flying, but only the airport had an approved approach. A one way flight to the airport wouldn't accomplish anything. Al Anderson picked up the phone and dialled the Claytons' estate. He distinctly heard two voices say "Hello?" after the first ring.

"Doctor Clayton? Is that you? This is Al Anderson."

"It's for me Jen. I've got it," said the doctor, and immediately heard Jen hang up the phone.

"Hi Al, will you need us to pick up Kyle tonight?" asked the doctor.

"Us?" asked Al Anderson.

"Yes, I was planning to do the flight with Jennifer Lamar. She's been hired to help us keep an eye on Kyle."

"Excellent. And she can fly a helicopter as well?" asked Al Anderson.

"Well according to her dossier she can. I was planning an initial assessment of her skills on this trip."

"That's right, I forgot about that. Tonight would be a good flying test with this weather. I've decided to transfer Kyle with our ground based transportation this evening. It's just not worth the risk in this weather. This is our second helicopter cancellation tonight. I expect they'll have Kyle home in the next few hours. We'll call you when we can confirm our exact arrival time."

"Okay, thanks for the call Al. We're here and ready to go. If the weather does break, I may possibly try a flight. If we do go, I'll park on one of the three helipads along the west ramp. If you see us your guys can load up and if not, we'll expect to see them back at the estate later on."

"I appreciate that—don't push the weather on our account. I'll instruct the flight crew to check and see if you've arrived."

"Anytime, talk to you soon," said the doctor as he hung up the phone.

He needed to let Jen know about the flight's cancellation and Kyle's arrival at Chalet Number Five tonight. He was still prepared to go flying tonight, but was also grateful to have the pressure of having to do the trip removed. He was still contemplating some training with Jen, even an engine start and a few vertical take offs would be an invaluable experience for Jen, especially at night. If they could climb above tree top level he might be able to check the visibility down below the estate. Unfortunately the valley below the estate would often tend to build up with clouds and fog.

This had caused serious problems in the past that previously resulted in two precautionary landings. Luckily, each time he'd managed to get his helicopter on the ground before losing his visual references. Both times his helicopter had to be parked overnight and flown back to the estate in the morning. In each instance he'd promised himself it was the last time he pushed the weather. One of these days he might

not have the luxury of a safe place to land. The risks of striking the main rotor, or the tail rotor blades, during any night landing were far greater than that of daylight operations.

James stood up, grabbed his flight bag off the desk and started to leave his office. He hadn't received clearance to use his cell phone and unfortunately Chalet Number Five was on the same line. He'd have to install a separate line to Chalet Number Five after Kyle and Jen moved in. James slowed down as he walked through the kitchen and tossed a few snacks in his coat pocket. As soon as he opened the door he knew he was taking his raincoat. The rain was still coming down, but not with the intensity of the earlier downpours.

James had parked his quad on an exterior porch off the north side of the house. A ramp to the porch had recently been constructed for Alexia's wheelchair which also provided an easy access point to shelter the quads. If nothing else, at least the seat was dry. James settled down in the seat on the quad, hit the start button and drove it down the ramp. He selected the high beam position on the head light and started the ride up to Chalet Number Five.

"Are you sleeping Kyle?"

"No. Does it look like I'm sleeping?"

"Well you haven't moved since we took off. Your head is still tilted back and your eyes still are closed."

"I'm working on a problem."

"What kind of problem Kyle?"

"Are you sure you want to know? Are you really, really sure you want to know?"

"Sure, tell me. What's your problem?"

"I'm trying to determine our speed."

"Oh, I know that, I've been up in the cockpit before."

"You think you know the correct answer? What's our present speed?" asked Kyle while starting to squint one eyelid.

"Yes, I think so," said the guard confidently as he repositioned himself in his seat. "We are going about five hundred miles an hour."

"I see. Is that airspeed or ground-speed?"

"That is the speed the pilot told me we were flying last week."

"That's probably airspeed. Ground-speed has been corrected for wind. Have you considered the rotational speed of the planet?"

"No. What's that speed?"

"It's about a thousand miles an hour at the equator. You have to correct that for our latitude."

"How do you do that?"

"You multiply the cosine of your latitude."

"What's a cosine?"

"I see someone was snoozing in their trigonometry class. What about the speed of our planet in orbit?"

"How fast is that going?"

"It's moving at about sixty-seven thousand miles an hour."

"No, I wasn't thinking about that."

"What about the speed of our solar system?"

"That's moving as well?"

"Yes, at about five hundred and eighty-six thousand miles an hour."

"Where is our solar system going?"

"It's doing a revolution within the Milky Way Galaxy."

"How long does that take?"

"It depends, between two hundred and twenty-five and two hundred and fifty million years."

"Is that it?"

"No, our galaxy, the Milky Way, and many other local galaxies are travelling towards a structure called the 'Great Attractor' at approximately one thousand kilometres per second."

"What's that Kyle?"

"No one really knows. All the galaxies that arrive there are missing huge amounts of mass. Explaining exactly how that happens will be one of the greatest discoveries in the history of science."

"Maybe you'll explain it one day Kyle."

"I often consider that problem, it's so profound. Thousands of galaxies accelerating towards the same location, then they begin to lose their mass."

"How far away is this 'Great Attractor?"

"It's about one hundred and fifty million light years away. If you traveled at the speed of light for that time you should be there. There's a good chance you may arrive early if you've corrected your calculations to factor in the increased acceleration when you're nearing the destination."

"Well that's good to know," the guard said with a smile.

"Unfortunately the Milky Way Galaxy is on a collision course with the Andromeda Galaxy, a well-known galactic cannibal with an immense appetite for other galaxies."

"Are you serious?"

"Yes, they're currently closing the gap at a rate of five hundred thousand kilometres an hour."

"That doesn't sound very good for the human race."

"The human race won't mind. Earth will be gone."

"What do you mean by that Kyle?" asked the guard who was now listening very intently to this small eight year old boy who still looked like he was taking a nap.

"Our Sun will have depleted its fuel before the galaxies collide."

"Then what happens? We all freeze to death?"

"No, once the sun depletes the hydrogen from its core it switches to fusing hydrogen into a shell outside the core. The sun will then expand to the 'Red Giant' stage."

"How large will it get?"

"Think of our Sun as a grain of rice."

"Yes."

"Now think of our sun as a basketball."

"Wow! And it's still hot?"

"Yes, its cooler, but still about five thousand degrees Kelvin."

"And what happens to our planet Earth?"

"Sorry, but the Earth's gravitational pull will create a tidal bulge on the surface of the sun. That 'bulge' will in turn increase the gravitational pull from the 'Red Giant' which will unfortunately pull planet Earth to a fiery demise on the surface of our dying Sun."

"Wow, that's incredible. Are you hungry Kyle?" asked the guard.

"That depends. What have you got?" asked Kyle as he opened both eyes, flipped around in his seat like the little kid he was and stared at the guard.

"I've got peanuts. Lots of 'Executive's Choice' peanuts."

"Thanks, I'll try some of those 'Executive's Choice' peanuts."

"Here you go," said the guard as he passed Kyle a few packs of peanuts.

"Let me get this straight Kyle. Our Sun is going to run out of fuel, then expand to hundreds of times its size and pull our earth inside?"

"I'd say that's straight. Is there anything to drink?' asked Kyle.

"I'll go and see what I can find," said the guard as he unbuckled his seat-belt and walked up front to check the galley.

James slowed down as he passed between the two garage buildings. He knew the Beaucerons had been tailing him as he left the house and preferred an interrogation on his terms. They took him up on his invitation and quickly moved in on the quad. James was not in the habit of ever removing valid scentlets and the dogs eventually blended back into the night. He continued along the dark path until he rolled to a stop at the entrance to Chalet Number Five. Leaving his quad running, he knocked on Jen's door and announced himself in a loud voice. Jen immediately opened the door and he could see she was prepared to leave.

"Did we get a dispatch?" asked Jen, trying to sound confident and keen despite the storm and darkness.

"Well, not really. We can pick him up if we want to, but the weather will probably stop us. I thought maybe we'll take a short flight and have a look first-hand."

"Great, give me twenty seconds and I'll be ready to go," said Jen trying to conceal her instant anxiety.

"Sure, you can follow me on your quad."

James sat on his quad as Jen locked the front door and started her quad.

"Are you ready?" asked James.

"Sure, lead the way," said Jen as she also turned on her headlight. "Are the Beaucerons out in this weather?"

"Of course," said James.

Jen reached down and confirmed her scentlets were still in place and started following James uphill along the wet cobblestone path.

After a ten minute ride the path started to level out as it entered a small grassy clearing on the top of the hill. The area was fairly well lit and a single narrow building was located by the edge of the clearing. As they started slowing down Jen instinctively knew she'd attracted the attention of the Beaucerons. Once again her sudden interrogation had taken place with her in the center of the pack. They took one more circle around James before finally resuming their night patrol.

"That didn't take too long," said Jen as they parked the two quads at the rear of the small hanger. It was a light blue metal clad building with a low level iron structure in front. "I don't see a helipad. Are we pushing the machine outside with a pair of handling wheels?"

"No, come with me and I'll show you," said James as he led Jen to the rear entrance door.

James unlocked the door and they quickly entered the hanger to escape the rain. Once he'd flipped on the light switches Jen could see an impressive black Bell 407 sitting on a pad about twelve inches off the floor. "It's a mobile pad system. The pad rolls outside under electrical power and back inside after you've finished your flight. It's very handy if you're by yourself and unable to push the helicopter out on your own."

"Yes, it looks like a great design," said Jen as she became more and more nervous.

"Why don't you start a daily inspection? There's a small step ladder up against the wall."

"Sure. Have you done a fuel-drain James?"

"No, we should do that. The drain pans are on the bottom shelf by the door."

"Okay, I'll get them ready."

"Thanks James. Can I do the drains inside?"

"Sure, the weather isn't ideal outside tonight."

Jen found a good drain pan and tried to remember the correct sequence for drains. Battery on—fuel valve off, sump drains but she knew it might be different with this machine. Jen had a long look around the cockpit. It was a well-equipped machine with a first class interior and an impressive layout. James had already installed a full set of dual controls, including pedals. Jen glanced up to the ceiling and flipped the battery switch on. The fuel valve was easily located and she put it in the 'off' position. Jen positioned the drain pan underneath the helicopter and drained a small amount of fuel from all three fuel cells.

Fuel valve on, boost pump on, was the next part of the drain sequence from what she could remember. Jen opened the pilot's door and put the fuel valve back in the 'on' position and glanced up at the circuit breaker panel located in the interior ceiling of the cockpit. This helicopter would have three fuel pumps; two electrical and one engine-driven fuel pump.

After she'd found the circuit breakers that turn the boost pumps on, she tried them one at a time and verified the left and right boost pump pressure from the fuel pressure gauge. Both pumps were running strong. Leaving one pump on, she picked up the small step ladder and then opened the engine access door and located the airframe fuel filter. Raising the drain valve underneath the canister released a steady pressurised stream of fuel. That would be captured in the engine pan and routed through an internal plumbing drain to the bottom of the helicopter. Immediately she realised she had forgotten to position a drain pan underneath and could hear fuel spilling on the timber pad below the helicopter.

"I've got it," yelled James as he quickly repositioned the drain pan underneath. "Did you check the fuel filter caution light while you're up there?"

"Not yet, I was going to do that next."

"Stay there, I'll help you. It's easier with two people." James pulled out the boost pump breaker and pushed in the 'caution' system circuit breaker. Multiple lights on the master caution panel illuminated along with the engine out and low rotor RPM horns.

James quickly muted the audio alarms and called back to Jen. "Okay, I'm ready. Press the red test button on the top of the filter."

"Okay, it's down."

"That's good, it's working," said James after watching the flash of the fuel filter caution light. James pulled the main 'caution' breaker and turned the battery off.

"You can continue your inspection of that side. I'll climb up and inspect the swash plate and main rotor head. Call me if you find anything that concerns you."

"Have you got a flashlight James?"

"Sure, there's one hanging above the counter to the left of the shop vice."

"Okay, thanks, I see it," said Jen as she removed the drain pans, picked up the flashlight and continued on with her inspection.

"We've got lots of choices Kyle," said the guard after returning from the forward galley of the Learjet. "You can have pop, water or juice."

"Coffee please, black with triple sugar."

"Kyle, I think you know what your dad would say if he heard you were drinking coffee black, with triple sugar."

"Yes, he would insist on a cup for himself, double sugar and flavoured cream."

"Well I wasn't really up there looking for coffee. I just checked in the bar fridge and don't even think about that."

"I won't. I don't like to drink when I'm about to fly. Do they have any apple juice?"

"I'll go and check again Kyle. I think there's some apple juice in the fridge."

"Thanks. Will you be talking to the pilots?"

"I wasn't planning to interrupt them. What did you want?"

"I'd like to do some flying if possible. Ask them if I can fly the instrument approach when we arrive."

"I'll mention it if I see them. Right now I'm just looking for some apple juice."

"Are they using Fair Trade coffee on this plane?"

"No, it's dark roast."

"Is dark roast good with triple sugar?"

"Stay there Kyle, I'll be back in a minute. Do you need any more peanuts?"

"No thanks. Do they have any cookies?"

"I'll have a look around when I'm back up there."

"Okay, maybe chocolate chip cookies if you find any."

"I'll see what they have."

"James, do you know about this small dent on one of the tail rotors blades?"

"Yes, it's been checked by an engineer and found to be within limits."

"Alright, everything seems good so far. I've checked all the fluid levels and everything seems okay."

"How much fuel do we have on board?" asked James as he finished inspecting the rotor head.

Jen opened the pilot's door and turned on the battery switch. "It's showing five hundred pounds on the fuel gauge."

"That's lots for tonight. About two hours of fuel, plus the reserve. Let's get the machine outside."

James climbed down and walked over to the hanger door. After pressing the 'up' switch, the hanger door immediately started to open. Jen had one final walk around the helicopter to confirm all the cowlings were properly secured and nothing had been overlooked.

"Jen, this switch controls the electric motor for the helipad. It has an automatic stop on each end." James hit the out switch once the hanger door was completely open and the pad began slowly rolling outside. After about three minutes the helipad came to a halt and James closed the hanger door. Jen walked to the back of the helicopter and started to rotate the tail rotor until the main rotor was ninety degrees to the fuselage.

"Why are you doing that Jen?" James asked.

"There are three reasons that I can remember. It confirms the main rotor tie-down has been removed and you have adequate main rotor clearance for a start-up. It also allows you to check the turbine is turning freely and isn't seized or frozen."

"Very good—you can fly from the right side Jen. Climb in when you're ready."

Jen opened the door and climbed in to the cockpit. It had a beautiful tan color interior and was extremely well equipped in the avionics department. Numerous instruments had dual installations for the pilot and co-pilot side. It took several minutes for Jen to adjust her pedals and seat-belts to fit her body. Whoever had been flying last time was much, much smaller. She didn't want to think about that.

"Well Jen, do you remember how to do a start?"

"I think we should review that James. I don't want to cook the turbine with a hot start."

"Trust me Jen, I wouldn't let that happen and the start is mostly automated on this machine"

They both sat still for a moment collecting their thoughts as Jen familiarized herself with the cockpit layout. The amount of noise produced from the rain hitting the

Plexiglas was surprising and the hanger door was mostly obscured by the dim light and raindrops on the window. Jen could feel her feet trembling on the pedals and knew things were about to get loud; very loud.

Chapter 12

The instructions to install a surveillance camera to watch the main entrance of the Claytons' estate seemed simple enough, however the logistics were now proving to be quite complex. The group of two men and their assistants were busy outfitting their small rental warehouse into a well-equipped fabrication shop that could quickly be modified to suit any specific needs. A wire-feed aluminum welder and assorted metal stock had been purchased this afternoon to facilitate the custom fabrication of various camera mounting brackets and assorted hardware. Depending on the duration of the surveillance system installation, it would most-likely operate on battery, or possibly even solar power.

Another complication was the existing camera system currently stalled on the granite walls of the main entrance. Installing a new camera far enough away to avoid detection of the existing camera system would require a night time installation and strong magnification powers for the new camera. One with remote manipulation capabilities would greatly increase its versatility compared to any standard fixed mount. Due to the short section of driveway before the main gate, the potential for an installation in the trees on the Claytons' estate was also a possibility.

After discussion of various possible systems it was decided to go with a small and powerful wireless IP camera. A nearby satellite Internet installation would also be required, but it would ultimately provide worldwide viewing access from any computer connected to the Internet. Additional purchases had included standard tree climbing gear and an assortment of ropes and rock climbing equipment. Tonight's bad weather would provide the cover they needed to properly inspect the location and hopefully begin preliminary work on the installation. It was imperative that the new system could at least provide a detailed view of any vehicles travelling into, or out of, the estate.

All four men were busy loading the van with tonight's equipment and they would soon be departing for the Claytons' estate, on West Cedar Drive. If everything went well after the initial recon they were planning to split into two groups with one group installing the IP camera and the other working on the satellite Internet installation. No one was really looking forward to working at night in the rain, but everyone knew it was the only real choice for this assignment.

"Did you ask the pilots if I could fly tonight's approach?"

"No Kyle, I didn't see them. I think they were probably in the cockpit, flying the plane. I did find a cold bottle of orange juice and a few packs of cookies."

"Do you know six cups of coffee a day can substantially reduce your chances of developing a myriad of degenerative brain diseases as you age?"

"Nice try Kyle."

"Maybe we can visit the pilots later and I'll discuss my request with them personally. They'll most likely be flying an ILS approach and that has to be one of my favourites."

"What's an ILS?"

"It's an acronym or abbreviation for an Instrument Landing System. It's quite simple really. It has a glide slope and a localizer. Once you've confirmed the identity of the selected localizer, and by the way, they use Morse code of all things, if you can believe it. Next you..."

"Okay Kyle, I'll see if we can visit the cockpit later in the flight. Have some juice and cookies."

"Thanks, maybe we can find a coffee at the terminal after we land."

"Sorry, but I don't think we'll be strolling around the terminal and drinking lattes when we get there."

"Yes I've concluded that. Were you implying that a person has some form of sociological dysfunction when he or she knowingly strolls about while consuming these lattes?"

"No, I don't think so. Did I say that?"

"I think you said that indirectly, just a mild suggestive inference perhaps. I'll have to try one the next chance I get, sitting down of course."

"Careful Kyle, you might really like them," said the guard with a smile.

James and Jen had completed two starts as he showed Jen about the automated FADEC system in the Bell 407.

A starting malfunction could easily destroy a turbine engine and pilots still needed to carefully monitor numerous gauges and always be ready to abort a start if any limits were about to be exceeded.

Jen carefully reviewed the events of the last two starts as she would be doing this one on her own.

"Flight controls, freedom of motion, set frictions."

She ran through all the initial checks and procedures.

"That look's good Jen, are you ready?"

"Yes, I think so."

"Okay, here goes..."

It didn't take her long to appreciate the machine's Full Authority Digital Engine Control system (FADEC) as she watched the machine practically start on its own. There was always something new being developed.

Gradually the rotors started turning and soon they were once again running at flight idle on the helipad. After several minutes they'd set all the required radio frequencies and navigational aids. The heaters and defog systems were also turned on to maximise cockpit visibility.

Windows could easily fog up under these temperature and moisture conditions, and James would always keep a few paper towels in the cockpit. James had his own personal helmet, and Jen was using a standard headset. They had both started talking over the helicopter's intercom system as it was now too loud to communicate without it.

Jen now had her right hand on the cyclic and her left hand on the collective. She quickly reviewed the basics in her mind—the cyclic controlled the direction of travel and the collective controlled the power. The collective control was similar to a large hand-brake located between the seats, with a motorcycle style throttle at the end. If she lifted the collective, she increased the power and if she lowered the collective, she decreased the power. She remembered that most turbine helicopters did not require manual throttle adjustments, once they were running at one hundred percent and ready for flight.

"Okay Jen, let's roll the throttle up to a hundred percent and get ready to lift off."

Slowly she continued to increase the throttle until the dual tachometer was showing one hundred percent rotor RPM.

"Let me know when you're ready to lift off and I'll stay light on the controls. When you've completed your checks try to hold a hover over the pad and if the winds are bothering you, move it into the clearing behind us. You remember the 'I-have-control' rule; if I take over the controls for safety reasons, I'll say 'I-have-control,' if not, you're still in control."

"Okay, I understand."

Jen slowly rolled the throttle back up to one hundred percent rotor RPM after the deceleration check. Her eyes kept constantly darting forward and sideways as she searched for any known references. Lifting off in rain and low visibility was a highly dangerous manoeuvre and it was critical that she always maintained her visual references. Right now the best references were the hanger door in front of the pad and a line of fuel drums to the right of the pad. Slowly she started lifting the collective between the seats while continuing to check the torque gauge on the instrument panel. Lifting the collective applied more pitch to the main rotors which increased the air flowing down through the rotors and also increased the torque displayed on the gauge. At fifty percent torque she could feel the helicopter getting light on the skids and the tail rotor pedals would soon have directional control.

Jen needed all her concentration to keep the cyclic centered as she slowly continued to increase power. The hydraulic systems on these aircraft made the flight controls extremely sensitive to control inputs. The tension in her legs made them feel like they were made of steel. Finally at about sixty five percent torque she could feel the helicopter starting to lift off the pad. The wind was stronger than she had anticipated and the helicopter suddenly started to rotate on the wet helipad, quickly and weather-cocking into wind. She was too late on the pedal correction and pulled up on the collective. The helicopter jumped off the pad and started climbing in an erratic hover, high above the pad.

"Watch out for the hanger roof. Your rotors are closer than you think. Back it up."

Jen tried to quell her fears, but the tension controlling her limbs just wouldn't subside.

"Is it clear behind us?" she asked, terrified of blindly backing up a helicopter, tail rotor first.

"I have control," said James.

Jen immediately felt a sense of relief and the blood returning to her legs.

"Jen, who do you think would check behind you if you were flying by yourself? Would you just cross your fingers and hope you didn't chop down a tree as you backed up tail rotor first?"

James switched on the landing lights and smoothly lowered the helicopter back into a steady hover above the pad. Jen remembered how these things were supposed to be flown.

"You have lots of rotor clearance with this hanger as long as you are over or behind the pad. I can tell you that the clearing behind you is mostly grass with no stumps or obstacles. You should never depart from anywhere without insuring your obstacle clearance."

"I know that. It's just the rain and darkness that's making everything so challenging."

"That's true, try it again."

James lowered the collective and put the helicopter softly back on the pad. This time he parked with the helicopter facing into the prevailing wind.

"Pick it up into a hover and start slowly climbing rearward while keeping the hanger and pad in sight. Are you ready?"

"Yes."

"Okay, you have control."

"Okay, I have control," said Jen as she prepared for another lift off.

This time she could anticipate the moment of lift off as she'd remembered how much torque was required to lift off the last time. Now that she was parked into wind also made a huge difference as she pulled it up into a hover. She wasn't rock solid by any means; however she was certainly beginning to feel more comfortable and her confidence was improving quickly thanks to the doctor's calm and professional manner.

"Keep practicing your lift-offs and landings and always keep the hanger in sight. I can see you're very smooth on the controls."

"Thanks, I'm doing my best. Does Kyle know how to fly this helicopter?"

"Yes, with his photographic memory he can recite the Aircraft Flight Manual word for word and he's smoother on the controls than anyone I know, including myself."

"Wow, that's incredible."

"I'm sure you'll see for yourself soon enough."

"Does he take solo flights with your helicopter?"

"Officially speaking—of course not. Unofficially—well, that's another story. I really don't mind him flying locally if he's in uncontrolled airspace. He likes to practice various hover exercises in front of the hanger and often takes local flights around the estate. By the way, your last landing was much better. Why don't you try and hover around the perimeter of this clearing while keeping your tail rotor pointed to the center of the field."

"Okay. My eyes are slowly starting to adjust to the rain and night lighting in this clearing. Kyle must be one of the youngest helicopter pilots in the country."

"I'm sure that's true, but I don't think the FAA would ever licence anyone under sixteen. Try climbing to a higher hover while you're doing these hover exercises, but don't lose you ground references."

"Okay, it looks like the clouds are just touching the tree tops around the clearing."

"You may be right. Don't take it up too high. We definitely don't want to be entering cloud."

"I'll be careful."

After thirty minutes of confined area manoeuvres, lift-offs and landings, Jen was starting to love the feel and power of this smooth black Bell 407.

The Learjet was experiencing much stronger turbulence than usual and everyone was now strapped in their seats as per the captain's instructions.

"How are we getting from the airport to the estate?" asked Kyle.

"I don't have any information on those plans yet. I'm sure something has been arranged for us, it always is. My guess is we'll be driving to the estate with this weather. What do you think Kyle?"

"You might be right. It depends on how low the clouds are. If the clouds are too low we'll be driving home, unless they've installed a private instrument approach for helicopters while I was away."

"I don't know if I like the sound of that. You mean that we'd be flying blindly inside clouds and then landing at the estate?"

Kyle turned slightly and looked at the guard speaking. "That depends on the sophistication of the system. You could probably do an approach with the two GPS map units in our helicopter, but it certainly wouldn't be legal. I know my dad prefers to see where he's going when he's flying a helicopter, so I doubt if he's installed any new navigation aids at the estate," said Kyle as he closed his eyes.

"I like his dad's rule," said one guard to the other, "If you can't see where you're going, then you shouldn't be flying."

"Yes, it's hard to argue with that," said the other guard.

Kyle opened his eyes for a moment at the subtle invitation to debate the topic further. "I like that rule too, notwithstanding the existence of exceptions of course," said Kyle as he again closed both eyes.

"Of course," said both guards simultaneously.

"I have control," said James as Jen was bringing the Bell 407 in for another landing attempt on the heli-pad.

"You didn't like my approach to the pad?" asked Jen.

"No, you're doing surprisingly well for someone who hasn't flown recently. I just want to have a good look at our current weather conditions."

The skill that James possessed was obvious the moment he took control and flew across the clearing and started a smooth vertical take-off towards the treetops. He continued his vertical climb while he kept the hanger and heli-pad in full view below. Once they'd climbed about a hundred feet above the treetops the distant city lights were now coming into view and James continued his vertical climb to the base of the clouds several hundred feet up. James knew the weather was probably acceptable for a night departure to the airport, but had no way of knowing that conditions wouldn't deteriorate and prevent a safe return.

"James, are you thinking about picking up Kyle tonight?" asked Jen as she kept her eye on the small clearing far down below.

"Well, we still have an hour and a half of fuel on board. Did you have any other plans?"

"No of course not—I'm ready if you are," said Jen with a smile. "Have you filed a flight plan or flight notification with anyone James?"

"No, actually I haven't, now that you mention it. Can you call Lisa on the satellite phone for me? I'll inform her about our intentions."

"Sure, do you have the new number?"

"Yes, I've got it right here." James handed Jen the new number and she entered the number on the keypad and hit the 'send' key. Moments later Lisa answered the phone and James explained the details of the flight and most importantly, when to expect to hear from them.

"Okay Jen, we're good to go. You have control."

Jen immediately felt uncomfortable assuming control in this situation. They were hovering in darkness, several hundred feet above the small helipad with only the distant city lights for references. James had kept the machine stable and nosed into wind despite the rain and darkness. Jen was almost immediately disoriented and couldn't stop herself from increasing the left pedal input to counter the crosswind forces on the fuselage. As total darkness quickly replaced the distant city lights the helicopter suddenly rotated violently into a downwind orientation and the view to the clearing below was lost. Jen immediately felt a sickening sense of panic as she began losing control of the helicopter.

"I have control Jen," said James calmly as he lowered the nose and started picking up airspeed. Within minutes James was flying at cruise speed and holding a set altitude as they proceeded south to the Columbia River approach corridor.

"What happened back there?" asked Jen, now feeling immensely grateful James was on board.

"You lost your situational awareness. Kyle or I will spend some time reviewing that later. Can you see the Columbia River up ahead?"

"Yes."

"Try to keep the helicopter at fifteen-hundred feet then turn right and follow the river out to the West. You have control."

"Okay, I have control," said Jen, instantly pleased at the new stability of cruise flight. James programmed the GPS units and set the correct approach frequencies in the VHF radios.

"James, I'm showing an YRX18 alert two kilometres ahead on the GPS moving map display. What's that?"

"Kyle has been programming the exact coordinates for most of the local hazards—'YRX18' to Kyle means 'wire crossing number 18'. That will be one of numerous wire crossings on the Columbia River. The height and proximity of the nearest hazard is always shown. Keep one GPS continually displaying the 'nearest' user waypoint information page—the GPS will compare our present altitude with the obstacle altitude. We have set it to provide an audio alarm if there is less than five-hundred feet clearance."

"That's a really great idea," exclaimed Jen.

"It's Kyle's idea. And yes, it's very useful at night and in poor weather conditions, provided he has the hazard entered. I'll do the radio work tonight and you can fly us into the airport. We'll be assigned a transponder code soon and then picked up on terminal radar shortly afterwards. Listen carefully to our clearance information as we enter the control zone and don't forget to monitor the hazard proximity information. This area is full of wire and tower hazards that won't be shown on terminal radar. What's our distance from the airport?"

"We're twenty-seven miles away and the GPS is estimating our arrival in sixteen minutes."

"Thanks Jen." James listened to the 'Automated Terminal Information Service' before contacting the tower.

"Do you think he's asleep?" asked one of the guards. "I doubt it, but you never know. Remember, he didn't get his coffee."

"I'm assessing the audio output from the engines."

"What for—is everything okay?"

"Yes, they sound normal at the moment. Generally they'll experience a subtle change in tone prior to any failure, unless it's catastrophic in nature. I may be able to provide the pilots with some advance notice of engine problems if I detect any anomalies in the acoustic signatures of either turbine engine."

"Well, if you have anything important to tell the pilots, just let us know and we'll get you up there right away."

"Thanks," said Kyle, knowing he had just arranged his visit to the cockpit of the Learjet.

The van had been driven inside the warehouse to simplify loading the required equipment for tonight's task. Everyone was double checking their own individual checklists prior to their departure and one of the assistants started opening the warehouse door. The rain continued falling outside and the wind was still gusting between the old concrete buildings. Driving to the estate in tonight's weather would take about forty minutes, without any unforeseen delays. Finally, after five hours of preparation, they backed the van out into the night and waited calmly as the last man closed the steel door and locked up the warehouse. As soon as he was done he quickly jumped in the van, and they started out on the night's assignment.

"I have something very important to tell the Captain," said Kyle suddenly opening his eyes.

Both guards jumped from their seats and hurried towards the cockpit door.

"Come in," said the captain, after hearing the multiple knocks on the door.

"Kyle has something very important to tell you," said the guard closest to the cockpit door.

"Well, bring him up here if he's not with you already."

"Yes Sir, thank you. I'll bring him up right away."

Kyle saw the guards returning and unbuckled his seat belt.

"The Captain is waiting to hear from you Kyle. Follow me and I'll take you up to the cockpit."

"Okay, thanks," said Kyle as he hopped out of his seat and walked up to the front of the Learjet. Kyle could tell at first glance they wouldn't be vacating their seats to let him fly and he was a bit old to be sitting on their laps.

"What's on your mind Kyle?" asked the captain.

"I've been detecting some intermittent rime ice accumulating on the leading edge of the starboard wing."

"Are you sure it's rime ice? How many types of ice do you know?" asked the captain.

"Well if you really have time for the answer I'm sure I can enlighten you about the various properties of ice and an interesting selection of types. As a naturally occurring crystalline inorganic solid with an ordered structure, ice is considered a mineral. An unusual property of ice frozen at atmospheric pressure is that the solid is approximately 9% less dense than liquid water. Ice is the only known non-metallic substance to expand when it freezes."

"Sorry Kyle, you said you observed some rime ice on the wing. How long ago?" asked the captain.

"Approximately three minutes and forty-three seconds ago," replied Kyle.

"Activate the de-icing boots, contact flight control and request an immediate decent to a lower altitude," the captain instructed the co-pilot.

"Are you certain we aren't flying through a temperature inversion?" asked Kyle.

"Correction—contact flight control and request a new clearance for the purpose of avoiding our present icing conditions."

"Right away Captain," replied the co-pilot.

"Thanks Kyle, we'll be doing our best to avoid these conditions as quickly as possible. Let me know if you notice any more ice accumulating on the wing."

"I'll continue my observations. We've probably just passed through a high concentration of super-cooled water droplets."

"Yes, you may be right. Thanks again for the information," replied the captain.

"We've been cleared to descend ten thousand feet to Flight Level 16," said the co-pilot.

"Flight level 16 acknowledged, please monitor the outside air temperature," said the captain as he initiated the decent.

"Yes Captain," replied the co-pilot.

Kyle tapped lightly on the captain's shoulder as he asked, "Excuse me for inquiring Captain. Are you monitoring the tower frequency yet?"

"No, we haven't switched over yet. Why do you ask?"

"Just wondering if you've overheard any recent inbound helicopter traffic?"

"What's the registration? I'll ask the tower after we change frequencies."

"No, that's okay. We shouldn't be broadcasting any form of public communication between our aircraft."

"Yes, good point. Well, you'll know shortly after we arrive, if you and the guards will be driving or flying home," said the captain suddenly aware that he'd just stated the plainly obvious.

The guards led Kyle back down the aisle and all three returned to their seats. Since the decent to a lower altitude the flight had become much more stable.

"Kyle, any sign of the ice you were telling the Captain about?"

"No, the leading edge of the wing is clean."

"That's great."

Kyle again focused on the mysterious phenomenon affecting his father's computer. It was inexplicable that hackers could somehow trick his reverse detection probes and re-direct his trace efforts to vague IP addresses in China. Recently he'd researched any and all available information on this worldwide 'GhostNet' method of protecting sophisticated cyber hackers. One thing was clear; whoever was responsible for implementing the 'GhostNet' was responsible for a wide range of cyber intrusion attempts, including those currently in progress at many leading-edge physics research facilities.

"Portland Tower, this is Bell 407 November five-five-zero-five."

"Go ahead November five-five-zero-five, this is Portland Tower."

"Good evening, you can check we're twenty miles East of the airport, inbound to the West ramp at fifteen hundred feet and estimating the field in eleven minutes.

"Good evening November five-five-zero-five- squawk Mode C transponder code 3425, and call five miles out."

"Roger, we'll call you five miles east of the field."

"November five-five-zero-five, check you are now radar identified."

"Roger, Bell 407 November five-five-zero-five."

"I'd never realised just how beautiful it is flying a helicopter at night over a city, even in the rain."

"Yes that's true Jen, especially these low level night flights. Not many people will ever have the chance to experience it."

"Shall I hold this altitude?" asked Jen while doing her best to maintain a direct inbound track to the airport.

"Yes, don't start a descent until after we've completed our five mile check-in."

"Okay James, holding fifteen hundred feet inbound."

"You're doing well. Remember it's a Mode C Transponder so the tower can monitor your altitude as well."

"Thanks for the reminder James. Do you know what aircraft Kyle will be arriving on?"

"I don't have the registration, but it will most likely be a Learjet. They know we will be parked on or near the public heli-pads and Kyle will certainly know this machine," said James.

"We're six miles back James."

"Portland Tower, Bell 407 November five-five-zero-five is five miles to the East requesting clearance to the helipads on the west ramp."

"Roger November five-five-zero-five, you can begin your decent and continue inbound. Hold short of Runway 22," said the ATC Controller.

"Roger Portland Tower, will hold short of Runway 22, November five-five-zero-five."

"Just start a gradual decent. Are you monitoring the other GPS for obstacles?"

"Yes James, just one tower three miles to the south of us."

"Okay, that's good. Do you have a visual of the airport and can you see Runway 22?"

"I can see the airport, but I can't see the runway yet."

"Just try and imagine where it should be located. It will be much easier to see when we're closer in. Don't forget to confirm your wind direction with the windsock when we reach the field."

"I won't. Will I be doing the landing?"

"Sure, you may as well get all the practice you can."

"Thanks. I think I have Runway 22 in sight up ahead."

"That's it. You'll be able to confirm it once you've seen the numbers painted on the runway threshold."

"Bell 407 November five-five-zero-five, you are cleared to cross Runway 22, wind is from 260 at 20, land on heli-pad three at your discretion."

"Thank you Portland Tower, Bell 407 November five-five-zero-five."

"Air taxi towards the apron and approach over the grass to heli-pad three. Can you see the windsock off to the north?" asked James.

"Yes, I have it now. The wind is coming from the west."

"You're doing well—don't worry if you don't put your skids right on the H, just keep it in the circle. Keep moving forward. That's it."

After a long approach, Jen felt relieved as the skids finally made contact with the wet asphalt.

"Not too bad, try picking it up and moving about fifteen feet forward, the back of your skids are just outside the heli-pad perimeter circle."

"Sorry James, let me try that again." Jen lifted it back up into a hover and slowly moved the Bell 407 forward before making a less than perfect landing."

"Good work, considering it's blowing twenty MPH. Let's roll the throttle down to flight idle for the required two minute cool down. It looks like we'll be shutting down here for a few minutes anyway."

"Portland Tower, November five-five-zero-five is down and clear on heli-pad three."

"Roger November five-five-zero-five. Have a good evening."

"Thank you, same to you."

"Jen, keep one of the radios on after we've shut down. I expect we'll be hearing from an inbound Learjet shortly."

"Okay James. Should I tie down the main rotor blades?"

"Let's wait and see how they react in this wind. They may be okay. Did you park the nose out of wind?"

"No. Why is that James?"

"It's a just an old habit from flying helicopters with two rotors Jen. It substantially reduces the chance of the main rotor striking the tail boom during shutdowns in windy conditions."

"No one ever taught us that, thanks."

James glanced up at the windsock and decided the winds were light enough to do a complete shutdown. "You can close the throttle whenever you're ready," said James.

The gentle chime sounded as the 'Fasten-your-seat-belt' sign illuminated. Kyle and the guards strapped in for the decent and approach to the airport. The captain had just announced an estimated time of arrival of twelve minutes from now and the current weather at the airport—moderate rain, with winds from the northwest at 20 MPH. At this altitude there was still nothing to be seen outside the windows except darkness. Kyle would be glued to the window throughout the decent trying to predict the exact moment the Learjet would break out of cloud. Depending on the captain's qualifications and the type of instrument approach, it could occur at a very low altitude with these conditions. Every approach has a Decision Height; a point where visual references with the runway environment must be seen or else a 'Missed Approach' with an immediate climb-out was next.

Kyle liked the excitement of watching the altimeter getting lower and lower as it closed in on the published 'Decision Height.' Most pilots, on the other hand, likely found that aspect of the approach to be the most stressful time in the cockpit, especially during poor weather conditions. The turbines decelerated gradually to a lower power setting as the Learjet began its descent. There was still nothing but darkness outside the windows and raindrops could be seen streaking by the exterior windows. One guard reached up and dimmed the overhead lighting while everyone remained quiet during the start of descent. Kyle straightened up in his seat and continued to press his face against the plastic interior window while cupping his brow with both hands. He promised himself the next time he was a passenger on a Learjet he'd bring along his own personal hand-held GPS. With that he'd always know the exact location and altitude of the aircraft.

"What do you think James? Should I tie down the main rotor in this wind?"

"Yes, it's probably a good idea. I was planning to check the oil levels and do a walk around the helicopter. If you can stay and monitor the tower frequency I'll tie the main rotor down."

"Sure. Are you positive it's a Learjet we're expecting?"

"I think that's the most likely. He almost always arrives in a Learjet."

"Okay, I'll let you know if I hear a Learjet contact the control tower."

"Thanks Jen, I'll be back in about five minutes."

Jen watched as James secured the main rotor and turned on his pocket flashlight. An aviation fuel truck was making its way towards them, but James could certainly decide if he wanted to take on extra fuel. She was impressed that he took the time to check the oil levels before the next flight. That was definitely another habit worth remembering.

"Should we drive past the entrance to the Claytons' estate or stop before it?" asked the driver.

"Let's stop before. We could be recorded while we're driving past the entrance."

"Okay, start looking for a place to pull over. The rock wall on the left is on the Claytons' property. Park by the next driveway on the right for now—we can scout out a better parking spot later. I don't want the van sitting on the side of the road all night."

With just enough room to pull off the road they unloaded two packs of gear and started formulating a plan for the night.

"How close does the satellite Internet station have to be to the IP camera?"

"They shouldn't be any more than five-hundred feet apart."

"Tell our assistants to find a secure place to park the van and they can catch up with us later. Tell them to call us on the portable FM radio, channel 16, when they're done. Let's get going. We'll need to do some signal tests before we select a location for the micro dish. On second thought, tell the assistants to stay with the van and monitor channel 16 on the FM portable. After our tests we can call them on the radio and have them bring the extra equipment we'll need."

"Alright, I'll let them know."

There was lots of verbal activity on the tower frequency, but still nothing concerning a Learjet. Just at that moment she overheard, "Portland Tower, good evening this is Learjet November four-three-zero-four."

"Good evening Learjet November four-three-zero-four."

"We are at check-point Lima, twelve thousand feet and estimating the ramp in fourteen minutes."

"Roger Learjet November four-three-zero-four, the wind is from 265 degrees at 20 gusting 30, the active runway is 22, next contact is at check-point Mike."

Jen could hear the rear left door opening and knew James was checking out the rear passenger compartment.

With rear seating for five, this helicopter was well suited for medevac purposes as it could accommodate one or two stretchers as well as two medical attendants. Jen could hear the rear door closing shortly afterwards. Despite the very limited visibility from the cockpit to the rear passenger compartment, she knew James was probably just sitting out the rain in the spacious rear seats.

"James, I just heard an inbound Learjet report at check point Lima and they're estimating the ramp in fourteen minutes."

"James?"

James opened the co-pilot's door and climbed back inside.

"Oh, there you are. I thought you were sitting in the back. An incoming Learjet is estimating an arrival time in ten minutes."

"Thanks Jen, you can start up the helicopter now. Kyle's strapped in the rear passenger compartment and ready to go."

"What!"

"How did that happen?"

"Welcome to the deceptive complexities of Al Anderson's world of logistics. Kyle and the guards were inside the cab of the fuel truck and we've just completed his transfer here instead of the estate. Even I didn't know."

"Hi Jen, is my father reviewing aborted start procedures with you this evening?"

"Hello Kyle. No. Why are you asking about aborted start procedures?"

"They'll be required shortly if either of you intend to start this turbine engine with our main rotor blades tied down."

"Oh thanks Kyle. I'll go and take care of that Jen," said James as he unbuckled his seat belts and stepped back outside.

"Thanks Kyle, I owe you one for that."

"One large coffee with triple sugar and we're even."

"You've got a deal Kyle. One large coffee with triple sugar it is," said Jen, unable to stop smiling.

Chapter 13

Professor Akkaim glanced up at the dusty electric alarm clock perched on the filing cabinet beside his cluttered office desk. Dust was a fact of life when you lived and worked underground. He'd previously requested a two o'clock meeting with the surveillance supervisor who was now almost five minutes late. Trying to take his mind off the man's annoying habit of being late, the professor continued to study the information he had requested on past and present employees of the Claytons' estate.

The supervisor knocked once with his right hand as he pushed the door open with his left.

"Sorry, I'm late. I've just received a confirmation on the Customs Service monitoring system that a Learjet just landed in Portland."

"Were you able to confirm Kyle Clayton's arrival?" asked the professor.

"Not directly. Portland was the destination printed on his customs notification and I'm trying to confirm the aircraft is in fact down in Portland."

"Don't you have four agents in Portland? Have them verify the aircraft was the same one that left Vancouver."

"I received an update from them this afternoon and they're planning to start the camera installation this evening."

"Oh that's right—will they complete the installation tonight?"

"Possibly—I'll get a progress report tomorrow," replied the supervisor.

"I want you to contact the two agents waiting in Salt Lake City."

"I thought their status was under review."

"That's correct, and the review is still ongoing. I did consider terminating their services, but decided instead to send them on another assignment. I want you to have them drive to Dayton, Ohio and contact us after they arrive."

"What's going on in Ohio?" asked the supervisor.

"When, and if you need to know, I'll inform you," replied the professor while glaring across the desk.

"Very well Professor, you know best."

"Still no developments on the two agents tracking Bill Riker's movements in Iraq?"

"No. Not a word."

"Have you had any success infiltrating the new phone service just installed at the Claytons' estate?"

"No, so far we've been unable to compromise the new telephone system installation and the doctor's computer is still disconnected."

"What about the cellular phones? We were getting information from them recently."

"Yes, we still have access, but they are rarely turned on."

"When was the last time one of their cell phones was in use?"

"Jennifer Lamar briefly switched her phone on last night, but she didn't make a call."

"Do you find that strange?" asked the professor, rolling a short, chewed up pencil between his dark, slender fingers.

"Not necessarily. It's possible she changed her mind or she may have been taking pictures."

"Can we obtain these images if that's what she was doing?"

"If she turns her phone on and tries to send them, well yes, we can definitely intercept the images. If the phone is turned on and they are stored in the memory, it becomes more difficult, but not impossible."

"I want to see what was so interesting that she needed to take pictures."

"Try and obtain those images as soon as possible."

"Yes, Professor Akkaim. Is there anything else?"

"Not at the moment. Let me know when the two agents arrive in Dayton, Ohio. Tell them to find a quiet hotel in the northern outskirts of Dayton. Sinzar Bakkir will be arriving in Santa Monica later next week and we'll also need someone there to discuss upcoming personal requirements and acquisitions."

"Okay Professor. I may have someone available in California, and if not maybe we can spare some men from Portland once the IP camera is installed."

"One more question. How is Kyle Clayton getting from the airport to the estate?"

"I don't have any information on that at all. We'll have a better idea of his activities after the new camera system is installed. It certainly would be nice to have someone providing information from inside the estate."

"Yes it most certainly would. I'm working on that now."

"That's such an excellent idea Professor! Let me know how I can be of assistance."

"Don't worry, I will. You can start by getting our two Salt Lake City tourists on their way to Dayton, Ohio."

"Yes, right away. I'll let you know if we receive any interesting developments."

"Let me know if you receive any developments, period."

"Yes of course Professor," said the supervisor as he rose from his chair and quickly departed the office.

Both men had now walked within four hundred feet of the Claytons' entrance gate. The night lighting around the gate was strong enough to reveal the position of the single camera mounted on the granite gate post. Even with field binoculars it was still too far away to determine if the camera was stationary or had remote control capabilities. Tonight's darkness and persistent rain greatly diminished the binoculars effectiveness. Proceeding further without a detailed understanding of the range and magnification capabilities of the gate camera would needlessly increase their risk of exposure and detection.

"What do you think?"

"This is close enough for my liking."

"Yes, I think so too."

"We're lucky to have so many tall conifers around here. They aren't easy to climb, but they'll provide good cover if we can install the equipment deep in the canopy."

"What side of the road do you want to use—this one or the across the road from the estate?"

"Let's move into the forest across the road. The trees on the estate may be taller, but they're not as dense as the stand across the road."

"Okay, let's work our way in there now and we can move closer to the gate once we're concealed in the forest. After we're in position we'll climb a couple of trees for a signal check."

"Did you bring a head lamp?"

"Yes, I have one in my backpack."

"Good, that's going to be indispensable for a night climb. Are you ready? The brush looks pretty thick and overgrown. Watch your eyes. It's going to be rough-going crashing through this wet undergrowth in the dark."

"You're not kidding. This stuff is almost seven feet high with patches of blackberry vines."

"What about the others? Should we call them on channel 16?"

"Wait until we've completed our signal checks, and then we'll know if we can proceed with the installation. At least they'll stay dry while they're waiting in the van."

"Yes, that's for sure, for a little while anyway."

"Watch your eyes. It's going to be difficult getting through this undergrowth. And make sure you don't turn on any lights."

"I won't. You can lead the way."

"Okay, let's go."

It had taken ten minutes to find a secluded location to park the van. A narrow overgrown logging road branched off into the forest across from the estate. It was slow going, inching along in darkness without any lights. One of them walked slowly in front of the van and eventually they found a small opening wide enough to turn the van around and park. They were now about two hundred yards up the logging road and well out of sight from anyone driving along West Cedar Drive.

"Do you think they tried to call us while we were moving the van?"

"Not a chance, I've been monitoring channel 16 on the van radio and they haven't called yet."

"Well let's give them a call and tell them where we are."

"No, it might compromise their position. We'll stick to the original plan and wait for their call. Between the climbs and signal testing it's going to take time to select the best location."

"Yes, you're probably right. I'm sure they'll need us soon enough."

"Yes, you're right about that."

After a brutal ten minutes of clawing their way through the wet underbrush, the ground was now becoming more passable under the solid canopy.

"What do you think? We should be well out of sight by now."

"Let's keep going a little further in and find the largest tree close to us."

"I can't see a thing, I need some light."

"I have an extra pen light you can use. Keep it pointed towards the ground and not towards the estate."

"I'm not even sure what direction the estate is in this darkness."

"Okay, let's stop here and try this tree. Heads or tails?" he said as he tossed a quarter down on the decaying forest floor.

"Tails"

They both located the fallen quarter with their pen lights and kneeled down to verify the winner.

"It's a head—I'm staying on the ground and you're climbing. If you get a strong signal when you get up there you may just as well stay there. You can hoist up anything you need with the climbing rope."

"I'm going to need the climbing spurs to make it up the first fifty feet."

"I can see that. Take a small saw with you and remove some branches on the way up. Don't forget to rope-in a few safety points during the climb."

"You don't have to worry about that, I learned my lesson a few years ago."

"Yes, I know about your fall. You were lucky you survived. I'll organize a small climbing backpack while you're getting your climbing gear on."

"Thanks. It's going to take a serious effort to climb the first part of this tree. I'm going to need my headlamp for this climb."

"I don't think that's a good idea. We can't have lights flashing on and off up in the tree tops."

"Well I'll need some light. Can you tape a penlight to my headband?"

"That's a minor improvement. Okay, pass me your headlamp and I'll get it ready."

"What about the solar panel? Are we installing that?"

"No, just drop the power cables down to the ground. We'll use batteries and then bury them later. That will be faster than installing solar panels."

"That's true, but we'll have to keep coming back here to change the batteries."

"At least they'll be on the ground."

"Good point."

"Pass me the backpack when you're done. I'll hoist up anything else I need later."

"Here, this should get you started. Call me on the radio once you completed a signal test."

"I will. Help me get my climbing belt around the tree trunk before I get started."

"Here you go. Good luck."

"Thanks, I might need it," he said as he stabbed his climbing spurs deep in the thick bark."

"I'll turn my radio on when you're getting close to the top."

"Okay, I'll talk to you then."

"They should have called by now. Let's try them on channel 16, just a quick radio test."

"Go ahead if you want, I don't think it's a good idea."

"Radio test, anyone copy on 16?"

"Give them a couple of minutes to respond."

"Radio test, does anyone copy this radio on channel 16?"

"Nothing heard, over."

"Let's take a walk and see if we can catch up with them."

"If we find them we'll have to return here for the equipment."

"I just think something's wrong."

"Alright, let's go and have a look around. Keep your radio on."

"Don't worry, I will."

After locking the van, both men followed the logging road out to West Cedar Drive, rain drowning out the sound of their footsteps.

"You answer it," said the older agent as he watched TV from the worn out hotel bed.

The younger agent rolled over and snatched the receiver from the phone between the beds.

"Yes—where? When—okay, why? Okay, understood," said the younger agent before hanging up the phone.

"Let me guess," said the older agent. "We're heading back to Portland in the morning."

"Wrong, we're driving to Dayton, Ohio and we're leaving now."

"What the ... Dayton, Ohio—now? I was just about asleep. Why?"

"They're not saying. Just check-in on arrival for further instructions," said the younger agent as he lay down on the bed and began rubbing his face with both hands.

The older agent sat up, put his feet down on the floor and pulled out his faded wallet. "Here's some cash. Pay for the room and I'll meet you at the car. We'll need fuel and coffee from the first gas station. Ohio is a long, long way away from here."

"That's for sure. Can I drive?"

"You can do the first shift, but remember the last time. We are not in any official rush," said the older agent.

"They said 'right away' on the phone."

"No, I repeat, no speeding," said the older agent with a yawn.

"I won't, you don't have to worry about that."

Jen had yet to lay her eyes on Kyle even though he was strapped in one of the seats behind her. Starting the helicopter and the night departure from the airport had gone well with a little guidance from James. Being familiar with any location certainly had its advantages, especially at night. It was lucky Kyle had reminded them about the main rotor being tied down.

"Jen, can you make the radio call to Air Traffic Control as we clear the control zone?"

"Sure, I'll try. Portland Tower, Bell 407 November five-five-zero-five is clearing your control zone to the southeast."

"Roger November five-five-zero-five, clear to the southeast, have a good flight."

"Thanks," said Jen into the microphone on her headset.

"I'll give you a three out of five for correct radio procedures Jen."

"Hi Kyle, I didn't know you were listening on the intercom. Three out of five—what did I miss?"

"Including your distance and altitude provides incoming pilots with additional detailed traffic information, improving the safety and separation of all arriving and departing aircraft."

"Thanks, that makes sense. I'll remember that next time," said Jen while trying to adjust her eyes to the growing darkness ahead, as the lights from the city gradually disappeared behind them.

The persistent rain was continuing to deteriorate the already poor night visibility.

"Just try and keep us flying east above the Columbia River for now," said James as he reprogrammed the moving map display on the GPS.

"What altitude do you want me to maintain?"

"Stay high enough to clear the wire crossings and low enough to stay out of the clouds."

"To be honest, it's getting harder and harder to see anything at all."

"I know Jen, don't worry. Try and keep scanning your flight instruments and remember, I'm here to assist you if it's required."

"Thanks."

"Stop, this is far enough. I can see the estate entrance up ahead. Can you see the camera up on the gate post?"

"Yes, let's move off the road. The other two should be around here somewhere."

"The height of the wall takes a dip over there. Let's try and climb up on top. Maybe we'll find their packs or ropes nearby."

"Alright, if a vehicle comes along we can lay flat on the wall. No one will be looking up here in this weather." It didn't take long to reach the base of the wet granite wall from across the road.

"Give me a leg up, I'll go first."

After negotiating several finger and toe holds, he pulled himself to the top of the wall and lowered his pack down to help his partner up.

"Let's stay on the wall and walk closer to the gate. We should see some sort of sign from them soon."

Both men approached as close to the security camera as they dared.

"Did you hear something?"

"No. Like what—voices?"

"Not voices, more like the sound of a branch, or small branches, breaking. Rustling leaves maybe."

"It's so hard to tell in this rain. Keep your eyes open for some light in the trees. They can't be climbing trees in total darkness. If we don't see anything soon we'll jump down and take a quick look around inside the estate."

"Okay, that's fine with me."

After close to thirty gruelling minutes he'd climbed as high as safely possible. Having underestimated the level of difficulty required to scale the bottom of the tree he was now physically exhausted and started roping-in his third safety point of the climb. Trimming off the ends of several overhead branches with a folding pruning saw, he managed to open up a suitable area for testing the satellite Internet signal. The testing gear was sophisticated for its size, but he'd completed the necessary calibrations earlier and would just have to wait while it scanned the sky, acquiring satellites.

Both men were now lying on their backs on the top of the wall, scanning the darkness of the tree tops within the estate for any sign of lights or voices.

"We should've stayed at the van for all the good we're doing here. Let's take a look around inside. If we don't find them we'll go back to the van."

"Okay then, at least we made an effort to find them. You can go first."

"Okay, lower me down with your pack straps."

"Tower to ground, do you copy on channel 16?"

"Ground to tower, I copy you five-by-five."

"The test results are in, we're clear for install."

"Excellent. I'll contact the van. What do you need?"

"We need the medium dish, two batteries and two extra coils of cable."

"Tower, this is the van crew and we heard your request. Where are you guys?"

"We're about two hundred yards inside the forest, directly across from the main entrance to the estate"

"No wonder we couldn't find you."

"You two aren't back at the van?"

"No, we're on the wall close to the gate. We thought you might be having some trouble."

"Thanks, I guess we should've checked in earlier. See you when you get here. Make absolutely sure you're not detected by the gate camera. Keep your lights off on the way in and minimize your radio use. It's extremely overgrown next to the road."

"Thanks for the information, see you soon."

Both men stood up on the wall. "Let's walk the wall back to the low spot. It's almost right across from the logging road."

"Sure, it's fairly easy walking up here if you're careful. Did you hear that?"

"What?"

"The same sounds as the last time—like leaves, ivy leaves, rustling. It's probably just my ears playing tricks on me with this weather."

"Let's go, and watch your step, this moss is really slippery with all of this rain."

"Thanks, I've noticed that. Let's go, I'm right behind you."

"Jen, start a turn towards the northeast and try to maintain your present altitude."

"I can't see a thing to the northeast. I can barely follow the Columbia River down below us," said Jen as she scanned intently for visual references.

"Correction—please climb another three hundred feet to two thousand and hold a heading of zero-seven-five degrees. Start cross-checking your flight instruments."

Jen smoothly initiated a left banking turn and pulled back slightly on the cyclic to initiate the climb. As she levelled off at two thousand feet she became immediately aware of a new warm sensation on the back of her neck.

"Dad—increase the map display scale on GPS 2, reset the directional gyro, and set both altimeters with the radar altimeter. Jen, what's the distance and direction to our closest hazard?"

Jen just realised Kyle had been standing on the seat behind her, his head directly behind hers, quietly observing everything in the cockpit through the gap by her headrest.

"The nearest hazard is 17 miles to the south. It's identified as YRXING 22," said Jen.

"Check wire crossing 22. Dad, set the terrain alarm on the radar altimeter to five hundred feet and switch the second GPS to the navigation mode. Please program the estate helipad as the destination waypoint."

"Okay Kyle, give me a couple of minutes for that."

"Jen, maintain at least sixty miles an hour and be prepared to climb immediately if you hear the radar altimeter terrain alarm."

"Climb? Are you sure about that Kyle? The clouds have been very low all evening."

"Considering we're already in cloud, initiating a climb is definitely safer than initiating a decent."

James was stunned by the seriousness of Kyle's statement. "In cloud—are you sure?"

"Can either one of you see anything outside—anything at all?"

Kyle watched as they both scanned outside the windows for several moments and knew they were fighting the onset of spatial disorientation. He knew that being well trained and aware of all the various possible illusions was a key aspect of survival in an instrument only environment. Kyle also knew that most flights that had ended in 'controlled flight into terrain' or 'graveyard spirals' had been caused by vestibular illusions, and later he'd make sure that Jen knew and understood the dangers as well.

"Trust the gauges Jen," said Kyle with his calm voice. "Fly us directly to the estate using your main GPS map display and not below twelve hundred feet on the altimeter. When you're within three miles start a three mile radius turn around the estate while holding an altitude of twelve hundred feet. I've noticed our fuel quantity is limited and just calculated two different 'point of no return' times depending on our alternate location."

"Sorry, Kyle, I should have taken on extra fuel at the airport. I certainly wasn't expecting you and the guards to be getting out from the cab of the fuel truck."

"We still have several options at the moment. Hopefully the weather opens up during our perimeter orbits around the estate."

Jen was now showing four miles away from the estate and concentrating intently on her instrument cross checks. The thing she remembered most about her training was never to focus on a single instrument. Always keep your eyes moving methodically throughout the instrument scan. Most of her limited instrument training had occurred in ground-based flight simulators. Never before had she devoted such a sustained level of mental concentration and determination to make the needles of the flight instruments behave the way she wanted; flying the gauges. Right now every minute that passed felt like an hour.

"There's a truck coming. Listen. Can you hear it?"

"That's not a truck. It's a chopper and it's getting closer. Come on, let's get off this wall and back across the road."

"I can't believe anyone is actually out here flying in this weather. I can barely see the tops of the trees."

"Hurry up, the lowest part of the wall is just up ahead. Now it sounds like the chopper is turning away from us."

"Maybe they're lost in the clouds?"

"We might see a fireball soon if they are. Let's move it."

Just as Jen was three miles from the estate the terrain alarm on the radar altimeter sounded.

"Dad, please reset the terrain alarm to four hundred feet. Jen, when you're three miles east of the heliport turn left to a heading of two four zero and begin a direct inbound track to the heliport. You should be directly into wind on your approach and please reduce your airspeed to sixty miles an hour. Maintain eight hundred feet on the dual altimeters. Use your GPS map to bring you in, and if dad doesn't assume control keep flying three miles past the heliport and commence another wide radius turn to the right."

"Listen, that helicopter is getting louder and louder. It's coming straight for us. Quick, we're almost there. I don't want to be seen walking around here on the road."

"Tower calling van on channel 16, do you copy?"

"Wait, they're calling us on the radio."

Jen could still feel Kyle's steady breath on her neck. Standing on the rear seat afforded Kyle a good view of everything that was going on in the cockpit.

"Dad, please increase the map scale on GPS 1 and Jen, please slow your approach speed to forty miles an hour. We'll be passing overhead the heliport in forty-five seconds, three hundred feet above ground."

Jen could see all the relevant details on the map display. It was showing the real time position of the helicopter and the exact track they were following as they approached the helipad which was clearly depicted on both GPS map displays.

"Jen, maintain your altitude and slow your airspeed to forty miles an hour. Dad, were the heliport lights on when you departed the estate?"

"Yes Kyle, the lights were on when we left."

Just at that moment they flew over a slightly illuminated, obscure haze.

"Nothing visual," declared James suddenly.

"Jen, maintain your present heading with an immediate sixty mile an hour climb to twelve hundred feet," said Kyle calmly.

Jen fought to comprehend her own eerie sense of vertigo and illusion as they passed above the glowing yellow halo of cloud, only to quickly return, blind, into the black darkness and rain.

"This is tower calling van on channel 16. Do you copy?"

"Hold it! This is where we climbed up. Pass me the radio."

Both men crouched down on the wall as he worked open the snap securing his radio on his belt.

"Here you go, it's on channel 16."

"Thanks. This is the van on channel 16. We copy, over"

"What is going on with that chopper? They just flew right over top of me and I didn't see a thing. They were so close I almost jumped."

"We don't know what's going on. They seem to be leaving the area again."

"Where are you two?"

"We're on our way back to the van to get your equipment. How will we find you?"

"Standby one—this is tower to ground. Are you still at the base of this tree?"

"Yes, I just heard your conversation. I'll tie a climbing rope on this tree and start making my way back towards the van. Use the rope to lead yourselves back here. Where are you parked?"

"About two hundred yards up the only road across from the estate."

"I know it, we walked right past it. And remember, no flash lights with this helicopter in the area."

"Copy that information, van out."

"Well at least we won't be spending the whole night searching for our remote Internet location."

"That's a great idea with the climbing rope. We can follow it right in with the equipment."

"I don't know about you, but I can still hear that chopper."

"So can I, let's get moving."

"Good idea, here's your radio. Can you lower me down with your pack straps?"

"Sure, can you grab my boot when I start coming down?"

"No problem."

He slid his radio back in the holster and bent down to secure his pack and the nylon straps.

"I've got to lie down and brace myself first. Okay. Grab the straps, I've got you."

Slowly the first man started down, found a few foot holds and dropped to the base of the wall.

"Thanks, your turn. Reach your leg down and I'll hold your boot."

As he stood up and started to reposition he heard a single distinctive noise; hard plastic hitting solid rock, once.

"Come on, what are you waiting for?"

"The radio just fell out of my pouch and dropped off the wall."

"That's high enough Jen. You can level off at this altitude. Maintain your heading until you're three miles out.

"Okay Kyle, almost there. I'm showing two point eight miles out."

"When you reach three miles, right radius turn, maintain present altitude and airspeed."

"Okay Kyle, I'm starting the radius turn."

"Your instrument flying skills are showing a steady improvement. Try to hold a three mile radius during the turn. It should be just less than ten degrees of right bank."

"Thanks Kyle."

"Let's leave the radio for now. I can still hear that chopper flying around and tower's waiting for us to bring the equipment. Next time we'll bring some rope to scale the wall and besides, they don't want us using any flash lights right now."

"Good thinking, give me a hand. I'm coming down."

"We better do some running, that chopper sounds like it's coming back in."

"Jen, you can start a right hand turn to establish another inbound track to the heliport. Dad, please reset the terrain alarm on the radar altimeter to three hundred feet."

"Radar altimeter terrain alarm—reset to three hundred."

"Roger, copy that Kyle."

"Jen begin a five hundred feet per minute descent to one thousand feet on the dual altimeters. Reduce your approach speed to sixty miles an hour."

"Descend to one thousand feet with a sixty miles an hour indicated airspeed."

"Jen—"

"Yes—"

"Watch your inbound track, you're drifting left."

"Sorry, I'm correcting my heading now. Okay, I'm holding an altitude of one thousand feet with sixty miles-an-hour airspeed and we're one mile out."

"That's looking good. Dad will take control if he confirms a visual reference."

"I'm standing by, Kyle."

"Jen reduce your speed to forty miles an hour at a half mile out. Maintain your inbound track and altitude."

"Roger, slowing down to forty miles an hour indicated."

"Look's good. Be ready for an immediate climb on this heading if you hear the terrain alarm."

"Roger, copy that Kyle."

"Jen, slow to thirty miles an hour, maintain your heading and altitude, and don't look away from the gauges."

"Roger, copy that."

Jen's peripheral vision was detecting the growing ambient light in the cockpit. The intensification of her battle between temptation and willpower continued as she forced herself not to look away from the instruments. Just hold the heading, hold the altitude, hold the airspeed and be ready to climb immediately if the terrain alarm sounded. Her brain felt like it was exploring the outer limits of her willpower and ability to maintain total concentration.

"Visual confirmed. I have control," said James as the tail boom of the helicopter dropped suddenly into a quick stop manoeuvre and the helicopter began a slow steep descent into the clearing below. Jen could hear the power increasing as the helicopter approached the pad and watched with amazement as James smoothly flew a 'no hover' landing, directly on to the wet helipad. Rolling the throttle to flight idle, James locked down the controls as they waited for the two minute turbine engine cool down.

Both men were drenched and exhausted when they reached the van. Once the doors were open they could hear the truck's mobile radio.

"This is the tower calling the van. Anyone copy on channel 16?"

"This is the van, go ahead tower."

"That chopper just landed somewhere up on the hilltop and I can still hear the engine running. Wait, I think it's shutting down now."

"Copy that tower."

"Wait until my partner gets back to the van and the three of you can bring everything back here in one trip, including the IP camera and the small black mounting bracket I made this morning."

"Roger, copy that tower."

"Thanks. See you soon, over."

James had completed the shutdown and the rotors had just now come to a stop.

"Welcome home Kyle, and thanks for your help."

"Sure Dad—that was fun. Nice flying Jen."

Jen's nerves were still recovering from the multiple, and illegal, instrument approaches to the estate in tonight's weather.

"Thanks Kyle. I may have to tack a few more coffees on our account after your help tonight."

"Thanks Jen. Perhaps we can keep that account confidential in the future?"

"What account Kyle? James, should we call Lisa and close our 'flight plan' or does she know we're safely back home?"

"Yes, our flight plan—she probably heard us land, but it wouldn't hurt to give her a call. Do you still have the number?"

"Yes, I've got it right here. I'll give her a quick call on my cell phone."

"Thanks Jen. I'll tie down the main rotors and open the hanger door. You and Kyle may as well stay in the helicopter while helipad rolls inside the hanger."

"Sure James, what a great system."

"Yes, it's perfect if you're going flying by yourself."

Jen called Lisa and officially ended their 'flight plan'. Kyle was still sitting in the rear passenger compartment as the helipad rolled on top of the tracks leading into the hanger.

James had the lights turned on and the hanger door was starting to close as Jen climbed out of the front seat.

"Thanks for the lesson James. It feels like I just had a year's worth of training in one night."

"Flying with Kyle is like that. I'd rather have my life in his hands than any autopilot or flight computer. You'll see that soon enough for yourself."

"Yes James, I believe I just did. Is Kyle going to the house or straight to Chalet Number Five?"

"Just ask him what he wants to do."

"Where do you want to go Kyle, the house or Chalet Number Five?"

"Did the new computers arrive? And if so, where are they now?"

"Yes, they are all ready to go in Chalet Number Five."

"Then can I go down to Chalet Number Five please? I should try and get back to work," said Kyle from the backseat.

"Sure, are you coming Kyle?"

"Not right away. I'm waiting for the hanger door to close."

"Why?"

"Well I find it very peculiar that we haven't seen the Beaucerons yet. Are they locked in the enclosure at the house? Why would they be locked up while you were both away? Something isn't right. They're always here and ready to interrogate anyone getting out of the helicopter."

"He's right James. Does Lisa have them locked up?"

"That would be very unlikely. She generally waits for my advice concerning anything to do with the Beaucerons. And now that you mention it, it is unusual—very unusual."

Jen stepped back to open the rear door when she noticed Kyle was holding the fire extinguisher.

"What's the matter?"

"Jen, are you interested in trading your scentlets for this fire extinguisher?"

"I'm sorry Kyle. We'll get that sorted out right away. Stay where you are and keep the fire extinguisher if it makes you comfortable."

"Any other 'self-defence' choices?" asked Kyle with a searching grin.

"We'll talk about that later. Wait here. I have to talk with your dad."

"James, we need a pair of scentlets for Kyle."

"Yes, I had a pair all ready for him and gave them to Lisa. She was planning to hide them in the kitchen. Listen, I'll drop off Kyle's luggage at Chalet Number Five, pick up the scentlets from Lisa, and then ride back up here. That should take me about fifteen minutes."

"Thanks James. I'll give you a hand getting his gear on the quad."

"Great. I'll get everything out of the baggage compartment. I should be able to take it all in one trip."

"Jen," Kyle whispered through the crack in the window. "You forgot the battery."

"Okay, thanks. I owe you one more—you know what. I'll be right there James. I'm just disconnecting the battery."

"Good thinking. I forgot all about that."

Kyle watched as they both walked out of the hanger, happy they didn't leave the hanger door open behind them. Kyle had the greatest admiration and respect for the Beaucerons, but also knew their code of conduct contained no provision for exceptions.

Jen came back inside the hanger, stepped up on the helipad and opened the rear door. When Kyle stepped out of the back she could see that he wasn't nearly as tall as she'd imagined him. His sandy blond hair was cut barber-short and although his teeth weren't perfect, they fit nicely within his well-guarded smile. He was wearing dark brown pants with a blue small check-shirt and a light brown jacket; its inner pocket had a plastic liner holding an assortment of pens and pencils. The hard black case containing his eyeglasses barely fit inside his shirt pocket, and his eyes; his eyes were the most striking shade of blue she'd ever seen. He was actually very handsome for such a young man and inexplicably, she couldn't help but sense his unusual intelligence the moment she gazed in his eyes.

"Jen, I could tell you were a little uncomfortable during the flight home tonight."

"Well, that's true. I really didn't appreciate the dangers of mixing night flying and bad weather. Even James didn't know we had accidentally flown into cloud."

"It can happen to experienced pilots as well and it's a known precursor of many 'Controlled Flight into Terrain' accidents," said Kyle.

"Do you think James would have tried to land at the estate tonight if you weren't on board?"

"No, I doubt it. He would have flown out towards the airport and requested a radar vector to return to 'visual flight conditions'."

"That sounds a little safer than what we just did."

"Maybe—except there wasn't enough fuel on board to complete the trip."

"Really—what would you have done if we didn't see the helipad on our last approach?" asked Jen.

"We would have tried one more approach, one hundred feet lower. Failing that we could have returned to the flat lands around Columbia River, descend into visual conditions and made a precautionary landing."

"Well Kyle, you certainly sounded competent while you were directing our actions from the back-seat."

"I always knew exactly where we were, and the minor deviations in your instrument flying abilities never compromised our safety."

"Are you sure?"

"Yes, I'm sure Jen. I could have told dad to take over sooner if I was worried."

"Just between you and me, you don't know how relieved I was to hear James say 'I have control' on the last approach."

"I knew. It's always safer to switch pilots when moving from instrument flight conditions to visual flight conditions. It was a good chance to give you some additional training on your first day of flying."

"Yes, that's for sure. I think I just heard James driving up to the hanger."

Both men from the camera crew had packed everything they needed for the installation of the remote Internet site and all the related camera equipment. When the third person from base station eventually returned to the van, they divided up the equipment and followed the light climbing line back to the base of the tree.

"This is base station calling tower on channel 16."

"Tower here, go ahead."

"Drop your rope and we'll make up the first load for your tote bag."

"Okay, send up the mounting brackets for the dish. Are the other two doing the camera installation?"

"We're working on a plan now. Unfortunately they managed to drop their radio inside the wall of the estate."

"Wait until we get everything I need up here and the battery power connected. After that, see if you can find a tree between here and the gate that will give us a good view of the entrance. They can go and find the radio later or pick it up the next time we're out here replacing batteries."

"Copy that tower, the first load is secure in your tote bag and ready to go."

"Thanks. I'll try pulling it up now."

"Welcome back James."

"Thanks Jen. These are for you Kyle," said James as he passed him the new pair of scentlets.

Kyle checked the expiration date, hopped back inside the helicopter and attached his scentlets.

"Okay Jen, I'm ready to go. I'd like to start hooking up the computers."

"Why don't you two take both of the quads down to Chalet Number Five, I've got a few things to do in the hanger and I'll pick up another ATV from the garage on my way down. Lisa said to stop by the house if you need anything, and if not we'll see you tomorrow."

"Great, thanks James," said Jen.

"See you both soon. And don't let Kyle keep you awake all night."

"I won't."

"By the way, did you see any sign of the Beaucerons?"

"No, but I did notice the kennels at the house were empty. As Kyle said earlier, it's very strange that we haven't seen them after landing here with the helicopter. Maybe you'll see them on the drive down."

"Okay, we'll keep our eyes open. Give me a call at Chalet Number Five if you need anything."

"Hey Dad, I'll let you know when I've made some progress on the computer problem."

"Sounds good, see you two later," said James as he closed the hanger door.

"Pick a quad, any quad," said Jen as she closed the hanger door behind her. Kyle jumped on the nearest quad, had the engine started and the lights on before Jen had inserted her key.

"Follow me," said Kyle he sped away from the hanger. Jen could only watch as his taillights disappeared into the night, down the steep cobblestone trail.

Chapter 14

James spent nearly an hour inspecting the Bell 407 after tonight's flight. He knew they were fortunate Kyle had been on board this evening or they wouldn't have made it home. Kyle was right; they would probably be sitting alongside the Columbia River needing a ride or fuel and quite possibly both. It was a classic example of just how quickly you could get into serious trouble flying during darkness and inclement weather.

Slipping into instrument conditions had happened without warning. Worse than that was the fact that they'd both been oblivious to the real danger they were in. Some of the most valuable lessons about flying often occurred after surviving a dangerous situation and tonight's flight was just such a lesson. James promised himself to be even more vigilant in trying to avoid a repeat of tonight's events. Even his personal fuel management procedures required improvement. There's never a good reason to run out of fuel in a helicopter and doing so at night during instrument conditions was the worst of all possible scenarios.

James walked to the back of the hanger and opened the overhead hanger door. He decided it was best to refuel the helicopter tonight despite the rain outside. He liked the peace of mind, knowing his helicopter was inspected, fuelled and prepared to depart on short notice.

"This is tower calling the camera crew on channel 16. Do you copy?"

"Go ahead tower."

"Have you finished the camera installation? Over—"

"Yes, it's mounted on a tree trunk about forty five feet high. We're just finishing up with the power connections."

"Do you have a clear view of the entrance gate?"

"We won't know until we test it. I'm staying up here with the camera in case it needs some final adjustments."

"This is the tower calling base station—have you opened the video stream on the Internet?"

"Yes, I'm just getting the video feed on my laptop now."

"How does it look?"

"It's as good as you'll get with these weather conditions."

"This is base station calling the camera crew on 16."

"Go ahead base station."

"Can you adjust the camera slightly to the right?"

"Sure."

"That's good there. Pan it down a bit. More, that's it. Are you on full zoom?"

"Not quite."

"Okay, slowly increase the zoom. Stop. That looks pretty good from my laptop."

"Tower to base station, the remote Internet connection is working perfectly. I'm going to start lowering some gear and preparing to climb down."

"Copy that tower."

"Camera crew, do you copy tower on channel 16?"

"Yes we copy, go ahead on 16"

"I'll be climbing down in ten minutes after I've locked in the new camera adjustments."

"Copy that. Let's all meet up back here and we can walk back to the van together."

"Copy that. See you soon. What about retrieving the radio we lost?"

"I'm not sure if we'll have time for that. We'll decide later. It's only a radio."

"Copy that. Camera crew clear on channel 16."

Kyle was standing outside the front door of Chalet Number Five when Jen drove up on her quad.

"Any sign of the Beaucerons Kyle?"

"No, I didn't see them. How was your ride down here?"

"It was wet and dark. Let's go inside and I'll get a fire started. We can light the Tulikivi as well."

"Sure, I want to start hooking up all the computers. They'll all function as one unit after I've finished the set up. What happened to the front door? It looks like a few bullet holes have been repaired."

"That's a long story Kyle. I'll tell you later," said Jen, surprised Kyle had effortlessly detected such a small deficiency.

"Nice, I'm already looking forward to that story. Did Lisa stock up a few groceries for the kitchen?"

"Yes, she packed a few boxes that I brought up here earlier."

"Excellent. Was coffee included?"

"Maybe, I haven't unpacked everything yet. Besides, coffee would probably keep you awake all night."

"No, twelve computers might keep me awake all night, but not a few cups of coffee," said Kyle, turning to hide his grin.

"Kyle, why do you need so many computers?"

"Have you ever heard of the 'GhostNet?"

"No, I don't think so. What's the GhostNet?"

"It's a highly sophisticated system designed to disguise the origin of computer hackers. It simply reroutes any detection efforts to random IP addresses in densely populated cities. They're usually, but not always within China."

"Why is that important to you?" asked Jen.

"Well, it's important to the integrity and security of scientific work throughout the world for starters. But more specifically, I believe we've isolated and quarantined the responsible nano virus within my father's hard drive. All our trace efforts in the past have always resulted in predictable GhostNet results. I'm trying to reconfigure the gate that redirects detection probes to the 'GhostNet' and reroute detection probes directly to the real computers involved in these cyber espionage attacks."

"Will the hackers know if they've been detected?"

"I can't answer that question yet. Of course being able to discover the origin of the hackers without their knowledge would be an obvious advantage, something I will no doubt be striving for."

"How long do you think it will take?"

"It's difficult to say. I've designed some new software programs that I'm hoping will speed things up."

"That's an interesting problem you're working on. Let me know if you need any help setting up the computers or with anything else"

"Okay, can I stay upstairs Jen?"

"Sure, it's best if you're on the second floor and I'll stay on the main floor. I like the fact there's only one entrance door to Chalet Number Five and I'm planning to make a few modifications on that tomorrow."

Jen locked up the front door and started a fire in the Tulikivi and the main fireplace. Each had a well-stocked wood box, filled with dry kindling and mix of split birch and alder.

Kyle was already upstairs working on the maze of cables underneath the main computer tables. Once again she had another chance to sit down in front of the fire. This time, with two night flights behind her and Kyle safely upstairs, she felt her first real sense of job satisfaction. James was right; this wouldn't be any normal nine-to-five position. Tomorrow she would try and purchase some additional security hardware for the main door; install a spyglass and possibly a door alarm.

In the silence of Chalet Number Five she could no longer ignore the sounds of her own hunger emanating from within her body.

"Kyle, I'm going to take a look in the kitchen and see what's available to eat."

"Good idea. We should have lots of choices if Lisa packed those boxes."

"Yes, Lisa packed them. Did you even have a dinner tonight?"

"I had the late night Learjet special, Executive Brand Peanuts served with chocolate chip cookies."

"Let me just check on our menu options."

"Thanks," said Kyle from the top of the stairs.

Jen lifted the two cases up on the counter and finished putting the groceries away.

"Kyle, would you like some breakfast for dinner? We could have bacon and eggs?"

"Bacon and eggs with coffee sounds excellent."

"How do you want your eggs?"

"Same way you're having them."

"Toast and hash browns?"

"Sure."

Jen had found everything she needed to make coffee and started off by brewing a full pot.

The lights inside the hanger provided some additional exterior lighting when refuelling outdoors at night. James had his own fuel bowser installed shortly after the hanger was completed. Unfortunately only one or two companies owned a truck capable of refilling his bowser due to the current condition of the helipad access road. Depending on the amount of flying they did, a full bowser generally lasted about two or three months. James finished pumping just enough Jet B fuel for about two hours flying with his required reserve. Just over five hundred pounds was his standard fuel limit when preparing the Bell 407. He could still cover a large area for medevac purposes and generally needed some additional justification to carry the extra weight of full fuel.

James walked inside the hanger and once again hit the switch that started the helipad moving slowly along its guide track and back inside the hanger. Because one person could not easily move the Bell 407 without help, this system was ideal for James and essential for Kyle.

Jen now had breakfast well under control and was impressed with the layout of the kitchen, including all the high end stainless steel appliances and a built-in dishwasher. She'd found anything she needed with ease and the cupboards were stocked with a wide selection of assorted staples, including sugar.

James always preferred private uninterrupted time for working on his helicopter. It was imperative to continually inspect all the various systems on the machine and to remain aware of any defects or ongoing maintenance issues. After locking the hanger he rechecked his scentlets and started walking down the path towards the house. It hadn't taken long to notice the smell of wood smoke drifting up the hill and he knew Jen and Kyle were getting settled in at Chalet Number Five.

"Kyle, are you coming down for your late night breakfast or do you want to keep working?"

"I'll keep working if I have a choice."

"That's fine. I'll bring you up something." Jen carried a tray upstairs with his breakfast and a large mug of coffee.

"Thanks Jen. Is that what I think it is?"

"Triple sugar, I'm not sure about the milk."

"No milk, that's perfect. I'll deduct one from the account."

"It's my pleasure. How's your super computer coming along?"

"I'm still downloading the new operating systems. It's going to take some time before they're all working together. Do you have a laptop Jen?"

"Well, yes I do. But it's not here at the moment."

"Okay, well you can show it to me later."

"Sure, don't let your breakfast get cold. I'll keep the coffee on downstairs if you need some more."

"Thanks Jen."

James walked past the turn-off to Chalet Number Five. If he hadn't needed a quad to reach the helicopter in an emergency he would have just walked all the way home. The absence of the Beaucerons was now becoming increasingly worrisome. He'd have to initiate a search if they were still missing tomorrow. James fished the keys out of his pocket as he approached the twin garage buildings. The quads were always kept in the same building and he knew there should still be two parked inside. It didn't take long to select a quad and get the machine outside and ready to go.

Within minutes James was riding the quad down the path to his house. As he approached he noticed a few lights were on in the kitchen and the automated dog kennels were all open and empty.

Jen was looking forward to her first good night's sleep in ages. She restocked both fires in the chalet and considered resetting her make-shift door alarm.

"Kyle?"

"Yes?"

"How's your coffee?"

"It was excellent, I've already finished it."

"Do you want another cup?"

"Sure that would be great, thanks."

Jen poured another mug for Kyle and brought it up stairs.

"It looks like lots of these computers are running now."

"Yes, but it's a long way from being fully operational."

"Kyle?"

"Yes?"

"Do you know that I'm now responsible for your safety?"

"Are you referring to the flight home?"

"Very funny. No Kyle, I'm very aware of who was responsible for our safety on that flight."

"I think you know what I'm trying to say Kyle."

"Not exactly Jen."

"We need to watch each other's backs."

"We may need two mirrors for that."

"It's just a figure of speech. It means that we look out for each other."

"I know what you mean," said Kyle with a grin.

"Kyle, do you need to go outside tonight?"

"I didn't have any plans to go outside."

"Then I'm going to set a simple door alarm tonight and I don't want anyone opening the front door except me, under any circumstances."

Kyle could think of a few sets of circumstances where Jen's life would depend on him opening the door, but that type of speculation wasn't called for at the moment.

"Of course, I understand."

"Thanks Kyle. I appreciate your co-operation. I may just have to brew another pot of coffee in the morning."

"That's the best time for coffee. Don't you think?"

"Yes, you're right about that." Jen locked the main door from the inside and rigged her plate on top of the door.

"Jen, are you expecting visitors?" said Kyle as he watched her set the plate from a chair.

"Kyle, you and I never want any uninvited visitors."

"Yes, I know. I get reminded of that every time I see my mother."

"I know Kyle, all the more reason to watch each other's back."

"I do like your door alarm. It's a little primitive perhaps, but it looks effective."

"Thanks Kyle, trust me, it's a proven design. Do you have everything you need upstairs?"

"Yes, everything looks good up here. I'm going to work a little longer and then I'll try to get some sleep. What are we doing tomorrow?"

"We should meet with your father and review your upcoming internship schedule. After that I'm open to suggestions. Maybe we can take a drive into town if you like. I need to buy a few things."

"Okay then, we'll decide in the morning. Thanks for the breakfast and especially the coffee."

"You're welcome. I hope it doesn't keep you awake all night. Goodnight."

"It won't, goodnight Jen."

Jen spent a few minutes tidying up the kitchen and retreated to her luxurious first floor accommodations. After another hot shower she slipped back underneath the thick eider-down duvet. The toll of tonight's inadvertent instrument flight had taken more out of her than she realized. She could only watch the news for a few minutes before turning off the TV and surrendering to her own fatigue.

The sound of Professor Akkaim's phone jolted his body upright from his unplanned nap.

"Yes?"

"Professor, we have some new developments to report," said the acting supervisor in the computer room.

"What have you got?"

"We have a streaming video feed from the IP camera at the estate entrance and we also have some images from Ms. Lamar's cell phone."

"Excellent! E-mail me the link to the IP camera. After that, print the images from the cell phone and bring them to my office ASAP. I want to see them right away."

"Very well Professor. I'll be there as soon as I can."

The professor hung up the phone and cleared his computer monitor while he waited for the link to the video feed. Within a minute he'd received the hyper-link. Professor Akkaim opened the link and inspected the image displayed on his monitor. The installation team must have installed a suitable lens shield as the lens appeared completely dry despite the obvious precipitation. The image wasn't perfect, but this would serve as an excellent surveillance tool, providing it continued to work properly and also remained undetected.

The supervisor knocked quietly on Professor Akkaim's office door.

"Come in."

"Thank you," said the supervisor as he settled into the only other chair in the room. "Did you have a look at the live video feed Professor?"

"Yes. It's not bad considering the darkness and rain they have at the moment."

"We're lucky the entrance area is illuminated at night. It really provides us twenty-four hour coverage."

"What about the pictures from her cell phone? And when did she use it?"

"She turned it on and made one short call this evening. We think it may have been to the estate. We're still waiting to confirm it's the newest number up at the estate."

"And how long is that going to take?"

"I'm not sure. They've installed a sophisticated new system that might not be easily compromised."

"You have virtually unlimited resources at your fingertips and you can't confirm the location of a single telephone number?"

"I hope to know soon. Every effort is being made to replace our lost connections with the estate phone line, and hopefully the computer as well."

"Let's see the images you were able to retrieve from her cell phone."

"This is what we've got Professor, four digital photographs," said the supervisor as he passed them across the desk.

He gathered the small stack of photos and tilted them towards his desk lamp for a closer inspection.

"She won't be travelling anywhere soon in that vehicle, not without a new set of wheels or a tow truck," said the supervisor.

The professor hoped his extended glare at the supervisor might reveal his disdain with the man for speaking the obvious.

"These images will require much closer scrutiny."

"I can have them printed and enlarged if you like. What exactly are you looking for?"

"Two of the images clearly show the licence plates have been removed. The photograph showing the right side of her Explorer shows a partial Oregon license plate on the vehicle beside her truck. I want you to zoom in on that partial plate and match it to the vehicle in the photograph. I want the address of that underground parking lot and I want it soon."

"Yes Professor, we can usually access state motor vehicle records. It may be possible to get an address depending on how much information we can get from the license plate."

"I don't care if you only have two numbers. With a partial photograph of the vehicle you should be able to find a match, and an address. Has the team installing the camera equipment returned to the warehouse or even checked in yet?"

"No, we haven't heard anything Professor."

"Well it was a routine assignment for them. The IP camera seems to be operating perfectly."

"Yes, I'll let you know when we hear from them and also if we get an address for her truck."

"What do you mean, if?"

"Forgive me, when, I mean when we find the address. Hopefully the other vehicle wasn't just visiting that location."

"That's unlikely. I'll expect to hear back from you soon."

"Yes Professor, we'll do our best," said the supervisor as he got up, happy to be leaving the professor's office.

James was glad to be back inside his home and settling in for the night. He had spoken briefly with Lisa before she retired for the evening. Her days were long and she was almost always the first person awake in the morning. James sat down in front of the fire and put his feet up on the warm stone hearth, steam rising slowly from his damp woollen socks. With no light but the fire, James allowed his mind to slowly explore the deepest of his own personal thoughts. Even after reliving every harrowing detail of tonight's flight he couldn't escape his underlying premonition that something, somewhere, was very wrong.

Kyle eventually finished his cold breakfast for dinner as his hot coffee and computers were distracting him from eating his meal. He was satisfied his father had made the right decision hiring Jen over Bill Riker. Granted, she did need some additional flight training, but overall she had handled herself reasonably well considering the circumstances. Kyle was already looking forward to some real training flights with Jen rather than just directing flight operations from the rear seat.

It was becoming apparent Kyle wouldn't finish setting up the computers tonight. He needed to pick up a few more items to complete the initial installation. So far the power modifications and the available Internet Service were adequate for the number of computers he was planning to use.

Kyle was hoping to start a forensic interrogation of his father's hard drive once his system was completed. He was confident the underlying virus remained in quarantine and he could soon determine exactly how it got in and how it functioned. It was obvious a port-scan had identified vulnerability in his father's system, and determining exactly how it entered was critical in designing security solutions for the future. Kyle still felt confident that it was only a matter of time before he would know the original source of the 'GhostNet' virus probing his father's computer system. Twelve computers working collectively should provide the analytical computing power he required to run his new software.

Kyle smiled as he glanced down at the large dinner plate balancing above the entrance door and then got up and unpacked a few things from his luggage. After brushing his teeth he too was lured into the inviting beds of Chalet Number Five.

James continued to watch the logs burn down, shifting them periodically with the long steel fire poker. He'd officially be on call in the morning and was scheduled to start an afternoon shift tomorrow.

James got up and peered outside through several windows, but still couldn't see any signs of the Beaucerons. He walked slowly down the hall for a night time visit with Alexia. Sitting beside her he realized just how predictable her sleeping behaviour was becoming. Nothing seemed to change. Her bed was tilted up thirty degrees and she slept on her back with same irregular breathing and both eyes wide open. Although she had a medic alert system available, it was extremely rare that she would actually summon the nurses during the night. James checked her pulse while she slept, then quietly kissed her on the cheek and went upstairs to bed.

"I'll need these images enlarged even further," said the shift supervisor to the computer technician.

"I've enlarged them already. It's just a poor quality image from a cell phone camera and too much magnification will only blur the image."

"And you think I don't know that! We need to determine the three numerals displayed on that license plate and match it to the vehicle."

"That's going to take a substantial research effort as we only have a partial view of the headlight, bumper and the front grille in this photo."

"Try and see if you can match the vehicle colour as well. A perfect color match should eliminate many different makes and models."

"I'm going to assign a couple of additional people to assist you with this task. I don't think the professor is any mood for extended delays locating the registered owner and address of this vehicle."

"Why is it so important?"

"The professor suspects the lady that's looking after Kyle Clayton may be living at that location."

"It doesn't look like she selected the best part of town judging by what's left of her vehicle."

"Well someone has a new set of wheels."

"More than likely someone has just *sold* a new set of wheels."

"You might be right about that," said the shift supervisor as he returned to his small office.

He notified two additional people to start working on the cell phone images. He was confident they still had the ability to access the State Motor Vehicle Branch computers, but first he needed some positive information about the vehicle in order to begin a search. With three people working on it they should have something to go on very soon.

It was still too early to know if the new webcam would have someone dedicated to watching it on a full time basis. It wouldn't take that much effort to install an additional surveillance monitor somewhere in his office wall until those issues were resolved. Ideally he needed a digital notification system that would alert him any time a vehicle passed through the entrance gate of the Claytons' estate. The installation team would have considered a motion detector for the webcam, but had apparently decided against it for reasons unknown.

The shift supervisor placed a work order for the installation of an additional monitor mounted on his office wall. It was marked as a low priority item as the estate was still only a surveillance target. Considering how long the webcam had been up and running, the supervisor was also wondering about the growing delay in receiving an update or completion report from the installation team. Delays of this nature certainly weren't unusual with remote location assignments taking place on the other side of the world. Once again he inspected the picture from the new webcam. The image was reasonably clear for a night time view and remained clearly focused on the estate entrance. Feeling impatient, he got up to check on the progress of the photo enlargement.

"Well, have you been able to determine the numbers on the licence plate?"

"Yes, we think so. We just got the image back from a high resolution digital magnification scan and we have the last two numerals. We have a three and a six."

"Good work! What about the vehicle type?"

"We're still working on that. We believe it's an older, possibly a late nineties Ford sedan, and the partial image of the headlight has been sent out for digital magnification. There's a possibility we have a part number printed on the lens and that would narrow the field of choices if it turns out to be legible."

"Well you're making some progress. Let's hope it's enough for the professor. I don't think he's in the best of moods today."

"We're working within the Oregon Motor Vehicle Branch data base as we speak. Domestic Fords registered in Oregon with plates ending with three-six number almost twenty thousand vehicles, so we obviously require some more information."

"We need the model, year and colour to have a list we can work with. After that we should be able to reduce it even further by eliminating any residential or business address that doesn't have underground parking."

"Let me know when you've narrowed down the list. I should have a Portland team available soon that could investigate all the locations on your list."

"You'll be the first to know once we have any new information."

"Thanks, I'll be in my office."

Professor Akkaim reviewed his most recent files on past and present employees of the Claytons' estate. He needed an 'inside' advantage; his own insider. The Claytons had a long history of dealings with various contractors and still did to some extent. Most were hired for short term projects and various servicing contracts. The medical staff contracted to provide long term care for Mrs. Clayton were unfortunately employed on a rotational basis. There was only one suitable employee working at the center of the Claytons' world and Professor Akkaim needed her in the palm of his hand.

The younger agent hit the brakes hard to avoid a group of deer walking along the highway. The sudden deceleration woke up his partner when his head fell hard against his chest.

"What's going on?" said the older agent massaging both eyes with his fingertips.

"Nothing much— I was just avoiding a few deer on the highway."

"You know, that's the problem with driving these secondary highways at night. I'll bet most people have no idea whatsoever of just how many vehicles collide with animals each year in the United States."

"How many are there—five thousand?"

"It's a little higher than that. It's about one and a half million accidents per year."

"You mean vehicle accidents?"

"No, I mean vehicles colliding with deer and other large animals."

"You must have your facts crossed somewhere. That can't be possible. How many vehicle accidents are there in the United States every year?"

"Over six million a year and over a hundred people killed every day."

"Wow! That's unbelievable," said the younger agent, remembering just how close he came to having a deer crash through his windshield.

"Do you know where I'm going with this?" asked the older agent.

"Let me guess. You want me to slow down."

"You know, you have a certain underlying ability to solve mildly complex problems at times. Yes, I want you to slow down and I also want you to pull over at the next place where we can get a decent meal. After dinner we'll switch positions and you can take a break."

"Okay, that sounds good. I guess that means we won't be stopping for any hotel breaks then?"

"Good guess. We'll be staying in the 'Cadillac Hotel' until we arrive at Dayton, Ohio," said the older agent.

"I've never been to Ohio myself. What about you?"

"Never, it's the first time for me as well. I have heard of the place so it can't be that small."

"Me too, maybe they're just repositioning us there or relocating us to a more central location," said the younger agent as he checked the time.

"It's possible, but I doubt it. I'm sure they have something in mind for us or they wouldn't have sent us this far on such short notice."

"Hopefully they'll fill us in on the details once we arrive," said the younger agent.

"Yes, I hope so too. We still have lots of ground to cover before we reach Ohio."

"Yes I know. It already feels like we've been driving for days."

"Relax—you can catch up on your sleep after we eat."

"Thanks, I'm looking forward to that."

The shift supervisor knew he needed to make continual progress on the latest task assigned to him by the professor. Extended delays in receiving new updates were just adding to the stress of the situation. Once again he decided to leave his office, visit the cyber labs, and personally inquire about the current status of their investigation.

"Hello again, has anybody made any progress identifying the vehicle?"

"Yes, we've managed to magnify and trace the part number displayed on the headlight lens."

"Excellent. What make does it belong to?"

"It's a 1997 Ford Taurus."

"Good work! How many of those vehicles registered in Oregon had plates ending in three-six?"

"There were two-hundred and fifty-six. We're still trying to access company records and match our color to the correct Ford paint code. That could eliminate almost two thirds of the vehicles on our current list."

"Perfect. What's the hold up?"

"The color was analyzed in the spectrometer, but we're still trying to match paint codes with the vehicle identification numbers from Ford's own production records. They ran three similar shades of blue in 1996. It shouldn't take long to locate the relevant information we need once we've penetrated Ford's main computer data base."

"I'm happy to see you're all making good progress," said the shift supervisor as he stood up behind the operator. "When will we know about the paint?"

"It should be any minute now. I'm really not expecting too much difficulty bypassing their security system."

"Okay, let me know right away. I'll be back in my office."

"Yes sir, I will."

Ten minutes after returning to his office he answered the phone after the first ring. "Yes?"

"I've got good news for you, we're in Ford's system and we've matched the color. It's Royal Marine Blue and we've reduced the list to forty five possible vehicles. I'm printing out the registration information on the remaining vehicles and we'll start by eliminating any business without an underground parking lot and any single detached residential dwellings shown on the list."

"Great. I'll be coming back down there soon."

"Give us about fifteen minutes and we should have a short list of locations with underground parking."

"Excellent."

"Why don't you try the next exit? It looks like there could be a place to eat coming up ahead on the right," said the older agent.

"Sure, we can fill up and stretch our legs if nothing else."

They turned on the parallel service road and rolled the Cadillac up to the pumps. A run-down gas station was the only business on this service road.

"I'll fill it up and you check if the cafe is still open," said the older agent.

"Okay, I'll take a look—back in a minute."

The younger agent watched the waitress approaching him through the glass door as he walked up to the entrance.

"I'm sorry Sir but we were just about to close."

"What time do you close?"

"Eleven o'clock on weeknights."

"Well my watch says it's ten to eleven, so I'd be grateful if you could find something to feed us. We don't know where else to eat at this hour and we've got a long way to drive. I'll make it worth your while."

"Well okay, we only get paid until eleven and I like to be closed up by then."

"Great, we'll take whatever is the easiest for you. I'll go and tell my partner. We're both starving."

The older agent placed the nozzle back in the fuel pump and replaced the fuel cap. "Are they still open?" he asked as his partner approached the car.

"They're just closing down, but I convinced them to make us something for dinner."

"Good, let's see what's cooking. I'll park the car and meet you inside."

"You know what I was thinking?" said the younger agent.

"No, what were you thinking?"

"Well, this place is closing soon and we could have ourselves some free gas, free meals and no witnesses if we played our cards right."

"I think you should take your cards and fold them as fast as you can. Save your enthusiasm for later."

"I just thought we could get away with it."

"Maybe, but these days a concealed camera could be installed anywhere. Overlook one of those in this state and you could end up strapped in the electric chair."

"I guess you're right, let's go and have some dinner."

Although the shift supervisor didn't always like Professor Akkaim he always tried to demonstrate his problem solving skills and showcase his ability to 'think outside the box' whenever possible. Finding this address was just such a challenge; this was the proverbial needle in the haystack and he wanted to be the one who found it.

Fifteen minutes had passed and once again he returned to his men working in the cyber labs. "Well, how is our list of possible locations looking now?"

"We have nineteen possible locations to check in Oregon, but only twelve are in and around Portland."

"That's excellent news! We'll begin investigating those locations after our Portland agents complete their last assignment. Any one of those locations could be the one we are looking for."

"Excuse me for a minute, I've got a call coming in," said the computer operator.

"Hello? Yes it is. Do you want to talk with Professor Akkaim? Okay then, yes we've all seen it and the webcam image looks great from what we can tell. No, we didn't know that. You're confirming a helicopter landed at the estate last night. Can you repeat that again? What kind of problem. Talk slowly. He was trying to find his radio and what happened? How is that possible? What do you mean he's gone? Did you search inside the grounds? Yes of course, I wouldn't either. Don't ask me, I'm not an expert on wolves. Is everyone else is okay? Why did he have to cut the rope? I see. Well you should start writing a detailed report when the three of you return to Portland. In any case I think you'll be getting a new assignment shortly. It's somewhere in and around Portland as far as I know."

The shift supervisor started tapping his assistant on the shoulder.

"What happened over there?" asked the supervisor.

"Just a minute," said the assistant as he turned around to look at his supervisor. "Do you want to speak to the shift supervisor? Okay, that's alright, I'll tell him. I'm sure he'll be talking with Professor Akkaim very soon. I'll be sending details about your new assignment shortly. Keep checking the secure fax number, RA-9 clear."

After hearing all the grim details from his assistant the shift supervisor walked slowly along the corridors and returned to his office. The new information from Portland was an extremely serious and troubling development. The loss of an agent and the failure to retrieve his body from a surveillance site could have grave repercussions. He'd been looking forward to reporting his team's progress about the search for the new address, but with the latest developments he'd unfortunately have to update Professor Akkaim immediately. He picked up his phone and dialled the professor.

"Yes?"

"Hello Professor. I have some new information and need to see you in person."

"Meet me in my office in ten minutes. What's it about?" asked the professor.

"It's about our affairs in Portland. I have good news and bad news, very bad news."

The Meadowlane Children's Sanatorium was almost one hundred years old. Two tall brick turrets framed the entrance of the two story brick facility and rusted steel bars guarded the grey glass windows. Its age and isolated rural location gave the sanatorium an unkempt look which was largely unnoticed due to the general lock-down of patients and the absence of visitors. It was initially built by local masons and served as a valuable quarantine facility in the fight against the rapid spread of tuberculosis. Only after a cure was found did the mandate gradually shift to a long term care facility for problem children diagnosed with chronic and incurable mental disorders.

Patients making good progress in the treatment of their various mental disorders were, unfortunately, never residents of The Meadowlane Children's Sanatorium. The secluded facility on the outskirts of Dayton, Ohio remained as one of the last available options for children unable to manage or cope in today's society. Sadly, even an institution like this had a growing waiting list with constant referrals from doctors across the country.

Sarah opened her eyes with a jolt to escape the same recurring nightmare in her mind. Something or someone was coming for her. She always woke up just before she could face her demons. Her sheets were soaked in sweat and her heavy breathing had been frantic, as usual during her nightmares. Gradually her sense of surroundings returned to normal. It was almost completely dark, but she could still see the shadows of the tall cottonwood trees emanating through the steel bars outside her small opaque window. This narrow room with soft walls was the only world she had ever known. Room number twelve, at the top of the stone staircase.

Chapter 15

Professor Akkaim was furious after reading the entire report about the incident in Portland. He had immediately sought confirmation that his agents had been travelling 'clean', without any ID, which was mandatory RA-9 protocol on assignments of that nature.

It certainly wasn't the first time they'd lost agents in the line of duty, but generally it involved an armed altercation, and only rarely was it accidental in nature. Whatever had happened the night before was nothing short of extraordinary and yet it was still entirely possible this was an isolated human-verses-wildlife conflict. Being in the wrong place at the wrong time could result in dire consequences at the best of times. Nothing in the report indicated the presence of any guards or vehicles anywhere near the perimeter wall. He read the report once again looking for any detail he might have missed.

Incident Overview: The operation to retrieve the radio was a standard elementary exercise. Two men joined at the waist by a length of rope; one scaled up and over the wall while the other controlled the rope and served as a safety anchor. Shortly after the climber disappeared over the top of the wall the anchor man felt the sudden overpowering tension on the rope, like a salmon snagged in a river current he was being hauled to the surface. His partner's agonizing screams began at the same instant and the anchor man panicked as he fought to resist the force pulling him up the face of the wall. Powerless to stop his vertical ascent, he finally removed his knife from its sheath. Driven by shear fear and adrenaline, he managed to slice his way through the rope holding them both together just before he reached the top of the wall. After falling to the base of the wall he realised the screams of his partner had stopped as suddenly as they started. No other sounds were heard during this terrifying and traumatic event that elapsed over a period of five to ten seconds, and all subsequent calls to his partner went unanswered. Stop.

The professor concluded that even the possibility of inadvertently lowering a man down on top of a sleeping bear couldn't be ruled out at this point. Certainly some form of wildlife, lethal wildlife, was instrumental in the reported events that occurred last night. Nothing else could explain what may have caused this unfortunate tragedy. It wasn't worth the additional risk of conducting an internal search on the Claytons' estate. If the agent's body was ever found on the property, people would probably suspect he was a thief looking for an opportunity to steal something valuable from one of these wealthy estates.

On the other hand, if he had somehow managed to survive the attack, there was still the possibility he might find his own way out. There was even a remote chance he could have retrieved the radio. After everything had been considered, the professor knew there was really nothing to do but wait. If a body was ever discovered on the Claytons' estate the story would quickly become 'breaking news,' and be broadcasted on all the local television stations. At least for now he had the luxury of his own private webcam, constantly monitoring the main entrance of the Claytons' estate.

Jen could smell the coffee before she could open her eyes. The craving for a cup of hot coffee was desperately looking for a role in the fading script of her meandering dreams. Finally she opened her eyes, rearranged the pillows and propped herself up on her elbow. Questions immediately began flowing through her mind as she analyzed her surroundings and collected her thoughts. The pleasant sounds and smell of wood burning inside the fireplace told her she wasn't the first one awake this morning. She hadn't slept in this late for weeks, maybe even months. The aroma of fresh coffee floating through Chalet Number Five was overwhelming and filling a large mug with hot coffee was the first thing on her 'to do' list.

Dressing quickly, she opened her bedroom door and walked out towards the kitchen.

"Good morning Jen. There's a pot of coffee in the kitchen."

"Thanks and good morning to you too. Have you been awake long?"

"About two hours. I didn't want to wake you."

"I must have really needed some sleep. Normally I'm a very light sleeper."

"That's the same with me Jen. I rarely sleep more than two or three hours."

"Well, I'm not that light of a sleeper, but it sounds like at least one of us will be awake most of the time."

"Good, it's going to be difficult to watch each other's back if we're both sound asleep."

"I can't argue with that," said Jen with a smile as she stepped up on a chair and removed the ceramic dinner plate from above the door.

"Well at least we didn't have any visitors last night."

"I can't argue with that," said Kyle as he started typing on his keyboard with astonishing speed.

"Kyle, how many words can you type per minute?"

"Not enough—it's never, never enough. It may be time to create a new universal language with a limit on the amount of letters in every word. A limit of four or five letters per word would easily give you enough possible combinations for most English words and also provide instant gratification to all the people suffering from low WPM scores."

"I've never even thought about that Kyle. I suppose English *could* be condensed somehow."

"Most certainly it could. Should we make another pot of coffee?"

"Yes, that's a good idea Kyle. I'll get a new one started in a few minutes. How is the new supercomputer coming along?"

"Excellent. It's been running my new diagnostics program for the last hour or so."

"Great! Any results yet?"

"Not yet, it's a complex program of random mathematical probes performing a complete interrogation of any and all data stored on my father's computer."

"How long will that take?"

"Unknown, it could be hours, days, maybe even weeks."

"That's incredible. Are you hungry yet?"

"Not really. We could eat at the house later. I'm sure Lisa wouldn't mind."

"Sounds good to me. When do you want to leave?"

"I'd like to keep working for another couple of hours if you don't mind."

"Not at all, I'll put another pot of coffee on and talk to you later."

"Thanks Jen."

"You're welcome."

Jen restocked the fires with wood, filled her mug, and returned to the comforts of her luxurious room. The weather outside had improved considerably from last night's storm and a nice day was shaping up. Jen settled back into her bed and tried to make some plans for the day. Deep down she knew that trying to stop the persistent reoccurring memories from last night's flight was still way beyond her control.

Losing a member of the team had shaken everyone to the core. Most people considered their own life to be worth more than the cost of a cheap radio. The two men who had stayed with the van were not as directly impacted as the one who was almost pulled over the wall along with his partner. He was progressively losing his ability to speak which was likely an ongoing symptom of severe shock. Last night he had eventually found his way back to the parked van on the edge of the logging road. Wandering like a lost zombie in the night, he'd shown up with his face drained of color and trailing a short piece of frayed rope cinched tightly around his waist.

His initial information wasn't clear, but the other men knew something had clearly gone wrong and a member of the team was missing. They all immediately returned to the scene at the wall and searched desperately for any signs, or sounds, of their missing friend. Not a trace of him was discovered and no one was volunteering to be the next man over the wall. Finally the team made a collective decision to return to the van and drive back to Portland. Remaining on this location until daybreak was no longer a viable option.

Instructions for their new assignment and the condensed address list had arrived by fax before they were back in town. After returning to the warehouse they unloaded the van and completed the required incident reports, detailing events from last night's accident.

Once everything was taken care of they all returned to the no-star motel where they'd been living. Everyone needed some sleep before they could start searching for her vandalized truck, abandoned in an underground parking lot. It wouldn't take long with such a short and manageable list. After studying the pictures of her Ford Explorer it was a safe bet that it wasn't going anywhere soon. Once they'd located the building it shouldn't be that difficult to find someone who knew the owner of the truck and what apartment she lived in.

Kyle had completed his setup and now had the combined computing power of twelve powerful computers running his new diagnostics software. Between Kyle and Jen they had finished off two pots of coffee before they were ready to leave Chalet Number Five.

"Do want the same quad as last night?" asked Jen.

"It doesn't matter to me, they're both pretty fast."

"You know we don't need to drive these machines at full speed everywhere we go."

Kyle was slipping on his helmet just as she was finishing her sentence. Jen had a pretty good idea of what was coming next and once again she found herself trying to start the only quad remaining in front of Chalet Number Five.

Kyle was waiting on his quad outside of the house when Jen pulled up. The Beaucerons were busy interrogating Kyle as Jen pulled up beside him.

"Well I see the dogs are back on duty," said Jen as she shut off the engine. Immediately they moved over to interrogate her and then proceeded on their rounds.

Lisa opened up the kitchen door as they were getting off their quads.

"Good Morning you two, I hope you're here for some breakfast."

"Morning Lisa, Yes, we're starving. Have the dogs been home all night?" asked Jen.

"No, they showed up about an hour ago. You didn't see them at Chalet Number Five this morning?"

"No, actually we didn't—no sign of them at all."

"Well, it's very unusual. James thinks they might have taken a deer down. A grounds keeper once found the remains of a partially buried animal that was probably the work of the dogs. With so much underbrush around here it's amazing it was even discovered. Unfortunately, deer occasionally manage to find their way inside these walls from time to time."

"Well that would certainly explain what was keeping them busy," said Kyle as he walked inside.

"That's what we think as well. Something else that seemed unusual was that they barely touched their food this morning. Anyway, the important thing is they've all returned unharmed. Would you two like some coffee?"

"No thanks. We've probably had too much already."

"Well you know where it is if you change your mind. Help yourself to anything you like. I have lots of food set out for everyone in the living room. James is waiting to talk with you in his office whenever you're available."

"Thanks Lisa, we appreciate that," said Jen for the two of them as they walked out towards the living room.

As they rounded the corner Jen could see the back of Alexia's wheelchair pushed tightly against the end of the table. A large red plastic bib had been loosely draped over her chest and tucked in the top of her neck brace. A tall attendant was struggling as he tried to spoon-feed her with one hand and manipulate her head and jaw with the other. Kyle and Jen waved to Alexia as they sat down for a small breakfast.

Like a pair of invisible diners, Alexia's blank expression showed no sign whatsoever of acknowledging their arrival. Jen didn't know exactly why she felt so uncomfortable, but she did know this was going to be one very, very fast breakfast.

Professor Akkaim also had a new dedicated webcam monitor installed on his office wall. He was privately still on pins and needles as a possible dead RA-9 agent lying on the Claytons' estate was the absolute definition of a loose end. He hated loose ends as they did absolutely nothing to make his world more comfortable or secure.

Surprisingly, he had yet to see a single vehicle arrive or depart through the main entrance gates.

He was now in the final stages of personally compiling the detailed instructions for the two men travelling to Dayton, Ohio. Careful detailed planning was underway to prepare and facilitate their mission through an elaborate ruse of written correspondence with the director of the Meadowlane Children's Sanatorium. Having compromised and studied the long term history of the director's personal and work-related computer files, it wasn't difficult for members of the cyber espionage team to assume the identity of a known out-of-state physician.

That physician was attempting to make all the necessary arrangements with the director, seeking the short term release of Sarah D. from the Meadowlane Children's Sanatorium. The permanent removal of each person's last name was a longstanding prerequisite for any patient committed to the Meadowlane Children's Sanatorium.

According to correspondence recently received by the director, Sarah D. had been selected and her participation was requested for a three week neurological imaging study, being conducted in an out-of-state university. The physician requesting her involvement with the study was a well-known expert in the field of schizophrenia and specialized in the rare, chronic and degenerative forms effecting children like Sarah D.

Protocols for the movement of any of Meadowlane's patients required a much higher level of standard security arrangements than normal and also stipulated that the immediate presence of at least two trained escorts was mandatory at all times. Details of the escort's arrival in Dayton, Ohio would be forthcoming once the director of the Sanatorium had authorized her release.

Professor Akkaim continued to finalize his instructions for the two men travelling to Dayton, Ohio. With all the preliminary arrangements mostly completed his men would soon be expected visitors at the Meadowlane

Children's Sanatorium. They would be arriving as planned, to pick up Sarah D. and supervise her return trip to the fictitious university study.

So far everything was going according to plan. All outgoing e-mail sent by the director to the university physician were being intercepted and rerouted to the RA-9 facility. Forging return correspondence from the university physician was a simple matter for RA-9 mission planners within the cyber labs.

The professor called his assistant to discuss his latest instructions and the various options available to send them to Ohio. They decided to leave a secure package containing his instructions at the main bus terminal in Dayton, Ohio. Addressed to an alias, it should be ready for a pickup, approximately eight hours from now.

The director of the Meadowlane Children's Sanatorium requested a meeting with the resident psychiatrist in his office for a brief consultation regarding Sarah D. The director routinely received requests to include certain patients in various studies throughout the country. Everything appeared to be completely in order with the latest application except the request to specifically include Sarah D. was unusual. It was widely accepted that her condition was past the point of no return; however, both men also realised the potential for cures or breakthroughs required occasional patient involvement in new psychiatric research programs.

"What's your professional opinion? Should we let her go?" asked the director.

"It's really hard to say. It's been almost four years since the last time we tried moving her, and as you know, that didn't go very well."

"That's exactly why we're having this discussion," said the director.

"Without a doubt, I'm concerned. They have an excellent facility at that university, but as you know, she can be dangerous without warning. She'll probably have to be sedated for the trip and I'd strongly recommend a straitjacket for the entire duration of her transfer. Every precaution should be taken to avoid a repeat of what happened last time and also to prevent our exposure to any legal liability during her time away from the sanatorium."

"That was my general assessment as well. I wanted your personal approval before I authorized the temporary transfer."

"I do appreciate you asking for my opinion. When are they expecting to move her?"

"Fairly soon I believe. We're still fine tuning the details and I expect we'll know more very soon."

"Let me know when you've arranged a definite departure time. The staff will need a couple of hours' notice to prepare her for travel."

"As soon as I know, you'll know. Thanks again," said the director as he stood up and escorted his colleague to the door.

The director returned to his desk and began drafting a response to the physician's latest e-mail. A temporary leave from the Meadowlane Children's Sanatorium to facilitate Sarah D.'s participation in the university's research project had been granted. Strict compliance with all of Meadowlane's standard precautionary measures was expected, and required, to ensure the safety of everyone involved in the handling and transportation of patients currently suffering from chronic severely-delusional forms of schizophrenia.

"Should we go and see my dad?" asked Kyle while watching as Jen finished her toast.

"I'm ready when you are."

The attendant was still struggling to feed Alexia, and it wasn't hard to see why such an over-sized bib was required. They both waved at her as they got up to leave and once again her expressionless gaze passed straight past them and fixated on an unknown point in space.

"Come on in," said James as he saw them approach his open office door.

"Good morning Dad."

"Hi James," said Jen as they both settled down in the two comfortable office chairs. James still had the blinds partially closed and it was surprisingly dark for this time in the morning.

"How was your first night together in Chalet Number Five?" asked James to whoever wanted to answer.

"It was great Dad. We had everything we needed and I finished setting up the computers. Thanks for ordering exactly the ones I'd requested."

"You're welcome Kyle. How about you Jen? Did you find everything you needed?"

"Yes, it was perfect. I may pick up a few security-related items today, but otherwise everything was excellent. Are the other Chalets as nice as Chalet Number Five?"

"Oh Kyle, she doesn't know yet?"

"It never came up in a conversation."

"I see. Well, I suppose that naming Chalet Number Five was really Kyle's idea. Alexia and I had always planned to build five chalets on the estate and Kyle suggested that we name them in reverse order. Although it was a novel idea at first, everyone liked it. It immediately gave us the feeling that we had accomplished all of our goals. When the next chalet is completed it's going to be called 'Chalet Number Four'."

Jen was smiling as she listened to the story of Chalet Number Five. Now that she was starting to know Kyle it seemed like a perfectly logical thing for him to do.

"Jen, is there anything you need that I can help you with? I know we have some issues with the damage to your Explorer and the Range Rover. I'm going to give you another five thousand for expenses. Can you think of anything else you need?"

"I don't know what kind of connections you have James, but some additional pieces of alternate personal identification would certainly be useful to have in my possession."

"I couldn't agree more and I know just the person who can help us with that request. Leave it with me for now. We may have to arrange for some photography sessions soon, but I'll give you the 'when and where'."

"Thanks. That would be great."

James removed a small unsealed envelope from his top desk drawer and passed it over to Jen. A quick inspection revealed another five thousand in US currency.

"Thanks James," said Jen.

"Anytime, just document your expenses and don't be afraid to ask if there's anything else you need."

"Thanks, I won't."

"Kyle, have you started studying the problems associated with my computer?"

"I have. It's undergoing an extensive interrogation as we speak and I'm confident nothing will escape my new diagnostic software program."

"That's great. I'm sure you'll find something soon."

Kyle rarely stated the obvious. Quietly he lifted both feet and curled himself up in the chair.

"Lisa was saying you thought the Beaucerons might have killed a deer last night?" asked Jen.

"It certainly seems like the most probable explanation to account for their extended period of absence. I suppose they could have been disoriented by the storm or the helicopter flying around last night. Whatever the reason, the most important thing is that they're home and everything has returned to normal."

"What about your inspection of the helicopter last night Dad—were there any issues after our instrument flight?"

"I didn't find any defects, but you're welcome to double check anything you like."

"I know. Did you take on fuel last night?"

"Yes, I filled it up to our standard level. Could you show Jen our fuelling procedures after the next flight?"

"Sure, I'll go over that with her."

"Thanks."

"Weren't you two planning a trip into town today?" asked James.

"We haven't finalized any plans yet, but a trip to town certainly is a possibility," said Jen.

"Well if you do, help yourself to whatever vehicle you want. I'll be starting a shift at the trauma center later this afternoon. I've also advised everyone to stop using their cell phones effective immediately and I'm just letting you know that you'll be receiving a new phone as well."

"Remember James? I did use it last night to call Lisa when we cancelled our flight plan."

"That's right. I forgot all about that. There isn't much we can do about that now. Just keep it turned off for now."

"I won't use it again, don't worry."

"I won't, thanks."

"I should also tell you both that I have a sealed envelope in my wall-safe. It's from Al Anderson and I expect it will contain all the details of Kyle's upcoming internship schedule over the next six months. Now he did promise me you will have a little time off before you leave so I've decided to keep the envelope sealed for a little longer. I'll be talking with Al Anderson later regarding obtaining additional identification for you Jen and I'll make sure that keeping it sealed a little longer won't cause any problems."

"James, I have an additional request."

"Sure Jen, what can I do for you?"

"Could we also acquire some additional identification for Kyle? Something I can personally keep in my possession?"

"I think that's a good idea as well. I'll include that in my request to Al Anderson when I'm talking with him. Very well then—why don't you two get out and enjoy your day. I'll catch up with you later."

"Okay, thanks again," said Jen as they started getting up from the chairs.

"Bye Dad. I hope the LDR isn't too high tonight."

"I hope it's not either, see you later."

Kyle and Jen walked back through the living room and out through the side kitchen door.

"Okay Kyle, what's the LDR?" asked Jen as they came to a stop on the porch."

"It's the life and death ratio. It's a system dad and I use to measure the success or failure of his previous shift at the trauma center."

"I see. So a ten-over-zero is good?"

"That's ten lives saved and no lives lost. A ten-over-zero is an excellent LDR Jen. I wish he had a score like that every shift, but he never does."

"Jen, let's go up to the garage and choose a vehicle for the day."

"Okay, sounds good. I liked the Range Rover I had last time."

"It's a nice vehicle, but maybe we should try something different today."

"Sure, let's go and have a look. You can choose a vehicle if you like."

"Sure. I can do that, no problem."

Professor Akkaim was informed the instant the director of the Meadowlane Children's Sanatorium sent an e-mail officially authorizing Sarah's release. Only minor scheduling details remained, concerning the exact date and time for the pickup. Once the agents had finished reading his instructions from the bus depot they could schedule the earliest possible time to remove Sarah D. from the Sanatorium.

The longer the delay in acquiring Sarah D., the greater the risk that something could complicate or jeopardize their plans. His instructions at the bus terminal also contained fake identification and outlined the obvious need to find an alternate vehicle for the pickup. *How* they acquired a suitable vehicle would be at the agent's discretion. They could transfer her back to the Cadillac after she was securely under control and in their possession. The professor glanced at the time and calculated the time difference. All the early preparations had now been completed. He wouldn't receive another direct report until his agents, and Sarah, were at least half way back to Portland, Oregon.

Sinzar Bakkir was still scheduled to surface in Santa Monica next week. Currently the central objective had remained the same. Kyle Clayton was not to be abducted by Sinzar Bakkir until after his tenure at the Central Fusion Research Complex 8. Not knowing any details about Kyle Clayton's schedule was frustrating for the professor, but hopefully that problem would change in the near future.

Sinzar Bakkir anchored his boat in a secluded bay on the north-western coast of Mexico. Yesterday morning he had docked at a local marina and completely restocked his boat with an ample supply of food and alcohol. He'd seen an opportunity to take a female tourist back to the boat, but decided against it. If she was ever reported missing there was a real chance that even his boat could be subjected to a search. He certainly didn't need to attract any unnecessary attention while anchored in this location. He was quite content to pass his days living on the boat as long as the food and alcohol were plentiful and the weather wasn't too severe.

Boredom was slowly becoming a factor and he was curious about who his next procurement targets might be. Planning his next abduction, always gave him a sense of job satisfaction. He cracked another can of beer and squinted through his worn out eyes as he tried to focus on some young people in the distance, diving off the front deck of their boat.

Jen went to unlock the garage service door and found it open.

"That's strange Kyle. Do you think James forgot to lock the door?"

"It's possible, but the quads are usually in the other garage."

"We'll just make sure it's locked properly when we leave. What car, do think we should take?"

"The black AMX is fun and very, very fast—but it's not the fastest. The truck and the van are boring, but I know for sure you'll love driving my dad's 2010 Ford Mustang GT-500. It has tinted windows and a Shelby Super Snake package that puts out about 725 horse power. It also handles really, really well."

"Should I ask you, how you know that?"

"You can if you like, but I expect you know the answer," said Kyle as they both smiled at each other.

Just at that moment they both heard some unusual faint scuffing sounds coming from further down inside the garage. Jen instantly turned off the lights as she motioned to Kyle to drop down low and stay put. After waiting for her eyes to adjust to the darkness, she pulled out her Glock 17 and began a slow methodical search of the garage.

As she came around the front fender of the black AMX, she could distinctly see the outline of Alexia in her wheel chair.

"Turn the lights on Kyle," she shouted as she stood up and holstered her gun. Once again, Alexia was totally oblivious to their presence. Her wheelchair was squeezed between the Range Rover and the black AMX. With the lights on, the dust on the truck clearly revealed Alexia's hand prints covering every square inch of the damaged area on the Range Rover. Staring into space, she continued to slowly massage the deep scratches along the side of the Range Rover.

"Stay there Kyle, we're taking the Mustang."

Soon they were outside and driving slowly down the driveway.

"What happened in the garage Jen?"

"I'm not sure exactly. Your mother was looking at the Range Rover."

"That used to be her favourite vehicle."

"Yes, I've heard that before."

"I'm going to tell Lisa about Alexia. They may be looking for her. I'll just be a minute," said Jen as she pulled up beside the kitchen door. Lisa opened the door and Jen told her of Alexia's whereabouts.

"Thanks Jen. Sometimes she just disappears around here. I'll let the attendants know. Bye."

"Bye Lisa. We'll be back sometime later today."

The Beaucerons were flanking the Mustang, but broke off their pursuit just before the gate. Jen started slowing down the Mustang as they approached the main entrance the gate. Once again it opened automatically and they were quickly on their way.

Finally, after almost twelve hours, the professor noticed the first vehicle on his new webcam. A late-model Mustang was leaving the estate. Unfortunately the tinted windows made it impossible to tell who was driving. Nevertheless, the importance of this new source of information could only improve as time progressed.

Professor Akkaim was notified immediately regarding the successful interception of correspondence between the director of the sanatorium and the impersonated physician at the university.

"How shall we draft the most appropriate response Professor?"

"Keep it short and professional. Thank him for releasing the girl on such relatively-short notice and also to expect to hear from the university personnel very soon. They'll want to know the most convenient time to arrive and escort her back to the university. Tell the director they are prepared to give them whatever notice is required to complete the necessary preparations to help ensure her safe transportation."

"Excellent Professor, it shall be sent immediately."

The director of the Meadowlane Children's Sanatorium was surprised at just how quickly he had received a reply from the physician conducting the study at the university. He was just about to call him directly and personally discuss the upcoming travel arrangements, and also confirm that he understood exactly what to expect while transporting and hosting Sarah D. The university did have an excellent reputation and it wasn't the first time he'd granted similar requests involving his patients' participation in their research projects. Any money funding new research projects in this field was welcome, and they certainly needed to do their part to facilitate and encourage related research whenever possible.

"Can you read that sign? I swear I need to get a pair of glasses. I haven't been to an optometrist in years," said the older agent.

"Dayton, Ohio, seventy two miles," said the younger agent as he opened his eyes while retaining his deflated posture. He was slumped against the passenger door with his arms crossed and barely managed to open his eyes before the sign flew past the Cadillac window.

"I'm pulling over at the next suitable location to change our plates and make a call on the satellite phone. I'm sure they're probably expecting an update from us already, and if we don't start checking in when they ask, well, there could be some unpleasant consequences."

"Yes, I know what you mean. They weren't happy with us last time. Sure, stop where ever you like. I can't wait to find out why they've sent us all the way across the country in the first place," said the younger agent with his eyes already closed.

James was having second thoughts about his decision to delay opening Kyle's internship instructions. Granted, it would have been nice for Kyle and Jen to enjoy their time off without having to worry about exactly what plans lay ahead. He, however, wasn't feeling the same benefit. He pulled his desk phone closer and dialled the number for Al Anderson. He was the only contact James knew that could possibly supply false identification for Kyle and Jen. He would certainly have expected James to review the schedule by now and would likely have expected a follow up conversation regarding the itinerary.

"The cellular customer, you are trying to reach is currently unavailable or out of the service area. Please leave a message after the tone."

"Hi Al—it's Doctor Clayton calling. Please return my call at your convenience."

James hung up the phone after leaving his message, somewhat surprised that he couldn't get through at this time of day.

He turned around and adjusted his blinds slightly to let in a little more daylight. In the distance he noticed one of the attendants pushing Alexia downhill towards the house. The weather had improved substantially from last night and he was happy to see his wife outside enjoying it. James stood up and walked over to the wall-safe. Gazing fondly at Alexia's youthful painting, he pulled on the frame and exposed the single dial on the door of the safe. James spun the dial and entered the combination that was permanently etched in his memory. He opened the door and reached inside, slowly removing the confidential letter.

"Excuse me Doctor Clayton, I didn't mean to disturb you," said Lisa from his partially open office door.

Startled, James quickly locked the safe and closed the hinged portrait of his wife.

"You may have startled me, but you're not disturbing me. What can I do for you?"

"Well it's about Alexia actually."

"What about Alexia? I just saw her being walked outside."

"Yes, Jen mentioned she found her inside the garage, next to the Range Rover with the lights out."

"That's a little odd."

"Yes, we thought so too. Her hand prints were all over the side of the vehicle."

"Which side?"

"I believe Jen said the passenger side, the damaged side."

"I know she liked that vehicle. I'll try and have it repaired as soon as possible. For that matter, I'll find a shop that will drive up here and pick it up. They could leave an unmarked courtesy car here until the Range Rover is returned."

"Whatever you think is best. I just thought you should know."

Lisa watched James as he sat down at his desk and placed a heavy paperweight on the confidential envelope he was holding.

"Thanks. It's really impossible to know what goes on in Alexia's mind these days. Thanks for bringing the matter to my attention."

"You're welcome. Are you driving in to the hospital later?"

"Yes, I'll be driving in later. Three twelve-hour shifts this week."

"Very well, call me if you need anything."

"I will. By the way, if someone calls from the gate intercom about picking up the Range Rover, make sure to advise them about our safety protocols. I'll leave the truck in the safe zone if I decide to have it repaired."

"Yes of course."

James reached for a phone book and leafed through the automotive section of the yellow pages. It wasn't worth getting the insurance company involved. On his second call he found a shop willing to come over and pick up the car. James put on a light jacket and walked up towards the garage. It wouldn't take long to drive the Range Rover down and park it in a safe zone next to the house.

After opening the garage it was hard for him not to be somewhat disturbed by the extent of his wife's hand prints on the side of car. Like a blind person examining a sculpture, this damaged area had been examined many, many times over. It was also apparent, that she had somehow managed to pull herself up out of her chair as her prints were all over the damaged roof. This was very surprising. The doctors had mostly given up hope of any further progress in her movement after all the various physiotherapy exercise routines they had tried previously.

He would definitely have to speak with her attendants concerning their lack of proper supervision of Alexia. Whatever her motives for such strange behaviour, she shouldn't be allowed to roam freely around the estate without supervision. James backed the Range Rover out of the bay and hosed down the truck before driving back to the house.

"Wake up. Can you change the license plates while I make the call?" said the older agent as he nudged his partner's shoulder.

"What plates do want?"

"I think I remember seeing a set of Ohio plates. Use them if you can."

"Okay, I'll see what I can find," said the younger agent as he opened the front passenger door.

Establishing satellite communications with RA-9 was a complex affair involving several security measures. His instructions had been minimized as usual.

"Use Personal ID number seven to pick up an envelope at the main bus depot in Dayton, Ohio."

Dial tone.

That was all he really needed to know at this point. They could pin-point his location, and hopefully the instructions would be self-explanatory.

Both men had a coded list of false identification papers known only to themselves and RA-9 supervisors. The younger agent had a personal identity list from one to ten and he had his own list from eleven to twenty. For whatever reason, the younger agent had been instructed to retrieve the package that was waiting for them in Dayton, Ohio.

"How did you make out?"

"You were right. We did have a set of valid Ohio licence plates in the truck and I've mounted both of them. Did you get through?"

"Yes, we'll know why we're here as soon as we pick up our instructions from the bus depot in Dayton."

"They didn't tell you the reason they sent us here?"

"Not a word about that. We've waited this long to find out, we can wait a little longer," said the older agent as he climbed back in the car. Maybe we can grab a meal when we reach the bus depot. The bigger depots usually have a cafe. Not only that, but we need some proper rest soon. We've been driving too long."

"I'll second that. Do you want me to drive?" asked the younger agent.

"Maybe later, try to locate and plan the best route to the bus depot. You can also organise your number seven identification papers. You'll be picking up our instructions once we've arrived at the bus depot."

"Okay, I'll bring up a city map of Dayton on the laptop."

"Sounds like a good place to start," said the older agent as he pulled the Cadillac back out on the highway.

"So Kyle, besides getting a coffee, where do you want to go first?"

"Let's pick up your laptop computer. I can start doing some network programming and possibly link your laptop with my system in Chalet Number Five."

"Are you saying you can operate your super computer remotely from my laptop computer?"

"Sure, why not?"

"I believe you. I just don't have the expertise to know how it's done."

"It will take some time, but it's definitely possible.

How do you like driving the Mustang?"

"It's great Kyle, a real pleasure to drive."

"I know," said Kyle as they exchanged smiles.

"I imagine I'm probably driving a little slow for your liking."

"That's okay, losing your driver's license is the last thing we need. How long will it take to get from here to your other place?"

"I'm not sure exactly. I would guess about thirty minutes."

"Can you count time in your mind?"

"What are you talking about Kyle?"

"If I told you to close your eyes and open them after thirty minutes, what would be your average margin of error after five attempts?"

"I have absolutely no idea. What about you?"

"I would say somewhere between five and fifteen seconds."

"How is that possible?"

"I just remember watching the second hand moving around a clock face. The speed does change depending on the size of the clock face, but it always takes one minute per revolution."

"And you can just remember that."

"Yes, when I concentrate I can see the movement of the timepiece clearly in my memory."

"I've never heard of anyone doing that before. It's really a unique ability."

"Perhaps, I haven't really researched the topic. What was my mother doing in the garage?"

"I don't know. I really can't say for sure."

Jen could sense the immediate change in Kyle's happy demeanour the second he started talking about his mother. It was easy to tell Alexia's condition was still a very sensitive topic.

Once again James sat down at his office desk and rechecked his messages. Still there was nothing at all from Al Anderson. He adjusted the blinds, dimming the light and turned on his office desk lamp. He stared at the stone paperweight for several minutes before lifting it from the confidential letter and piercing the envelope with his letter opener.

After skimming through all the preliminary correspondence, he arrived at the schedule laid out on the last page. Kyle's primary internship would begin at the Central Fusion Research Complex 8 in California starting with an initial six week stay. His internship would consist of three, two-week semesters.

The first would involve on-site design and engineering. The second semester would focus strictly on state-of-the-art methods of laser amplification and the third semester would study the complex computing systems required to run the project. Starting date was to be announced. That would be followed by eight weeks at the Livermore

Plasma Research Center and then a third internship at the University of Saskatchewan Physics Department lasting for three months. A scheduled six week break at home had been allocated between each of the three different internships.

It was still unclear to James if Kyle would remain on the facility the entire time, or be permitted to leave each day. There was also no mention of any provisions to accommodate Jen, and that would most certainly have to be discussed once he had managed to contact Al Anderson. James knew that even Kyle might prefer to work on the CFRC-8 premises full time. At his age, his mind was like a giant insatiable sponge, sucking up every bit of new information he could lay his eyes on.

The timetable laid out in this letter would take them almost to the end of the year. That wouldn't end Kyle's contractual obligation with the US government, but he'd be receiving one of the most sophisticated science curriculums in the country, and was also receiving a generous compensation package throughout the program's duration. James folded the letter, placed it inside the envelope and returned it to his wall-safe.

At least for James, the speculation was finally over. Numerous details still had to be worked out, but he could now plan ahead with some degree of certainty. The Central Fusion Research Complex 8 in California was a massive project on the leading-edge of laser fusion research that only rarely interned a few select students. There wasn't a doubt in his mind that Kyle would be extremely excited to begin his internship at CFRC-8.

James decided to see what Lisa was cooking for lunch before he prepared to leave for work. He'd have a discussion with Kyle and Jen later, after he'd spoken with Al Anderson.

Professor Akkaim had just been notified that his two men in Ohio successfully contacted a shift supervisor several minutes ago. Judging by the coordinates of their call they would soon be picking up his personal instructions concerning Sarah D.

He looked up at his wall monitor and watched as the small car approached the Claytons' main entrance. He could clearly see a hand reaching out and operating the intercom buttons. Shortly afterwards the gate opened briefly and allowed the vehicle to enter.

The professor paced back and forth as he wondered who might be visiting the estate. As long as his missing agent was unaccounted for, anything was possible. He quickly picked up his phone and dialled the shift supervisor.

"Hello."

"Were you watching the monitor ten minutes ago?"

"Yes."

"Then who do you think just arrived at the estate?"

"I'm not sure. I was able to enhance and record the license plate, but we couldn't see the driver."

"I want you to start keeping detailed records of every vehicle passing through those gates."

"Yes, of course Professor, we were already doing that."

"Wait, have a look at your monitor right now."

"Stand by. Okay, it looks like the Claytons' Range Rover about to leave the estate."

"And who's driving now?" asked the professor, feeling increasingly agitated.

"I'm not sure who's driving."

"Just make sure your keeping detailed records of all movements through that gate."

"Don't worry Professor, everything is being recorded," said the supervisor to the dial tone.

This time the professor had a good front row view as he watched a young man with dark blue coveralls driving the dark green Range Rover away from the estate.

"Jen, you know how sometimes your imagination can form an image in your mind?"

"Of course, there's nothing wrong with that. Why do you ask?"

"Somehow I didn't really imagine you would keep a place in this part of town. What attracted you to this area?"

"It wasn't really an attraction—it was more of an immediate necessity. I needed to find a safe place to hide my truck. I needed a place with underground parking."

"Are places with underground parking safer?"

"Any place can be dangerous Kyle. Remember what I said, we need to watch each other's back."

"Can you please lean forward and turn slightly to the left," said Kyle as he glanced over in her direction with a smile.

"I have to say your navigation skills are showing signs of improvement. I think I can see the bus depot from here."

"If your eyesight was corrected you could've seen it half a mile back," said the younger agent.

"Give it a few years. Your eyesight will deteriorate as well."

"I doubt it. Should I pick up the envelope? Or do you want to eat something first?"

"Have you got the correct identification sorted out?"

"Yes I have."

"Then go and pick up the envelope and bring it back here. We'll decide about eating after we know the reason they sent us to Ohio."

The older agent shut off the car while he waited for his partner to return. Five minutes later he could see him walking back over to the Cadillac with a manila envelope under his arm.

"Did you have any problems?"

"No, no problems at all."

"Good. Pass me the envelope," said the older agent.

"Here you go. Hurry up and open it."

The older agent opened the envelope and carefully reviewed the two pages of detailed instructions.

"Well, what was the reason for the big panic to get us over to Dayton, Ohio?" asked the younger agent impatiently.

"Just a minute, let me finish reading this. Okay. It looks like we have to contact the director of the Meadowlane Children's Sanatorium and schedule an appointment to pick up a resident patient. All we know so far is that her name is Sarah D. We'll be impersonating two university employees hired to transport her back to an out-of-state university for a fictitious research project. Once we have her she is to be unharmed and returned to Oregon. We are supposed to check in for further instructions after we are at least half way back to Portland."

"They sent both of us all the way out here to pickup one young girl, some child from a hospital. I don't believe it. They could have hired some local babysitters. This mindless daycare job is going to be a piece of cake."

"Don't be so sure," said the older agent as he leafed through the rental car listings in the local directory.

"There's a highlighted safety warning that stipulates a minimum of two trained attendants must be present at all times, unless she's securely restrained or confined within an appropriate facility."

"I hope they don't run any background checks on the people coming to pick her up," said the younger agent unable to contain his laughter.

"They've included new identities for our use during the pickup. Any background inquiries would have been intercepted and the appropriate reports provided," said the older agent.

"We'll know soon enough if they find us suspicious. One way or the other, she'll be leaving with us," said the younger agent.

Chapter 16

None of the three men had slept well in their cheap motel. Most of the time, they tried to keep a low profile by cooking inside their small room, with a sparsely-equipped kitchenette and a burned-out electric hotplate. Today was different; they were now one man short, demoralized, and determined to start the day with a proper breakfast for a change.

Driving together in the same van, they stopped at a small 'hole in the wall' and piled into an old restaurant booth covered with dirty orange vinyl. The man with the missing partner sat on his own, facing the other two men.

"Are all three of you boys' having coffee this morning?"

"Yes, three cups of coffee and some menus please."

"Menu's on the chalkboard by the kitchen. I'll bring your coffee over."

"Thanks," said the man who had installed the satellite dish last night. "It's going to be difficult adjusting to a three man team. I wonder if we'll be getting a new replacement."

"It's a little early for talk like that don't you think!" yelled the single agent as he reached across the table and grabbed the front of his shirt with both hands.

"You men had better settle down over there if want to be served, we don't need any trouble in here," said the waitress as she approached the table.

"Sorry, there won't be any trouble Miss."

The man slowly settled back down in the booth as the waitress dropped off three coffees.

"Just relax—we'll work as a three person team today. It may take a little longer to search the address list, but I'd say there's a good chance we'll get the ones in Portland done by tonight. Okay?"

"Okay, sorry I lost my temper, but I'm still really upset."

"I know, you two guys had worked together for a long time and you're right, I'm sorry. I shouldn't have said that. Let's all just try and relax and eat a proper breakfast. After that we'll find a detailed city map, mark down all our locations, and plan the search from there. Are we all agreed?"

"Agreed. Okay—let's order some breakfast. I'm starving," he said as he turned and tried to catch the fleeting attention of the waitress.

"Is that your apartment block?" asked Kyle as Jen drove the Mustang slowly past the front of the aging low-rise.

"Yes," said Jen feeling a sudden sense of embarrassment.

"Two more questions. Why do all the buildings look the same and why aren't you stopping?"

"They all look the same because it must be the cheapest way to build a low-income housing development and I'm just having a look around the area before we stop."

"Looking for what?"

"I'm just looking for anything out of the ordinary."

"I see something out of the ordinary Jen."

"What's that?"

"An almost new Mustang GT-500 with tinted windows driving slowly through a mostly-dilapidated low-income housing project," said Kyle, smiling as he studied his surroundings through the darkened glass.

"Well that's true. We probably should have chosen a different vehicle. Next time we will. This is exactly where someone vandalized the Range Rover the last time I was here."

"Why?"

"I don't know. Unfortunately some people don't need a reason to damage other people's property Kyle."

"There's always a reason, always a reason."

"You're probably right."

"Jen, are you planning to park on the road or underground this time? I could stay here and watch the car if you like."

"Thanks, but no thanks, I want us to stick together and not split up. It's safer that way. I think this time we'll park underground. At least it's only the tenants who are able to open the gate."

"Do you know any of the tenants living here?"

"No, but it should narrow down the number of people with access."

"I agree. Statistical probabilities are such a fascinating subject."

After completing a careful recon around the area, Jen slowly lifted the turn signal control arm and immediately took a hard right turn, driving down a steep concrete hill towards the rusted underground parking gates.

All three men finished eating everything served on their breakfast plates.

"Can I get you gentlemen anything else?" asked the waitress while stopping to pick up their plates.

"No thanks. Just bring us the bill please."

"Sure, right away," said the waitress.

"I'll take care of the bill and meet you guys back at the van. Do we need to stop at the warehouse and get the address list?"

"No, I've got it with me."

"Great, we can start the search right away using the GPS for navigation and we'll try to buy a proper city map when we get a chance."

"Sounds good, see you guys back at the van."

"Hi Lisa, how's your day going?"

"Great James, you should have seen the young man from the auto body shop. He was so frightened I didn't think he was ever getting out of that courtesy car," said Lisa, with a grin.

"I take it the Beaucerons were sizing him up. Other than that, everything went okay?"

"Yes, everything was fine after I walked over and escorted him to the Range Rover. He was never in any danger parked in the 'safe zone', but those dogs can be more than a little intimidating."

"They're just doing their job."

"Yes I know. Anyway, he said it should be ready in a few days and he'll call before he returns the Range Rover. I hung the keys for the courtesy car on the hook beside the kitchen door. Do you want anything for lunch?"

"No thanks. I'll find something later on," said James as he turned and walked away.

There was no point in starting the van until every address in Portland was entered into the GPS. They didn't need to be wasting time driving needlessly back and forth across town.

"How's it going?"

"I've got two more to go."

"Is that all of them?"

"No, we have fifteen addresses within Portland's city limits and another ten spread out across the state of Oregon."

"Well let's hope we don't have to start looking outside of Portland. Has this list been narrowed down as far as possible?"

"Yes, and according to our instructions each address has underground parking and a 1997 aqua-marine Ford Taurus registered to the owner.

Hopefully one of these locations have, or had, a dark grey Ford Explorer with missing wheels parked beside them."

"So, where should we start?"

"Let's start with the closest one in the GPS. It's a ten story apartment complex about fifteen minutes from here."

"How exactly are we planning to get inside these buildings?"

"I don't know, we'll figure that out as we go. Each place is going to be different and most of them will have security systems to deal with. We should get started."

"Okay, we're both ready. Let's go."

The chrome fingertip controls on the black leather door console smoothly lowered Jen's tinted window exposing the underground gate control mounted inches away on the stained concrete wall. Jen paused as she recalled the last time she stopped in front of this security barrier. Her Ford Explorer only passed once through this entrance, a one way only trip, 'sorry, no returns'.

The gate was a folding steel grid design which took forever to open, constantly crying for lubrication as it struggled to lift itself vertically. High concrete walls boxed the cairn tightly on both sides and Jen recognised the onset of those familiar uncontrolled nervous sensations developed in Iraq. Glancing in the rear view mirror she could see two figures in dark clothes slowing down on the top of the hill behind her. The cries of this slow wailing gate had probably summoned young delinquents for years, following cars in and out of their own personal automotive superstore.

"Hold something Kyle, hold tight" said Jen, almost serenely. Instinctively she raised the power window with her left finger while shifting into reverse at the same moment. She had learned enough lessons in Iraq to recognize a closing box with deteriorating tactical options.

With a full extension of her right foot, she pressed the accelerator pedal as far forward as possible and held it there. The sudden and explosive power of the super-charged V-8 engine instantly responded to her command. Dark smoke started rising from the melting rubber as the spinning rear tires momentarily fought for traction. The pressure from the locked shoulder belts continued to press firmly into their chests as the car accelerated backwards up the ramp like a missile from a launcher. The Mustang was airborne when it flew across the sidewalk and both men scrambled away desperately trying to save their lives.

Jen had no intention of sticking around for any formal introductions with these two. A well-timed shift into low gear created a dark seamless burnout as they departed the area in a cloud of black smoke.

"Nice!" said Kyle with the biggest smile Jen had ever seen.

"Let's do some shopping instead. Maybe we can look for a new laptop."

"I can help you with that."

"Thanks Kyle, that's great."

"I know a nice coffee shop inside a large shopping complex."

"I'll bet you do. That's perfect, let's go!"

"So, what's next?" asked the younger agent. "Are we just going to go along with this charade, or should we just storm the place."

The older agent casually ignored his trigger happy partner as he gradually pulled off the highway in a cloud of dirt and dust. He came to a stop across from a strip of old and neglected, single story motels.

"Have a look inside the trunk for our small case with the forged identifications. Sort through our papers and choose something appropriate. Make sure you get a bundle with a valid credit card as well, and don't forget to check the expiry date. We'll need it later. I don't want you using the new identification we just received, or the alias you used at the bus depot."

"Okay. Then what should I do?"

"Take your bag, rent a room and get cleaned up. Try to find something to eat around here and I'll be back to pick you up, right here, in two hours."

"What are you going to be doing?"

"Same thing, different motel," said the older agent.

"Okay, I'll need a few minutes to organize some things in the trunk."

"No problem. Do you need any more cash?"

"No, I'm still okay thanks. Wait here for a few minutes and watch what room they give me."

"Why should I care about that?"

"Well, if I fall asleep you'll know where to find me."

"If you fall asleep—I'll be leaving you behind. Remember, two hours," said the older agent as he started the car and watched his partner sprint across the dusty two lane highway.

He waited just long enough to have a general idea of where his partner was going before driving away. Fighting the onset of fatigue was becoming a real problem and even the use of direct caffeine injections couldn't be ruled out. He needed to contact the director of the sanatorium as soon as possible. Acquiring Sarah D., as planned, would give them both days, and potentially weeks, before anyone even knew or cared that she was missing. By that time they would be long gone.

Professor Akkaim picked up the phone and called his shift supervisor.

"What's the current status of your Internet connection with the Oregon Motor Vehicle Branch?"

"Why do you ask?"

"Why? How dare you question my question?"

"Sorry Professor. We aren't maintaining a link at the moment, but it's always been fairly easy to penetrate their system."

"Then I want you to acquire all the available information associated with the license plates of any vehicles passing through the Claytons' estate entrance. You can start with the first three on record, the blue Mustang, the Range Rover and the other small car that arrived this morning."

"Certainly Professor, that shouldn't take long. I'll send you an e-mail with any information we find and continue to research the license plates of any new vehicles coming or going, until instructed otherwise."

"I'll be awaiting your reply."

After the older agent finished checking into another motel he walked over to a nearby payphone and placed a call to the director of the Meadowlane Children's Sanatorium.

"Good morning, Meadowlane Children's Sanatorium."

"Good morning. Is it possible to speak with the director?"

"Who shall I say is calling?"

"It's Earl Jackson."

"Oh yes, Mr. Jackson. I believe he's expecting your call. I'll put you through."

"Thank you."

"Good Morning, this is the Meadowlane Children's Sanatorium. How may I help you?"

"Yes, good morning. It's Earl Jackson. I'm here with my son to pick up a patient and transport her to the university research project."

"Yes, yes, I've been expecting your call. Are you in Dayton now?"

"Yes, we've just arrived. What time would be convenient for us to stop by and pick her up?"

"We'll need a little time to make the necessary preparations. How about four hours from now?"

"That's fine with us. We'll look forward to seeing you in four hours. Bye for now."

"Thanks for the call Mr. Jackson. We'll see both of you later."

The older agent checked his watch and returned to the hotel. He was uncomfortable using the father and son identities provided, due to their general lack of resemblance. Four hours should be enough time to finish all of their preparations. They needed to find a hardware or industrial supply store to purchase some additional supplies and locate and rent another suitable vehicle. The sanatorium was about thirty miles out of town. Most importantly, they also needed to find a suitable location to park the Cadillac. Somewhere secure and yet secluded enough to transfer Sarah D. from the rental car and back into the Cadillac.

The older agent closed the door to his room and prepared to make a pot of motel coffee. He too would have to guard against falling asleep in his motel room. Four hours can pass by quickly and they needed to be fully prepared.

The professor heard the chime of his incoming e-mail. As expected his latest inquiry had yielded some new information. The Mustang and the Range Rover were both registered to James Clayton. The other small vehicle however, was registered to Straighter Line Auto Body Ltd.

in Portland, Oregon. Whatever reason they had for visiting the estate wasn't known.

The director of the sanatorium contacted all the staff in charge and updated them on the timing of Sarah's departure. A list of preparations was drawn up that would begin with Sarah's feeding. Her transfer was estimated to last about eight to ten hours, depending on traffic, and a doubling of her normal meal portion was ordered from the kitchen. For every one's safety, including hers, Sarah had always been banned from using any utensils during feeding. She was typically always fed within room number twelve and her room was cleaned and serviced during her yard time. She would need to be fed and cleaned, dressed for transport, and also safely restrained and medicated, prior to her departure from Meadowlane Children's Sanatorium.

The younger agent finished eating his meal and double checked his watch. It felt good to get cleaned up, but he was starting to push his personal limits for going without sleep. The short naps on the road helped, but they couldn't replenish the depleted REM sleep account. He needed to keep moving. Service was unbearably slow in this cafe and he still had to return to his room, pack up, and be on the highway to meet his partner.

Sarah D. had been lying in bed staring at the door for an undetermined period of time. Initial efforts to foster new interests in various activities included classes in artwork, knitting and general crafts, all of which had proved unsuccessful.

She had arrived years ago with only scant personal possessions that included two medium-sized rag dolls. Although one had been destroyed in a previous outdoor altercation with another patient, staff had permitted her to keep the last remaining doll, Sally, because she simply became totally unmanageable without her. Occasional exceptions to certain institutional rules could sometimes make real differences in the daily 'quality of life' issues for patients within the sanatorium. Most of the staff knew that 'Sally' would be travelling with Sarah anywhere she went, and today's trip would not be an exception.

Sarah's rapid onset of Type 1 Schizophrenia at such an early age was a rare exception to the general development of the disease in the overall population. Even today her exact subtype was a topic of continued professional debate however her chronic underlying condition as a Paranoid Schizophrenic was never in dispute.

The older agent was surprised to see his partner running across the road just before he arrived to pick him up. He had fully expected he might have to wait or even start searching for him.

"How are you, my Son?"

"My son—what are you talking about?"

"Here's your new identification. You're now Jeff Jackson and I'm now officially your father, Earl Jackson."

"I'm not comfortable with that. Take a look in the mirror, that's a bad plan that could very well jeopardize the success of this entire operation."

"For once, I agree with you, but the arrangements have already been made. They're expecting both of us in two hours and we've still got plenty of things to do."

Sally was hanging off the edge of the bed, her hair clutched tightly in Sarah's grip when the metal food gate snapped open. Two foam plates quickly appeared on the door ledge and the metal gate snapped shut.

'Something's Wrong Sally, WRONG! They NEVER, NEVER, NEVER bring our food on separate plates.

Careful! Watch out! Something's WRONG, RIGHT SALLY, WRONG! SARAH! Get your useless gargantuan body out of bed, NOW SARAH! Start eating that food! QUICK! HURRY! Before Sally gets into it!'

Her auditory hallucinations had started at such an early age they were now a normal part of Sarah's life. Unfortunately when the nature of the auditory commands became too dangerous for Sarah and those around her, her distraught single mother was running out of options. The development of Sarah's increasingly bizarre behaviour eventually left her mother with only one final option; the permanent confinement of her only child within the stone walls of the Meadowlane Children's Sanatorium.

"Have a look in the directory for an industrial supply store," said the older agent.

"Okay, what do we need?"

"Well, some sort of uniforms for starters."

"Uniforms—what are you talking about? We'll never have time to get the proper labels we need to make them look official. What would workers in a place like that be wearing anyway?" asked the younger agent.

"I don't know, white pants, white shirts maybe."

"Let's skip the uniforms. We're just stopping by to transport her."

"Okay, we might have to. Take a few minutes and study this information we've received. We need to have our stories straight if they start asking us any questions."

"Okay, there's an industrial supply store a few blocks down the road. Anything else?" asked the younger agent.

"Yes, we need to find a van, maybe a newer panel van without windows."

"I can see the place coming up ahead on the right. What do we need here?" asked the younger agent.

"Rope, tape, wire, shrink wrap, tubing, tie wraps, anything that might come in handy. Just use your imagination. Hurry up, we have to keep moving."

"Okay, let's see what they've got in here."

Jen followed Kyle into the electronics store and watched as he started walking down the long isle displaying the laptop computers. Suddenly he came to an abrupt stop towards the end of the isle.

"This one," said Kyle as he lifted it up and felt the action of the keypad.

Jen had quickly scanned some of the nearby price tags; it was a high end unit, but not the most expensive one on display.

"This one it is Kyle."

They notified a sales rep who commended them on their choice and continued on with the standard sales pitch concerning warranties.

"I'll maintain it," said Kyle.

"There are no user-serviceable parts inside that unit young man," said the sales rep.

"Thank you," said Kyle. "We'll take this one without the warranty."

"Alright then, how will you be paying for this?"

"We'll be paying with cash."

"Very well, I'll work out the total for you."

"Is there anything else you need Kyle?"

"Yes, just a few cables and a case of memory sticks."

"I can help you with those over here," said the sales rep as he found exactly what Kyle was looking for. The total came in at just under three thousand dollars and Jen paid for it with the cash James had given her this morning.

"Let's find something to eat Kyle. I didn't eat enough this morning."

"Sure, let's see what's available."

Sarah's routine had been the same for years. After her daytime feeding she would be escorted though the wash-down personal hygiene gantry and then dressed in a clean smock and allowed access to a small private outdoor area.

'Something's Wrong! Right Sally! Wrong! Wrong!'

Sarah could hear footsteps coming down the hall as she ran back to her bed and crawled quickly under the blankets. She heard the knocks on her door and the keys being inserted into her door lock.

"Let's go Sarah, it's wash time and it's a beautiful day outside. Come on, let's go."

"I'm coming, I'm coming. Don't rush us," said Sarah

"Leave Sally here, she'll be safe," said a voice from the hall.

'I told you! Told you! Right Sally! Something's Wrong! They're trying to separate us! Divide and Conquer! Wrong! They're taking me away, leaving you alone. It's Wrong! I know it, wrong! I know you know we know, it's wrong! Wrong! Right Sally! Wrong!'

Each man eventually gained control of one of Sarah's arms and coaxed her out of bed and up on her feet. After standing her up between them, they worked to escort her slowly down the hall. After they had reached the personal sanitation area, they'd sign her off to a pair of female attendants who tried their best to assist Sarah wherever possible. The sanitation gantry was equipped with various suspended retractable pressure washing hose lines fitted with assorted attachments. Sarah had come to despise this institutional cleaning routine, but knew it was the final step before she arrived at the small outdoor enclosure.

All of Meadowlane's patients had virtually identical extremely short haircuts to facilitate general inspections and drying, and also to minimize the requirement for any personal grooming. After the basic hygiene procedure, the two female attendants secured the back straps on Sarah's light blue smock, put on her slippers and escorted her the short remaining distance to the outside area.

She was often left unattended for brief periods of time as the area was under constant video surveillance. Generally she spent most of her time walking backwards in tight circles around the inside perimeter of the fenced enclosure.

The daily management and administration of medications varied considerably between all the resident patients. Current adjustments to Sarah's prescriptions were underway in an effort to reduce safety concerns for everyone involved in today's patient transfer. Most of her medications would be increased in order to keep her properly sedated and manageable during her trip and until her expected arrival at the university research project.

Both agents had each selected a wide assortment of potentially useful industrial supplies before departing the store. After a short drive, the older agent parked two blocks past the entrance to a car rental agency.

"I'll wait here. Just pull up behind me after you've rented a van and you can follow me out of town. The highway follows a small river and hopefully it won't take us long to find a suitable location to park the Cadillac."

"What about the rental? Are we returning it or should we rent it long term?" asked the younger agent.

"I think we'll try and return it, but keep it open-ended if you can. Just tell them you're not sure of your plans yet."

"Okay, wait here," said the younger agent.

After fifteen minutes the older agent watched as a late model white panel van pulled up behind him while flashing the headlights. He immediately turned the key and started the still-warm engine of the Cadillac. Both vehicles were quickly out on the road and leaving town.

"Did you have enough to eat Kyle?"

"Enough for now," said Kyle as he continued working with Jen's new laptop.

"Anything else you need while we're in town?"

"Not really. I've still got lots of work to do with the computers at Chalet Number Five. I'm going to design a network that will allow us to remotely interface with the main computers from both of our laptops."

"That's a good idea. Do you want to go back to the estate?"

"Sure, anytime you're ready."

"Maybe we should we have some dessert first?"

"Good idea!" said Kyle with a smile.

Two male staff members escorted Sarah from the outdoor area and back to room number twelve. A physician was waiting inside her room to administer the required medications for the day. Both men sat her down and restrained her briefly while she received a single injection and a variety of pills with small cups of water.

'Too! Too many! Way too many!! Way too many Pills!! Something's Wrong! Wrong! Right Sally! Wrong!'

"Can I have a word with you men in private please?" asked the physician while stepping out into the hall.

'Secrets! They're keeping Secrets! Wrong! Wrong! Right Sally! Wrong!'

"Are you men able to pack a travel bag for Sarah? She is going to be leaving shortly."

"Sure, we can do that. How long will she be gone?"

"I believe she'll be gone for about three weeks."

"When is she leaving?"

"Very soon." said the physician.

"Leave it with us. We'll get something ready for her."

"Thanks. I'll catch up with you later," said the physician.

The younger agent turned off the secondary highway and followed the Cadillac down towards the river. The road was steep, rocky and overgrown and when they reached the river one car and a small truck and camper were already parked in the small clearing beside the river. A short time later they managed to turn the vehicles around and drive back out to the highway. Time was becoming an issue; they needed a safe place to park and soon.

The two male attendants located a medium-sized soft travel case and packed whatever general items they could find from the main supply rooms, including extra towels, smocks and slippers. As they opened the door to room number twelve they could see Sarah had fallen asleep in the same chair. The men dropped the bag inside the door and went for a quick break.

Sarah's eyes opened the instant the door closed and she managed to lift herself out the chair and walk across the room. She quickly grabbed Sally by one leg and stuffed her deep inside the travel case. After zipping up the case she walked back over, climbed in the chair and closed her eyes.

'I go you go we go, right Sally!'

They had driven almost five miles until they spotted another road leading off in the direction of the river. Once again the van followed the Cadillac, creeping down an even steeper narrow road towards the river. This road was rougher than the first and the Cadillac kept grounding out on large rocks embedded in the road.

They were committed now and there was no way of turning around. Even backing out would prove to be a difficult challenge. Finally the road levelled off next to a rocky riverbank along a section of fast flowing rapids.

The river was much slower at the first location and the people parked there were likely fishermen. Time and options were running out; this place would have to do. The older agent secured the Cadillac as the younger agent struggled to turn the van around.

"It's best if I drive," said the older agent.

"Why is that? Because you know where all the big rocks are?" said the younger agent with a laugh.

"One of the reasons the Cadillac handles so well on the highway is because of its low clearance, it's not an off-road vehicle as you'll find out later when you try driving it back up this hill."

Wishing he'd kept his mouth shut, he opened the front passenger door of the rental van and climbed in.

"Are we taking any equipment or supplies with us?"

"No, just take your personal weapons. We should be able to bring her back without any problems. The sanatorium is only a twenty minute drive from here. We'll use the time to work on our story."

"Yes Father, anything you say," said the younger agent in a condescending fashion.

The search of the underground parking lots was going much slower than expected. It had taken nearly two hours to get inside the first building on the list. The parking space belonging to the registered owner of the Ford Taurus was empty and the two adjacent spaces were occupied by other vehicles ruling out the first location. While conducting surveillance on the second building, the men casually followed a postman to the front door of the building. In one silent move from behind they tranquilized the unsuspecting postman with a direct hit in the back of neck from a short-range blow dart. His set of master keys was quickly removed and he was stuffed in a closet to sleep it off.

The next four buildings were quickly accessed with the master postal key, but no sign of the Ford Explorer was detected. The next location was a low income housing project on the other side of town.

"Come in," said the director as his secretary knocked lightly with her knuckles and cracked the door ajar.

"Just to let you know, I can see a vehicle driving up the road."

"Oh, Thanks. I've been expecting Mr. Jackson and his son to arrive and pick up Sarah, they're right on time. The attendants should have been making preparations for her departure. Can you tell them to finish their work and escort her to the front door?"

"Certainly, I'll inform them immediately," said the secretary as she closed the door and went on her way.

"What's the plan Father?" asked the younger agent.

"We're parking as close as possible to the front door, and then walking inside to pick up Sarah."

"Both of us are going inside?"

"No, I'm leaving you with the van. Get in here fast if you hear any shots. And if not, then open the side door and look as if you're making preparations for her."

"There's less danger of someone making a 'verbal mistake' if only one of us does the talking. Remember, be polite and only talk if you absolutely have to."

"Yeah—yeah—yeah, I understand," said the younger agent.

One of the male attendants unlocked Sarah's steel door and two female attendants also entered her room. Sarah was heavily sedated and as a precaution the women fitted her with a large disposable transport diaper and fastened her smock.

The men then entered the room and they all worked to get her into an institutional over-sized canvas coat used for transporting certain problem patients. The sleeves were double the normal length and after crossing her arms in front of her body the ends of the sleeves were buckled down tightly behind her. Six suitcase handles were securely riveted to the coat, one above each shoulder, one on each upper arm and the last two attached to the upper back of her coat.

"I can't see that stupid doll anywhere so grab her bag and let's go," said one of the male attendants.

In Sarah's heavily sedated condition it took every-one's effort to lift her out of the chair by the suitcase handles and manoeuvre her out of the room.

"Good afternoon! You must be Mr. Jackson," said the secretary as she noticed the older stranger slowly approaching her glass office door.

"Well, of course, that's right, yes I am. I'm Mr. Earl Jackson. I'm here to see the director."

"Yes, Mr. Jackson. Follow me please, he's expecting you." The secretary led him down a short hall and knocked again on the director's door.

"Come in! Please come in!" said the director as he stood up and reached out to shake hands. "You must be Mr. Jackson. We've heard so much about you. Is your son coming in?"

"No, my son Jeff, Jeff Jackson, I like to call him J.J., he's just adjusting the seats and making a few preparations to ensure our guest's utmost travelling comfort."

"That's great. I have a few forms you'll need to sign before you leave and the attendants should have her outside anytime now. So what do you think about the new university research physician?"

"They were lucky to land him, that's for sure," said the older agent, suddenly very nervous. "I don't mean to be rude, but we have a long drive ahead of us. What forms would you like me to sign before we get going?"

"Just a couple of release forms. Here you are. Two signatures on each form please."

The day shift physician will meet you both outside for a quick briefing about Sarah D. and also to assist with her loading."

"Excellent, I appreciate that," said the older agent as he reached down to sign the forms. "There you are sir. It was sure a pleasure to meet you. I should get going and meet everyone at the van."

"Oh Mr. Jackson—"

"Yes—" replied the older agent nervously.

"Here are your copies of the release forms. They'll be expecting these when you drop her off."

"Oh, yes of course. How forgetful of me. Thanks again. Bye for now."

"We're all hoping you three have a safe trip, Mr. Jackson," said the director with a concerned look.

The younger agent looked up in time to see the commotion at the front door. It looked like four or five people were trying to guide Sarah D. in his direction. She was larger than he expected—much larger. It was as if she was half asleep when she approached the van and her coat was covered with handles. Just then he noticed his partner running up to the van with several papers clutched in his hand.

"Hello, hello everyone, just stand back and we'll make some room here for Sarah. One of the attendants passed over her bag and he wedged it under the rear bench seat.

"Just run the seat-belts through the handles. That's the way we normally do it."

"J.J., can you slide that seat up?" His son was oblivious to the name.

"Excuse me, my Son! Can you please slide that seat forward?"

"Sure Father, I'll try."

"Sarah, I'd like you to meet Mr. Jackson. He'll be taking you on a little holiday today," said the day shift physician.

'Traitor Traitor! You'll pay later!'

"Hello Mr. Jackson, how nice to meet you."

"Hi Sarah, it's so nice to meet you too."

'Liar Liar! Burn in Fire!'

"This is my son, Jeff," said the older agent.

'In a Pigs Eye! Liar Liar! Burn in Fire!'

"Hello Jeff, how nice to meet you," said Sarah as she watched them both cinch down her belts. The younger agent had momentarily reached out his arm to shake her hand before he realised his embarrassingly awkward gesture.

"She looks to me like she'll be fairly comfortable back there. I've included some contact numbers for you both in case you have any questions or happen to run into any problems. All the additional medications should keep her controllable for the next ten hours. It's about a seven or eight hour drive from here to the university and they'll take over administering her medications from there," said the physician.

"That's good to know, bye. Thanks for all your help," said the older agent as he started the van and his partner slid the side door closed with a bang.

"Let's get out of this insane asylum," said the younger agent. "Just what exactly are we supposed to do when she starts running out of her medications?" he demanded, tired and increasingly agitated himself.

"We'll deal with that problem later," said the older agent as he put his foot on the accelerator. He studied the strange face intently staring back at him from the rear view mirror and knew they'd just picked up much more than they had bargained for.

'Something's Wrong! Wrong! Right Sally! Wrong! Quiet Sally! Keep very very, very quiet! Liars might be listening! Never! Ever! Trust a liar Sally! Don't even think, don't even think about a single word! And remember Sally! Until we're told! Stay in the Bag! Deep in the Bag!!'

Chapter 17

"Jen, didn't you want to buy something for the front door?" asked Kyle.

"I was thinking about looking for a few things, but it's not that important."

"There's a building supply store in the complex if you want to take a look. I don't mind," said Kyle.

"Sure, we can have a quick look. I was just going to buy a couple of deadbolts and a glass peephole for the front door. It won't take long."

"Follow me Jen, I'll show you where it is."

The three agents slowed down as they neared the next address on their list. Most of the buildings all looked the same and the underground parking area was locked.

"Should we try the postal master key?"

"You can try if you want, but it's very unlikely to work this far away from where we acquired it. Let's just have a chat with the building manager."

They parked the van on the street and walked up to the main door. After checking the door and finding it locked he pressed the buzzer marked 'Manager.'

"What do you want?"

"Hello, we were wondering if you might have any suites for rent."

"If you don't see a 'For Rent,' sign on the front lawn—then Get Lost!"

"Sorry for the trouble."

"Now what—there aren't any names on the buzzers."

"Buzz another apartment. We need to get inside."

"I'll try this one. Room 231."

"Hello," said a woman's voice through the speaker.

"Good afternoon Miss, this is Mark from the Viceroy Overhead Door Ltd. We're here to service the garage gate and the manager must be away today. He told us to contact the lady in room 231 and you would let us in."

"That's strange—the manager is almost never away."

"Yes I know, he's always been here every other time we've come to service the door."

"Well okay, maybe he's just away from the intercom or something. I guess I'll let you in. I have no idea why he'd ask me to let you in."

"Thank you kindly. We have a busy schedule today and it's greatly appreciated."

"Were those the only items you wanted Jen?"

"Yes that's it. Are you ready for the drive back home?"

"Sure, I can still do a few things on the laptop even if we don't have any Internet service."

"I can see that. Soon they'll all be connected together."

"That's right Jen. You're going to love this new laptop and all of its capabilities."

"Great. I'm looking forward to trying it."

Jen kept a vigilant watch for anything, or anyone, out of the ordinary while they walked back to the Mustang. Fortunately she didn't notice any new vehicle damage as they unlocked the doors and prepared to leave the shopping complex.

"That was easy, let's check the underground parking area first. There's no point in wasting our time if we're in the wrong building."

"Exactly, should we take the stairs or elevator?"

"Let's split up. You two take the elevator and I'll take the stairs."

Some people enjoyed listening to police scanners and others liked to listen to airport radios. This building manager liked to monitor every spoken word on the building intercom system. He'd heard this type of scam many times before from the various delinquents trying to get inside his building. He quickly shed his red terry bathrobe and dressed in more suitable attire.

He was always well armed when leaving his apartment to enforce building security, and his shortened baseball bat was standard equipment. Just to verify his suspicions he typed 'Viceroy Overhead Doors Ltd' in a computer search and found nothing. Chain smoking as usual, he fumbled to light another cigarette before he started unlocking his heavily fortified apartment door.

The man who ran down the stairs was the first to reach the underground parking area. He couldn't believe the Ford Explorer was parked almost directly in front of him when he opened the door. Still missing all four wheels and sitting on the orange milk crates; this was definitely what they were looking for. Even the aqua-marine Ford Taurus was parked beside it, leaving no doubt they had the correct building. The elevator doors opened and the other two men walked over to inspect the scene.

"Excellent! Let's get some pictures. What a stroke of luck. All we need now is the apartment number."

The building manager wore a full length oilskin jacket to conceal the unregistered sawed off shotgun at his side. A standard side-by-side twelve gauge with a modified stock and short barrels would provide ample close range stopping power in almost any situation. He started his slow methodical patrol of the building hallways, from the top floor working down. He was always exempt from the no smoking rules when dealing with any building-related security issues.

A 'Blue-K9' hands-free phone with voice activated calling was clipped to his left ear for additional security. After completing the top floor patrol he descended one flight of stairs and started working the second floor. The display above the elevator door indicated the elevator was still on the lowest level, in the underground parking area.

"We don't need that many pictures. Just make sure you take some that show both vehicles in the same frame. Try to match the photos to the ones we've seen in the file."

"Okay, I'll take a few more shots. What about the apartment? Are you planning to just walk around the building searching door to door? The manager didn't sound too co-operative."

"No, he didn't, but he doesn't even know we're in the building."

Just then the manager pushed hard on the door to the basement at the same instant the camera flash went off.

"Hold it right there—security!"

The three agents were still surrounding the car as the manager raised the twin barrels of the shotgun into plain view.

"Hello Sir, we were just examining the vehicle. Could you tell us where we might find the owner of this vehicle? We have a few questions."

"I have a few questions myself. What's the nature of your business in my underground parking lot?"

"We're a team of insurance adjusters from Eastport Insurance Agency. We're conducting a confidential investigation into what we believe may be a fraudulent claim involving this vehicle."

"I see. Why wouldn't you know where the owner lived?"

"We believe that information may have been misrepresented by our client."

"How did you manage to get inside my building?"

"A man was leaving through the front door and he offered to let us in. He mentioned the manager was usually away this time of day."

"Directory Assistance, do you have a listing for the 'Eastport Insurance Agency?"

One agent opened the clear cellophane wrapper of a large cigar and put it to his lips.

"I'll be the only one doing any smoking in this building" said the manager as he waited for a response on his Blue-K9 phone.

"Fine, I won't light it until I'm outside."

"I'm sorry, the number you have requested is not listed in our directory," could be heard by everyone from the earpiece of the Blue-K9 phone.

"Oh we've just moved into our new office two weeks ago. You'll have to ask for their new listings. Here's one of our business cards with any information you might require," said the man with the cigar.

He placed the artificial cigar in his mouth as he removed his wallet and started edging closer to the manager. He watched his wallet carefully as he extracted a new business card and held it out for the manager. With a sudden blast of breath and meticulous timing he shot a micro-dermic dart squarely in the front of the manager's throat the moment his gaze touched the crisp new business card.

The manager collapsed instantly to the cold concrete floor. At the same moment everyone heard the screeching noise of the parking gates as they started to open. The dosage in the dart was sufficient to instantly drop a much larger man, but not quite lethal.

"Hide him under the truck—he'll be out for a while. Let's check his suite for a building directory."

"I don't know. What if he doesn't live alone? Besides, there's going to be a car driving by here any second."

"You're right. Take a quick impression of his master key and push the old man under the truck. We can always come back later. I'll retrieve the dart."

The three men finished their work in seconds and casually walked up the single flight of stairs and straight out the main entrance.

James was working in his office when the phone rang. Reaching across the desk he picked up his phone

"Hello."

"Is this James?"

"Yes, speaking."

"It's Al Anderson returning your call."

"Hi Al, I was trying to contact you earlier."

"Yes, I got your message earlier on—there have been a few new developments today and I didn't want to speak with you until I knew exactly how things were going to play out."

"What are you talking about?"

"Did you get a chance to review Kyle's internship schedule yet?"

"Yes. I took a quick look at it anyway."

"Great. Has Kyle and his companion, Jennifer Lamar, seen the documents yet?"

"No, just myself."

"Have you told them anything about the schedule?"

"Not a word. I believe it said the starting date was to be announced."

"That's correct—the schedule at this point is still the same, with only a couple of changes."

"What kind of changes?"

"They've moved the schedule forward at the Central Fusion Research Complex 8 in California."

"How far forward did they move it?"

"Well, I'm sorry to inform you, but we'll be dispatching a Black Hawk helicopter that should be arriving on your estate by 10 p.m. tonight."

"But Kyle only just got home Al."

"I know James, it couldn't be helped. They're on schedule to test fire the laser array sooner than planned. This way Kyle will be involved during the entire preliminary setup and calibration phases of the experiments. As you know, his first internship is scheduled to last about six weeks and then he'll be back here for a six week break. I'll promise you that."

"What about Jennifer Lamar?"

"Well we've done some additional background checks and we've decided she's a good security companion for Kyle and we're willing to support and sanction her as well. That said, Kyle will remain within the confines of the CFRC-8 facility during the entire six weeks. They have excellent accommodations and he'll be granted full access to all the equipment at the facility. We'll also be sending Jennifer Lamar away for five to six weeks of advanced tactical helicopter training in California and she should complete her course about the same time Kyle's finished."

"She's going to like that. Are they both flying out tonight?"

"Yes."

"Well okay then, I know we have a long term commitment with you so I guess we'll make the necessary arrangements at this end."

"Glad to hear that. Is there anything else I can do?"

"Yes. We were wondering about acquiring some additional, forged identification documents for Kyle and Jen. Can you arrange that somehow?"

"Certainly, that's probably a good idea. I'll get the ball rolling on this end, later on in the week."

"Well, thanks for the update. I'll be at work tonight. Please call me if there are any changes."

"Of course I will. I feel better about calling you since you've changed the phones. Has Kyle made any progress regarding your computer problem?"

"Not yet, but I know he's still working on that."

"CFRC-8 has one of the most powerful super-computers in the country located on the premises. I wouldn't be surprised if he's given access soon."

"No, neither would I," said James knowing that was almost certain.

"Thanks Al, bye for now."

Jen slowed the Mustang down as they approached the entrance to the estate. Kyle had been working on the new laptop during the entire drive home. Jen was nearing the entrance gate when the doors began to open.

"Stop!" said Kyle suddenly.

"What for?"

"I'm showing an Internet service signal."

"Is that unusual?"

"Yes, just keep driving slowly towards the house."

"How is it now?"

"It's starting to fade out. We are up on a hill so the signal could be getting reflected somehow. Still, it's a very curious anomaly."

"Kyle, take a look behind us. Are you wearing your scentlets?"

"Don't worry about that, it's the first thing I check every morning," said Kyle.

Jen pressed a little harder on the accelerator to give the Beaucerons a better workout. "Do you want to stop at the house Kyle?"

"Sure, we may as well. I think my dad's going to be working later and we've got time for a quick visit."

"Okay, sounds good. Whose little car is that?"

"I don't know. I've never seen it," said Kyle as they rolled to a stop in front of the house.

"Wait here a minute Kyle, I want to check on this vehicle and don't worry—I'll be watching you the whole time." Jen threaded her way through the panting dogs and knocked on the side kitchen door.

"Hi Jen, you don't have to knock here, just open the door and let yourself in."

"Thanks Lisa, we were planning to come in. Who owns that small vehicle parked outside?"

"Oh, that's just a courtesy car they dropped off when they took the Range Rover in for repairs. They should be finished in a few days."

"Okay. Thanks, we'll be right in." Jen walked over to the Mustang and escorted Kyle inside. "Lisa, have you seen James around?"

"Yes, he was working in his office. I'll tell him you're here." Lisa walked over to his office and stepped through the open door as James was removing Kyle's confidential file from the wall-safe.

"Hi James, just wanted to let you know that Kyle and Jen just stopped in."

"That's great! Lisa can you fix an early dinner for the three of us upstairs in the loft, and ask them to meet me up there shortly?"

"Sure. Is everything alright?"

"Well yes, but we just had a slight change in Kyle's plans. They're both leaving tonight."

"Tonight—where are they going on such short notice?"

"Well you know, they always like to keep those details confidential."

"Oh that's right. Top secret, confidential CIA stuff," said Lisa with a smile. "Do Jen and Kyle know about it?"

"No, and please don't mention anything. I'll be discussing the details with them soon."

"Certainly, my lips are sealed."

"Thanks Lisa." James locked the wall-safe and returned to his desk. He could use the extra time to carefully examine the details of Kyle's upcoming schedule.

"I spoke with James and he wants to meet you both for an early dinner up in the loft. You two can make yourselves comfortable up there if you like."

"Thanks, we'll wait upstairs," said Kyle as they walked away towards the loft.

The older agent slowed down and pulled over just before their turnoff. He waited patiently until the road was clear of traffic before turning and driving down towards the river.

"What about this rental van? Are we returning it?" asked the younger agent.

"Yes, we'll drop it off at the same place we rented it from," said the older agent.

"What about you-know-who in the back seat?"

"Listen, just keep quiet for now. We'll discuss that after we park the van."

"It's going to be so much fun going on a vacation. Don't you think so J.J.?" said Sarah. "We're talking to you, J.J."

"Hey, she's talking to you," said the older agent to his partner.

"Who's J.J.?" said the younger agent as he scratched his head.

"You are, remember, you're Jeff Jackson, J.J." said the older agent.

"Oh, that's right. I've got it. I'm just a little tired. What did you mean Sarah when you said, 'we're' talking to you?"

"Oh, silly me—did I say that? I meant I'm talking to you, of course."

'Keep quiet Sally! Don't even think about another word!'

"I'm sure glad you're such a good driver Mr. Jackson. All of us would surely be dead and burned alive if a wheel slipped off the edge of this steep narrow road. Hey look! I can see a river down at the bottom of the hill."

"Yes, I can see it Sarah. We'll be stopping there for a little while." said the older agent.

"Why are we stopping by the river?" asked Sarah.

"We just need to pick up our other car before we can get going on our vacation," said the older agent.

"Why on earth do we need so many cars?" asked Sarah.

"The other one is a luxury car. It's a much nicer car for going on vacation," said the older agent.

"Word, new word, heard a new word! What's luxury mean?" asked Sarah.

"It just means that it's a little more comfortable," said the older agent.

"Word, new word, heard a new word! What's comfortable mean?"

"It just means that you're feeling more relaxed, generally free from stress and anxiety," said the older agent.

"Word, new word, heard a new word. What's anxiety mean?"

The younger agent jumped around in the passenger seat and shouted at Sarah. "Listen to me! Just keep quiet and stop asking so many stupid questions or I'll make sure you stay quiet."

"We're sorry J.J." said Sarah as she started giggling softly.

"Don't worry about my boy, he's just a little over tired right now," said the older agent.

"I am not—over tired! She is really starting to get on my nerves," yelled the younger agent.

"Word, new word, heard a new word. What's nerves mean?"

"We'll tell you later Sarah. Right now we need to park this van and get you into the Cadillac. Just you and I, J.J. can drive the van for a while," said the older agent.

"That's great! It's going to be nice driving in the front seat," said Sarah.

"That's not going to happen. I'll be coming back after I return the van and I want the front seat."

"Okay J.J."

"You-know-who can stay in the back if you like," said Sarah as her giggles turned to laughter.

'We'd rather look at the back of their heads anyway, Right Sally!'

"We'll be back in a few minutes Sarah," said the older agent.

'Something's Wrong! Wrong! Right Sally, Wrong!'

The agents parked the van in the clearing and walked over to the Cadillac.

"What exactly are we going to do with her for the next few days? There's no way she'll ever fit in the trunk," said the younger agent.

"I know. We're going to have to wrap and tube her the way that Sinzar does or else maybe try to find some drugs for her. She's still manageable like this, but who knows what's going to happen after her drugs wear off. For now let's stick with our original plan. We'll try to get her in the Cadillac, return the van, and then start driving back to Oregon. We need to check in at the half way point for further instructions," said the older agent.

"Okay, we'll try it your way, for now. Do we have any tinting film in the trunk? It would be nice if the rear windows of the Cadillac were darkened while she's in the back," said the younger agent.

"No, I don't think we've got any. You could try and buy some in Dayton before you return the van," said the older agent.

"Good idea. Do we need anything else?"

"Yes, you better buy some extra blankets and enough groceries for a few days. We can't just leave her in a hotel parking lot unless she's secured and the windows are tinted—besides, it could be risky bringing her inside our hotel room. Let's go and try to get her moved over to the Cadillac. I'll drive it right up beside the van first. Let me do the talking," said the older agent.

"Alright—I'll wait for you by the front of the van."

The Cadillac started up easily and the older agent manoeuvred it as close as possible to the side of the van. He shut off the car, walked around and slid open the van door.

"Sarah, we really have to move you over to the Cadillac. I'll unbuckle the seat belts for you."

"Mr. Jackson, is everything okay?"

"Everything is fine Sarah—we just need to get you inside the other car."

"My bag is in the way. Can you please put it in the other car first, please Mr. Jackson?"

"Of course I can. I'll pass it over right now."

'I go you go we go, Right Sally!'

"You're a kind man Mr. Jackson. We thank you so much," said Sarah.

"Give me another minute to undo these seat belts and let's see if you can move on your own."

"How is everything going?" asked the younger agent.

"Everything's fine, just wait over there for now." said the older agent.

"Can you move on your own Sarah?"

"I'm trying—it's really hard with this coat on."

"Let me pull you along with the handles on your coat."

"Okay, you can try if you want."

'Closer, closer. Keep moving those hands closer! Now! Bite him! Bite him hard! Now!'

"No!" screamed Sarah.

"What's the matter Sarah, I'm just trying to pull you by these handles. I'm only trying to get you moving."

"Okay, I think that's starting to help. Tell me when my feet get close to the ground."

"That's it Sarah, keep coming, good girl, you're almost there," said the older agent. "You're doing great—just duck your head when you're getting in the car, perfect. I'll do up your belts and we'll get going."

'Now! Now! Bite him now!'

"No!" yelled Sarah again.

"Look Sarah, you have to wear them. It's against the law to drive without seat belts," said the older agent.

"Yes, of course Mr. Jackson."

'No! Stop thinking about that Sally! We can't! Not yet! No! No! No!'

"I'll be back in a few minutes Sarah," said the older agent.

"Okay, thanks for your help Mr. Jackson."

"I'm surprised you managed to move you-know-who over to the Cadillac without my help," said the younger agent.

"Well she seems fairly cooperative as long as she's on her medications. I've decided to drive the Cadillac for now. Follow me into town and you can finish the shopping and load up the trunk before we return the van," said the older agent.

"Okay, but I still think we should prepare her the way Sinzar does. She won't cause us any trouble if she's done like that."

"We might have to, we'll know soon enough. Are you ready to go?"

"Sure, you can go first. Don't hit too many rocks," said the younger agent.

"That's right. I was going to let you drive up this road, but decided I didn't want the bottom of the Cadillac destroyed."

"That's very funny, Old Man."

"Yes Child, I thought so too. I'll talk to you later, after we get to town."

"Hi Sarah, are you ready to start travelling again?"

"Yes Mr. Jackson. I'm sure glad J.J. has his own car. I'm also really, really glad that he's not coming on the vacation with us."

"Well I'm sorry to tell you, but he may have to join us again later."

"I'm sure you and your child know what's best, Mr. Jackson."

'No! They most certainly do not! We'll decide what's best and when! Right Sally!'

Jen and Kyle were both studying the computer monitor when James walked into the loft.

"Sorry about the early dinner invitation and the short notice."

"That's okay Dad, I know you're planning to go to work later. This way we won't have to worry about dinner tonight and I'll be able to keep working on the computers in Chalet Number Five."

"Well, I have some news for the both of you," said James as he laid the confidential file on the table.

"What kind of news Dad?"

"I finally had a long talk with Al Anderson this afternoon."

"Oh, did you get a chance to discuss the new identification papers?" asked Jen.

"Well yes, we talked about that as well."

"Hello everyone," said Lisa as she began setting the table. James lifted Kyle's file from the table.

"Hi Lisa—would you mind giving us another fifteen or twenty minutes before we start eating?"

"Sure James, no problem whatsoever. See you soon," said Lisa as she walked away.

"Can he help us acquire any forged identifications?" asked Jen.

"Absolutely, he'll start working on that next week."

"That's excellent. Mr. Anderson must have a few resources at his disposal," said Jen.

"He has more than a few Jen. Listen, I'll get right to the point. Kyle, you will be starting a six week internship at CFRC-8 which I'm sure you know is the Central Fusion Research Complex 8 in California. Their schedule has been moved ahead and they're planning some laser fusion experiments in the very near future. You have a full time curriculum involving all aspects of the project. How does that sound to you?"

"That's fantastic! That is exactly what I was hoping for."

"Jen, you've been booked for five weeks of advanced tactical helicopter training in California while Kyle is at CFRC-8, and afterwards you'll both return here for a six week break."

"I don't know what to say? Five weeks of tactical training will cost a fortune. Who's covering that?"

"Let's just say Uncle Sam will be picking up the tab."

"I'm still stunned. When is all this going to happen?"

"Ten o'clock tonight. A Black Hawk helicopter is scheduled to land at our helipad and fly you both out tonight. Pack what you want. Anything else can be acquired later on."

"Will Kyle be allowed time away from CFRC-8?"

"No, he'll be there on a full time basis for six weeks. Trust me, he'll probably be running the place after a few weeks."

"So he'll be out of contact?"

"Let me worry about that Jen. I'll evaluate the situation later and contact you on the laptop," said Kyle.

"Are we flying the Black Hawk from here to California?" asked Kyle.

"Sorry Kyle, I don't have any of those the details."

"I hope so," said Kyle.

"Let's just relax and enjoy our dinner. I won't be here when they pick you up. Don't forget to pack some valid scentlets for your return trips. Al Anderson will handle any personal requirements or logistical details while you're away. Hi Lisa! Perfect timing, I think we're all ready for some dinner now."

"Sure, here's something to get you started and I'll bring the rest up right away," said Lisa as she disappeared down the stairs.

"Are you driving or flying into work tonight Dad?"

"I was planning to drive. There's plenty of room to land a Black Hawk helicopter near our hanger if we keep our machine inside. The weather looks good tonight and you can leave an outdoor light on if you want. Don't worry about the quads. Just leave them beside the hanger."

"Okay, thanks Dad," said Kyle as Lisa started serving dinner.

Professor Akkaim was reviewing the latest update from the Portland agents. Surprisingly, they did manage to locate the building with the Ford Explorer on their first day of searching. It would be only a matter of time before they found out if she kept an apartment in the building. Now that he knew the building address he could instruct his cyber team to compile a list of valid phone numbers belonging to the apartments in the building. It seemed likely that her apartment would be among the ones that didn't have a registered telephone line. That would certainly be useful information the next time his team planned a visit to the building unless the building manager suddenly became co-operative. Judging from the details in their report, that seemed highly unlikely.

Unfortunately there was still no confirmation on Sarah D.'s abduction, and for now there was nothing more he could do but wait for them to check in. It was still possible they might receive some electronic verification, but it would be inappropriate to launch any inquiries at this point.

Constant monitoring of the estate had revealed only minimal vehicle traffic. The Mustang had returned today, but with the tinted windows it was impossible to know who was inside the vehicle. The ongoing mystery of his missing agent remained unresolved, however that was far more preferable than having his body discovered somewhere on the grounds.

Despite all his dedicated manpower he still didn't feel like he had the upper hand concerning any of Kyle Clayton's day-to-day activities. That information would become increasingly important once Sinzar Bakkir was brought in to plan Kyle's abduction. Sinzar's scheduled meeting in Santa Monica wasn't really necessary at this point, but with the ongoing security arrangements nobody ever really knew how to contact him.

"Why are we stopping out here on the highway Mr. Jackson?" asked Sarah.

"It looks like J.J. needs something from the automotive supply shop," said the older agent.

"Why didn't you just park beside him in the parking lot?"

"No real reason Sarah."

'Lies, lies and more lies!'

"I'm getting hungry Mr. Jackson. When do we eat?"

"Well, J.J. is going to do some grocery shopping soon. We'll have lots to eat after that Sarah."

"By the way, what happens when you run out of your medications Sarah?"

"The numbers start coming back."

"The numbers—what are you talking about?"

"Nothing—I don't want to think about the numbers."

'If you know what's good for you! Right Sally!'

"I'm sorry Sarah, we won't talk about that anymore," said the older agent.

"I like Salt and Pepper potato chips. Make J.J. buy me lots of them, okay?"

"Sure, I'll tell him."

"Thank you so much Mr. Jackson."

'Patience pays Sally. Sooner or later you'll get your chance! Right Sally!'

James stood up as he picked up Kyle's file from the table.

"Let's get our goodbye's out of the way. Kyle, I hope you have a great trip down at CFRC-8. And Jen, you can give me a few flying lessons after you get back here."

"Thanks for everything Mr. Clayton. We'll see you in five or six weeks."

"You're welcome Jen. I hope you have a great time in California."

"Bye Dad. Thanks, I'll be in touch. Hope you get some good LDR scores while I'm gone."

"Thanks, I hope so too. Remember, everything is highly confidential. Don't discuss any details with anyone."

"We won't."

James returned to his office and Kyle and Jen took some dishes down to the kitchen.

"Oh, you two didn't have to do that," said Lisa as she started trying to unload them.

"That's okay, we were coming down anyway," said Jen.

"We'll be going away on business for a while. Thanks for the great dinner and we'll see you when we get back."

"You only just got home. Oh well, I'll see you two when you get back here. Be careful. Bye."

"We will. Bye Lisa." Kyle and Jen waved as they walked out of the kitchen.

"Let's park the car and drive the quads up to Chalet Number Five," said Kyle.

"Sounds good, let's go."

James locked up Kyle's internship schedule in his wall-safe. He wasn't happy Kyle and Jen were leaving so soon because he liked having them around. He was pleasantly surprised how well they seemed to get along, but he also knew his son's insatiable appetite for knowledge would be satisfied once he started working at the new science facility. Checking his watch, he realised he'd be late for work if he didn't leave immediately.

"Now where are we going Mr. Jackson?" said Sarah.

"To the grocery store and then J.J. has to drop off the van."

"Is he going to get the potato chips for us?"

"Yes, I'll tell him."

"You better tell him before he goes shopping."

"Yes, I will." The older agent drove up alongside the van and motioned to his partner to roll down the window.

"Hey, buy some chips when you're in the store."

"Excuse me please Mr. Jackson. Tell J.J. to buy about ten bags of Salt and Pepper potato chips."

"Hey J.J., I think maybe you better pick up about ten bags of Salt and Pepper chips."

"Ten bags—what the... for? I've never even heard of Salt and Pepper potato chips."

"Listen to me! Just do it and meet me out on the highway."

The older agent quickly drove out of the parking lot and parked on the side of the highway.

"Are we parking out here for no real reason again Mr. Jackson?" asked Sarah.

"He should be along soon with your chips Sarah."

"We know why you're parking on the highway Mr. Jackson," said Sarah as she started thrashing around in the back seat.

'Don't worry Sally! Just wait! Wait! Till the time is Right! Right Sally!'

"Settle down back there. J.J. will be dropping off the groceries soon and I'm sure he'll have some chips for you."

"Sorry Mr. Jackson. I'll be good. I promise."

'Shame we can't keep a promise. Right Sally!'

Twenty minutes later the older agent watched as the van pulled up behind him. He calmly pressed the trunk release as his partner approached the rear of the Cadillac.

"All of these groceries will never fit in the trunk."

"Well, load up what you can. Put the chips and whatever else you can't fit in the trunk up here in the front seat. Do we still have that galvanized bucket in the trunk?"

"Yes it's in there. Why?"

"Just put it in the front seat for now. We need to drop off the van and start travelling. I'll wait for you on the highway a few blocks past the car rental yard."

"Why so far away?"

"We don't want anyone connecting the rental van with the Cadillac."

"Okay, I'll see you there after I return the van."

"Do you always park on the side of the highway Mr. Jackson?"

"Sometimes the car has trouble with reverse gear and this just makes parking a little easier."

"I just knew you would have a good reason Mr. Jackson."

'Lies! Lies! and more Lies!'

Kyle was waiting by the door to Chalet Number Five when Jen arrived on her quad.

"What took you so long?" said Kyle with a smile.

"Oh you know, just a little slow getting the engine started, but I'm working on it. Soon I'll be waiting for you. Do you have much gear to pack Kyle?"

"No, I've barely even started unpacking. What about you?" asked Kyle as he ran up the stairs.

"It's the same for me. I'm travelling pretty light at the moment."

"I want to finish the networking links between our computers before we go. I'll be searching for a way to tap into the processing power of the supercomputers in California. If I do manage to get them working, even part time on my new diagnostic program, we might find the source of the GhostNet cyber intrusions much sooner."

"Do you want me to take the new laptop Kyle?"

"Yes, that's why I want to finish everything tonight before we leave. We can't quite watch each other's backs, but we should be able to stay in contact. You'll also have shared access with the systems here if you need additional computing resources."

"That sounds great. I'm going to make sure everything is locked up here and start making some preparations for our departure tonight. If you need a hot pot of anything, just let me know."

"Thanks, I was already thinking about that Jen."

"How much longer are we going to keep waiting for J.J.?"

"I can see someone walking along the highway towards us, it's probably him."

"I don't think he really wants to go on a vacation with us. Let's leave him here."

"I can't do that Sarah."

"I'm afraid of him Mr. Jackson. I don't think he likes me."

"Oh, he just needs to get to know you a little better Sarah."

'Don't believe a word Sarah, Lies! Lies and more lies!'

"Maybe you're right Mr. Jackson. Is he still walking towards us?"

"Yes, I can see him now, he's almost here."

"Which direction are we going for our vacation?"

"We'll be traveling west Sarah."

"Okay, that sounds interesting. Any direction is new to me."

The younger agent opened the door and climbed in the passenger side.

"Did everything go alright when you returned the van?" asked the older agent.

"Yes, everything seemed normal as far as I could tell. I think they were sorry to get the van back so soon. What's going on with all these potato chips?"

"Sarah wanted you to buy some for her."

"Yes, thank you so much J.J. I haven't had Salt and Pepper potato chips for years."

"They didn't have that kind so I bought barbecue instead."

"Word, new word, heard a new word. What's barbecue?"

"It's just a way of cooking something over hot coals. I'm sure you will like the taste of them."

"We can't wait. Can you untie the straps on the back of my coat? I need my arms and hands to eat potato chips."

"Sorry Sarah, I don't think we can do that," said the older agent.

"Why not—you can trust me."

'Or not! Right Sally!'

"We're just following our instructions," said the older agent.

"J.J., figure out some way to feed her that will work. I need to focus on driving."

"Don't worry, I know exactly what will work, watch this!" He ripped open three bags of chips and filled the galvanized bucket. Reaching over to the back seat he pulled the handle over the back of her head and left the bucket hanging below her face.

"How's that Sarah?"

"Thank you J.J., this should work fine."

'Nobody makes us eat from a bucket. Nobody! Just be patient Sally, we'll get our chance! I'll be ready Sarah! Don't worry, I'll be ready!'

"Did you find any tinting film for the windows?" asked the older agent.

"Yes I did, but it won't be easy fitting it properly," said the younger agent.

"We can do a temporary job on the outside of the windows instead. Just apply it, get the bubbles out and trim the perimeter with a utility knife."

"That will be much easier than trying to do the inside of the rear windows with you-know-who in the back seat."

"You-know-who can hear you J.J. It's not nice to talk about people sitting behind your back. Mr. Jackson, please whatever you do Mr. Jackson—don't let the numbers start coming back again. Keep them away!"

"What is she talking about?" asked the younger agent.

"I'm not sure. She obviously has some kind of bad experience whenever she starts to see these numbers. They must be some form of hallucinations or something, and the prescription drugs probably keep them away."

"Some numbers are good, some bad and some really, really, bad and I don't want to talk about any of them," said Sarah.

"What do you mean by that?" asked the younger agent.

"I mean, I just told you, I don't want to talk about them, if I talk about them, we'll think about them.

'We can't hide from the numbers Sarah, you should know that. There's nowhere to hide if the numbers come to call.'

Sinzar Bakkir had meticulously prepared his boat for any uninvited guests before slipping away in the darkness. He rigged the galley doors to a breakaway detonator connected to a plastic explosives charge attached firmly to the top of the main fuel tank. If anyone opened the door to his boat it would be the last thing they ever did.

Wearing khaki shorts and a Hawaiian shirt, dark glasses and a safari hat, Sinzar had easily joined a group of tourists boarding a bus to the U.S.A. After passing through the border the bus was heading directly for Las Vegas, Nevada, which left him ample time to make his appointment in Santa Monica.

He had timed his visit to coincide with a large Shiner's convention in Las Vegas, and a following one starting in L.A. Once he had acquired the customary outfit he would blend in anywhere in Vegas. It wasn't the first time he'd tagged along on the coattails of various conventions and wouldn't be the last. The general public seemed to have an unspoken aversion to him anyway and once he'd found a new purple flat-top hat with gold tassels, everyone would definitely go out of their way to avoid him.

Sinzar liked Las Vegas and needed to be sure he didn't get overly carried away with life's darker temptations. Although he held an important rank in RA-9, he absolutely couldn't afford to miss his upcoming meeting in Santa

Monica, California. One chance for contact each month was the mandatory part of his long term arrangement.

Professor Akkaim rolled his chewed up pencil repeatedly between his fingertips as he watched the monitor on the wall. The small vehicle from the auto body shop was leaving the estate. The image was clear and this time there was no doubt; James Clayton was driving.

Immediately he picked up his phone and called his assistant.

"Yes."

"Are you in contact with the three agents in Portland?"

"I'm expecting to hear from them a little later. They've been working long hours and are probably getting some rest."

"I have a new assignment for them."

"What a most excellent thought Professor! What's inside's your mind?"

The professor hated hearing this mutated English expression, 'what's inside's your mind', but fought off the desire to verbally reprimand his assistant.

"I want them to locate and investigate the business called Straighter Line Auto Body."

"Should we be looking for anything specific?"

"No, just investigate their premises. I want to know if the car James Clayton was just driving today is currently at that location, and why."

"Okay, I understand Professor. I'll give you an update as soon as I have some new information. Is there anything else?"

"Yes, there is something else. I also have a message for the two agents travelling back from Ohio."

"Yes, the ones trying to bring the girl you requested?"

"That's right, and for their sake she had better be with them. I want them to send me some digital pictures of her."

"I'll pass the message along. Do you want just a passport-style photo?"

"No, actually I want some more dramatic photos, ransom-style, depicting the fact she's clearly been abducted and we are holding her captive or else. Those type of photos. Do you understand exactly what I'm asking for?"

"Yes, I think so Professor. Does she have any current orders protecting her from physical harm?"

"Yes, that was a standing order in their first set of instructions and I don't see any reason to change it at this point."

"Very well. I'll take care of those requests personally. Have you decided who's going to meet with Sinzar Bakkir yet?"

"I like to keep you on a need-to-know basis, so if there is some valid justifiable reason that you need-to-know, I may possibly inform you."

"Yes of course, Professor. My sincerest of all of the apologies and thank you for your most valuable time."

Jen was relaxing by the fire when Kyle eventually came downstairs and settled down in front of the hearth.

"Are you excited to be going to this place for six weeks Kyle?"

"Yes I am, it was my first choice of all the possible locations in North America. Do you know what they're working on down there?"

"Not really. Isn't it something to do with lasers?"

"That's right. It's the most advanced laser fusion research facility in the United States. In a nutshell, they're trying to create the temperatures and conditions required to initiate a controlled nuclear fusion reaction within the complex. Once I've finished my first internship, and when we have some extra time, I'll explain everything to you in much greater detail."

"That sounds so interesting. I'll be looking forward to learning some more about that Kyle."

"You might have some new things to teach me about flying as well."

"I hope so, that depends on how extensive the tactical training course is going to be. Did you make any progress with your 'GhostNet' interrogation programs tonight?"

"As a matter of fact I have. One continent has been ruled out."

"That's interesting—which one?"

"South America is now off the list."

"So the interrogations really could have originated in China?"

"That's still possible, but it's not confirmed at this point. The diagnostics program will automatically update us with any new information concerning my ongoing 'GhostNet' investigation."

"Great. What about contacting each other? Should we set up a regular time for communications? Or how do you want to do it?"

"Let me try and arrange that over the first few days, depending on how our schedules work out."

"Good idea Kyle. Can you show me what you've done with the new laptop?"

"Give me five minutes Jen and I'll bring the laptop downstairs."

"Don't be long, we have to leave soon. I want to be up there before they land. Somehow I don't think they'll be wearing any scentlets."

"Sure Jen. I'll be right down."

"Excuse me please. I think I have to use the ladies' room."

"Sorry, but I can't see a ladies' room anywhere on this highway so you're just going to have to wait. How are you doing with those potato chips? Do you want me to put another bag in your bucket?" said the younger agent.

"Sure, another bag would be great. It's hard to stop eating them when they taste so good."

'Just bring me those little pink fingers, bring them close! Nice and close! He deserves a good lesson, don't you think so Sarah!'

The younger agent opened another bag, turned around and started dumping the bag in her bucket.

'Do it! Do it! Do it now!'

"Stop!" screamed Sarah at the top of her voice.

"What's your problem?" asked the younger agent as he dropped the empty bag on the floor.

"Oh nothing J.J., the bucket was just filling up so quickly it startled me a little."

"Don't be so paranoid," said the younger agent as Sarah began crunching away at the chips in her bucket.

'Wrong! Wrong word! Right Sally! Wrong word! He has no idea what that word means! No idea at all! Not yet! Right Sally!'

Kyle had almost finished his instructional demonstration about how to use the laptop when Jen glanced at the wall clock.

"Kyle, what you've done here is incredible. I'm totally impressed, but we have to leave right away. Are you still wearing your scentlets? Have you got everything you need?"

"Yes twice."

"Here, put some of these earplugs in your pocket."

"Sure! That's a good idea."

"Okay, I'll start strapping our gear down on the quads."

Jen opened the door slightly to check for the dogs, but they were nowhere to be seen. This time she started her quad right away and then secured her travel gear. She left most of her weapons behind as she and Kyle would soon be separated for the duration of the trip.

Kyle dropped his bag by the door and Jen started strapping it down on his quad. Just as she was about to start looking for him he came running out the front door with his laptop.

"We've got some more news."

"What news Kyle? We have to go."

"Antarctica has been eliminated."

"Antarctica? Did you think someone might be attacking our computers from there?"

"The program is conducting an initial process of continental elimination and if we're patient, and lucky, the program will continue operating until it pinpoints the location. Hey, can you hear that?"

"Yes, it sounds like a very powerful helicopter heading this way."

"It must be the Black Hawk, let's go."

Just as they started their quads Jen turned and saw the three Beaucerons blocking the pathway.

"Just relax and let the dogs verify our scentlets. It's unbelievable how they just appear out of nowhere at the same instant we step outside. Let's get going. If we try driving slowly maybe they won't follow us up to the helipad."

"No chance of that, they won't be able to resist the sound of the incoming Black Hawk."

"You're probably right. See you at the top."

They had planned their arrival perfectly, leaving them just enough time to unpack the quads and get in position for a pickup. The Beaucerons retreated back into the forest as the Black Hawk approached the tree line and started a slow, steep approach.

The engine noise and downdraft from the main rotors was overwhelming as it continued its decent down towards them. They had been spotted by the landing lights and Kyle tried to marshal them with hand signals towards the best available landing area. They could have been better prepared with eye protection for the inevitable dust storm caused by the hot pick up.

They stayed in position as the Black Hawk touched down and both of them kept constant eye contact with the pilot. Moments later, he signalled a 'thumbs up' with his gloved hand and they approached the machine. The side door slid open and Kyle and Jen passed up their gear and climbed inside. Two pilots where sitting up front and the other crew members in the back handed them each a helicopter helmet and directed them to their designated seats. Within a minute they were securely strapped in their seats and plugged into the intercom.

"Intercom check—do you copy?"

"Yes, I hear you loud and clear," said Jen.

"Copy you five-by-five," said Kyle.

"Great, welcome aboard. We'll be flying dark for most of the trip and dropping Kyle off first. All set?"

"All set!" said Kyle and Jen at the same instant.

The turbines started to wind back up to one hundred percent and the powerful machine lifted into a hover and continued to climb effortlessly over the trees.

They both watched quietly as the pilots turned off all the exterior lights and dimmed the instrument panels before switching them over to an eerie green combat lighting. Now operating in dark mode, the pilots set a course for southern California as the Black Hawk vanished from sight in the clear night sky.

Chapter 18

"It looks like you're having some trouble getting to sleep," said the older agent.

"Nobody could get any sleep with you-know-who snoring like a freight train in the back seat. I don't know what's worse, the snoring when she's asleep or the questions when she's awake."

"Why don't you take a sleeping pill? I think we've got a bottle somewhere in the trunk. I'll keep driving while you get a few hours of sleep if you like. You know what's strange? Sometimes it sounds like she's almost going to stop snoring, and then she just starts up again," said the older agent.

"You know what that sound reminds me of?" asked the younger agent.

"No, what does it remind you of? Something loud, that's for sure."

"You remember the sound of an old beer fridge? She sounds just like an old beer fridge when the compressor's used to start up."

'Old Beer Fridge!'

"Only she keeps making that same sound over and over and over again, and it's driving me crazy. Why should I have to take a sleeping pill? Let's just fill a needle with tranquilizers, inject her in the neck and knock her out for good," said the younger agent.

'Let me out! Now! Now! Now! I told you, I can't! I can't Sally! Not yet!'

"Just take a look at her back there. Her head is tilted so far back it's probably causing her to snore. Pull the bucket a little and see if you can tilt her head forward to a normal position."

"I don't know why you want to bother. Let's knock her out, throw in a few tubes and I'll wrap her up in shrink-wrap like a spider's breakfast."

'Spider's Breakfast!'

"Just try pulling on the bucket. Even you snore some nights when your head's tilted back."

"Well, if that's what I sound like when I'm sleeping then promise me you'll kill me in my sleep."

'I promise J.J.! I Promise! Quiet Sally! Just keep quiet!'

"Normally I just throw a few pillows on top of your head, which always seems to work. Try pulling her bucket."

"Oh okay," said the younger agent as he turned around and reached for the top edge of the bucket.

"Just see if you can pull her head forward," said the older agent.

"This really feels strange," said the younger agent.

"Why? What do you mean?" asked the older agent.

"I'm pulling with almost all my strength and nothing's happening—nothing at all."

"I wonder if she's had a seizure or something like that, because her neck isn't moving at all. Do you think that's even possible?" asked the younger agent.

"I guess anything's possible. Are you pulling with both hands?"

"Hang on a second. Okay, now I'm pulling with both hands. Any harder and the handle is going to break off. Let's just stuff a pair of socks in her mouth and wrap her head in duct tape. That will keep her quiet for good," said the younger agent.

'We'll show you what 'quiet for good' means! Right Sally!'

"See if you have any luck waking her up," said the older agent.

"I'm pretty sure if I filled this bucket with ice cold water from the next river and dumped it over her head she'd wake up."

"Try making some noise first," said the older agent.

The younger agent turned around in his seat and opened the glove compartment. After digging around inside he found a large adjustable crescent wrench on the bottom.

"This should work," he said. Spinning around in his seat he started banging on the side of her bucket.

"Sarah, it's time to wake up. Wake up Sarah. Time to be quiet, Sarah!" yelled the younger agent.

"If she doesn't stop snoring I'm going to shoot her right between the eyes. Roll her electric window all the way down, just for a minute," demanded the younger agent.

"What are you planning to do?" asked the older agent.

"Plug your ears," said the younger agent as he pointed his revolver out the window and fired three shots next to Sarah's head. Seconds later Sarah tilted her head forward and opened her eyes.

"Good morning J.J. I must have dozed off after eating all those potato chips. Did you know the window back here is wide open? Why are my ears are ringing?"

"No idea Sarah? Maybe you've got tinnitus?"

"Word, new word, heard a new word. What's a tinnitus?" asked Sarah.

"That's when people hear ringing sounds in their ears," said the younger agent.

"I've got that," said Sarah.

"I'm sorry to hear that Sarah."

'Lies! Lies and more Lies!'

"Do you want me to refill your bucket?"

"Sure J.J., I bet you know the way to a witch's heart," said Sarah, unable to stop giggling.

"You don't even know what you're talking about. Stay still while I refill your bucket," said the younger agent.

"Okay, you seem so cranky and overtired J.J. Have you thought about getting some sleep?" said Sarah.

"No! I am not cranky or overtired! What made you say that?"

"Your father told me when you were out running errands for us."

"You told her I was cranky and over tired?" screamed the younger agent at his partner.

Before he had a chance to answer Sarah started laughing uncontrollably at the top of her lungs.

"What's so funny?"

"Nothing J.J.—It's a just a little secret we've got, but I promised not to tell."

'Don't even think about that! Not when he's here! Right Sally!'

The three agents watched each other as the hotel phone rang several times. Finally an agent reached over and picked up the receiver.

"Yes."

"I & R Straighter Line Auto Body, no delay" was all he heard before the phone went dead.

"Did we get some new instructions?"

"Yes, investigate and report on Straighter Line Auto Body. No delay."

"That was it?"

"That was it."

"Start with the telephone directory and see if you can find an address."

"Okay, I'll take a look. Straight, Straighter Line, here it is. Okay, I've got a Portland address. What do you want to do?"

"Go and investigate it of course. Let's get moving, we'll find something to eat in town."

"It's going to be hard finding a place that's open now."

"You're right, let's find the auto body shop first. Maybe we can just break in and have a look around."

"Okay, sounds good. I'll see you outside."

"Okay. I'll be right there."

Sinzar dusted off his new purple hat after cutting off the insignias and adjusted it slightly for fit. The previous owner wouldn't be waking up for some time and Sinzar was certain he didn't know what hit him.

He still had some time to kill and could never seem to resist the magnetic pull of the dazzling casinos. The neon lights, the music and the women had an inexplicable way of drawing him inside.

Although he loved the blackjack tables, sitting alone and playing the slot machines was much safer. Every now and then he'd hit a small jackpot to replenish his supply of nickels. The key to playing a long time was drinking slowly. If he could hold his consumption at one drink an hour, he wouldn't have to worry about losing his self-control, random altercations, falling off his chair, or even worse; an alcoholic blackout. He hated waking up in strange places without any recollection of the night before, or even worse, finding a pair of swollen black eyes staring straight back at him from a mirror in the morning.

A simple prepaid arrangement with his waitress always worked the best; one drink—every hour on the hour with no exceptions. Pulling hard on the lever, his eyes lit up with excitement as he lined up three oranges in a row. With a yelping "Yes!" he clasped his hands together as the oncoming rush of nickels filled the silver trough.

The three agents drove by the cinder block shop on the outskirts of town. It was located inside a small fenced compound with an assorted collection of vehicles scattered around the yard. Slowing down beside the fence had triggered the motion sensors and activated the security yard lighting.

"Start by making a list of the vehicles you can identify and get the plate numbers if you can. I think it makes more sense to come back when they're open. It won't be that much longer."

"I agree, it's not worth the risk of a break and enter when we could probably walk right in later. Let's just find a place to eat and come back later."

"Look! I'm in charge here and our instructions said 'no delay'. Let's find a place to park nearby and have a look inside. Take your weapons and choose something quiet to hit the security lights. We'll need them out first."

"How far away do you want to park?"

"Not that far. We'll be the only ones walking around here this time of night and we might need to leave in a hurry. On second thought, back up and I'll shoot out the security lights with my small calibre first. I don't want to get caught inside if they're hooked into an alarm system."

"Okay. I like that idea better."

"Yeah, so do I."

The lights were an inexpensive residential design, but it still it took seven shots to remove all four flood lights.

"Let's take a little drive around the block and we'll come back and make sure everything is still quiet. Check inside our locksmith case and bring at least two impression tools. We'll just cut our own key in the van and then we'll have our own if we ever need to come back here."

"Alright, everything seems quiet and I can't hear any alarms. Slow down beside the fence and I'll use the roof of the van to hop over. I'll be right back after I've made the impressions."

"Hurry up. We'll be waiting for you right here."

Sinzar Bakkir's pockets were becoming heavy with nickels. He knew it was time to call it a night, but for some inexplicable reason he was never able to leave with any winnings in his pocket. He played until he'd lost everything; the same way he'd always played. He decided to stay for one more drink and play the machine until his nickels were gone, promising himself that if he kept on winning, everything was going to his waitress.

The driver watched as both men dropped down from the fence and returned to the van.

"That didn't take long. Did you make a key impression?"

"Yes, I made two. I didn't see any windows and there's only one steel entrance door."

"Do you have the blanks to cut the key?"

"I'm just checking them now. I think so. I've got a good selection of blanks."

"How long will it take to cut the key?"

"It should only take a few minutes. Find a place to park and we'll take a quick look."

Leaving one man with the van, the other two walked back over to the compound, scaled the fence and inserted their key. It took several attempts, but the new key finally turned and opened the door. They waited for any sign of an alarm before entering and turning on the lights. The small body shop had an empty paint booth in the far corner and only two vehicles were inside.

"Isn't that the Claytons' Range Rover?"

"It sure looks like it. I'll check the glove compartment, the registration should be inside."

"Don't touch anything. We'll cross check the plates later. It looks like they've still got some more work to do before they'll be ready to paint. Write down the information from the other car, it might be a courtesy car. I don't see any damage at all."

"Do you see anything else?"

"No. I don't see anything else suspicious in this place—it's just a small shop. Let's get out of here."

"That's fine with me. I'll get the lights."

Everything was still quiet when the men returned to the van and they wasted no time departing. A report would have to be called in before they could start looking for a restaurant.

"Listen, I want you to take something to make you sleep. We can't both be sleeping at the same time," said the older agent.

"This is getting ridiculous, give me five minutes with you-know-who and we won't have to worry about her until we arrive in Portland."

"Word, new word, heard a new word. What's a ridiculous?"

"Look! Keep quiet back there or else."

"Or else what J.J.?" said Sarah as she started giggling uncontrollably.

"Or else this!" screamed J.J. as he spun around and flipped the bucket upside down on her head. "Are you comfortable now?"

"Well I don't know, let me try it out," said Sarah as she started banging her head hard against the glass in the rear door.

"Hey, stop that or I'll stuff you in the trunk."

"I heard you say that you-know-who wouldn't fit in the trunk and I know that you know I know who you-know-who is J.J."

"If you don't be quiet I'll put your head in the trunk and throw away the rest of you."

'That's it! Let me out! Quiet Sally! I mean it! Stay in the bag!'

"I'm sorry J.J. I should try and get some sleep while I can. We'll both be awake if the numbers come to call."

"Look, I have no idea what you're talking about. If you can keep quiet then maybe I'll take the bucket off your head."

"Can I have some more potato chips? The other ones fell on the floor."

"Only—if you promise to keep quiet."

"What about my pills? I think it's time for all my pills. I hope you didn't forget to bring my pills J.J. That could cause trouble."

'Real trouble! Right Sally!'

"We'll find something for you, don't you worry about that."

'We'll find something for you, don't you worry about that! Right Sally!'

"We're just glad you didn't forget to bring my pills J.J."

"We can't just keep on driving and driving without getting any sleep. We barely slept on the trip out here," said the younger agent.

"I know we're both getting tired. Let's get off the highway and find a secluded place. Maybe we can apply the tinting film."

"Okay, let's take the next exit and we'll see what we can find. It wouldn't take more than an hour to tint the back windows if we both worked on it."

"Sounds good. I'll find some special medicine and a heavy blanket for you-know-who and maybe we'll all get some sleep."

"Is it going to get cold J.J.?"

"Yes, it might get colder during the night."

"Won't we be there by then J.J.?"

"There was a little change in plans, they are going to need you for a new more important research project, but it's a lot farther away."

"How much farther away is it J.J.?"

"It will take at least a couple of days to get there."

"That's the longest trip we've ever had J.J. I see why you want some sleep."

"Everyone needs sleep Sarah."

'I'll put him to sleep! Permanently! Not yet Sally!'

"Hey, there's an exit coming up on the right," said the younger agent.

"I see it. Let's give that one a try. We're a long way from the next small town."

The fruits on the slot machine were slowly beginning to blur. At ten minutes past the hour Sinzar was still staring at his empty glass. He just couldn't remember if the cocktail waitress had forgotten to bring him his next drink or if he'd already finished drinking it. As always, no one had bothered him when he wore his purple flat-top hat. Fishing around in his pockets he could feel his dwindling collection of coins. He needed to make his way out of the casino, find a hotel, and be on a bus in the morning. It didn't take long to locate his waitress on the other side of the room. He held his hand high up in the air until he finally caught her attention and waved her over.

"Where's my drink? You're almost fifteen minutes late."

"No Mister Shiner, you've already finished your drink."

"Are you sure?"

"Yes, I'm positive. The receipt will have the exact time I ordered it printed on your tab."

"How do I know you didn't drink it or sell it to someone else?"

"There are at least seven cameras continuously recording this area. I'm sure somebody from security or the manager can review a tape if you want to make an issue about it Mr. Shiner."

"Why do you keep calling me Mr. Shiner?"

"Well—because your hat is similar to a purple Shiner's hat." Sinzar brushed his forehead with his hand and realised he'd completely forgot about his new purple hat.

"How much do I owe you?"

"You were paid up until six o'clock and I've been running a tab since then. You owe me sixty-five dollars and thirty-five cents."

"Are you kidding me? That's preposterous! Is that for only one single drink?"

"No, Mr. Shiner, that's for seven drinks. It's two in the morning."

"Oh, yes, so it is." Sinzar pulled out his wallet and made a point of showing her the thick bulge of bills inside.

"Here you are Missy, take this hundred and bring me three more drinks."

"I'm sorry, I can't do that. We had a deal, remember? I was only allowed to bring you one drink every hour. You made me promise."

"Are you sure? Did I really say that?" asked Sinzar, perplexed with his seemingly vacated mind.

"I'm positive."

"Okay, well if that's the case, then I want you to keep the change, and take these coins as well."

"Thank you Mr. Shiner. Will you be riding in the parade tomorrow?"

"Parade—why are you asking me about parades?"

"Well, maybe I'll see you tomorrow. Take care Mr. Shiner. I have to get back to work now. Bye."

"Bye."

Kyle and Jen could hear the Black Hawk reducing power and initiating the approach to the Central Fusion Research Complex 8. They were still operating in dark mode and looking ahead they could see the yellow helipad lights illuminating from the far end of the huge facility. The machine closed in on the pad with expert precision and the pilot landed smoothly in the center of the painted circle.

"This is your stop Kyle," said the pilot after rolling the throttle down to flight idle.

"Are we shutting down?" asked Kyle.

"No, just a quick drop off and pilot change. One of the crew will escort you off."

"Thanks, great flight," said Kyle.

He took off his helmet and moved over to Jen. "Bye Jen, check your e-mail. I'll talk to you soon," said Kyle as loud as he could.

"I will, see you soon," Jen shouted in his ear while they shook hands.

One of the crew members unloaded Kyle's bags and escorted him over to the two men waiting beside the helipad. Jen watched as the co-pilot jumped out from the front and walked around to the side door.

"Come on up front Jen, you can fly us back to the training base."

For some reason she was caught completely off guard. It didn't even cross her mind that they might offer her a chance to fly this Black Hawk.

"Thanks, sure, wow! I'd love to try this machine."

"Do we have any detailed maps of this area?" asked the older agent.

"No I don't think so, nothing showing the secondary roads. Did you see the sign we just passed?"

"Do you mean the sign about the campground?"

"Yes, there's a public campground about five miles from here. Let's take a look when we get there."

"Okay, it won't hurt to check it out. I'm not sure how to get back out on the highway if we keep driving this way we might have to backtrack to the last exit," said the older agent.

"When are we stopping at the ladies' room?"

"We're still looking for one of those, but we haven't seen any yet."

"When am I going to get my medications?"

"I'll look for them the next time we stop."

"That's good, I need them soon because I can feel them coming."

"What are you talking about? I don't see anything coming."

"I told you J.J., I don't want to talk about it."

"We'll good, just keep quiet then."

"I'm hungry J.J., What are you making for dinner?"

"I'm making potato chips for the main course and if you keep quiet, maybe I'll give you a bag of chips for dessert."

"Okay, we'll try our best."

"Does your imaginary friend like eating potato chips too?" said J.J. as he burst out laughing.

"I don't have any imaginary friends J.J. What's it like having only imaginary friends J.J.?"

"I have lots of different friends, don't you worry about that."

"That's not what I was told. I heard you didn't have a single friend in the world, and even a starving dog wouldn't be your friend if you had ten steaks on a barbecue."

"And just who told you that?"

"That's a secret and I promised not to tell."

"Did you tell her that?" screamed J.J. at his partner.

"No, I didn't say anything about that at all. She's making it up."

Sarah burst out in another fit of uncontrolled hysterical laughter.

"Keep quiet or you won't be getting any more chips."

"You can't just starve people because they laugh at you. What's the matter with you J.J.?"

"Nothing is the matter with me, just be quiet and I'll give you another bag of chips. Okay?"

"Okay J.J."

'He'll be quiet when he stops breathing! Right Sarah! Right Sally!'

Sinzar stumbled straight into the front doorman as he was leaving the casino.

"Hey there mister, watch where you're walking." Sinzar had to fight off the urge to break the doorman's nose with his forehead.

"Find me a taxi."

"Sure. Can you see those five taxis lined up beside the curb at the bottom of the stairs? Ask the driver at the front of the line."

Sinzar gripped the handrail firmly and slowly made his way down the several flights of concrete stairs and fell into the back seat of the first taxi.

"Find me a hotel close to the bus station."

"Do you have a reservation?"

"No, but I'm with the Shiners."

"Do they have a reservation?"

"How should I know? Forget about the reservation—just find something close to the bus station."

"I'll see what I can find. It's always harder to find a room this late at night."

The driver glanced back and noticed Sinzar, slouched against the door and trying to stay awake.

"Just find me a room as soon as you can."

"Okay, I'll see what I can find. Do you care about the cost?"

"No, the price doesn't matter. Just find me a room."

"If money doesn't matter, I'll find something for you, we're in Las Vegas."

"Slow down, that campground is coming up on the right."

"Are we going camping?"

"Just ignore you-know-who and take the turnoff up ahead," said the younger agent.

"It's not polite to ignore you-know-who J.J."

"Some of these places are only open during the summer months. I can see a gate blocking the road just up ahead."

"Stop by the gate. I want to read the information board and take a quick walk around."

"Well, what did you find out?" asked the older agent as his partner returned to the van.

"This place is only open from May to September and the gate is locked with a chain and a medium size padlock."

"Perfect, let's break the gate open and stay the night. This place will be deserted this time of year," said the older agent.

"Should I cut the chain or shoot the lock?" asked the younger agent.

"There's a new cut-off wheel on the cordless grinder. Try cutting the chain with that. It's quieter than shooting out the lock."

"Okay, give me a few minutes."

"Mr. Jackson, is J.J. trying to start a fire with all those sparks? Is that thing a giant birthday sparkler?"

"No Sarah, he's just opening the gate with a grinder so we can start camping. It looks like a private camp ground, for members only."

"That sounds really exciting."

'Something's wrong Sally! Wrong! Wrong! Wrong!'

"You're right, that didn't take long at all to cut through that chain. Drive forward and I'll close the gate behind you."

The younger agent closed the gate and carefully repositioned the lock and chain on the gate latch.

"Hop in, let's go and find a campsite. They might even have some firewood around this place if we're lucky."

"Are we going to have a real fire J.J.?"

"Why do you ask?"

'Liar! Liar! Burn in Fire!'

"Its cold outside and real fires are just so exciting."

"When are you planning to do our check in?" asked the younger agent.

"Let's discuss that later, in private."

"Okay. Sounds like a good idea."

"Most of these sites all look the same, a picnic table and a fire pit. Which one do you want?"

"Keep driving around until we know the whole layout. If we see a pile of firewood we'll find a site close by."

"There looks like a shed or something up ahead."

"It's an outhouse and a wood shed. Let's find a place near here."

"How about this one—number fifty-four?"

"It looks alright, let's pull in and park here." |

"Okay, number fifty four it is."

"What about—?"

"Yes, J.J., what about you-know-who? The girl wearing a straitjacket, tied in the back seat with a bucket hanging from her neck? Is that who you were wondering about J.J.?"

"Lock her up inside the car and let's have a look around."

"Would you like to be locked up all day J.J.?"

"Keep quiet. We'll be back soon and maybe you can go for a walk later, if you behave."

"Can we walk backwards J.J.? I love walking backwards."

"How can you see where you're going?"

"I can't, but I can see where I've been."

"I dreamed you could walk backwards J.J."

"You did?"

"Yes I did. You walked backwards off a cliff and we never saw you again." Sarah burst out laughing as loud as she could while they locked the doors and opened the trunk.

"What do you need from the trunk?" asked the younger agent.

"I need the satellite phone. I'll check in early from here. It seems like we might have finally found ourselves a nice private location."

Sinzar struggled to make sense of his surrounding environment as he gradually regained consciousness. He was lying in dense brush and his scraped hand immediately found the egg sized lump on the back of his head. He knew without checking that he had lost his wallet. Despite his complete lack of memory for the last part of the evening, he did remember one small detail; climbing into cab number eighty eight. That small detail was inexplicably etched in his pickled mind. He could now start planning his return encounter with the driver of taxi number eighty eight. That was a given. He might even book a future vacation to Las Vegas, just for the pure joy of hunting down the man who had robbed him.

He reached down and felt his legs for the spare credit cards taped inside them. He should have known better than to be out drinking on the job. Killing time and drinking on his boat was one thing, but drinking in public always ended in some type of trouble. From what he could tell he was in a public park a couple of miles from the downtown lights, with no idea of the time other than it was obviously still dark.

Clawing around blindly, he found his purple flat-top hat lying nearby in the dirt. He picked it up, brushed it off and repositioned it on his head to cover the growing lump on the back of his head. He knew exactly how to make a lump like that; he'd made many like that himself. In fact, that's just how he'd acquired his latest purple hat with gold tassels; with a boot sock full of coins.

Sinzar adjusted his gait to minimize his stagger as he began walking towards town. He thought he might even have time to hunt down the taxi driver before leaving Vegas; he had always been a man who enjoyed planning his work and planning his own personal revenge wasn't any different.

Professor Akkaim was immediately notified about the call from his agents. The abduction of Sarah D. had seemingly gone off without a hitch. On the off-chance the director of the Meadowlane Children's Sanatorium had bothered to inquire about the safe delivery of Sarah D., the agents would now be well out of the state.

The instructions were passed along concerning the photos he had requested and hopefully they would be sent back soon. From what he could tell, the agents were, so far, managing reasonably well with their new captive. He could appreciate the additional difficulties they might face with his directive not to harm to her, at least for the time being.

Sinzar would soon be appearing in Santa Monica to pick up his instructions. Unfortunately, it was still too early to provide any confirmed abduction targets for Sinzar Bakkir. Standard procedures dictated a one month delay if his package wasn't waiting at the predetermined location in Santa Monica. There was no other choice; Sinzar would arrive to find nothing and know to return to the same location, same date and time, one month later. Alternate targets were generally substituted in these circumstances, but this time Professor Akkaim didn't want him distracted with any additional assignments. He desperately needed a new source of detailed information, and soon. Until then it wasn't even worth repositioning Sinzar until he knew exactly where to send him.

It was rare that Sinzar was held for an additional month, although this wasn't the first time that it had happened. The professor knew he would be disappointed, but also had no doubt Sinzar would find some way of amusing himself with his unexpected time off.

The latest report from Portland clarified the most likely explanation for the small car on the Claytons' estate. With the discovery of the Range Rover in the body shop, it was almost certain that the small car at the estate was a courtesy car provided by Straighter Line while the Claytons' Range Rover was being repaired and repainted.

If that in fact was the case, it could potentially offer a possible way inside the estate in the future. There had been no recent confirmed sightings of Kyle or Miss Lamar and that needed to change soon. The professor needed to be continually aware of their movements and any recent activities.

The older agent had completed his satellite phone call to RA-9 and both agents were finishing their walk through the campground. All the sites were empty and it didn't look like anyone had passed through the entrance gates for some time. The campground had an old outhouse building, a ground water pump, and two partially-covered wood sheds.

They had yet to be restocked for the season, but each shed still contained about a half a cord of split wood from last year.

"Did they mind you checking-in early?"

"What do you mean?"

"I thought we were supposed to phone in when we were halfway home," said the younger agent.

"No, they didn't mention anything about that. They were glad we had her, and also the professor wanted some pictures sent back as soon as possible."

"What kind of pictures?"

"They want pictures of Sarah, pictures of her in a captive hostage situation, pictures that depict a threat or risk of personal harm."

"They said that?"

"Yes."

"*Exactly* like that?"

"Yes."

"Okay. I'll be more than happy to take care of that."

"She can't be hurt. You do remember that, don't you?"

"Of course I do. Maybe I'll just scare her a little for a realistic effect."

"What do you have in mind?" asked the older agent.

"Nothing yet, but I'll think of something. I'm already looking forward to it."

"Don't get too carried away."

"I won't. What's that banging noise?"

"Come on let's go! It's coming from the car!"

Sinzar had walked for what seemed like hours until he'd found his way back to town. He needed to check the bus schedule before he did anything else. Traveling to Santa Monica was now his main priority. He could always catch some sleep on the bus if he had to. He was still trying to get his bearings when he found an open gas station whose attendant provided directions to the bus depot. With a stroke of luck he'd been only been five blocks away at the time and was now almost through the front doors.

It was still dark outside and Sinzar headed directly to the washrooms to get cleaned up. He looked like he'd been run over by a vehicle; unfortunately his efforts at controlled drinking had certainly failed his expectations last night. He washed up as best he could and kicked open an empty stall door then sat down and retrieved a credit card and an identification pack. He'd seen a bank machine in the main terminal and walked over and withdrew the daily cash limit before approaching the glass ticket wicket.

"When is the next bus leaving for Santa Monica and how much is a one way ticket?"

"Bus number 1160 is leaving in exactly one hour from now and with taxes it's $183.40."

"Give me one ticket," he said as he passed over two hundred dollars.

"Here you are, a single one way ticket to Santa Monica departing from gate 16. Kindly arrive ten minutes prior to the departure time."

"Okay." Sinzar put the change in his pocket and walked over and sat down on a counter stool in the cafe.

"Would you like a coffee and a menu Mr. Shiner?"

"Sure. Would you have anything for a headache hiding behind that counter?"

"I'll see if I can find something for you."

"Thanks, I really need something this morning."

"Yes, I can see that." The waitress dropped off a coffee and placed four pills on the counter.

"Is that enough for you Mr. Shiner?"

"That's just right. Thanks."

"She's got that bucket stuck on her head and she's banging the window again."

"Help—help! Help! Help! Help me! They're beating me again! Help me!"

"Stop that, no one is beating you. You're hitting the windows with your head when you're thrashing about, that's all."

"I am? It got so dark, and I thought J.J. was beating me again."

"Relax—nobody can hear your cries."

'You won't hear your own cries J.J. We promise! Quiet Sally! Keep Quiet!'

"I need to go to the ladies room."

"Just a minute, we'll be back in a few minutes."

"Hurry up!"

"What are we going to do about this situation?" asked the older agent.

"We can't just let her use the outhouse on her own. Let's rig up a high line or something so she can walk around in the forest."

"What do you mean?" asked the older agent.

"We can rig a tight line between two trees with a choker hanging off that line. Tie her up and attach the other end of the choker to her jacket handles so she can walk back and forth."

"Okay, sure that's not a bad idea. Do we have a choker?" asked the older agent.

"Yes, I saw a few wire chokers in the auto spares box. We can double them up to increase the length."

"What about the pictures?" asked the older agent.

"I'm working on an idea for that. Let's just get her secured for now."

"Okay. I'll get the rope and some chokers," said the older agent.

"Try to find some large tie wraps as well. It looks like we're going to have to untie her hands for a while, as far as I can tell. I'll go and look for the best location to rig her up."

"Okay. I won't be long," said the older agent.

"Hello out there! I need to go to the ladies' room. Can anybody hear me out there? How many times do I have to tell you?" yelled Sarah.

"Just wait a minute. We'll let you out in a few minutes," yelled J.J.

"What are we going to do about her medications?"

"Let's just give her some different pills. I'll just tell her that they're her pills. She'll never know," said J.J.

"The power of placebos is well known. You know, that might just work. What do we have that we could give her?" asked the older agent.

"There might be something in the first aid box, other than that we only have the caffeine pills in the glove compartment."

"I don't know if that's such a good idea. Maybe just a couple wouldn't hurt," said the older agent.

"Okay then, let's use these two trees over here for the high line. It's fairly open and she should be able to walk back and forth without that much trouble."

"I see you brought your appetite Mr. Shiner. Are you coming or going?"

"I'm going."

"We'll at least you were smart enough to keep some money for your return trip. Some people are so stupid they blow all their money then wake up broke in some skid row park in Vegas. Can you believe it?"

Sinzar could feel his temper building and his blood pressure rising.

"Just give me my bill Madame."

"Madame—did you just call me a Madame? What exactly is it you think I do here Mister Shiner?"

"I'm sorry. Here, keep the change."

Sinzar slapped a hundred dollar bill hard on the counter and got up and walked away.

"Thanks! Don't fall off your tiny little tricycle."

He had a very low tolerance for any escalating verbal arguments and knew it was sometimes better to just get up and walk away before he completely lost his temper.

Sarah could feel the onset of the numbers forming in her mind. It was a condition that had largely been kept under control by her medications, but its repeated manifestation had caused numerous problems in the past. Certain numbers were starting to float into her subconscious thoughts.

For Sarah, they were as clear as day, drifting by in ever changing sizes and colors and shapes. Unstoppable, always in motion, no matter how hard she tried it was impossible to visualize them as a stationary number. Each number had its own distinct personality and associated meanings, ranging from subtle pleasant notions to the most compelling directives that she was often powerless to control.

"Hello! It's time for my medications and I have to go to the Ladies' room right away. Can you hear me out there?"

"Okay okay—we're coming. We have to secure some lines to your coat handles before we can untie your jacket."

"J.J., give me a hand back here," asked the older agent.

"I'm attaching some carabineers on here. I might be able to use them later."

"Just hang on and we'll get you out soon."

"Are we going camping?"

"Yes, we might camp here for a while. I don't know yet. Okay, J.J. Just unclip those lines on the handles and start pulling her out the passenger side."

'Closer Punk! Not yet Sally! Not Yet!'

"What's in her bag?" asked the younger agent.

"Personal lady's things, just take it easy. I'm coming. Where are you taking me?"

"Just over here a little farther. I'm going to clip you to this high line and then you can use the ladies' room."

"I don't see a ladies' room around here."

"It's a nature room. It's what the jungle ladies use when they're camping. I left you a roll of paper over by the tree."

"There, you can walk back and forth between these two trees for now."

"Okay then, you'll have to untie me and you're not allowed to look."

"I don't think we should untie her. Do you?" asked the younger agent.

"We have to, one arm anyway. I don't think she can undo the other straps behind her back."

"I still don't like it. Let's tie wrap her elbow to the lowest handle on the coat first. I think that should work."

"Okay Sarah, we are going to untie one arm while you use the ladies' room and we promise not to look," said the younger agent.

"It's almost time for my pills. I can feel it."

"We're getting those ready for you right now."

"That's a good idea. I need them right away. I can feel it. Remember, don't look."

"Let's get some wood over here and make a fire," said the older agent. "I don't want her unattended unless she's really secure."

"Okay, we'll wait then."

"Yes, I think that's best. Sarah, I'm going to give you ten minutes and after that you're getting strapped back in your jacket."

"What about the fire?"

"As soon as you're finished, we'll light a fire, okay?"

"Okay J.J."

'Liar! Liar! Burn in Fire!'

"Here, give me a hand for a few minutes."

"What do you want to do?" asked the older agent.

"I want to get another rope tied off tight between these two trees high above our camp site."

"What's that for?"

"I'll show you later, just climb up that tree. I'll throw the rope across and you can secure it around the trunk."

Within ten minutes they had a rope rigged tightly between the trees about twenty five feet above the campsite.

"Throw this climbing rope over the high line and we'll rig her up with that. Hey Sarah, ready or not, here we come."

"I'm ready to go. Did you bring my pills?"

"We've got them ready over at the car. Stand still while we strap up your sleeve behind your back."

"What about the chokers?" asked the older agent.

"Leave them attached to the coat handles, we'll rig her up with those back at the campsite."

"Have you got her? Come along Sarah, we'll find your pills and something for us to eat."

"Do we have more potato chips?"

"Yes. I'll refill your bucket for you later."

"Thank you J.J. Are you still going to make a fire?"

"Yes. Would you like that Sarah?"

"Yes, I love fire."

'Liar! Liar! Burn in Fire!'

"Rig her chokers up to the end of that line hanging over the high line. I'll secure the free end."

"Okay, Sarah, this is just like the other rope, you can walk back and forth a little between these trees for now. If you start behaving badly I'll tie you to a tree trunk and you won't be able to go anywhere."

"Do I get to take my pills now?"

"Sure, just a minute, we'll be right back."

"What are we going to give her?" asked the younger agent.

"Give her a couple of caffeine pills—it's all we have right now."

"Okay Sarah, can you tilt your head back, open your mouth and close your eyes."

"Like this?"

"Perfect, I'm just going to drop these two pills in your mouth. Now, can you swallow them?"

"Yes. Like this?" said Sarah as she gulped them down.

"Yes, that was perfect."

"Where are the rest of my pills?" asked Sarah, looking confused.

"How many do you usually get?"

"Eight. I always get at least eight, sometimes more."

"Okay, let's just do the same thing, three more times."

"Then can you fill my bucket?"

"Sure, I'll find something for you after that." He double checked her rigging and walked back over to the car.

"How did that go?" asked the older agent.

"Fine—I had to give her a few extra pills because she said she always takes eight."

"Well she won't be getting any sleep tonight. Let's bring some wood over and get a fire ready to start. Is she secure?"

"You bet—the straitjacket's back on and she can't move far with that arrangement."

"Why did you bother with putting up such a high line?"

"You'll see soon enough," said the younger agent.

Jen had finally settled into her new private accommodations at the training camp. Getting a chance to fly a Black Hawk on her first night had been incredible. The recent flights with James had prepared her for this flight even though it was a larger and much more powerful helicopter. The crew made her feel like a part of the team from the moment she lifted off to the time they reached the training base. She had managed to bring the machine in for a complete landing without ever having to relinquish control back to the captain.

They had given her an informal night time tour of the camp and she had helped herself to a few snacks before being issued a comfortable room for her stay. Jen unpacked her bags and put her few clothes away in the dresser drawers for a change. The camp had Internet and it didn't take her long to set up her new laptop. Kyle had yet to check in, but already she could see a new development on his diagnostic GhostNet program. A flashing alert had indicated that Europe had just been eliminated as a possible source continent. Jen knew that Kyle would know about the latest development as soon as he started his own laptop. Jen signed off and got ready for her first night's sleep in the new camp.

"We were lucky to find this dry wood here. How much do you think we'll need?" asked the older agent.

"Let's bring a few more armloads over there anyway," said the younger agent as they both stacked split-wood on their left arms.

"What about the pictures? We should get them done as soon as possible. I know there's a good digital camera in the trunk of the car," said the older agent.

"Okay, why don't you go and look for that while I get the fire ready," said the younger agent as they walked back to the campsite.

"I'm hungry J.J., you promised to bring me more chips."

"You just wait where you are for now. Can't you see I'm busy? Hey! What's the length of those blue climbing ropes in the trunk?" asked the younger agent.

"I think most of them are one-hundred foot lengths."

"Perfect, that should work fine. Can you bring one over here by the fire pit?" asked the younger agent.

"Sure, give me a minute."

"It should be really easy starting a fire with this wood," said the younger agent as he admired his unlit fire.

"Here's the climbing rope you wanted," said the older agent as he walked up and dropped it on the ground.

It took several tries with a small log tied to the end of rope until the younger agent managed to toss one end of the rope over the high line above the campsite.

"Hold on to the free end for a minute," said the younger agent to is partner.

"Hey Sarah, I just need to rearrange these lines on your coat. He wrapped the chokers through all six suitcase handles on the back of her thick canvas jacket. We're going to bring you over a little closer to the campsite."

"Can I please sit close to the fire?"

"I think we can arrange that," said the younger agent.

Once he brought her over he tied the free end of the line to the back bumper.

"What are you doing to me J.J.?"

"Just be quiet," demanded the younger agent.

"Help—help! Help!" screamed Sarah as loud as she could.

"Scream all you want, nobody can hear you. I just want you to have a really good view of a bonfire."

"Help—what are you doing? Help me!"

The younger agent pulled out a roll of duct tape, attached a rag to the tape and wrapped it three times around her mouth to keep her quiet.

'This is wrong Sally! Wrong! Wrong! Wrong!'

He started up the Cadillac and drove it slowly forward as the line tightened and began to hoist Sarah straight up in the air. She was suspended almost vertically in her canvas straitjacket, high above the unlit bonfire. Unable to speak, she had no control of the numbers flooding into her terrified runaway thoughts.

She was scared, really scared and knew that not even Sally could help her until she got out of the bag. She had to let her out. There wasn't any other way. J.J. had to go, for good.

"What about the bucket? Should we take it off?" asked the older agent.

"No, leave it hanging there for now. Did you find the digital camera?"

"Yes I've got it here in my pocket. Are you going to take those pictures?"

"Sure, pass me the camera," said the younger agent.

"Now what are you doing?" said the older agent as he tossed him the camera.

"Back the car up a little and I'll tell you when to stop. I want her hanging right above the fire."

"I hope you're not planning to light it," said the older agent.

"Of course I'm planning to light it. Didn't I tell you? We're having a giant pot roast for dinner," yelled the younger agent as he winked at his partner.

Sarah was flailing around and kicking her legs frantically as the younger agent tugged her foot and started her turning in a slow awkward spin.

The younger agent pulled his partner aside and whispered in his ear.

"I've changed my mind, I'll light the fire and you start driving forward, very slowly. I'll tell you when to stop. I need some good close-ups that really show the fear on her face."

"Okay, watch the fire, the wood's very dry."

"You don't have to worry about that, she'll be okay up in the air. Hurry up, start driving forward. Remember, slowly."

"Say goodbye to the world Sarah. Say goodbye Sarah."

'Make him pay Sally! Don't worry Sarah! Roses are Red! J.J.'s Dead!'

The younger agent had taken almost twenty excellent photos, but when he lowered the camera he could see thick grey smoke starting to billow out from Sarah's canvas coat.

"Quick!" he yelled as loud as he could.

"Quick what?" asked the older agent.

"Pull the car forward as far as you can then bring me the fire extinguisher."

The older agent slammed the car in gear and quickly drove it forward.

Only her feet had been visible in the rear view mirror and they shot straight up when he pulled forward. Just at that moment her canvas coat burst into flames.

"Back up the car! Now! Hurry! Fast as you can!" screamed the younger agent to his partner.

He quickly kicked away at the burning bonfire while his partner rushed to move the car. When the car shot backwards Sarah started free falling in a ball of flames and stopped just above the scattered bonfire bouncing like a dead man cinched in a hangman's noose.

The younger agent pushed her hard to start her swinging back and forth as he sprinted to the car and grabbed the fire extinguisher. He pulled the safety pin and pointed the nozzle directly at her before squeezing the handles together. One solid shot extinguished most of the flames and he pulled her foot hard to spin her around and blasted her again with the fire extinguisher.

The younger agent, his own hands now singed, worked feverishly trying to smother the back of the burning jacket. As he snuffed out the last of the glowing embers still burning in her leather straps he called his partner over to help. He reached up and carefully removed the remaining duct tape and lifted the bucket handle over her head.

"Go and fill this with water," demanded the younger agent as he passed it over with his outstretched arm.

Her face and everything else was covered in white retardant and he could see her eyebrows were singed as well. He knew it was lucky she was almost bald or it could have been much worse. His partner returned in less than five minutes with a bucket of cold water.

"Thanks—pass me the water," said the younger agent when his partner returned.

He took the bucket and poured half of it on Sarah's head and used the rest on her hands and the burnt areas of her heavy coat.

"I knew that wasn't a good idea. I just don't know why I let you try it."

"Relax Old Man, the wind must have thrown some embers a little higher than I expected. That's all. I'm sure we got some great pictures."

"J.J. tried to kill me. He tried to burn me alive. Please, don't leave me alone with J.J. I'm begging you, please."

"Sorry Sarah—that was just a little accident."

"Oh, you mean a little roast you-know-who alive accident J.J.?"

'Tick Tock! Watch the clock! When you sleep, your heart will stop! Right Sally!'

"Let's untie the rope from the bumper and secure the free end to that cedar tree over there. She'll be able to move around a little, but I can't see her getting into any trouble while she's wearing that straitjacket. Here Sarah, you can sit on this stump and I'll find you a blanket to dry off."

"Thank you Mr. Jackson, you're so kind. I thought J.J. was going to roast me alive on a bonfire."

"I was and if you don't behave yourself you know that's exactly what I'll be doing."

"I'll be good J.J. I don't want to be a giant pot roast. Have you roasted other people alive?"

"Sure, plenty of times."

'Liar Liar! Burn in Fire! Burn! Burn! Burn!'

"Okay, I'm going to send all of these pictures on the satellite up-link. Can you get the fire going while I'm doing that? And then we'll find something to eat."

"Sure, maybe we can get some sleep as well."

Sarah sat down close to the fire and watched with amazement as they placed the burnt logs back in place and soon had a raging fire going again. The older agent filled her bucket with chips and hung it over her head. Instantly she was pressing her head deep in the bucket and eating them like a crazed, starving animal.

'Eat for me! Eat for you! If you're not here! I'll eat for two! Right Sally!'

"Ticket please, Mr. Shiner. Are you not bringing any luggage with you today?"

"Do you see any luggage Mr. Bus Driver?"

"I was just checking. Please don't take any offence. You know sometimes people forget their luggage right here in the station."

"Okay, no luggage. I travel light. How long is the trip Mr. Bus Driver?"

"With stopovers, it's about fourteen hours."

"I need to get off in Santa Monica."

"You're in luck, that's my last stop. I'll make sure you get off there as well."

"Thanks. I might be asleep."

"No problem. Enjoy the trip Mr. Shiner."

Professor Akkaim was immediately informed once the first images of Sarah began arriving. The duct tape covered a portion of her face, but her expression of total terror was unmistakable. For once he was mildly impressed with the work of these two agents. He had a good selection of photos to choose from and these were exactly the type of images he had hoped for. Even the timing was perfect.

He needed to work out the exact details of a notification plan and it had to be implemented without delay. This could give him the advantage he and the whole RA-9 operation desperately required. He decided to begin drafting the notification personally as it was much too important to leave to any junior assistants. It was imperative his instructions were sent out the moment he finished his work.

Sarah had never felt so awake. For some reason her medications weren't working properly.

She couldn't escape the smell of her charred canvas straitjacket. In many ways the long sleeves and boots had saved her hands and feet from the hot flames. She could already feel the charred leather straps of the back of her jacket were beginning to relax their grip. The numbers were now dancing around her mind like the embers flying from the fire. They were starting to form shapes—there was no doubt about it. The numbers were coming.

"Sarah, move back from the fire. You're sitting to close," yelled the younger agent.

The closer she sat to the flames, the more intense the numbers became. She couldn't shut them out if she tried.

"Oh okay. J.J., but I can't move the stump without my arms."

"Here use this one," said the younger agent as he rolled up another round and stood it up a little farther back from the fire. Sarah managed to rise to her feet and move over to the new stump.

"I'm thirsty J.J."

"Keep quiet and maybe I'll find some water for your bucket."

Three times Sarah had glanced at J.J. and each and every time the number eight drifted by. Number eight was one of the truly bad ones, devoid of morals, completely overpowering and probably the worst number of all. Sarah knew it was only a matter of time until it happened again.

"I don't know about you, but I'm going to find a snack and have a quick sleep in the car," said the older agent.

"Go ahead. I'll keep the fire going and watch you-know-who for a while."

Sarah carefully reached out with her leg and pulled a burnt log closer to her stump.

"I'm tired. I need a rest and I'm going to lie down."

"Go ahead! Just don't get to close to the fire."

"Don't worry about me J.J."

"Don't worry, I won't," he said with a sneer and a grin.

Sarah slowly inched the log closer and closer to where she was sitting. She then lay down beside the stump, making sure to press the leather straps firmly against the glowing embers of the smouldering log.

'The Roses are Red and the Violets are Blue! The Dead get Red and the Dead turn Blue! Right Sally! Just like last time!'

Chapter 19

Lisa flew through the kitchen and caught the phone on the fifth ring. "Hello."

"Is this the Clayton residence?"

"Yes it is, how can I help you?"

"Good Morning. I'm calling from Straighter Line Auto Body. I wanted to let you know that your Range Rover is finished and we're ready to deliver it."

"Oh, that's great."

"Would this morning be a convenient time for us to return your vehicle?"

"Sure, I'll be here all day."

"Excellent, will our courtesy car be available for a pick up as well?"

Lisa glanced out the window and saw the small car was still parked out front. "Yes, it should be here all day."

Lisa hadn't talked to James this morning but she'd definitely heard the helicopter taking off at dawn. He'd mentioned the possibility of doing some relief work at a different hospital and it wasn't at all unusual for James to be commuting with his helicopter.

"Excellent, thanks for the information. We should be dropping off your vehicle sometime this morning. Bye for now."

"Thank you. Please make sure your driver calls the house from the front entrance intercom for security instructions."

"Sure, I'll pass that message along before we dispatch him."

"Thanks for notifying us first. Bye."

"You're welcome. At Straighter Line Auto Body we always like to call our clients before we return their cars. Bye for now."

As promised the bus driver had woken Sinzar at the bus depot in Santa Monica. He hadn't been able to sleep during most of the trip but he'd obviously nodded off somewhere along the way. After checking the time he eventually managed to hail a cab from outside the bus depot.

"Good day Sir! Are you going downtown to the Shiner's Hall?"

"No Thanks, maybe later. Take me to the Super Six-Pack Motel on Sixth Street. Drop me off a couple of blocks before we get there. A little walking will do me some good"

"Sure. No problem, we should be there in about twenty minutes. Is this your first time in Santa Monica?"

"Look! I know how to get to the Super Six-Pack from here so don't even think about driving me all over town."

"I wouldn't dream of taking advantage of someone like that, especially someone as honest as a Shiner. So you're just here visiting then?"

"Yes, I'm meeting some of my brothers later on."

"Well at least you'll have some nice weather for the next few days."

"Good, I hope so. Pull over at that convenience store up ahead. I need to pick up a few things."

"Sure, I'll wait for you out front."

"Don't even think about leaving," he threatened.

Sinzar withdrew some extra cash from the bank machine and bought a toothbrush, a package of disposable razors and a few other items to take with him to the motel. He was already looking forward to having his own room and getting cleaned up after his little misadventure in Vegas.

"Thanks, let's get going," said Sinzar to the driver as he climbed back in the rear seat of the cab.

"Sure, right away."

The gentle rain and warmth from the flames had lulled the younger agent to sleep as he sat beside the fire. He was dreaming about an exotic tropical rain forest when a shivering chill suddenly awoke him. The fire was nearly out and the rain had been soaking through his clothes while he slept. For one startling instant he thought Sarah might have actually escaped her tethered prison. As his eyes adjusted to the darkness he could see she was still lying on the ground, her burnt clothes blending right in with the dirt surrounding the fire pit.

She had become so dirty with soot, mud and ash that only the whites of her eyes were visible. He didn't remember her being quite so black earlier on, but now she looked like an alien creature, glaring straight at him from the ground.

He stood up and piled some new wood on the burned-out logs. With these conditions he gave it a fifty-fifty chance of relighting on its own. With the steady drizzle tonight, he might have to throw some gas on the fire if he really wanted to get it going again. Five minutes later the wood pile was starting to smoke with increasing intensity and he walked over to the parked Cadillac. He opened the back door and got in, somewhat surprised that his partner didn't even flinch when he slammed the rear door.

Lisa answered the intercom from the main entrance gate and directed the driver to proceed to the safe parking area. The Beaucerons were working somewhere on the property but she hadn't seen them for at least a couple of hours. A few minutes later she watched as the driver parked the Range Rover inside the marked safety area. She was relieved to see it was the same young man who had picked up the vehicle the first time.

"Hello, Mrs. Clayton. I'd like to thank you for selecting Straighter Line Auto Body for all your vehicle requirements. Would you like to inspect the work we've just completed on your vehicle?"

"Oh, I'm not Mrs. Clayton, and I don't think that will be necessary. I'm sure if there's any problems Doctor Clayton will contact you immediately."

"That's fair enough. Here are the keys for the Range Rover. I'll need to ask you to sign this release form. It just acknowledges that you've received the vehicle in good condition."

"Sure, that's fine. I can do that, there you are. That should do it."

"Thank you, here's a copy for your records. Are the keys inside the courtesy car?"

"No, just a moment and I'll find them for you."

Lisa stepped inside and quickly found the keys for the car. "There you are. Thanks for everything. Remember to stay inside the vehicle at all times when you're leaving."

"Don't worry about that. I was delayed picking up the flowers and now I'm late for my next delivery."

"What flowers? Who are the flowers for?"

"I have no idea. I was just told to pick up a box from the florist and leave the box in the back of the Range Rover."

"Who paid for them?" asked Lisa.

"Like I said, I have no idea. They're gift wrapped in a flower box and everything was prepaid. Honestly, I don't even think I was supposed to mention it. Please don't tell anyone that I told you."

"I won't tell a soul, I promise. Bye now."

"Bye, and thanks for keeping that quiet."

Lisa watched as the young driver started the car and drove carefully down the driveway. The weather was warm and dry and while she watched him drive away she noticed Alexia slowly inching her wheelchair down the winding gravel path towards the parked Range Rover. Lisa knew that James had just finished warning the nurses, in no uncertain terms, to never leave Alexia unattended. She walked over to the Range Rover and called the nurses on the mobile phone. Within two minutes she could see them running down the path to intercept Alexia and then watched as both nurses pushed her back up the trail.

Sinzar tipped the driver generously before getting out of the taxi. Walking two extra blocks hadn't really been necessary but Sinzar knew that even a little exercise and fresh air generally made him feel better.

"Room 236—turn right at the top of the stairs. I hope you enjoy your stay," were the last well practiced words he heard from the elderly woman working the front desk.

After entering his room and locking the door he dropped his plastic bag on the desk and collapsed on the bed. It seemed like ages since the last time he'd actually laid down on a proper bed.

He picked up the remote control and flipped through all the available TV channels. As he surveyed the room he realized he was in a divided room; his least favourite in some ways, and yet his favourite in others. For the moment he didn't have any unknown neighbours living behind the hollow shared door, yet he was always consumed by the irresistible temptation to pay some sleeping strangers a surprise visit during the middle of the night. Just the thrill of walking inside their room as they slept gave him such an intense adrenaline rush he felt like a junkie getting his fix.

He rolled over and set the radio alarm clock for two hours from now. His new instructions were due to arrive in less than three hours, and a couple of extra hours of sleep might prove invaluable if he had to check out right away.

Lisa hung up the phone and locked the front passenger door of the Range Rover. Nobody really knew why Alexia was so seemingly attached to that vehicle. As she walked around the side she couldn't help but glance in the back, and sure enough a beautiful gift wrapped flower box was lying behind the rear seats. Could they have been for Alexia? How could she have known flowers were being delivered today? Glancing around to check if she was alone, she slipped the key into the rear hatch and opened the back door.

It was a classy long narrow box, professionally wrapped with a festive bow and matching ribbon. As she examined the box she could see a small tangerine envelope tucked underneath the impeccably tied bow and ribbon cross. She carefully slipped it out from underneath the ribbon and read the small dark writing on the unusual envelope.

'For the eyes of Lisa Only' was written on the front of the small sealed envelope. She used the key in her hand as a letter opener and carefully unsealed the thin envelope flap.

A matching card was enclosed and Lisa opened it eagerly with intense curiosity.

My Dearest Lisa,

It's taken years to find you and I wanted to send you a small gift to express my deepest love and appreciation for everything you've ever done to help me. I hope I can count on more of your assistance and devotion the next time you hear from me.

With Love, your abandoned, discarded daughter, Sarah.

Lisa tilted her head back in a state of shock. How could Sarah have possibly found her after all these years? She was like the needle in a haystack on the other side of the country. It seemed completely impossible; it just had to be a mistake, a remarkable coincidence. There just wasn't another explanation. Lisa reached down, picked up the long flower box and closed the rear hatch of the truck.

It was rare to see such a fine flower box used at all these days. She returned to the house and found her favourite ornate glass vase and placed it beside the sink. If it was a mistake it certainly wasn't any reason she shouldn't enjoy the beauty of the flowers. Lisa carefully lifted the lid off the box and watched helplessly as it suddenly dropped from her paralyzed fingertips to the floor. The smell hit her first; musty, decaying, dead. There must have been close to a dozen roses. A dark variety, almost a blood red in colour, and every single one of them obviously long dead. It was as if they'd been stolen from a cold forgotten headstone in a remote neglected graveyard. She couldn't even bear to touch them, let alone lift them from the box.

Lisa quickly picked up the lid, put it on the box and carried everything out to the backyard fire pit. Minutes later she managed to light the box with her lighter and watched in an uneasy fear as the fire gradually flared up and consumed the box. Nobody needed to see or know anything about this disturbing gift. Lisa could only pray this was just a bad dream.

The instant J.J. slammed the rear door of the Cadillac Sarah resumed her frantic struggle in the muddy dirt next to the fire. There wasn't any question; she was gaining ground in her battle to escape the torturous confinement of her bulky straitjacket. The burnt leather straps were finally starting to relax their grip. The mud and dirt she had smeared on her face provided all the cover she needed, and the overdose of caffeine just fuelled her increasing desperation. J.J. had almost roasted her alive—and deep down she knew Sally couldn't wait to pay him back, once and for all.

With a sudden adrenalin-fired spasm, she knew one of the many leather straps had just snapped. It didn't give much overall, yet there's a distinctive noise when a leather strap breaks, and she had definitely just heard it. The numbers were rampant now, flowing constantly through her thoughts and she felt herself getting closer and closer to the breaking point. Past that point everything was out of her control and she'd likely become a totally submissive servant to the bizarre and unpredictable thoughts flashing through her deranged mind.

Sinzar's hand pounded down repeatedly on top of the annoying noise blaring from the clock radio. He was positive that he'd only just closed his eyes and obviously he must have set the alarm incorrectly. After finally managing to silence or break the alarm he checked the time with his watch. Incredibly, there wasn't any mistake; he had definitely been sleeping. It wouldn't be long now, he couldn't help trying to predict where his new assignment would take him and the misfortunes and upheavals he was about to inflict on his new abduction targets.

He had just enough time for a shave and shower before his instructions would be dropped off. Sinzar turned up the volume on the TV before he started getting ready. As he washed his face he realized just how swollen the back of his head was. His night of uncontrolled drinking in Vegas could have very easily cost him his life. Instantly he began thinking about his next visit to Vegas and his future surprise reunion with a certain unsuspecting taxi driver.

"Hey! Wake up! Where is she? Where's Sarah?" yelled the older agent after he awoke suddenly without reason.

"Don't worry Old Man, everything is under control. She's over there by the fire."

"What fire?" said the older agent as he tried to look through the rain soaked window into the surrounding darkness.

The younger agent wiped the condensation off the cold wet glass. "How long were we sleeping?"

"I'm not sure, maybe a couple of hours," said the older agent as he started the car and turned on the heater.

"I'll go and make sure everything is alright with you-know-who. I don't want you starting to get all paranoid."

"I'm not getting all paranoid I just want to know where she is. That's all."

"Okay fine! I'll be right back," said the younger agent.

"You might want to bring a flashlight. Here, take this one."

"Thanks! I was just thinking the same thing," he lied.

Sinzar felt like fifty bucks after getting all cleaned up. He knew this routine all too well. With the layout of this hotel his instructions should be safely in place within the next few minutes. Although it would happen on the floor above him, he never wanted to know the identity of the person delivering his package, and he certainly didn't want his identity discovered by anyone.

Sinzar watched the second hand for a few more minutes before picking up his keys, stepping into the hall and closing the door behind him. When he reached the next floor he strolled casually along towards the pop machine at the end of the hall. The setup was always the same; a cold pop machine with an adjacent ice machine.

Looking around carefully for anyone, or anything, out of the ordinary, Sinzar quickly hopped up on the ice machine and felt around on top of the adjacent pop machine for his instructions. In a panic he frantically scoured every square inch of the machine with his hand. He couldn't believe it. There wasn't anything at all. No package.

For some reason he'd been overlooked. He knew it was possible, but highly unlikely that someone actually had a valid reason for failing to deliver his package on time. Under the circumstances he could afford to continue waiting in his room before he started making any alternate plans. If nothing was dropped off soon he'd be expected to return here on exactly the same date and time next month.

Sarah was almost invisible lying in the wet black mud surrounding the fire pit. If he hadn't brought the flashlight with him he could've easily stepped on or tripped right over her.

"Wake up! We're getting ready to leave our little campsite and I need to get you back inside the car. Did you hear me?"

We need to do it and we need to do it soon! Right Sally!

"Hello up there. Is that you J.J.? I didn't hear your footsteps with all this rain coming down."

"Stand up and I'll unhook some of these lines. You can dry off when you get in the car."

"Thank you so much J.J. I think I may have some dry towels with me."

"Yes you do. I saw some in your duffel bag."

"Excuse me? Did you just say—you looked in my bag? You looked in a lady's private bag and rummaged through her strictly personal belongings?"

"Sure, we're in charge here and we'll look anywhere we feel like looking. I saw that stupid doll of yours with the red stained hands."

'Stupid Doll? Wrong! Wrong! Dead wrong! We know different! Right Sally!'

"Well the important thing is I've got some dry towels. Do you have any more chips J.J.?"

"Bring your bucket and I'll fill it after we've got you secured in the back of the car. I think we still have a couple more bags of chips?"

"I certainly won't forget the bucket J.J., it's still around my neck. Are you going to untie these ropes?"

"Yes, just stay still. I'll start working on them now."
"Excellent. It's going to be a real treat to get out of this rain."

"Okay, you're clear of the ropes and I've got you by your coat handles, let's go."

"I'm going, I'm going J.J. Just take it easy. Didn't anyone ever teach you that it's rude to rush a Lady?"

"No, darn it! I must have missed school that day. Keep going, the car is just up ahead."

Lisa's mind was still spinning from the dead flowers. No matter how she looked at things nothing made any sense. After all of these years of hearing nothing whatsoever about her daughter—today a box of dead roses arrives at her home? She was already thinking she'd probably have to tell James. He at least he might have the resources to get to the bottom of this. He was the one who had chosen the body shop. How were they connected? Could James somehow be involved? She just couldn't stop thinking about it. Why? Why this after so many years?

The cell phone was lying beside the fridge and connected to the charger as usual. As she walked by her phone a small flashing light stopped her dead in her tracks. Her inbox display was reading: 'New Text Message'.

Her frayed nerves had taken just about all they could take. Nobody left messages on that phone and she didn't even know the first thing about texting. She picked up the phone and blindly started pressing buttons with her trembling fingers.

Sinzar paced back and forth across the hotel room. Although he knew minimal contact was always the safest option, he felt ignored, taken for granted. As the head of the RA-9 Human Procurement Division, part of him desperately wanted an explanation. He'd invested considerable time and effort in order to live up to his half of the arrangement. He was here, on time, and they weren't. If he'd known this was going to be the end result of all his efforts—he would have still been drinking on his boat in Mexico, or maybe even entertaining himself in Vegas.

Lisa found the menu on her phone and immediately noticed the message in her inbox. After a few frantic clicks on the phone's keypad the new message was displayed.

Message 1: SHE'S UNDER THE SEAT: Caller: UNKNOWN.

Lisa almost dropped the phone. Under the seat—what seat? Who's under the seat? Was this message really intended for her? Could it be wrong number? It had to be. Her mind was spinning—this just didn't make any sense whatsoever. Lisa's mouth and both eyes suddenly flew wide open and she bolted out the door running at full speed towards the Range Rover.

Sinzar settled back on his bed and turned on the television. He flipped through all the available stations at least twice before narrowing down his selection. Sinzar loved watching soap operas when he was alone, but would never dare disclose that secret to anyone.

Under these circumstances there wasn't any standard protocol for exactly how long he was required to wait. They've had an entire month to figure out how to get his procurement instructions to him on time. He should have turned on a dime and left the instant he realized there wasn't anything waiting for him. That would surely teach someone a lesson. The professor would make them pay dearly if their incompetent tardiness had resulted in a one month delay of any RA-9 procurement plans.

Sinzar found a comfortable position on the bed as one of his most endearing soap operas was almost set to begin. He flipped back to the guide channel and tried to decide on which two soaps to watch next. Three in a row, he could wait another ninety minutes before checking for his instructions one last time. Sinzar hopped up and placed the 'Do Not Disturb' sign out on the hallway doorknob, then locked the deadbolt and jumped back on the bed. He secretly couldn't believe his luck with the television schedule, he had some serious catching up to do with all three of these popular soap operas.

Lisa fumbled with the keys until she managed to open the front passenger door. She cautiously reached under the passenger seat and found nothing.

'She's under the seat' rang out in her mind as if someone was shouting at her. Reaching under the driver's seat her hand landed on a large envelope. Lisa pulled it out from under the seat and winced immediately when she saw her name scrawled on the outside. Shaking visibly, she sat down inside the Range Rover and locked the door.

All her instincts told her to prepare for the worst. She held the envelope close to her as she looked around for anyone else nearby, and then tried to summon up enough courage to open it. Using one of her keys she slowly ripped open the top of the large envelope.

The small stack of enlarged photos, were immediately evident. Her blood ran cold as she inched the stack of photos out from the envelope. There wasn't a single doubt in her mind, even after all these years, that the terrified girl sadistically suspended above the licking flames of the bonfire was her daughter, Sarah.

Lisa could feel her tears dripping off her cheeks. What was happening here? After forcing herself to look at every one of these graphic images she found a single sheet of paper at the bottom of the pile.

Dear Lisa, only you and you alone can save your daughter. Will you abandon her again, like the last time? We need your assistance regarding Kyle Clayton's upcoming schedule and accurate information concerning his future whereabouts. In exchange your daughter will be released unharmed. If anyone else is informed of this correspondence you will be personally responsible for your daughter's unfortunate and merciless demise. You can expect further contact soon and you must immediately burn everything you have just received.

This wasn't any honest mistake or case of mistaken identity; this was clearly intended for her and nobody else. It was amazing that despite all the years that had passed by, just looking at these deplorable images Lisa was absolutely positive this was her daughter.

There wasn't any question that the images might have been staged. They were real. Nobody could fake the facial expressions she had just witnessed. Sarah was obviously mortally terrified and fearing for her own life. Lisa's mind was made up; she had to act, and she had to act soon.

Lisa stuffed the photos back in the envelope and concealed them inside her shirt. After locking the Range Rover she walked back out to the fire pit and burned everything she'd just received. The photos and the box of dead flowers were quickly reduced to a pile of dirty ashes. Lisa stirred them up with a poker and walked back towards the house. She felt a strange sense of calm and now knew exactly what needed to be done.

"Have you got her strapped in back there, or do you want some help?"

"I don't need your help Old Man. I've got her seat belt on and when she's dry I'll find some chips and fill her bucket."

"How in the world did she get so dirty that fast?" asked he older agent.

"I don't know, for some crazy reason she just seems to enjoy rolling around in the dirty mud," said the younger agent as he climbed in the front seat.

Sarah could see the outline of the older agent's head and a second outline of the number eight. With increasing skill she continued manipulating her arms as she fought to keep her head perfectly still.

"How do you like the camping trip so far?" asked the younger agent.

Sarah slowly tilted her head back and started to pretend she was falling asleep. Just at that instant she could feel another burnt leather strap give slightly. It wouldn't be long until she could manage to free her arms from the heavy canvas straitjacket. She could feel her travel bag just under her right leg.

'Soon Sally, very, very, soon.'

Sarah tilted her head further back and closed her eyes just enough that she could still see through her eye lashes. She adjusted her position gradually until she could watch the rear view mirror without opening her eyes.

"Well I'm ready to leave. Are you?" asked the older agent.

"Sure, stop up at the gate and I'll open it for us."

"Okay, sounds good. It looks like you-know-who is finally starting to get a little sleep back there. Strange, she's not even hungry anymore."

"Yes, that is strange now that you mention it."

'Not hungry? We're not hungry? Well you're right! We're starving! Right Sally! Starving for revenge!'

Sinzar's mind had been completely preoccupied during the last three soap operas. They acted like a hypnotic drug, luring him completely away from his day-to-day thoughts and the worries and concerns of real life. He was an unseen observer in the private lives of others, which was not unlike certain aspects of some of his own assignments. He picked up the remote and raised the volume on the television.

Time for one final look upstairs and if nothing was waiting for him he was free to go. Sinzar had made up his mind and wasn't planning to wait around any longer. He opened the deadbolt and walked quietly out the door, upstairs and down the hall. Once again he looked around, and then hopped up on the ice machine to check for any new instructions. Still there was nothing there, absolutely nothing.

Normally an unexpected month off would trigger the anticipation of an unknown exotic vacation. This time the pull back to Vegas was just too strong to ignore. He couldn't escape the presence of the swollen lump and the pain coming from the back of his head. Now he'd have some time for planning—time to plan exactly how a certain cab driver, was going to pay for his previous actions. Once his business was concluded he might even stay a little longer just to visit a few extra casinos.

Sinzar got back to the room and gathered up his few possessions. Glancing in the mirror he proudly positioned his purple hat on the top of his head, picked up the thin plastic bag and disappeared down the hall.

Lisa calmly made herself a cup of tea and walked deliberately upstairs to the loft to formulate her plans. She needed to calm down, really calm down. She couldn't afford to raise any suspicions concerning any recent changes in her behaviour. Everything needed to be exactly as it was this morning and every other day before that.

Her next concern was to study the exact details of where and when James would be scheduled to work. She needed to plan all of her actions with the utmost care and caution. She had no doubt the threat to Sarah's life was real and she had no intention of letting her down again. Lisa calmly finished her tea and went downstairs to start preparing the next meal.

"Slow down. I'll open the gate for you" said the younger agent.

"Thanks. Make sure you remember to arrange that chain just the way it was before we got here."

"Of course I will. You didn't have to tell me that Old Man," said the younger agent as he slammed the door shut. The older agent drove through the gate and waited up ahead.

Sarah tried to settle her thoughts and figure out what was going on. Just then the door opened again and Sarah could see the second person again. No matter what she tried to think about the figure eight loomed large above the passenger seat.

"Well a little sleep is better than none, let's get back out on the highway and keep heading west," said the older agent.

"Go west young man. Isn't that what they used to say when you were a child, Old Man? Hey, I wonder if they've found a way to deliver all the special order pictures we sent them?" asked the younger agent.

Sarah had been following the conversation along with a casual interest but now she was suddenly clinging to every word.

"I don't think they could've delivered them so quickly, but you never know. The professor has been going to a lot of trouble acquiring you-know-who and I'm sure he had a good reason," said the older agent.

"Speaking of her, do you think you-know-who is sleeping back there?"

"I think so, she been pretty quiet since we left the campground."

Sarah's ability to manipulate her arms forcefully without moving her head was continually improving. She was close, very close, to extracting her right arm from the weakening confines of her extended sleeve. If she could manage to get one arm out, just one arm, she was as good as free.

"Do you think anyone will even bother trying to save her?" asked the younger agent.

"Sure, they wouldn't have gone to all this trouble if nobody cared for her."

"I guess you're probably right. I can't imagine who would. Maybe it's her parents?"

"Yes, most likely it's something like that." said the older agent.

Sarah fought to contort her hand and wrist while trying to move her elbow further and further back to clear the sleeve.

'COME ON! WORK TO BE DONE! HURRY UP AND GET ME OUT OF THIS BAG!'

Sally's demands were becoming more and more desperate, but Sarah just had to keep quiet. She knew she couldn't risk talking to Sally right now because she was supposed to be sleeping. It was also extremely lucky that J.J. didn't toss Sally and her bag on the bonfire earlier on. For now she had to stay focused and definitely couldn't give up hope.

Her priority was to break free from whatever was holding her sleeves behind her, and soon. She was positive that at least two straps had already broken. How many more were there? All she could do was to keep testing the restraints with all her force.

Slowly she started to inhale as much air as she could and then began forcing even more gulps of air deep into her lungs. When she couldn't hold another gulp she lunged forward and pulled sharply with all her might—nothing. Undeterred, Sarah focused methodically on her problem and continued repeating the same procedure over and over. Something had to give sooner or later.

"I think we're going to have to try and clean her up somehow?" said the older agent.

"What for?" asked the younger agent.

"Just take a look at her. She can't be seen by anyone looking like that. We definitely need to do something, but I'm not sure—what's the best way to go about it?"

"We can roll the back windows down at the next truck wash and I'll use the coin operated pressure washer on her."

"No, you listen to me Child—we won't be doing any pressure washing inside this car."

"You listen to me! Don't you ever, ever, call me child again or I promise you'll regret it!"

"Just relax and try to get some more sleep," said the older agent.

"Okay, hey let's just cover her with a tarp, nobody will notice her then."

"Maybe, we'll see, it's dark right now so it's not that important anyway."

Lisa could hear the helicopter circling above the estate. James had been away for the entire day as usual. Generally it took him at least a half hour to reach the house after landing, depending on if he walked down or drove the quad. She knew he probably wouldn't be staying up very late tonight after he'd finished his dinner. From what she could tell so far it looked like he'd be leaving early again tomorrow.

Would it happen tonight or tomorrow? She needed to make a decision. She knew it would be safer tomorrow after James went to work, but she didn't want to let Sarah down if someone showed up demanding information tonight. She methodically finished setting the table as she'd done so many times before. Everything that she needed to prepare for tonight's dinner was done and all the food was ready to be served.

Her mind was running in overdrive. She would need her digital camera ready to go and complete with fresh batteries. Nothing could be left to chance. If James took the helicopter tomorrow morning she would do it as soon as she heard him take off. In the distance she could hear the sound of the quad's engine as James was approaching the house.

"Hi Lisa, something smells good around here."

"Thanks James, we're having roast chicken tonight, one of your favourites."

"That's great! I'm starving! I see somebody dropped off the Range Rover today. Did you happen to look over their body work?"

"Not really. I don't know much about things like that. I told them you'd be taking a closer look after you got home. What did you think about it?"

"Actually, Alexia and her attendant are outside sitting beside the Range Rover right now so maybe I'll take a look later on."

"Very well James. Are you ready to eat now, or would you rather eat later?"

"Sure, just give me about ten minutes to clean up and I'll be right back."

"Okay, I get something started."

Lisa walked over and slightly lifted the window blind with a single finger. Alexia had reached up and gripped the door handle of the Range Rover with one hand and the other was moving in circular motions on the passenger side of the car. Her head was tilted all the way back and her attendant was sitting nearby, reading a novel.

"Why don't you try to get some more sleep yourself? Who knows how long you-know-who is going to be sleeping back there. If she wakes up again you'll never get any sleep."

"I can't argue with that Old Man, maybe you're right. Wake me up when you need a driving break."

"Don't worry, I will. We won't be making any good time unless we sleep at different times."

"Do you think I don't know about that?"

"Relax! Just take it easy, you know I'm just making conversation."

Sarah continued her determined assault on the remaining strap or straps on the back of her jacket. As more and more of her medications wore off, her adrenalin and dogged determination just continued to increase. Inhale as much air as possible and tilt forward while thrusting her elbows out to the sides. She knew that bit by bit she had to be making progress.

Jen was adapting quickly to the new training routine at the base. There was very little daytime flying scheduled over the next few days as she was about to start her required Night Vision Goggles (NVG) training this evening. They were used more often than she realized and she couldn't believe how much they improved a pilot's night time vision capabilities.

She had enough free time to boot up the laptop, but she was starting to worry now because she still hadn't heard a word from Kyle. The laptop was coming to life with astonishing speed and immediately she noticed another flashing alert. Once again Kyle's diagnostic GhostNet program was indicating another continent had been eliminated. This time it was Australia. She quickly fired off an e-mail to Kyle asking him to try his best to establish contact with her and try to keep in touch on a regular basis.

"James, would you care for any dessert tonight?"

"No thanks. I think I'll slip out quietly before the others show up for dinner. We had an extremely busy day at work today and it looks like more of the same tomorrow."

"Well a good night's sleep never hurt anyone. Are you flying the helicopter in tomorrow?"

"Probably, that depends on the weather forecast. Anyway, thanks for dinner and excuse me for leaving so early." "Sure that's fine. Goodnight. I'll say hello to the others for you."

"Thanks Lisa, maybe I'll see you in the morning, Goodnight."

Lisa walked out towards the front door and casually glanced over her shoulder to see if James had gone to his office or upstairs to bed.

Sarah started packing air into her lungs like a mechanical compressor. Slowly, gulp after gulp of air was being forced down inside her. All the caffeine pills were keeping her wide awake and increasingly agitated. Anxiously she waited for the older agent to look away from the rear view mirror before coughing and violently lunging forward with all her might.

Something happened, and what just happened in that instant was unmistakable. She knew that she'd finally broken the last remaining strap locking the dirty canvas sleeves behind her back. As the heavy sleeves fell down behind her she remained perfectly still as she contemplated her next move. She needed to get her arms out of the sleeves but still appear to have them both secured in the normal position. Keeping her eyes closed and pretending to snore ever so quietly she carefully manipulated her arms within the jacket until she finally managed to free both arms. Discreetly she placed the sleeves back in position and tucked in the ends securely behind her back.

'Let me out! It's payback time! Get me out of this bag!'

"You can count on it Sally! Just keep quiet!"

"Well, well, look who is waking up back there. You've been pretty quiet since we left the campground."

"No, nightmares, normal nightmares, that's all—I just opened my eyes for a second but I'm sure I still need a lot more sleep. Please! You really should try and keep quiet when a lady is sleeping."

"Sorry, I was sure I just heard you talking."

"Wasn't us. It was probably just the wind. Hey! Keep your big prying eyes on the road while you're driving!"

Sarah slowly slipped her hand out from under the heavy canvas jacket and then cleared her throat just long enough and loud enough to drown out the sound of the zipper opening.

'Better say your goodbyes to the world J.J., while you still can!'

"No Please! Not again!" screamed Sarah knowing she was losing her ability to control her actions.

"What's your problem back there?" asked the older agent.

"Did you say my problem? What problem? No problem, wait, I think maybe you meant, your problem. Yes definitely, it's going to be your problem and keep your beady little eyes on the road!"

Seconds later Sarah's searching hand locked onto Sally's neck and yanked her violently out of the bag before quickly stuffing her inside the canvas straitjacket.

'Ready Sally?'

Chapter 20

Jen adjusted the green ocular lens on her set of Night Vision Goggles as they worked through the checklist prior to lift off. It felt awkward wearing a helmet and these goggles on her head, but already she was becoming fascinated by their capabilities. It was a dark night outside, but she could clearly see the green landscape almost as if it were daytime. It wasn't any wonder that the use of these goggles was becoming so widespread for so many different night missions.

"Roll up the throttle when you're ready and make your departure towards the Southwest Target Range. I want you to get adjusted to your new night vision before we continue our training."

"Yes Sir! I'll advise flight ops of our intentions."

"Sounds good."

Kyle had clearly impressed all the staff at CFRC-8 from the moment he arrived. After joining the small group of gifted students doing various short term tenures at the facility, it was readily apparent that his unusual abilities and photographic memory were quickly leaving the others far behind. Not only that, but his dedication and work ethics kept him working longer than a new physician interning at a hospital. He just couldn't get enough of this place. The sheer size of the facility, all the leading-edge physics being used in the laser fusion project itself, the supercomputers, everything fit him like a glove. He even dreaded going to sleep for the fear that he might miss something.

Every tiny detail, including time management, was critical. The arrays of lasers and the ongoing amplification of the laser beams was a complex feat of engineering. He wanted to lay his eyes on every single piece of equipment within the entire facility. He was only now starting to gain limited access to the supercomputer.

He should have almost two hours to evaluate the present criteria for an upcoming laser shot. Testing on the lasers was now being done much more often as all the baseline data collected was critical information that was required by the supercomputers. When the real attempts at laser fusion began, the computers would require the precision to adjust the timing of the laser array within a billionth of a second. Each one of hundreds of lasers had to strike the fuel pellet at exactly the right place and time to cause a fusion reaction.

Kyle felt he could complete his work in about ten minutes before his allotted time was complete. During those ten minutes he planned to try and link this supercomputer to his own personal system. It would most certainly speed up his own GhostNet diagnostic program and, if possible, he would try to create a cloaked-link to network with Jen's system as well. He also knew he was long overdue with the check-ins that he had planned with Jen.

"Pull up! Pull up! I have control!"
"Uh Roger, you have control. Why did you do that?"
"You were flying us directly toward a row of trees."
"I don't understand. How could that happen?"
"It's a common occurrence with new night time pilots on the gunnery range."

Jen had flown three approaches targeting the concealed remnants of an old tank destroyed many times over from previous helicopter gunships.

"I was just making a few more corrections before firing."

"The illusion is called Fascination or Fixation, specifically, Target Hypnosis. That's precisely what we are watching out for with our new students. Just like instrument flying, you have to keep your eyes moving between different gauges and sources of information."

"Of course, thank you. I was lucky you were on board."

"Yes, that's true. Come around again from the north and try another targeting run. Just don't get fixated on adjusting your aim. Fire only if you think you're on target."

"You actually want me to fire a live missile?"

"Yes I do. We're loaded with four SS-10 Anti-Armour missiles and we're out here to use them."

"Yes Sir! I'll do my best!"

Professor Akkaim was becoming more and more aggravated at the constant stream of construction delays plaguing the underground project in Iraq. Manufacturing problems in the nearby plant dedicated to growing KDP crystals was another ongoing concern. If and when all the problems were sorted out, it would still take about two months to grow each batch of crystals. Each completed crystal was almost the size of a microwave oven. Even at full capacity, they needed more time to grow the required number of crystals. As a laser beam passes through a KDP crystal the infrared light is converted to ultraviolet light and every laser needed to pass through a crystal on its way to the deuterium fuel cell. Only small shipments of KDP crystals had been trickling in and almost all the other sectors of the project were continually behind schedule. Overall, more expert help was desperately needed in all areas of the project.

He still had some planning to do concerning the ongoing plans for Lisa's daughter Sarah, and the steps required to retrieve any relevant information Lisa might or might not provide. That would also determine if there was even any point in keeping Sarah alive once he had seen what she had to offer. Of course there was the possibility Lisa might also be of future use as well, but keeping Sarah alive for any extended period would obviously be problematic, and likely unnecessary.

His technicians had recently verified that Lisa had received their last text message. He needed some good reliable information, and soon. The professor glanced up at his monitor displaying the image of the Claytons' entrance gate. It seemed like that image never changed on his monitor. Not even one single vehicle had passed through the gates of the Claytons' estate since the Range Rover had been returned.

Lisa woke up abruptly from her sleep. She was lying on her back and immediately her mind started rehearsing everything over and over. The camera was ready, new batteries were installed, and the digital memory card was cleared. The combination for the Murphy wall-safe had remained safe and secure with her for years.

She used to dream about the lengths she would go to protect the Claytons themselves and of course, the combination of the safe and any valuables inside. Never in her wildest dreams did she imagine the possibility that she might be the person breaking into it. She could clearly see moonlight filtering through the polyester curtains and into her bedroom.

Almost for sure James would be taking the helicopter in today. At least the weather didn't look like it was going to be an issue. Lisa glanced at the clock and decided to get up before the alarm. She was usually the first person awake anyway, and nobody would know, or care, if she was up a little earlier than usual. Everyone needed new scentlets this morning, and to make sure she would never forget it, she always kept the replacement pair inside her shoes. She took an extra-long shower to try and relax her nerves before getting dressed, changing her scentlets and going downstairs. It was critical that everything appeared perfectly normal this morning.

Jen was surprised at just how much she was enjoying this advanced tactical training. The base had a variety of different helicopters available including the most common gunships found in the US Military. The combination of night training and live-fire exercises was about as far from boring as it got. She had fired four live missiles last night, missing above the target on the first two shots, low on the third, and a direct hit with the fourth. Clearly this type of training was only for a select few, and she couldn't even imagine the cost of an SS-10 missile.

Jen rolled over and opened up her laptop. Even though her night training allowed her to wake up later in the mornings, they always had something planned for her. The computer came online so fast she thought she might have forgotten to turn it off. A light was blinking on the GhostNet diagnostic program and she could see a message from Kyle on the desktop.

"Hi Jen—hope you're enjoying yourself over there. The GhostNet diagnostics will be working much faster now. I'll be monitoring it as well when I have the time. Everything is totally awesome over here. Fly safe."

Jen was glad to have finally heard from Kyle, although she wasn't really that worried about him with all the high level security in place at the Central Fusion Research Complex 8.

She clicked on the light and immediately noticed another continent had been removed from the list of possibilities. With a blank stare she realised that China, their prime suspect, was now off the list. Whoever had the capabilities to infiltrate James Clayton's computer was starting to have a smaller and smaller world in which to hide.

Checking her daily schedule she noticed a one hour time slot this afternoon was booked with a photographer. It looked like Al Anderson was taking the necessary steps to acquire the new identification they had requested. Jen signed off and rolled back into bed wishing for just a little more sleep. So far nothing had changed with her overall schedule and she would still finish her training one week before Kyle was finished.

"Good Morning James. Would you like some coffee?"

"Good Morning Lisa. Have you ever seen me start a day without coffee?"

"Sorry. I guess I've said that so many times it's become a habit."

"Did you change your scentlets this morning?"

"Yes I did, and thanks for reminding me. Have you seen the Beaucerons this morning?"

"No, but I heard them out on the porch earlier on. It looks like it's going to be another beautiful day. Are you taking the helicopter in this morning?"

"Yes. I'm going to check the weather forecast first, but it looks like a go from what I can see."

"Do you have time for breakfast before you leave James?"

"Sure, maybe something quick. How about making your world famous breakfast clubhouse with a large orange juice for breakfast?"

"Sure. I'll bring it out to you in a few minutes."

"Great. I'll go and check the weather forecast."

Sinzar slowly opened the plush red drapes on his tenth floor hotel room. This view of Las Vegas was second to none, and after just wasting his time on the last useless jaunt to Santa Monica he didn't care what they charged for this room. No luxury was spared; it had a stocked beer fridge and also a large screen digital HD TV complete with full-service on-demand entertainment programming.

He was definitely going to catch up on every single episode of all of his favourite soap operas. With three restaurants, two casinos and a mall downstairs he might not ever have to leave the building, except of course, for a little unfinished business with a certain cab driver.

Sinzar reached up to feel the lump on the back of his head. The swelling was slowly going down, but it was still at least the size of a golf ball. He kicked off his shoes and lay down on the massive king size bed. He was already beginning to see the positive side of this unexpected month-long vacation in Vegas.

Lisa could now hear the distant drone of the helicopter running at the top of the hill. She poured herself a coffee and waited to make sure James was really gone and not returning home for some unknown reason. She needed to calmly collect her thoughts, go to her room, pick up the camera and then make her way downstairs to his office.

She nervously glanced over at her cell phone on the counter and was relieved to see everything on the display appeared normal. It suddenly dawned on her that she hadn't given any thought to the topic of fingerprints. Lisa quickly reached out and pulled a narrow kitchen drawer open. She still had one new pair of yellow rubber gloves that she removed and placed in her apron pocket. Ten minutes had passed since James had taken off. She put her coffee cup in the dishwasher, rinsed her hands and walked upstairs to her room.

She was still wearing her red short sleeved dress with a cotton kitchen apron tied around her waist. Two large apron pockets would hold everything she needed, including a standard flashlight. Lisa made her way downstairs checking carefully for any signs of other activity in the house. Everything was quiet, as usual. Nobody was ever awake this early in the morning, except for Kyle.

Lisa slowed down in front of the tall oak doors to Doctor Clayton's office. Quietly she slipped the door key into the lock and opened the tall doors. The office was still very dark except for a little light coming between the curtains. Lisa could feel her anxiety levels starting to soar. No time to waste. Lisa removed the yellow gloves from her pocket and pulled the tight fitting rubber gloves over her shaking hands. Glancing around, she walked over to Alexia's portrait above the coat hooks and suddenly came face to face with the young Alexia. She had never realized just how beautiful she had been when she was younger. Reaching up she pulled on the frame and opened the door concealing the Murphy wall-safe.

Lisa spun the dial clockwise, then anticlockwise past the number, and finally clockwise one more time. Finally she grasped the short chrome lever and pulled the unusually thick door open. The sight of the gun startled her immediately. She had next to no knowledge about firearms and wasn't even sure if it was loaded or even how to check it. The gun, two boxes of bullets and several stacks of cash were sitting on top of a small pile of large yellow envelopes. Lisa reached in and picked up the handgun. She was surprised by the weight of the firearm. It was the first time she ever actually handled a real firearm. It weighed five times what she had imagined.

Carefully she removed the gun and placed it on the desk. Then she removed both boxes of bullets and the three stacks of cash. Each bundle was clearly marked $10.000 US. She had never seen that much cash in one place before. Lisa pulled her flashlight out and examined the envelopes carefully. It didn't take long to realise exactly what she was looking for as it was clearly marked.

CLASSIFIED DOCUMENTS: US LEVEL II SECURITY CLEARANCE REQUIRED

KYLE CLAYTON'S CONFIDENTIAL INTERNSHIP SCHEDULE 2011

CONTENTS PROTECTED BY ORDER OF THE CENTRAL INTELLIGENCE AGENCY

VIOLATORS WILL BE PROSECUTED UNDER THE FULLEST EXTENT OF US LAW

Lisa quickly glanced at the other envelopes, but nothing else had anything to do with Kyle. To be safe she removed the stack of envelopes and placed them on the desk next to everything else. She needed everything to go back in exactly the same order. Separating the envelopes into two piles, Lisa removed Kyle's envelope and brought it around to the front of the desk. The red wax seal had clearly been pressed and marked CIA. Luckily for her the envelope had already been opened or that would have caused a huge problem for her.

Reaching over she turned on the desk lamp, opened the envelope, and slid several sheets of paper out and onto the desk. After clearing some space she laid out three pages side by side under the desk lamp. She turned her camera on, checked the settings, and tried to zoom in on the papers. It was next to impossible to photograph all of the pages at once; she was just too close. Lisa stood up on a chair and focused the camera on each page individually.

Finally the resolution looked like it would work and she took two pictures of each page. The automatic flash activated for each photo despite the annoying two or three second delay. Quickly she checked the images on the viewfinder and confirmed the contents of the documents could clearly be seen on the photos. Lisa climbed down off the chair and carefully placed the pages back inside the envelope. Then she placed the envelope back in the pile and walked back over to the safe, placing the stack of envelopes back in the exact position she found them.

Walking back to the desk she picked up the three stacks of cash and placed them carefully back in the same position. Once again she retrieved the two boxes of bullets. One had been opened and it was the one sitting in front. Finally she went to the desk and picked up the heavy firearm. She was just terrified handling this gun and not knowing if it was loaded made it that much worse. Lisa could feel her hands were soaked with sweat inside the tight yellow gloves. Holding the firearm she pauses to remember just exactly how it was positioned when she first opened the safe.

Just at that moment, she heard a loud metallic bang and turned instantly as the office door swung wide open. Alexia was in her wheelchair and her eyes and mouth flew wide open in a state of shock when she saw Lisa. Frantically, Alexia started trying to spin the wheelchair around as Lisa realised she was pointing the weapon straight at her head. Lisa stood frozen in time as she watched Alexia escape out the door and listened while the wheelchair slowly picked up speed down the hall. Lisa took a deep breath then carefully replaced the firearm in the wall-safe and locked the door. Finally she reached over for the picture frame and gently closed the door to conceal the wall-safe.

Once again she was standing face to face with Alexia and realized everything had just changed and that things would never be the same again. Lisa casually straightened up the office and walked back upstairs to her room. This time around, nothing at all was going to stop her from helping her daughter. She was going to do anything that needed to be done, no matter what. Deep down she knew she was transforming to a colder, calculating woman.

It was impossible to know Alexia's true mental state. Was she shocked because she saw her breaking into the safe or because she had accidentally pointed the firearm at her head? Could she tell anyone? Or even manage to communicate properly with anyone now or in the future? She was now a potential problem, a major potential problem, a loose end, an unknown variable, and most calculating people preferred to eliminate the presence of all unknown variables.

Sarah's head was tilted all the way back and she was continuously swaying her upper body back and forth from side to side. Her eyes were almost closed as she kept pretending to snore while making sure she was as loud and obnoxious as possible. Her strange repetitive motion had been going on for several hours and she had no intention of stopping anytime soon. The distraction was also allowing her to prepare and manipulate Sally exactly the way she needed her underneath the heavy straitjacket. Having Sally in her hands under the jacket gave her a tremendous sense of confidence and power.

'Nobody can hurt us now. Right Sally!'

"How much longer do you think we have to keep you-know-who with us?" asked the younger agent.

"I don't know anything that you don't know," said the older agent.

"Can you say that again Old Man? You have no idea how much I just love to hear you say that."

"I'm talking about you-know-who Child. Don't get me started."

"I told you before. Don't ever call me child, Old Man!"

"Listen. What do you think? We will be keeping her with us until we are instructed to do otherwise. It's that simple."

Sarah was listening keenly to every word.

"What if there was a little accident or something happened beyond our control?"

"Look, put some ear plugs in your ears and try to get some more sleep. We've still got a long way to drive until we get back."

"We better get some new orders about you-know-who soon, and that's all I'm going to say."

Sarah was now completely off her medications. The memories of how Sally got her red hands were coming back clearly now. That boy should have known better than to try taking Sarah's things, especially in the middle of her favourite class at the sanatorium.

Lisa had done every single thing that was asked of her so far. She paced back and forth in the kitchen while constantly watching her cell phone display as it lay charging on the counter.

The new replacement scentlets were laid out for everyone in the usual location and so far only she and James had claimed their replacement sets. She then removed a medium pressure cooker from the well-stocked pot drawers and placed it on the back of the gas range. Earlier on, she had checked the utility cabinet on the outside porch and found a small tin of penetrating oil. Dropping to her hands and knees, she opened the cabinet doors beneath the double sinks. After rummaging through the cabinet for some time she found exactly what she was looking for. She diluted the penetrating oil with one cup of vinegar and poured it into the pressure cooker and then added the entire contents of the bottle she'd just found.

She paused for a moment before taking one deep breath and picking up Alexia's pair of scentlets. In a trance-like state she watched as they sank like eels to the bottom of the pressure cooker. After she had finished, she added everything else, then locked the lid down and placed it at the back of the gas range on a medium flame. She set the timer on the range for twenty minutes and gradually adjusted the flame to a low simmer.

Lisa thought about the stacks of cash and everything else in the safe. A small sense of comfort came over her knowing that she had the means to help herself to anything inside that wall-safe if she really needed too. With a practiced glance around the kitchen she flinched when she saw her phone slowly starting to rotate. The phone wasn't ringing, but the vibration mode was making it slowly spin around in one spot on the counter. A second later it was in her hand and she clicked on the message icon displayed on the small illuminated screen.

'Place our information inside the garbage bin located at Site 16 in the Willow Breeze Campground by 3 p.m. today. Your daughter's life depends on it.'

Lisa checked the time. She had things to finish first, but she knew she could make it there on time. Lisa wasn't really sure how to develop or print the images so she decided she would just make a waterproof package for the camera and drop that off instead. She looked up the address of the campground and refreshed her memory with a street map on the best route to get there. It would take her close to an hour if all the traffic flows were normal.

The timer went off as she folded up the map and walked over and turned off the flame under the pressure cooker. After everything was done, cleaned up, and put back in place she went to her room and picked up everything she needed for her trip to town. It wouldn't hurt to leave early in any case, as she didn't want to be late under any circumstances. Lisa locked up and picked up the keys to the Range Rover.

It was somewhat strange not to have seen anyone else during the morning, and of course Alexia might still even be suffering from shock. It was impossible to say. The Range Rover started instantly and soon Lisa was on her way to town. The Beaucerons shadowed the Range Rover as it made its way down towards the main entrance gate.

Professor Akkaim watched on his monitor as the gates to the estate opened. He couldn't help himself from rubbing his hands together in anticipation. For once everything was going according to his plan and he would soon be getting exactly what he wanted; inside information on the exact whereabouts of Kyle Clayton, and hopefully also on Jennifer Lamar.

Sarah kept on slamming her upper body from side to side while snoring with all her might. She knew perfectly well that she was keeping J.J. awake, as intended. Sarah could feel the sharp point in each of Sally's red palms. Knitting was the only thing that kindled her interest when she was in the sanatorium. She was always the slowest in the group, with each stitch taking her close to minute, but she didn't care. Many times she would even bite her own tongue as she focused intently on the intricate coordinated motions required to knit every single stitch.

Later on, when the teacher showed the class how to knit sleeves, Sarah was so impressed she begged her to try the special knitting needles. They weren't the ordinary style; these were two knitting needles connected to each other with a thick plastic line.

After almost two weeks of work, Sarah had two rows started on a sleeve when that hyper boy grabbed it away from her after class and pulled all her knitting apart. He was laughing at her hysterically while he destroyed her precious work. During her fit of rage she knew she had been bad, but he deserved it. She needed to hide the bloody needles fast, and all she could think of was to thread them into Sally, up one arm, around, and back down the other arm. Sally had kept them safe inside her all this time, but they both knew they would be getting used again; very, very soon.

The drive to the campground was uneventful and Lisa began driving slowly along the road, winding through the willows and past some of the first camp sites. A large branch was blocking the entrance to campsite number 16. Lisa parked the car and walked into the empty campsite. There was a small pile of wet wood next to the fire pit, but it certainly didn't look like anyone was using the site. There were a few people using the campground, but it wasn't full by any means. Looking around to make sure she wasn't being watched, Lisa opened the garbage container and dropped her package inside.

Bending down by the fire, she picked up a small boulder a little larger than a baseball and brought it back to the Range Rover. Once again it started beautifully and Lisa drove out of the campground. She would have to pray they kept their end of the bargain. She desperately wanted to see her daughter again and most of all she wanted to help keep her safe and out of danger. Lisa had done everything that was asked of her and that was all she could do for now. After leaving the campground she pulled off on the side of a highway by an overgrown access road. She slipped the Range Rover into four wheel drive and waited for a break in the traffic. When the road was clear, she put it in first gear and drove the Range Rover about a hundred yards up the overgrown road. There was no place to turn around so she stopped, set the hand brake and turned off the engine.

"Pull over right now—you-know-who is going in the trunk."

"Just relax. I told you nothing is going to happen until we get new instructions. Have you been using those wax earplugs? Why don't you listen to some music with the headphones on?" said the older agent.

"Promise me that if we get new orders, new orders that say they don't care what happens to you-know-who, I get to fix that problem permanently. Promise me you'll stop in the middle of the highest bridge we can find and I personally get to throw her over the railing."

"As I said, we have to see what they say the next time we check in."

Sarah could feel the two sharp knitting needles fully protruding from each of Sally's red palms.

Soon Sally!

The agents working in Portland wasted no time in checking the garbage container in campsite 16 at exactly three o'clock. When they realized a camera had been dropped off they drove directly back to town to transfer the images onto a computer. They all knew Professor Akkaim would be waiting anxiously for any new information they might have acquired.

An hour later they watched as the images were transferred from the digital camera and over to a computer. Everything was clear and legible, and they immediately took all the necessary security precautions to transfer the files over to the professor. He received them and knew at once, without a doubt, that this was the upper hand he had been praying for. The fact that Kyle was already at the Central Fusion Research Complex 8 simply couldn't have worked out any better. It was in the best interest of the entire RA-9 operation to allow Kyle to continue learning every single detail he could while he was in the Central Fusion Research Complex 8. He would almost certainly become one of the best assets the RA-9 project had ever acquired as long as he was properly motivated.

Sinzar had passed out immediately after lying down on the bed and awoke several hours later in almost exactly the same position. He continued to lie there as he waited for his mind to fully awaken. Reaching over to the side of the bed he picked up the phone and ordered some food from the hotel's room service. He was feeling hungry and didn't want to go out on the town without a proper meal first. An hour later he was outside, walking the side streets of Vegas until he eventually came across a small costume shop.

A pair of brass bells rang overhead as he opened the door to the shop.

"Evening Sir. Can I help you find something?"

"Just looking thanks, my wife's friends are having a costume party later on."

"Let me know if I can help you with anything. Everything in the store is for sale and most things can also be rented, if you like."

"Do you have a changing room here?"

"Yes, right over there. See me first before you use it."

Sinzar took his time looking through all the costumes hanging on the racks. The selection of accessories and masks was impressive.

"What about make up? Do you have anything I could use if I needed some?"

"Sure, everything's for sale here," said the odd little shopkeeper. "There's a make-up desk with a mirror beside the changing room. If you want to use it, just help yourself."

"Thanks, I might just do that."

Lisa was sitting in the Range Rover collecting her thoughts. The camera had been dropped off on time and she was sure she had the images they needed. She opened her cell phone and rechecked the instructions to make certain there had been no mistake. She had dropped it off on time and in the correct place. She could only pray they would notify her soon and confirm Sarah's well-being, and also her location.

She briefly considered back-tracking to the campsite and attempting to see who would be picking up the camera, but decided it was just too risky. She would stick to her original plan for now. Lisa opened the driver's door and removed a floor mat and the rock she'd picked up beside the fire. Walking around to the front of the Range Rover she held the floor mat directly over the left front signal light. She held the rock firmly and struck the floor mat with a sharp blow shattering the signal lens. Checking the time to make sure she could drive home during daylight hours she hit the floor mat again and completely shattered the driver's headlamp. She threw the rock as far away as she could before cleaning every small piece of glass from the gravel road and replacing the floor mat.

She planned to pick up a few groceries on the way home just in case James was wondering why she had gone to town. It was just plain bad luck that somebody had collided with the Range Rover while she was away shopping and then fled the scene without even bothering to leave a note. Lisa started the Range Rover and turned to look over her shoulder before slowly backing down the narrow overgrown road leading to the highway.

Sinzar had picked out a women's wig with medium-length greying hair. After trying on various clothing combinations he was satisfied with his final choice. He wanted to look elderly and well off, yet also frail and vulnerable. The mink fur coat and matching hat went well with the over-sized purse, and for an extra fifty the odd storekeeper had provided his surprising skills and talents as a makeup artist. Sinzar was so grateful for his assistance that he let him live. Sinzar smiled quietly to himself when he gazed into the full-length mirror. He had to admit that he didn't even recognise himself it was such a good outfit; absolutely perfect for his needs. Sinzar walked for a couple more blocks until he found a small strip mall where he stopped to pick up a few additional items before carrying on to the casino.

"When are you planning to make your next check-in call Old Man?" asked the younger agent.

"I don't think they are expecting to hear from us until we get back to Portland. So to answer your little question, I'll contact them on the satellite phone when we get back to Portland. Is there anything else on your little mind?"

Sarah suddenly switched from snoring loudly too giggling quietly. Sarah's head was still tilted all the way back and she kept swaying from side to side like a precision timepiece.

"Perhaps I could offer a small suggestion Old Man. What do you think about this idea?"

The younger agent pulled out his loaded handgun and levelled it at the older agents head.

"Drive this car directly to the next rest stop. Get the satellite phone out and make a call to professor what's his name. After that I'm sure he'll say were finished with Miss Psycho, and then I want you to drive straight to the highest bridge we can find. Do you understand me Old Man? I've had it with this whole situation."

Sarah's giggles turned to laughter, loud and obnoxious laughter.

"I know you're upset and I can't say I blame you. I'll call them from the next rest stop. They will probably be done with her soon anyway. Now just relax and put that gun down."

"Not this time Old Man!"

Although the images of floating numbers persisted in her mind, the number eight was completely associated with J.J. Sarah stopped laughing and once again pretended to sleep. Gradually she began pulling the sharp needles from Sally's red palms until they were exactly the length she wanted them. Sarah grasped each of Sally's stuffed red hands inside her own with a grip so extraordinarily strong she could feel she was about to lose control and maybe do something really, really, bad.

'You do it, okay Sally. I'll do it Sarah, Don't you worry about that!'

"Slow down Old Man. I want to read this highway sign coming up," said the younger agent while still holding the gun at his partner's head.

"What did it say Old Man?"

"Next Rest Stop 5 Miles"

"Perfect, let's just hope that the professor gives us the green light to get rid of you-know-who, and if he doesn't, well let's just say something might just accidentally happen to you-know-who," said the younger agent with a laugh.

"I know you know I know who you-know-who is," said Sarah without warning.

"Shut up and go back to sleep before I shoot you both right here and now. Start slowing down, it looks like we're almost here."

They pulled into the rest stop and several cars and trucks were already there. Some were parked and a few other vehicles were still running next to the washrooms. The older agent parked the Cadillac down at the far end of the parking lot.

"Go and make the call Old Man. Where's the satellite phone?"

"It's under my seat," said the older agent quietly.

"Take it out slowly and go make the call."

"It might be hard to get a connection here. We may have to wait until we're higher up in the mountains," said the older agent.

"Leave your gun here and go make the call. Don't come back here until you have the answer I want."

The older agent dropped his gun on the seat, pulled out the satellite phone and walked away from the parking area.

Sarah had quietly taken Sally out from under her coat while the agents were arguing in the front seat. She had heard enough and the time to act had come.

"Say your goodbye's J.J."

"Shut up you fat..." were the last words he spoke as the full length of the sharp knitting needles plunged deep into his ears.

Sarah watched helplessly as Sally's bloody hands kept stabbing him deep inside both ears, over and over again. Even though she was holding Sally's hands she felt powerless to stop the violent attack. J.J. slumped over against the door and Sarah pulled Sally away and over into the back seat of the Cadillac. She quickly pushed the needles back inside Sally's arms and placed her down in the bottom of her travel bag. A moment later the older agent opened the front door.

"Hey wake up. Professor Akkaim wants a word with you."

As the older agent held out the phone in his left hand, he instantly rammed a long thin metal skewer through the younger agent's temple. It passed right through his head with almost no resistance. Blood immediately began flowing down over his ears and onto his shoulders. For a moment the older agent thought it was strange there was no reaction, but also knew anything was possible with fatal brain injuries such as the type he had just inflicted, especially considering he may have actually just fallen asleep.

The younger agent's actions were so serious there was simply only one available remedy. He hadn't even bothered trying to call the professor. Organizations such as RA-9 would never function properly if everyone just disregarded the established chain of command anytime they wanted. He was sure Professor Akkaim would have handled the problem in a similar fashion if he was in his shoes.

The older agent walked to the back, opened the trunk and brought back two blankets. He tossed one in the backseat over Sarah and then pushed J.J. down in front of the seat and covered him with the other blanket. The older agent started the car as if nothing had happened and merged back out on the highway.

Sarah couldn't speak even if she wanted to. She was in a state of shock. She had just watched J.J. being killed. Twice. First by Sally and then by the older agent. In a delayed reaction of sorts, Sarah was now too scared to move and didn't know what to do. The numbers were almost gone and she was starting to feel sick to her stomach.

"Try to get some rest back there Sarah, we've still got a long way to go," said the older agent.

"Can't you just keep quiet—we're trying to get some more sleep back here?"

The older agent wasn't really sure exactly what Sarah had just witnessed. It wasn't that important right now. He needed to dispose of J.J. and the sooner the better. It wasn't long until they were following a larger river. Under normal circumstances, fire or acid would be the preferred method to conceal all traces of person's identity. This was different. This wild river would carry him quickly away from any bridge site and they were now in a very sparsely populated area. The older agent wasted no time and slowed down to a stop on the next bridge.

In less than a minute all of J.J.'s pockets where empty and he was dragged from the car and thrown over the rail. Sarah had watched everything while she pretended to sleep. She still had no idea what to do and felt more and more anxious the longer she went without taking her proper medications.

"Excuse me Madame. Are you waiting for a taxi?"

"Well maybe. I'm waiting for a telephone call first, and then I'll probably need one."

"That's fine. Let me know whenever you're ready."

"Everything looks so professional. I bet you must have fifty taxi's working outside this casino."

"Yes that's true, even more on weekends."

"It's all so very impressive! I'll let you know when I'm ready to leave."

Twenty minutes passed by before Sinzar spotted the taxi he wanted.

"Okay, I'm ready to leave. I'll take that one if you don't mind. Eighty-eight's my lucky number."

"Sure Madame, no problem."

"Here you are young man! Keep this for your trouble."

"Thank you so much Madame! I think that's the biggest tip I've ever got!" said the attendant as he opened the back door.

Sinzar slid awkwardly across the back seat with his dress and heels until he was sitting directly behind the driver.

"Hello Sir. I would appreciate if you could find me a hotel for the evening," said Sinzar in his best elderly female voice.

"What price range are you looking for Lady?" asked the driver.

"Price is no object. Nothing could stop my winning streak this evening. I'm just glad I happened to bring my big purse tonight."

"Well if that's the case I'm sure we'll manage to find something suitable for you this evening."

"I certainly hope so. I wouldn't want to be carrying this much money around Las Vegas by my little old self, that's for sure."

Sinzar quietly started preparing a few items inside the large purse on his lap.

"I know a small hotel close to a large park that often has late night vacancies."

"Excellent. I was hoping you would be so helpful Sir."

Sinzar fashioned his own custom wire garrotte using a pair of common four inch lag bolts as handles. The same simple design he had used many times before. He didn't have any plans to really kill the driver, just to remind him to think twice the next time he planned to beat and rob his drunk and elderly clients. He was more interested in his two thumbs and eight fingers, for he knew it would be difficult to steal things without them.

The garrotte would cause the driver to instantly raise his hands where they could be promptly secured by heavy tie wraps. A liberal application of Super Glue would quickly bond his lips and eyelids and a common pex-tube cutter would make removing ten digits child's play. Sinzar estimated he could complete the entire operation in less than thirty seconds as this particular glue bonded instantly on contact.

"Why are you stopping here in the park?" asked Sinzar in his most vulnerable elderly female voice while putting his surgical gloves on.

"We have a little mechanical problem Lady."

"Isn't this where you usually stop to assault your victims before robbing them?"

Sinzar was wrong. It only took him twenty-five seconds, so he opened another tube of glue and sealed both hands together to stop the bleeding, the stubs of one hand glued to the stubs of the other hand. Thumbs to thumbs, and fingers to fingers.

He could feel himself smiling in a whimsical way as he thought about how he could have been a good surgeon in some other lifetime. He was just so naturally inclined at performing these simple types of debilitating and disfiguring surgery. With both hands behind his head and glued together through the head rest, the driver wouldn't be going anywhere soon. Sinzar disposed of all the items he had needed in a variety of different locations during his walk back into town.

After returning the costume, he went directly back to the hotel room to catch up his soap operas. He was especially looking forward to trying the new luxury shower with all the multiple shower heads. He knew it was just his nature, but he absolutely hated having any unfinished business to take care of, even if was just minor stuff. Now he could truly relax and enjoy everything Las Vegas had to offer someone like himself.

Lisa pulled up to the entrance gate of the estate and waiting as the doors slowly rolled open. She didn't notice any sign of the dogs as she passed through, but that in itself wasn't unusual. She would be a little late getting dinner ready tonight, but James probably wouldn't be home before then anyway. Emergency Trauma surgeons rarely worked seven or eight hour shifts. Luckily there were still lots of daylight on her trip home and Lisa didn't have to worry about being stopped by the police for driving with a shattered headlight.

As she drove closer to the house everything looked the same as it was when she left. Lisa stopped by the house and unloaded the groceries she'd picked up on her way home. Leaving them on the porch she walked back over to the Range Rover. This time she drove it a little farther up the drive towards Alexia's addition. After two attempts she had finally parked the Range Rover exactly where she wanted it. The left front corner was facing directly towards Alexia's large window and the front left wheel was just off the crushed gravel and just outside of the marked safety zone. It was so close that nobody other than her and the Beaucerons would ever notice it wasn't inside the safety zone.

It was only a matter of time until Alexia noticed the damage to the Range Rover. After that, one way or another, she would eventually find a way to examine it. Lisa walked back to the house and brought in the groceries. When she had finished putting everything away she plugged her cell phone back into the charger and left it on the counter.

She was desperate to hear something regarding her daughter. Had she been saved because of her actions? Had her daughter been released? Was she still being held hostage? Had she been executed? All she could do was whatever she was asked, and to try and make sure there weren't any loose ends. Lisa turned around suddenly and could barely contain her delight as she noticed Alexia's pair of replacement scentlets had been picked up from the kitchen.

"Do you know that we know that you know that we know something really, really, really bad just happened to J.J.?"

"What are you talking about? Look, just forget anything you think you might have seen happen to J.J., okay? He won't be bothering you anymore."

"What if he gets out of the river?"

"Trust me. You don't have to worry about that."

"Why? Because J.J. is gone! Gone-gone-gone and he's never ever coming back."

"Do you mean what we think you mean?"

"I don't know what you think I mean or why you're always talking as if there are two people sitting in the back seat. Do as I say, stop talking about him and forget anything you saw happen."

"Okay then, we'll try to forget everything we saw you do to the tall child. He had it coming anyway."

"Just what did you two see anyway?"

"We didn't see anything at all! Besides, we've already forgot about everything you did to him with that little sword."

"Try to get some rest. Maybe I'll take your jacket off later if you behave yourself."

"The jacket—oh yes—the jacket. I forgot to mention that—J.J. was trying to take it off when you were outside using the phone."

"J.J. was trying to take your jacket off while I was gone?"

"I believe that's what I just said."

"Why would he do that?"

"How on mother earth should we know? We don't know what goes on inside the child's mind?"

"Okay, forget it. I'll finish taking it off for you later."

"Thank you so much. I'm sure that will be much more comfortable. Do you have any more Salt and Pepper chips?"

"I don't know, but I'll find something for you to eat tomorrow. I need to keep on driving right now."

"Okay. Did J.J. go down to hell?"

"Get some sleep unless you want to go and join him."

"Okay, we're asleep."

'We could send him down to see J.J. anytime we want!! Right Sally!'

Lisa was having second thoughts after putting all the groceries away. By boiling the scentlets this morning in penetrating oil, a bottle of odour remover, and a box of cloves, she knew that they were most certainly disabled for good. Still, she wasn't completely positive that Alexia was even wearing them. Now she was really beginning to doubt her plan. Maybe Alexia had already forgotten everything that had happened. Still, her daughter's life could be at stake and she wasn't going to discard her again.

Lisa slowly opened the blinds with her fingers and glanced up towards the Range Rover. It wasn't too late to change her plans. No, she'd made a decision and now she needed to stick with it. Just then she could see the blinds starting to open up on Alexia's front window. Alexia had moved her wheelchair slowly up to the center of the window and sat like a disabled gargoyle overlooking the grounds. It looked as if she was almost instantly transfixed on the damaged Range Rover as she gazed down from high above. There was no turning back now, the trap was set and the prey had just seen the bait.

Chapter 21

Jen was starting to relax next to the warm fire burning inside Chalet Number Five. The last six weeks had passed by faster than a ten day spring break. Five weeks of intense training had added over a hundred hours to her logbook, as well as a current helicopter instrument rating and several new type-endorsements. Ever since she'd returned last week, James had been trying to give her extra flights in the Bell 407.

She was gradually evolving from a low-time student to a well-trained pilot, and also becoming increasingly familiar with the local terrain and the layout of various area hospitals. James had been flying with her a few times and tried to dispatch her for the occasional medevac flight now that she'd completed her training. This morning at the hospital helipad, James had simply opened the door and stepped out from his Bell 407 after telling Jen that he'd call her when he needed a flight home.

It probably wouldn't be long until she'd be once again flying under Kyle's critical eye. His six week internship at the Central Fusion Research Complex 8 was now almost over, and he would be back home anytime. So far no arrangements had been made with her regarding Kyle's return flight back to Portland. If the instructors had neglected to teach her anything during her training, he would be the first person to notice it.

She hadn't seen Kyle at all since they'd parted ways at the CFRC-8 helipad six weeks ago. Kyle had only left a few brief messages and it wasn't hard to tell how absorbed he was in the entire laser fusion process and the facility itself.

Her suspicions were that Kyle wouldn't even want to leave CFRC-8 if he were given the choice. Jen realised she would have to try and pull him away from the scientific lifestyle he'd been leading, and get him involved in a few regular activities during his short break from CFRC-8. That task would be challenging for anyone, but it would most certainly end up becoming hers. The truth was she really liked Kyle and was looking forward to his return.

The computer system he'd built weeks ago had been running the entire time they'd been away. She knew Kyle had, most likely, continued to develop his various diagnostic programs while they were both away, and that he had almost certainly been networking with the supercomputers from CFRC-8. She had monitored the continual progress of his diagnostic program as it had continued to systematically eliminate all the other continents and was now searching for the exact origin of the GhostNet cyber-attacks.

As time went on Kyle's diagnostics program had focused in on the Middle East countries and constantly narrowed the scope of the search. With Kyle devoting his spare time to this project, Jen wouldn't be surprised if he pinpointed the exact location anytime now.

Glancing out the windows she could see it was starting to get dark, but the weather was still looking fairly good. So far, all of her flights with James had been during daylight hours and, despite her recent training, she had no intention of ever being forced to make another instrument approach back to the estate. She had learned enough to know the real danger they had exposed themselves to that night and how lucky they were to have survived. They'd repeatedly told her the old adage during her training: Use your experience to avoid getting into situations that you will need your experience to get out of. It hadn't taken long to learn the wisdom of those words.

Jen got up and added another log to glowing embers in the fire. She had stopped for a late lunch and coffee with Lisa this afternoon, and was now ready to leave the minute James called. It was really the first chance she had to learn about the details of the accident with the Beaucerons.

Kyle was about fifty miles south of Portland enjoying a spectacular sunset as he flew the Black Hawk northbound. This time the pilots had allowed him ride up front and were very comfortable with letting Kyle fly, even though the pilot in command operated the pedals for him. After six weeks at CFRC-8 he knew it wouldn't hurt to have a quick holiday from the facility, as long as it was really short.

Flying the Black Hawk was a pleasure and he had remembered every detail about the last flight he took with Jen. Even though he was sitting in the rear seats, he could virtually recreate the entire flight in his mind from his ability to keep track of time and remember everything he experienced. He knew the pilots probably wouldn't let him land back at the estate, but the next time he had the chance to fly, they just might. It wasn't easy for the pilots to hide their obvious fascination for Kyle's seemingly effortless precision flying abilities. He could maintain the heading and altitude almost as well as the helicopter's auto-pilot system.

Jen was starting to wonder when James would call. It was definitely going to be dark for her flight, even if he called right now. She had done the pre-flight inspection this afternoon and was fuelled up as well. She had definitely noticed a change in both James and Lisa's behaviour ever since she returned to Portland. Hopefully they would be back to their old selves after Kyle got back.

Understandably the attack on the nurse had upset everyone. Alexia had managed to slip away from her apartment and manoeuver her wheelchair almost down to the lower parking lot when one of the nurses noticed she was gone. She bolted down the path and managed to catch up with her as she neared the parked Range Rover.

The Beaucerons were gathering close by and acting in a strange and unusual way. They were continuously circling Alexia's wheelchair in a predatory manner with their heads dropped and growling amongst each other. The nurse instinctively placed herself between the dogs and Alexia and then pushed her wheelchair around some shrubs in the garden and back onto the path. In that horrifying instant when they launched their attack, she realized she'd forgotten to change into her new scentlets.

If it wasn't for Lisa running to her aid with a fire extinguisher things could have been much, much worse. She must have heard the screams as the dogs teeth pierced the flesh on her legs and brought her to the ground. Lisa had seemingly appeared out of nowhere, and seconds later she was blasting each dog in the face with a full charge from a large fire extinguisher. Lisa was, without question, 'Her Guardian Angel', as far as the nurse was concerned.

Pressure from the authorities had been mounting to have the Beaucerons put down, but James objected and threatened a lawsuit if anyone tried to take any action against his Beaucerons. He had maintained from the very beginning, they were only doing what they were trained to do.

The nurse had made a critical error in failing to replace her scentlets on the correct date. With almost one hundred and forty stitches, she had paid a high enough price for her negligence. Initially James didn't even want the nurse working for him any longer, but his sympathy for her injuries and her courageous protection of Alexia eventually made him change his mind. He was certain she would never again forget to change her scentlets in the future. He had treated her personally when she first arrived at the trauma center. Lisa had called for the ambulance herself, and it just so happened, that James had been working at the nearest hospital. He knew instantly that the nurse must have been wearing an expired pair of scentlets. She was in stable condition after about two hours of surgery and, despite her injuries she would almost certainly retain the use of both legs.

Jen could feel herself slowly drifting off to sleep when the distant growl of an approaching helicopter snapped her back to reality. It had to be Kyle returning from the CFRC-8. Nobody had mentioned that he was returning, and in all likely-hood, if Al Anderson was in charge, then nobody else would have known. It had to be him, unless maybe James was getting a ride home with another medevac machine. That was also a very realistic possibility. In any case, Jen picked up an iron poker, spread out the logs in the fire, and got what she needed to take up to the helipad. The Long Ranger was on the pad ready to go, so if it was Kyle, they would have to park out in the center of the clearing.

Jen locked up Chalet Number Five and started up an ATV for the drive up to the helipad. She was carrying a new pair of scentlets with her just in case it was Kyle coming home after his first internship in California.

Sarah's behaviour had improved considerably since she started taking the new drugs. The older agent had stopped in a small town on the way back to Portland. He had done some research the last time he was online and compiled a list of common medications prescribed for paranoid schizophrenics. Later that evening he broke into a small drugstore with ease, and after a considerable amount of time spent searching and reading labels he managed to locate some of the drugs on his scribbled list. He had originally planned to stay in Jen's apartment building, but decided Sarah was still just too unpredictable to ever be left alone, even though he'd been experimenting with slipping different medications into her food.

Once it was clear that Professor Akkaim's extraordinary instructions that Sarah was to be kept alive and also unharmed were true, her type of accommodations and her exact location would be completely at his discretion. Sarah couldn't really be housed in an apartment building unless she was completely silenced with duct tape. That worked well for short term situations, but it was problematic for any long term basic survival care.

The older agent had provided a brief account of what happened to his partner, but the professor had virtually no reaction whatsoever to the younger agents recent disposal. It almost went without saying that any acts of insubordination within the RA-9 organization would be dealt with in a similar manner.

He needed her to be completely isolated from people so he had rented a remote dilapidated hobby farm in the rural outskirts of Portland. It had been abandoned for several years and the owner was more than happy to accept a six month cash payment in advance, with no questions asked. He was highly unlikely to find a tenant for this property even if he offered it for free.

Several run down out buildings were still standing, but just barely. One was a large low-level chicken coop, and also an old barn and an old garage. Over grown blackberry bushes were in the process of consuming the defenceless structures. The house was a run down two bedroom farmhouse that must have been at least eighty years old. It had a rotten wrap-around porch with holes in the deck planks and several broken windows. It was in sad need of repair, but for the older agent's purposes it was ideal. Sarah could scream and snore all she wanted up here and nobody would ever hear her. She still needed to be restrained, but not as severely as before.

The older agent had set up an ingenious system of four double-loop rubber tension straps attached to the four sets of handcuffs on Sarah's wrists and ankles. The tension straps were secured through the opposing walls, which allowed Sarah only limited movement around the center of the room. A thin mattress and a makeshift bucket provided for bare necessities.

She had a sleeping bag opened up for her blanket, and after Sarah had finally persuaded him to let her use her 'Lady's Bag' as a pillow, she seemed much more content. The older agent had been boiling two pots of smaller new potatoes on a Coleman stove in the barn, as she seemed quite content eating cold potatoes and drinking pop. The older agent travelled back to town, on most days, for his own needs, and occasionally picked up a bag of burgers from various local drive-ins on the way home. This was always a huge treat for Sarah to get a bag of hamburgers and she was just like a kid at Christmas, devouring the cold burgers with the utmost savage-like enjoyment. It was certainly unusual for the older agent to be tasked with this sort of work, but knowing the insubordination policies at RA-9, he wasn't about to start questioning his orders.

Kyle could see the faint lights of the estate coming into view.

"You did great Kyle! I was sure we were flying on auto-pilot the whole way back. If you don't mind I better take it in for the landing. Okay, I have control."

"Sure you have control. Thanks. I like the feel of this machine and hope to get the chance to fly it again."

"Well you can fly it again if I'm in command. I'll promise you that."

"Great! It looks like my dad's Bell 407 is parked outside on the pad. Is he home?"

"I'm not really sure, we'll know soon I imagine."

The co-pilot turned on the Night Sun landing lights and illuminated the whole clearing like a summer afternoon.

"Nice!" said Kyle. "We have one of those on our helicopter, but it's not as strong as this one."

"They're great when you need them, I know that for sure." The pilot in command had a good look around for any loose debris before lowering the Black Hawk down into the clearing. Fortunately the rotors on the Bell 407 were properly tied down or they would have had to land on the far edge of the clearing. Kyle could see Jen standing by the side of the hanger watching their arrival. Once the pilot had settled the wheels on the ground he rolled the throttles back to flight idle and gave Jen the 'thumbs up' to approach the helicopter. The flight engineer rolled the rear side door wide open and Jen jumped inside.

She flashed the scentlets at Kyle and quickly helped him lock them around his ankles. In a matter of minutes they were back outside next to the hanger and watching as the Black Hawk's turbines spooled up and started to 'vertical' straight up from the clearing.

"Good to see you again Kyle."

"Good to see you too, Jen. How was your training?"

"It was fantastic. I've got a lot of stories to tell you about that."

"Great, they let me fly the helicopter almost all the way home."

"Nice. I have an endorsement on them now."

"Cool. Were you training on a Black Hawk?"

"I was training on a variety of machines actually and also night and live-fire training as well."

"That's great Jen. I'm sure you can probably show me a few things now."

"I don't know about that. Did you have a good time at CFRC-8?" asked Jen.

"Yes, it was totally fantastic. I don't think I've ever learned so much about one topic in such a short period of time. They'll be ready to start conducting actual laser fusion tests very soon. If they can successfully harness fusion energy at this facility, it will be a turning point for the future for mankind."

"That's really exciting, you'll have to give me the layman's explanation later."

"Sure, my pleasure. Are you staying at Chalet Number Five now?"

"Yes, I've been there since I got back last week. It's been a nice and peaceful change. James has been keeping me busy doing some flying as well."

"Excellent, well he's obviously happy with your flying then, or he wouldn't let you take the machine by yourself like that. Congratulations!"

"Thanks Kyle. Do you have any new developments on the GhostNet diagnostic program?"

"No, it's getting close to locating the IP address, but no details yet. It's still working in the general vicinity of Iraq and Iran. Let's go and get some coffee."

"Sure, I'm still expecting to fly out and pick up James later on tonight."

"Don't hold your breath waiting for that. My dad can work some extremely long shifts when he's in ER. You might not hear from him until tomorrow morning."

"Yes, I am starting to realize that now. Okay well, let's go. The logs in the fire should still be burning and easy to light when we get there."

"Good. I'll fly out with you to pick up dad later on."

"Thanks Kyle, but I think we had better wait and see what time he calls first," said Jen, feeling suddenly awkward with her babysitter's tone of voice.

"Sure, sounds good. I'm ready to go when you are."

"Take your time. I just noticed one of the dogs moving around by the edge of trees," said Jen.

"Okay, I'll be right behind you."

"No, I want you to ride in front of me. Keep it slow. I'll watch your back."

"Okay, I'll try."

Lisa had to feed Alexia this evening as the on-duty nurse left unexpectedly to attend an urgent family matter. She wheeled her up to the end of the table and draped two towels over her neck and chest. It was almost impossible to pry her lower jaw open. The harder she tried the more Alexia clenched her teeth. It had been many weeks since the incident in the office, but still there was no way of knowing what was really going on in her mind, if anything.

It was becoming apparent she might need to try some different tactics in order to get a feeding tube inside her. She certainly wasn't in any mood to be spoon-fed like a baby this evening. Lisa suddenly pinched Alexia's nose tight with the thumb and fingers of her left hand and covered her mouth firmly with palm of her right hand. How easy it would be. Lisa lowered her face right above Alexia's and peered straight into her eyes. She could see the shock in her face as her eyes opened wider and wider. After nearly a minute she released her grip and watched as her mouth opened wide and she started frantically sucking in air. Slipping in a flex feeding tube was now child's play and Lisa rolled the IV gantry over beside her wheel chair.

A few minutes later Alexia was starting to settle back into her normal vegetative state as the drip continued to supply some basic fluid nourishment. Although keeping Alexia alive was certainly a personal risk, she was generally becoming less and less concerned about Alexia as time went on.

The Range Rover had been promptly repaired and was now securely locked up back in its original spot. It was hard to imagine any thoughts still going through Alexia's mind. Lisa walked back into the kitchen and fixed herself a mug of tea. She had heard the large helicopter landing and then departing from the top of the hill. She wasn't always privy to everything that went on with the helicopters, but she did know from the itineraries that Kyle could be back anytime. That certainly was the most logical explanation as she could tell from the sound that it wasn't the Bell 407 that belonged to James. In any case she needed to start making some basic plans to be ready to feed whoever it was that just arrived.

Later on Lisa walked back out to check on Alexia and was startled to find the feeding tube hanging down from the gantry and dripping on the floor. She quickly inserted it back into Alexia's open mouth and assumed she must have forgotten to secure it properly. It would take at least another hour before she could remove it and then push Alexia back to her own personal room for the night. Hopefully the on-duty nurse, or a replacement, would get back before then.

Kyle was up the stairs and working on his array of computers seconds after walking through the door.

"How's the supercomputer Kyle?"

"Well, it's nothing like the system at CFRC-8, but it's been making steady progress. I was able to network with this system on several occasions when I was in California and increase the efficiency of the software that's running the program."

"That's great! When will we know where the cyber-attacks originated from?"

"I still can't say for sure, soon I hope. It's continually focusing on a smaller and smaller area in the Middle East."

"What on earth would somebody from that part of the world need from your father's computer?"

"Impossible to say, for all we know it was just a random attack, computer to computer. Anything's possible and jumping to conclusions based on only speculation is generally an exercise in futility."

"Well Kyle, I'm looking forward to your complete and comprehensive evaluation of all the data when you're ready."

"You can count on that."

The older agent drove the Cadillac up the private road leading back out to the property.

'He's home! He's here! Heard him! Back in the bag Sally!'

Sarah grabbed Sally by the neck and stuffed her deep down inside the bottom of the duffel bag. "Keep quiet Sally!"

"Are you awake, Sarah?"

"Yes, your car woke us up when you got home. Did you bring hamburgers?"

"Yes, two bags, one for each of you," said the older agent.

"Thanks, she said I could have them all."

Sarah quickly opened the first burger she pulled out of the bag. A triple dose of her medications had been crushed and mixed in with the condiments of several burgers.

All-in-all Sarah was becoming less and less of a problem for the older agent. It was unfortunate that everything might be changing soon. The older agent dropped a newspaper with the current day's date on the mattress next to Sarah and took two pictures with his cell phone. They could both hear the engine of another vehicle as it made its way up the narrow farm road towards the buildings. The older agent quickly picked up the newspapers and shut the door to her room as he walked outside to meet the driver.

Lisa nearly jumped out of her skin when she noticed her cell phone once again slowly rotating on the stone counter top. She had done everything they asked her to do. She wanted to see her daughter more than anything else in the world.

"As promised Dear Lisa. Stand by."

Moments later a grainy image appeared on her cell phone. It wasn't the most detailed picture of Sarah's face because she was eating something, but the picture did show the front page of that day's local newspaper. She was alive and possibly even staying close by. Lisa simply couldn't ask for more under the circumstances. After weeks without contact this was fantastic news. She was elated beyond words. Once again her phone started to vibrate.

"Stand by for instructions."

The men were getting out of the van as the older agent approached them.

"Is she ready to go?"

"Not quite, but she'll be ready soon. I gave her a special dose of pills tonight. Wait here and I'll let you know when she's ready to go."

The older agent waited outside for a while, and when he opened the door Sarah was out cold on the mattress.

"Come on in, we're going to need everybody to get her inside the truck."

Together they fitted Sarah back into her canvas straitjacket, dragged her outside and loaded her inside the cube van.

"Is that everything?"

"Yes, I think so."

"What about her bag?"

"Just leave it where it is."

"Don't you think it's strange that the professor is allowing this one to live?"

"Yes, I do, but I wouldn't recommend questioning his reasons."

"Is everything arranged at the other end?"

"Are you questioning the competency of your superiors?"

"No, I would never do that!"

"Good, just start driving back to Portland and carry out your instructions, then wait for my call. I'll let you know when to proceed."

"Okay, talk to you later."

The older agent watched from the sagging old porch as the van turned around in the mud and started driving down the narrow road.

Lisa had no idea how tight she was holding the phone until she realized the phone was trying to vibrate.

"If you want to see your daughter, leave Alexia outside the front entrance in one hour, alone. Sarah's location will be provided after the task is completed."

Lisa almost dropped the phone. Alexia! She thought they wanted Kyle.

That meant she would have to wheel her all the way down the driveway in the dark. There wasn't any suitable vehicle to drive her down there in the wheel chair. What if somebody saw her? The scentlets! She had to change Alexia's scentlets and change them quick. Lisa quickly located a valid pair of scentlets and ran to the dining room to change them. Once again Alexia's feeding tube was out of her mouth and dripping on the ground. Her head was tilted all the way back and her mouth and eyes were wide open. There wasn't any time left to try and finish feeding her.

Lisa rolled up the tubes and put away the IV gantry. Bending down in front of the wheel chair stirrups she lifted Alexia's robe above her ankles and started removing her scentlets. After almost five minutes she had secured both new scentlets and nearly fainted when she noticed Alexia was staring straight down at her in a state of paralyzed shock. What was the time? She needed to know the time, exactly. She had forty-seven minutes remaining before Alexia had to be sitting outside the entrance gate, alone. There were still lots of things to do and no time to waste.

It had taken both men considerable effort to remove Sarah from the back of the cube van. In her apparent unconscious state she was of absolutely no assistance to them whatsoever. They had backed the truck up to the end of the picnic table and slowly managed to slide her out and place her on top of the table. Eventually they rolled her over and dropped her down to the bench and then finally down below the table.

They were using the same campsite Lisa had used when she delivered the camera. It was impossible to know when she might be waking up with the assortment of medications she had just consumed. The campground was quiet tonight, and unless somebody decided to take this exact spot, she would probably just sleep under the table all through the night. They knew somebody would be picking her up eventually, although that, and her general well-being, wasn't really a concern to either one of them. They were simply following orders. Drop one off, pick one up. Having no reason to stick around, they started driving closer to the Claytons' estate to wait for the next phone call.

Professor Akkaim adjusted the monitor for the best viewing angle of the Claytons' front entrance gate. He had been waiting for a long, long time for this night. Orchestrating all the components of his latest requisition had taken meticulous planning and everything was finally coming together like clockwork. He knew that privately, he might be criticized for his unusual leniency involving the mental patient, but the truth of the matter was that he could probably continue to count on Lisa's assistance in the future, anytime it might be required. She would know just how easily her daughter could be abducted again in the future. He enjoyed having this power over her as he did with almost everyone he abducted to work on the RA-

9 project. Any minute now Lisa should be opening those two gates and pushing Kyle's comatose mother outside.

Lisa put on her jacket and draped a woollen blanket over Alexia. She knew she would have her out there in time, but with not much to spare. She was so nervous about the entire situation her hands were trembling uncontrollably, and as much as she tried, she was unable to stop them. If anyone showed up now she would be hard-pressed to come up with a convincing explanation. Closing the front door behind her she started pushing Alexia away from the house.

The Beaucerons hadn't missed a move and were following them along the edge of the safe area. Soon their paths would converge and an interrogation would be inevitable. Alexia was tilted all the way back and lying almost prone on her back with her feet stretched well forward. The dogs converged on them the instant they left the safe parking area.

All three had surrounded them briefly and then moved away. Even with the correct scentlets such night-time encounters were uncomfortable at best. The wind was starting to pick up now and Lisa struggled harder and harder as they moved further away from the house. Finally she realized Alexia was squeezing the hand brakes tighter and tighter as she continued to try and stop the wheelchair from moving away from the house and out into the dark. Lisa finally pried Alexia's tight fingers off the brakes and managed to get moving again.

Small bits of branches were starting to fall from the trees as Lisa was getting closer and closer to the gate. She folded the blanket over Alexia's head as she pressed the button to open the gates. The dogs were off to the side and lying in wait for anyone, or anything, that might want to try their luck passing through the open gates.

Lisa rolled Alexia's wheelchair outside the gates and paused to study her surroundings. She decided to turn her wheelchair around and push it off to the side of the road and into a shallow muddy ditch next to the stone wall. She wouldn't be able to get her chair back up to the road without someone's help. Lisa tucked in the blanket around Alexia as best as she could, before she had to leave her there on her own. Hopefully the wind would die down before any larger branches started falling down on her.

There wasn't any sign of anyone waiting to pick her up so she walked back inside the estate and stared out through the vertical bars of the closing gates. She had the strangest sensation she was being watched, and knew it was quite possible that she was. Anybody could be hiding out there in the forest, watching her every move. There was dense cover and trees everywhere that could easily conceal someone. With one final look around Lisa could see Alexia was still sitting there motionless and facing the wall. She wasn't even trying to move the wheelchair, so she turned and started walking quickly back up the driveway towards the house.

Professor Akkaim had watched Lisa's every move. Alexia was outside the gate as requested, and on time. He was slightly uneasy about not seeing her face, but he could easily wait for confirmation before telling Lisa where her daughter was, provided of course that he didn't change his mind. He wasted no time in contacting his waiting agents to inform them about Alexia's location. He knew she needed to be collected soon, and the sooner the better.

The older agent pushed hard to open the heavy wooden doors on the old abandoned chicken coop. There were gaps in most of the worn out cedar boards around the outside of the structure, and the several rows of old battery cages had likely produced eggs on a small scale years ago.

The older agent had to demolish one bank of the wire cages to make room for the hearse, but he eventually he managed to squeeze it in between two remaining rows of cages. The overhead rafters were starting to sag in the center of the low building, but there was still just enough clearance to accommodate the raised roof of the black hearse.

It had been purchased in new condition from an out-of-state dealer, and then delivered to a nearby location three days ago. The older agent had walked almost four hours until he reached the prearranged pickup location. The hearse was supplied with everything they needed for the trip, including two coffins. Although stealing a local hearse would have been much less expensive and a simple task, purchasing one with all the appropriate paperwork was safer as nobody would ever be out looking for it. The older agent had set both coffins up on a ramp he had constructed behind the rear doors of the hearse.

Once they were filled, one person could easily slide them down the inclined ramp and into the back of the hearse, if he needed to. The ongoing modifications to the new water and oxygen supply tanks were almost finished. The connections to the coffins were concealed by connecting them to the front end of each coffin and running the lines underneath the tufted red velvet interior. Each coffin had its own independent supply system capable of providing just enough air and water to maintain life.

The older agent was taking care of all the last minute modifications on the hearse, but could easily call for extra help if he wanted it. So far it looked as if he had everything under control, but he still needed to test the new generator that he installed behind the barn. He'd been working on a crude wooden structure of timbers and also an enclosure for the generator in his spare time.

Fortunately there was an endless supply of old hand-cut lumber lying around this property which must have had a small saw mill working close by in the past. Gradually most things were starting to fall into place, but he still had a lot of electrical wiring to complete before everything was finished.

Lisa was almost completely out of breath after she stepped inside the front door. It was hard to believe she had just done exactly what she had just done. Alexia was now completely on her own, outside the safety of the estate walls and facing any number of unknown possibilities. For all she knew she could have just signed Alexia's own death warrant. She had no idea who, or what type of people, she was really dealing with.

Her mounting insecurities were causing her to second guess herself over and over again. She should have told James everything from the beginning. James and Al Anderson would have found a way to deal with the situation. She felt like she was getting close to a nervous breakdown when the front gate buzzer sounded on the kitchen intercom panel. What if James was at the front gate? She was starting to feel like she was about to lose it completely.

"Yes, this is the Clayton residence."

"Thanks for your co-operation. You'll find your daughter exactly where you dropped off the camera. If you say a word to anyone, you won't get her back alive the next time we take her."

Lisa tried to speak, but was too stunned and choked up to talk. Did they really drop Sarah off at the campground? Maybe it was just a trap to get her out of the house? Maybe they just wanted her to drive to a secluded place for her own execution? Maybe they were planning a double execution? How did she ever get herself into such a corner? No, she had to go. The more she thought about her new situation, the more she realised she could never return home.

She needed to start a new life for her and for Sarah. She had to. Besides, James and Kyle would never forgive her if they found out what she had done to Alexia; handed her over without an ounce of concern for her safety. Just put her outside the gate, just like taking out the trash. She really did have to leave. She was officially out of choices.

Lisa quickly ran upstairs and started packing everything she could fit inside her two suitcases. She desperately wanted more options, but she couldn't think of anything else to do. She would need to get the keys for the van and bring it down from the garage as soon as possible. Then she needed cash and there was only one place to get that.

After she finished loading up the van she would have to take another trip to the Murphy wall-safe. Face to face with Alexia. There wasn't any other way. She could only pray that nobody would show up before then. She slid both her suitcases under the bed and went to pick up the van. The Beaucerons followed her every step of the way and then she remembered they hadn't been fed today. They would have to make do on their own. Lisa had heard the helicopters running at the helipad earlier and broke into a run. She didn't want to see Kyle or Jen. She needed to keep moving as fast as she could, no turning back now.

Professor Akkaim had watched with amusement as Alexia kept trying hopelessly to get the blanket off her head. She was like a cat trapped under a tight bedspread, testing every possible direction for a way out. The agents had arrived swiftly, and although the wheelchair was awkward, they had it out of the ditch and inside the cube van in no time. A few wraps around Alexia with an industrial roll of shrink-wrap had her sealed tightly in her seat. They placed a loose cardboard box over her head and secured it temporarily with additional shrink-wrap. Minutes later they had fastened the cargo straps between her wheelchair and the internal wall cleats and Alexia was almost secured for transport.

After the wheelchair was secured they lowered the rear door and locked it in place. The professor had taken full advantage of this opportunity to watch his men in action and he couldn't resist the urge to time them on his stopwatch and assess their overall proficiency and performance. He was disappointed that it had taken them almost ten minutes to secure an elderly lady in a wheelchair. He picked up the phone and leaned back in his chair while he placed another call.

Lisa parked the van right outside the front doors and quickly ran inside to get her suitcases. She had stuffed them with all the clothes she could find as she knew Sarah would need lots of things as well. She dragged the heavy cases down the stairs and loaded them into the back of the van. She wanted some type of distraction and considered setting the entire house on fire, but decided against it. James would have more than enough problems as it was.

She quickly grabbed another pair of rubber gloves from the kitchen and ran back down the hall to the office. This time was different; she could feel the panic setting in and just wanted the gun, the money and to get going as soon as possible. Lisa ran through the open doors to the office then pulled hard on the picture frame to expose the wall-safe. It took several attempts to get it open because she was in such a hurry and she couldn't stop her hands from shaking. Finally it opened and she reached inside to pick up the bundles of cash.

She knew instantly that the gun was gone along with the open box of bullets. She also noticed several coats had been pulled from the coat hooks below the safe and tossed on the floor. What she was thinking seemed impossible or almost impossible, but right now she didn't have time to worry about it; she had to get out of there. She grabbed the cash, locked up the safe and left the room in a sprint. After speeding recklessly along the driveway, she hit the brakes and waited as the gates started to open.

Something in her mind told her that Alexia might still be sitting outside the gates. It didn't really matter anyway because if she was she had no intention of stopping. Lisa glanced around quickly as she sped away, but didn't see any sign of Alexia. Then she realised they would never divulge Sarah's location unless they had picked up Alexia. Lisa started driving as fast as she dared. She was very lucky to have gotten away unnoticed and could only pray that her only daughter would be alive and waiting for her.

Jen was about to try and get a new weather update when the phone rang.

"I'll get it, it's probably my dad," said Kyle.

"That's okay Kyle, I've got it. I'll let you talk to him in a minute."

"Hello."

"Hello. Is this Jennifer Lamar?" asked the person on the phone.

"Yes it is. Who's calling please?"

"It's the dispatcher from the hospital with a message for you from Doctor James Clayton. He wanted me to call and ask you if you could pick him up in an hour and a half at the same place you dropped him off. He said he'll be ready and waiting to go."

"Sure, that's fine. You can tell him I'll be there to pick him up."

"Great. I'll let him know. Thanks."

"You're welcome, thanks for the message. Bye."

"Bye for now. Fly safe!"

"Sounds like dad might be too busy to make the call himself, as usual."

"Yes, but I'm sure somebody is grateful for his attention right now."

"You're probably right about that. Okay, well that's great! We're going flying, night flying!"

"We—are going flying? Are you sure you don't want to stay here and get some rest Kyle? It's dark now and you must have been awake for a long time now."

"Yes, that's true. Just like I always am, besides I can't wait to go flying with you after all your new training."

"Well okay then, it's nice to have you with me anytime."

"Thanks Jen. By the way, I have some new information on the diagnostics program."

"What kind of new information?"

"The origin of the GhostNet intrusion is located in Iraq, close to the border with Iran.

"Are you saying you've almost found the needle in the haystack? What's over there anyway?"

"I can only see images of the general area. Here's the strange part, this two year old air photo data isn't showing much of anything in that area. From the images I've studied so far, it's mostly just a maze of different pipelines and dormant oil wells throughout the whole general area."

"Do you really think that's the location of all these GhostNet cyber-attacks?"

"I don't know for sure, but it is according to the program I designed. I'll have to recheck everything and see if I've missed something. It certainly looks like something might be wrong. There's really nothing there, at least not when these air photos were taken. Did you get the latest weather forecast?" asked Kyle.

"Yes, I checked it online and every thing's fine for the flight."

"When do you want to leave?"

"I think we should leave in about fifteen minutes."

"Sure, I'm ready whenever you are. Are the pedal extensions in the helicopter?"

"Yes, they're in the back. Let's get going now and we can install them, along with the dual controls."

"Sure, sounds good!"

Lisa was lucky not to have been pulled over during her frantic road race up to the campground. She slowed the van down to a normal speed as she reached the entrance and pulled into the campground. She could feel her emotions building inside her as she got closer to the campsite. She had to be prepared for anything and wished she had the gun with her. Lisa parked at the entrance to the campsite and shut off the engine. There wasn't any sign of anybody using the campsite at all; no sign of any vehicles, and no sign of any tents or fires.

Lisa could feel the tears welling up in her eyes as she started to realize what a fool she'd been. How could she have let herself trust a group of unknown strangers? She should have kept her trust in those she'd known for years; James, Alexia, and Kyle. She could feel herself start to physically collapse as she staggered towards the dark picnic table. All she could do was hold her head in between her hands and let the tears flow. She knew she was losing it, and then she heard *it* through her sobs. It was faint at first, but she definitely heard the sound of someone breathing or grunting, right from underneath the picnic table.

She slowly inched the toe of her foot forward and recoiled instantly when she felt it stop below the table.

"Sarah! Oh My God! Sarah! Sarah my sweet darling! Is that you?"

Wishing she'd brought a flashlight with her, Lisa lay down on the bench seat and tried to reach over and touch Sarah's motionless body. All she could feel was the rough tent-like fabric, and what felt like several large suitcase handles attached to it. The smell of smoke and burnt soot was all over her hands, and so far she hadn't even managed to budge her.

Lisa put both feet on Sarah's strange coat and started to push her into a slow steady rocking motion. It was all she could do to rock her gently back and forth and keep talking to her. She had to still be asleep and Lisa did whatever she could to try and keep her comfortable. She was next to her now and that was by far the most important thing for this moment in time. Hopefully she would wake up soon and Lisa could start the healing process with her daughter. Lisa moved herself down under the table and tried to put her arms around her daughter; that's exactly where she wanted to be when her daughter finally woke up.

The older agent shut off the diesel generator when he saw the truck driving up the old farm road. He had just finished testing all the various auxiliary equipment that required power from the diesel generator. Among other things, this location had an ideal view of any approaching vehicles and was generally well suited for their needs.

The suspension on the approaching truck looked like it was broken as it tried to navigate through the maze of large potholes. He pulled the huge barn doors closed and started walking back towards the farm house. Ten minutes later the truck was slowly backing up to the stairs to the porch. The truck was covered in fresh mud from driving up to the property. Steam was still coming out from under the truck where the water had contacted the hot exhaust pipes.

Both men stepped outside and walked around the back of the truck and opened the rear door. Incredibly, the wheelchair was still standing upright inside the back of the cube van, almost completely wrapped in shrink-wrap. Two men climbed inside the back of the truck, then untied all the anchor straps and rolled her to the edge of truck.

"Do you need a ramp?" asked the older agent.

"No, she doesn't weigh much" said the men as they lifted the wheelchair down between them and set her up on the porch.

"Where do you want her Boss? Any lights working in this place?"

"Not yet. You can still see what you're doing. Just wheel her in through the front door and leave her in the middle of the room beside the mattress."

Several minutes later they walked back outside and closed up the back of the truck.

"We left her just where you wanted. It's hard to tell if she's even alive under all that shrink-wrap. We opened the plastic around her head to make sure she was still getting some air."

"Good, thanks for your help. I'll finish prepping her later."

"Okay, we have to get going."

"Okay. Thanks for your help."

Lisa could hear Sarah's breathing becoming louder and louder. No matter how hard she pulled the strange handles on her coat she couldn't seem to shift her into a more comfortable position. Suddenly Sarah started swinging her arms around wildly and yelling "No! No! No! Sally! No! No! No!"

"Easy Sarah, easy, just take it easy Sarah. You're having a bad dream, that's all."

"Are you in my dream?"

"No Sarah. I'm your mother, Lisa."

"I don't have a mother."

"Yes you do and I'm here with you now. I'm never going to leave you again."

"Again, did you leave me before, Mother?"

"Yes baby, a long time ago when you were sick, but I've come back for you now."

'Liar! Liar! Liar! Right Sally! Sally?'

"Where's Sally?" asked Sarah.

"I don't know Sally. Was she with you before? Is she here now? Who is she? You can tell me, I'm your mother."

"Sally said she was sorry."

"Sorry for what my dear?"

"We can't tell. I'm so hungry. Do you have any hamburgers or Salt and Pepper chips?"

"No, we're going on a little vacation first and I'll buy you lots of hamburgers and chips as soon as I can. I promise."

"You promise?"

"Yes."

"Cross your heart and hope to die?"

"Yes baby, cross my heart and hope to die. Come on and let me help you into the car. I'm going to find a nice hotel where you can get a proper rest. After that we're going to travel until we find the perfect place to start our lives all over again, right from scratch, just you and I. Would you like that baby?"

"Yes Mother. I need my bag, but I don't think I need the scratch?"

"Okay then. Where's your bag Sarah?"

"I don't know. It's in the room."

"What room sweetie?"

"The room in the jailer's house and I know I'll have to walk backwards for a long way to find her."

"Okay baby, I'll drive nice and slow and we'll keep looking for your friend," trying to sound hopeful.

"Okay Mom, I'm ready to go now."

"Let's go baby. We're going to start our new life right now. I'm so happy I found you darling."

"Okay Mom, but don't you ever tell Sally you're taking me away from her, ever."

'Because she'll kill you, Deader than Dead!'

Sarah suddenly burst out laughing hysterically as loud as she possibly could.

The older agent lit a couple of small candles and sat down on the stained counter as he contemplated Alexia and how best to deal with her. It was as if she was in a constant state of hibernation. He wasn't sure if she needed to be secured in the same manner Sarah was or not. So far she hadn't moved a muscle. It was obvious how the neck brace and wheelchair constrained her, and with all the bulky blankets under the shrink-wrap it didn't seem like she was any type of risk to anyone, nor would she have any chance of escaping.

Still, after watching her intently for any sign of life, he decided not to take any chances. He set her in the middle of the room and secured all four rubber tethers to each corner of the wheelchair. If she was able to move, it would only be a short distance in every direction before she would come to a stop. Positioning her out in the middle of the room would make things much easier later on if by chance he was instructed to re-wrap her for transport. Even though he had yet to receive any official 'instructions' concerning her, he was quite sure this one wouldn't be around for long. Same stuff—different place, that's all.

In any case he still needed more time to work on the coffin supply systems inside the hearse. They needed to function perfectly on their own because if they failed, the outcome was always the same.

"How are those pedals Kyle? Can you reach them alright?"

"Yes. They're perfect. Nobody else ever uses these pedal extensions and I'm not growing that quickly. Are you taking any extra fuel for this flight?"

"No. What for? I have the same amount of fuel that James does every time he takes off from here."

"Yes I see that. I was just curious if you'd changed the quantity for your own personal reasons."

"No, I think it's an appropriate amount for an optimal mix of range and power requirements."

"Sure, I agree. Besides the flight to this hospital should only take us about twenty minutes each way."

"Are you ready to start the engine?"

"Sure, everything looks good on this side and I've already untied the main rotor."

"Do you want to fly Kyle?"

"No thanks, maybe a little later. I want to watch how you're flying now that you've finished all your advanced training."

"I can feel myself getting nervous already."

"Don't worry about that—you're not on any type of check-ride. I'm sure you had lots of those during your training anyway."

"You're right, I did."

"I bet they showed you all sorts of things I've never even tried. Anyway, just relax and enjoy the flight. I know it's dark outside now, but the weather looked good at sunset. Did you file a flight plan Jen?"

"No actually I didn't, but the hospital dispatcher knows we're coming over to pick up James."

"Well that's true. What about Lisa? Does she know?"

"I'm not sure. I talked to her earlier on, but we didn't discuss that."

"Do you want me to call her?" asked Kyle.

"Sure, give her a quick call if you like. Here, you can use my cell phone. I'll get the machine ready to start."

"I'm calling her now, but I'm just getting an 'away from the phone or out of the service area' recording."

"That's strange, our flight plan with central dispatch should be fine. Let's do some flying!"

"Sounds good to me."

"By the way, did you ever check into that Internet anomaly yet?"

"What are you talking about?" asked Jen.

"Remember when we briefly picked up the Internet service close to the estate, when we both flew in here last time."

"Oh, that's right. Really I forgot all about that. Was it really that unusual?"

"Well, getting Internet service from no apparent source can be a little unusual."

"We can investigate it tomorrow if you like Kyle, just let me know."

"There's no rush, let's keep it for something to do on a rainy day."

"Okay, I'm sure we'll figure out the reason once we put our minds to it."

"Yes, I'm sure you will too."

"Okay Kyle, I'm going to start up the machine."

"Good, I'm ready for that. I've always loved the sound of a turbine engine starting up."

"Me too," said Jen with a smile as she pressed her thumb down on the starter button.

Working on the coffins after dark was next to impossible so the older agent set up a propane lantern to continue working into the night. He needed to install extra oxygen bottles for this trip because of the long distance between here and the small airport where the coffins would be transferred to an aircraft. The tanks would have to be refilled or replaced at that point, but that wouldn't be his concern. His problem was to have both support systems installed, operational, and tested, before the coffins were sealed and loaded. He continued working in the back of the hearse as a half dozen rats ran freely about the old coop, oblivious to his presence.

Access to the coffins after they were occupied wouldn't be easy, so he needed it done right the first time if he was going to be successful. The rats were now becoming used to the vehicle and running right across the roof of the hearse really amplified the sound of their feet on the metal roof.

After he finished he climbed out from the back of the hearse, picked up the lantern, and started walking up towards the house. When he opened the door he was surprised to see Alexia's wheelchair was knocked over. The chair was still secured, but she was lying on her left side on the mattress with her head on Sarah's duffel bag. All the shrink-wrap was starting to loosen up, but it looked like she was sound asleep. He picked up the old blanket and tossed it over her. It wasn't clear how she managed to do that, but she didn't look like she was going anywhere soon, that's for sure.

"Jen, it looks like you're using a new procedure for your take off. Did they teach you that on your training course?"

"Yes, just for confined area take offs. We climb straight up from the pad until you're out of the hole. That way, if you have an engine failure you still have a helipad directly below you."

"Did they give you any surprise engine failures during vertical take-offs?"

"Yes—and they scared the living daylight's out of me."

"Nice. How high above the pad were you when they cut the power?" said Kyle while trying not to smile.

"We did some 'vertical autos' back to the pad from about forty to fifty feet."

"Did you do them yourself or was the instructor flying?"

"He did several demonstrations and I did several by myself after that. That was a good lesson."

"Cool. Those are all about your split-second timing. Well it's not hard to see you're a lot more comfortable than you were before. You're also becoming very steady."

"Thanks Kyle. Do you want to look after the communications for this flight?"

"Sure. I'll be happy too."

It had taken Lisa considerable time and effort to get Sarah out from under the table and into the back of van. Riding in the front seat wasn't an option and eventually

Sarah was lying down across the backseat and propped up on some old quilts Lisa had thrown in the van. She couldn't use a seat belt in this position, but at least she was lying down low and mostly out of sight. They had been driving for almost fifteen minutes when Lisa started slowing down for the stop sign.

"Have you seen Sally?"

"No, honey—I haven't seen anyone at all."

"Are you stopping at the stopping place?"

"What's that honey?"

"Are you stopping at the stopping place and why are you calling me what bumble bees make?"

"Oh that's just an expression."

"Word, word! Heard a new word."

"It's a nice word you say to someone you like Sarah. And yes, I guess we are stopping at the stopping place."

"Turn left, now, right now honey."

'Stay where you are Sally, just stay where you are!'

"Bell 407 November five-five-zero-five, its central dispatch. Do you copy?"

"Roger central dispatch, we copy you five-by-five."

"What's your current position and ETA at the hospital?"

"Our estimated time of arrival at the hospital is twenty minutes from now and we just departed two minutes ago. We're currently three miles southwest of the estate and en-route to the hospital."

"Copy that. Are you able to drop in for a possible medevac flight on your way in? A motorist reported a serious motor vehicle accident nearby with one possible fatality and another person with serious injuries. If you could stop in, evaluate the situation, and possibly bring that patient back to the emergency helipad, we'll be ready and waiting for you when you arrive."

"Certainly, we have a stretcher on board. What are the coordinates or location?"

"I don't have the GPS coordinates for you yet, but it's along Highway 16 next to a bridge. It looks like the vehicle had a direct hit with the concrete abutment at the east end of the bridge."

"Kyle, do you know where Highway 16 is?" asked Jen through the intercom.

"Yes. Roger central dispatch, we copy your request and we're on our way. We're estimating about seven minutes to the scene of the accident."

"That's great news, let us know when you're inbound to the hospital."

"Roger, will do. Bell 407 November-five-five-zero-five clear."

"Where exactly are we going, Kyle?"

"Just head south for a few minutes until we spot the highway."

"Do you want to fly Kyle?"

"No, you're doing fine, besides you've been the one doing all the flying lately."

"Okay, sure. Let me know if you have any safety concerns."

"I will, don't worry about that," said Kyle with a grin. "I can see a few lights from the highway up ahead. Do you have them in sight?"

"You must be talking about the only car I can see moving down there."

"I am. Highway 16 isn't used much at all this late in the evening. We should be able to see the river soon. It will be flowing in from the north."

"How do you know that's the right highway Kyle?"

"Easy, there's only one bridge around here that crosses Highway 16."

"Can we land there? What about wires?"

"I don't know about wires. We'll have to do a good recce with the Night-Sun lights. I'm sure we can land right on the bridge if there isn't any traffic. Okay, slow down Jen, I can see what looks like the river up ahead. We should be able to see the bridge shortly."

"Okay, I'm slowing down and turning on the Night-Sun."

"I can see the bridge just up ahead. Jen, keep slowing down and bring us in a little lower. I have a visual of the vehicle now. It looks like they hit the abutment at a high rate of speed."

"Can you see any wires Kyle?"

"Not yet, but keep us circling above wire height while I look for poles. They're easier to see than wires. Hold a low slow orbit around the bridge so I can have a good look around with the landing lights."

"Okay, the wind is calm and I think there's enough room to land on the bridge. Oh—My—God! That's looks like a body hanging over the bridge railing way up in front of the car. I can also see another person still in the car. From here it looks like most of the front windshield is shattered or gone," said Jen while trying to hide the panic in her voice.

"Hold it! Okay we've got some wires crossing the river just downstream of the bridge. Just make your decent on the upstream side and then move over above the bridge. That looks good Jen, keep it coming down nice and slow and try to land facing the wreck. Clear on my side, you've got lots of room. It looks like we're going to be the first ones on the scene unless an ambulance has already left," said Kyle as he watched the skids contact the bridge deck.

"No, we're first. I can't see any other vehicles here. I can clearly see another partially ejected body halfway through the windshield and almost out on the hood of the car. Should I shut it down Kyle?"

"Not yet, as dad always says, time is critical. I'll stay on the controls while you go and evaluate the situation."

"Okay, sounds good.

The skids are down and clear and I'm rolling the throttle back to flight idle, you have control."

"Roger, I have control," said Kyle.

Jen unbuckled her shoulder belts, unplugged the intercom cable and jumped out of the machine. Still wearing her helmet, she ducked down and sprinted towards the first victim draped over the bridge railing.

Instinctively, she reached out and grabbed the wrist to check for a pulse, but the stiffness of the arm and the cold temperature of the skin sent a shock-wave through her body. It was an older woman who was badly cut up and appeared very dead. She had obviously been ejected through the windshield, but it was strange to see such an advanced state of rigor mortise in a victim. This must have happened some-time-ago. After confirming there was definitely no pulse, Jen released the woman's stiff arm and ran over to other victim.

He was an older male who was also almost ejected, but stopped by the steering wheel of the car. These two couldn't have been wearing seat belts or else they must have failed during the crash sequence. Jen quickly grabbed his wrist and concentrated as she tried to feel for a pulse from this victim. Shortly afterwards she felt it; he was still alive and the pulse was strong.

Despite the limited light from the landing light and the noise of the helicopter she knew he still might have a chance. His face was almost completely covered in blood from what must have been injuries to the top of his head and scalp, but the trauma surgeons might be able to save him if they could just fly him to the hospital in time.

"Hello? Sir, can you hear me? Don't worry—we're going to get you to a hospital. I'll be right back," yelled Jen over the high pitched wail of the running helicopter. There was no answer and Jen ran back over to the Bell 407. She knew they were fortunate to have a stretcher with a set of wheels on board, or it would have been extremely difficult to load and move a patient like this on her own. She slowed down to make eye contact with Kyle before running underneath the spinning rotors. Kyle gave her the 'thumbs up' to proceed and then signalled her by dragging a finger across his throat. Jen didn't want him to shut down, so she motioned with her finger by spinning circles above her head which meant—'keep it turning'.

She opened the baggage compartment and removed the stretcher kit and the folding wheel set. It didn't take long to realize she should have been a lot more familiar with this piece of equipment, and how to use it. She vowed to practice setting up this stretcher until she could do it in her sleep, and while wearing a blindfold. Finally she lowered her head and pushed the stretcher as fast as she could back over to the mangled vehicle. After one small height adjustment the stretcher was about the same level as the top of the vehicle hood. She stepped on the wheel locks with her foot and immobilized the stretcher.

"Hello Sir! Try to hang on—we're here to help you. I need to move you out on the hood and across to the stretcher. Can you hear me?"

The man looked like he was drifting in and out of consciousness, probably from internal injuries and blood loss. Jen knew that if they were going to save him they had to act fast, really fast.

She pulled as hard as she could on the driver's door handle, but it was just too badly damaged to move. Most of the side windows had also been broken out during the crash.

"Sir, can you manage to pull yourself further out and up on to the hood of your car?"

She wasn't getting any verbal response at all except for the continual moans from the victim. Jen jumped up on the hood of the car and sat down face to face with the bloody man. After carefully positioning her feet on the windshield frame for leverage she hugged him around the torso and pulled with every ounce of strength she had. The man started screaming as she slowly manoeuvred him out from the wreck. She knew this wasn't exactly standard first aid protocol, but she didn't have much choice. She had to take charge and needed to act fast.

Finally he was lying down on the hood of the car and Jen managed to roll him over and onto the stretcher. Seconds later she had a blanket over him was pushing him towards the running Bell 407. Kyle had his thumb up as she approached the helicopter and she continued to walk directly under the spinning rotors. Luckily, because of her recent training, she was familiar with the ambulance configuration kit used on this machine and knew how to use it. She worked away as fast as possible until the stretcher was secured in the back of the helicopter, and then struggled to get the door closed and ready for flight.

She had heard Kyle rolling up the throttle and knew from the increasing down-wash of air outside he was ready to lift off the second the door was secured. Jen locked the door and instantly felt the machine lift off as it started climbing straight up into the night.

Jen located the intercom jack and plugged in her helmet and secured her seat belts.

"How is he doing?" asked Kyle as he pulled every last bit of allowable engine power.

"It's hard to say for sure, but I think you'd better hurry!"

Jen rolled him over on his side so he wouldn't swallow his tongue or suffocate in his own blood. His face was covered in blood from going through the windshield and almost certainly the moaning was being caused from the pain associated with any number of unknown internal injuries.

"What's our time to the hospital?" asked Jen as she looked at her watch.

"I just called them and advised them we'll be landing in eighteen minutes."

"Copy that, down at the hospital pad in eighteen minutes. He seems to be gurgling or having some kind of trouble breathing. I going to have a closer look and make sure his airway isn't obstructed and preventing him from breathing. Did they ask you for a current status report on the victim?"

"No, actually they didn't ask me about that. How is he doing anyway? Do you think he'll survive the eighteen minute flight to the hospital?"

With one explosive move, Sinzar's left hand had grabbed Jen's helmet and pulled her face down hard onto his bloody chest. Locking her head in his iron grip, he felt her futile resistance quickly fading away as his right hand calmly injected the large syringe, deep into the side of her neck.

Chapter 22

The new diesel generator fired up on the second pull. The older agent carefully adjusted the throttle before closing the lid of the makeshift enclosure. After checking his watch he quickly ran over to the small electrical fuse box, arriving seconds before the prearranged time. Wishing he had tested the circuit breakers first, he switched both 30 amp breakers on at exactly the same time.

Two large outdoor halide lamps slowly illuminated and started working together in a perfectly coordinated pulsating sequence. They were mounted on the front wall, high above the doors to the old wooden barn. One was installed on each side of the wall and both lamps were pointing directly to the north. The pulsating lights illuminated the entire area in front of the barn and caused a strobe light effect that gave everything an unusual slow-motion illusion.

Kyle yelped as the needle suddenly pierced the top of his right shoulder.

"I'll bet you're familiar with Benzodiazepine. If I squeeze this syringe, I think you know that all three of us will be dead very soon," said Sinzar calmly through the intercom.

"Yes, it's a tranquilizer," said Kyle knowing he was exactly right and fighting the onset of shock symptoms.

"That's the one, only this concentrated solution is my own special blend. Tried and true," boasted the man behind him.

Sinzar reached over Kyle's other shoulder to the electrical panel on the ceiling and systematically started pulling out the circuit breakers, row by row, to shut down all the radios, transponders, lights and navigation equipment onboard the helicopter, leaving only the two electric boost pumps running to supply fuel to the engine.

"Maintain your altitude and fly south using your compass."

"Where are we going to?" Kyle heard himself asking subserviently.

"Just keep flying south," commanded a voice from behind his head.

"Is Jen still alive?" asked Kyle, desperately hoping to hear any sign or sound of her voice from behind him.

"Just keep flying south," repeated the voice breathing down on his neck.

"What do you want with us?" pleaded Kyle as his options became almost nonexistent.

"Shut up! Do what I say, and don't speak unless I tell you to. Do you understand me?" said the man with growing agitation.

"Yes," said Kyle nervously after quickly evaluating the man's short temper and deciding not to test its limits.

Just then they crested a ridge line and the distant strobe lights came into clear view.

"Fly directly towards the pulsating lights."

"But they're expecting us at the hospital," pleaded Kyle.

"I said shut up! Nobody is expecting you anywhere."

Kyle had to struggle to fight his fear. Not knowing who was sitting behind him, where they were going, or why, and the stabbing pain from the needle lodged deep in his shoulder. Kyle quickly calculated the distance from the estate using speed and time.

"Start an approach towards the lights, we're going to land in front of those strobe lights," demanded the man behind him.

"What about wires? It's dark and we need to assess the approach direction and the landing area."

"Don't worry about that, just do as I say. Fly directly towards the lights and land in front of the building, nice and close, and facing the doors."

"Okay." He hated the fact that he really didn't have a choice. He hated that it felt so submissive—but that was the only word Kyle that could bring himself to say.

The older agent kept glancing at his watch and looking out into the night sky. He didn't know for certain when the helicopter was scheduled to arrive, or exactly from what direction. So far there weren't any aircraft lights to be seen, and with the noise from the generator it was next to impossible to hear anything approaching. Luckily the location was quite remote, and although he knew they were creating an unusual night time display, the truth of the matter was that nobody was likely to see it. After almost ten minutes he finally detected the noise of an approaching helicopter.

There were no lights whatsoever, but the there was no mistaking the sound as it continued getting louder and louder. Finally he could see it coming into view, slowly increasing in size and descending directly towards the barn. He walked back over to the electrical panel, took shelter and waited for them to land. The wind from the down-wash blasted all the loose debris around the area, and off the walls, before the machine finally landed in front of the barn. After he was sure they had finished shutting down and the rotors had stopped, he flipped the two circuit breakers and killed the large outdoor lights.

"Now what?" asked Kyle, feeling more and more hopeless, about the present situation he was in.

"I told you to shut up and keep quiet! I'll be the one asking the questions."

Sinzar kept the syringe pressed into his shoulder as the older agent opened the front door of the helicopter.

"So we finally have the boy. Nice work!"

Kyle was suddenly frozen with fear as he recognised the man standing outside.

"What do you want to do with him now?" asked the older agent.

"Do you have a pair of handcuffs with you?"

"Yes," replied the older agent.

"Is the other one here yet?" asked Sinzar.

"Yes, she's up at the house."

"Okay, cuff him and bring him up to the house for now. You'll have to come back and help me with the one on the floor beside me. She won't be moving for a long time."

Sinzar waited until the older agent had handcuffed Kyle to his wrist before pulling the syringe out of Kyle's shoulder.

"Good. I'll see you back here in a few minutes."

The older agent tugged on Kyle's arm to get him out the door and moving away from the helicopter. It was still very dark as they made their way down towards the farmhouse. A faint light from the lantern glowed through the small windows as the two of them approached the house.

"You people are making a big mistake! I'm sure you probably wanted my identical twin brother, Kyle."

"Nice try Kid, just keep quiet." said the older agent.

They both started walking up to the steps to the porch and stepped into the dimly lit room. Kyle let out a gasp as things came into view.

"Oh no, Mom!" Kyle shrieked as he struggled to run towards her.

Seeing Alexia lying on her side in the wheel chair was a complete shock. The light was enough for Kyle to see around the room and he suddenly became very scared and started shaking uncontrollably. The older agent stood Alexia's chair back up and tossed the blanket over her. Her chair was still secured by the tethers in the center of the room and the older agent unlocked the handcuff from his wrist and attached it to the main frame of the wheelchair.

Kyle leaned over and hugged his mother while trying to fight away the tears as he embraced Alexia tightly in his small arms. The older agent dimmed the lantern before he walked out of the room and back to the helicopter. Kyle waited for a couple of minutes before whispering into Alexia's ear.

"It's him! It's him Mama. I'm sure of it! He's the man who shot you and killed Ivan that night. He isn't wearing his gold glasses, but I remember his face. It's him Mama, I'm positive. He's the man who shot you."

They both remained locked together without moving for several minutes before his mother suddenly took his small hand in hers, and guided it into her side pocket under the blanket. Kyle felt them right away and instinctively knew what they were. They were bullets. Inexplicably, Alexia had about a half dozen loose bullets in her pocket and she was definitely trying to give them to Kyle. He quickly dropped them deep inside his socks and was still stunned at what his mother had just done. It was the first time he realised without a doubt that she hadn't completely lost all of her cognitive capabilities.

"There you are, you've got a few rolls of shrink wrap around here I hope."

"Yes, of course. We've got the masks and everything else we need here," said the older agent.

"Good, let's get her ready for shipping," said Sinzar.

"Do you want to prep her here or down at the house?"

"Are there any rafters in the ceiling of the house?"

"No," said the older agent.

"Okay, help me get her into the barn and we'll hoist her up on a rope. It's easier when you can spin them."

"Sure, I'll light a lantern and find some rope in the barn."

"Sounds good! I'll wait here for you."

Sinzar found a rag and tried to clean some of the fake blood off his face until the older agent returned.

"Everything is ready in the barn. I'll take her arms and you can take her feet if you want."

"That works. Let's do it," said Sinzar as he hopped inside the helicopter, and together they dragged Jen out from the back of the helicopter and carried her to the barn.

"Lie her down. I want to search her first."

Sinzar opened her jacket and realized that not only was she armed with a side holstered Glock 17, but that she had undone both holster straps and the gun was almost out of the case. It was lucky he had the element of surprise and injected her in the neck, or he could have very nearly been shot.

He quickly deactivated her phone by removing the internal battery. After several minutes he had collected an impressive selection of discreet lethal weapons, most of which he looked forward to adding to his own personal collection.

"Good, let's get that rope tied around her chest first and then we can hang her up from the rafters."

"Sure. What about the boy?" asked the older agent.

"Just wait until she's hanging and then you can bring him back up here. I want him to watch her getting prepared so he'll know exactly what's in store for him."

"Good idea." said the older agent. "I'll go down and get him once she's secured."

"Okay, don't say anything about the lady in the wheel chair. We want him to think she's getting prepared for shipping as well."

"Sure, not a word," said the older agent.

The older agent pulled on the rope while Sinzar lifted Jen up and together they hoisted her six inches off the ground. Sinzar grabbed her hair and held her head upright while the older agent went to work taping the full oxygen mask to her head and hooking up the modified intake lines. He carefully inserted his IV lines into her forearm and taped the excess tubing securely along her arm. Several leads were taped in place to collect vital signs for a small electronic monitor. Ongoing intravenous sedation was generally used for longer trips involving prolonged incapacitation. It was imperative everything was correctly positioned and secured before they wrapped her.

"Good, now you can go and bring the boy back," said Sinzar satisfied with the initial work they'd done.

Sinzar checked the syringe for the appropriate dosage, then removed a thick black woollen ski hat from his pocket and slid it over the top his head. It wasn't a complete disguise by any means, just a black trapper style ski hat with large ear flaps, but that was better than nothing.

Kyle finished stashing away the small pile of bullets as he heard somebody walking up the stairs to the porch. He buried his head into his mother's neck brace and hugged her tightly as the older agent walked into the darkened room.

"Don't worry about your mother. You should be seeing her again soon. They'll take good care of your two friends as long as you're working out okay."

"Where are you taking us?" pleaded Kyle as tears started forming in his eyes.

"Sorry, I said no questions. Come with me."

The older agent unlocked the handcuff from the wheelchair and locked it to his wrist. He brought Kyle's arm up behind his back in an arm-bar and pushed him up towards the barn.

As they entered the barn, Sinzar was taping Jen's wrists and ankles securely as he spun her slowly on the rope.

"Jen!" screamed Kyle as soon as he saw what the man was doing to her.

"Handcuff his arms to the post behind you so he gets a front row seat. Keep watching boy, because you're next," said Sinzar as he watched the older agent handcuff Kyle's arms behind the vertical timber post.

Kyle's mind immediately started to process every dark and ugly feature of the man's dimly lit face. He could see he had gone several days or more without shaving, but that didn't matter to Kyle. It was a face he would never, ever forget.

Sinzar put on some gloves and grabbed a large industrial roll of shrink wrap and started wrapping it around Jen's lower legs. Then he picked up an old broom and passed the handle through the center of the roll.

"Start spinning her when I tell you," shouted Sinzar to the older agent.

Moments later Sinzar held the broom handle in both hands as the spinning roll began to unravel and efficiently wrapped Jen into a tight plastic cocoon.

Kyle was sobbing at the futility of his situation. He so desperately wanted to help, but there was nothing he could do. He knew he may have a chance with the bullets, but without the use of his hands his choices were severely limited.

"Say goodbye to this one as well if you want, but you never know, you just might see her again if you're useful to the professor."

"Who are you and who's the professor?" yelled Kyle frantically.

"No questions, remember, no questions," said the ugly man in the black trapper hat with over-sized ear muffs.

Sinzar trimmed the shrink-wrap with a utility knife and tucked in all the loose ends. He then gave Jen a slow spin as he stepped back and admired his work.

"One down, two to go," said Sinzar as he pulled the small black case from his pocket and walked up behind Kyle.

Sinzar guided the needle with astonishing precision directly into an artery and moments later Kyle was slumped over in the front of the post.

"What do you want to do next?" asked the older agent while trying to be helpful.

"Let's cut her down and get her inside a coffin. It won't take long to make the connections with these quick-lock connectors after she's secured inside the hearse."

"It shouldn't take more than five minutes and we can start preparing the boy."

Together they cut Jen down and moved her over to the adjacent chicken coop.

Sinzar opened the first coffin and placed Jen inside.

"Did you bring the packing foam?"

"Yes, I've got about six bags below the table," said the older agent.

"Okay, I see it," said Sinzar as he reached below the table and pulled out a bag.

Once Jen was in the coffin, he double checked the mask and the connections, then started pouring out the small pink foam pellets as he pressed them in tightly around her body. It had taken two bags to completely cover her and they both had to press down hard to close the lid. They would need the last four bags to secure Kyle because of his small size. It was a really snug fit, but keeping them both completely immobilized should also help stabilize them for the long trip.

After she was hooked up and secured they came back to the barn and repeated exactly the same procedure on Kyle. He took far less time to complete due to his size and weight. Both men were professionals and worked quickly and efficiently together. Finally, after testing the oxygen and water systems on both coffins, they locked the back door of the hearse.

"Do you need my help finishing up here?" asked Sinzar.

"Can you stick around and help me get the helicopter moved into the barn?"

"Sure," replied Sinzar.

"Good, I'll go and start the generator."

The older agent fired up the generator and started to unwind the steel cable from the electric winch.

"Are you just planning to drag it inside? Don't you need handling wheels?" asked Sinzar as they both pushed the barns doors wide open.

"No, I found a few pieces of old pipe that we can use for rollers."

"Okay, good idea, let's try it," said Sinzar.

Between the two of them they slowly winched the helicopter inside the large barn and closed the doors with several meters to spare. Together they walked back over to the chicken coop and opened the old wooden doors.

"Well that's it for me around here. Is everything ready to go with the hearse?"

"Yes. Keys are in the ignition, she's full of fuel and ready for anything."

"Well I'm ready to roll. I'm sure you can take care of the loose ends around here after I'm gone. Do you need any clarifications?" asked Sinzar.

"No clarifications required. Have a good trip."

Sinzar nodded as he opened the door and stepped inside the front seat of the luxurious hearse. The engine started flawlessly and moments later he pulled out from inside the dark rat infested chicken coop and started driving down the road.

"What's that awful smell?" said Sarah as she came around a corner on the highway.

"They must be fertilizing the fields with fish or something."

"Word! Word! Heard a new word! What's a fertilizing?" asked Sarah.

"Oh it's when they put fish or chemicals into the soil for farming."

"Okay, grow fish, for growing fish, growing confused, okay, never-mind, drive for five, no ten minutes and turn left. No right. No left. That's it. Drive for ten minutes past the stink, nine minutes now, and turn left."

"Are you sure Sarah?"

"Yes, Sally's waiting and I know she's upset and starting to get really angry. Nobody likes to be abandoned and left behind like rotten garbage. Right Mommy?"

"No, of course not my dear."

'Liar! Liar! Burn in Fire!'

"No Sally! Stop it! Stop it!" screamed Sarah.

"What's the matter with you my dear, are you okay?"

"Just drive for seven more minutes and then turn left up the long bumpy road."

"Okay don't worry Sarah, we'll find her."

'Shut Up Sally! I Mean It Sally! Just Shut It Right Up! All the Way Right Up!'

The older agent finished loading the various small tools and equipment back into the Cadillac. It hadn't taken him long to remove the lights and electrical panel as everything was a temporary installation in the first place. After that was done he walked out behind the barn and picked up a five gallon gas container and started walking slowly back down to the farm house.

He could see the lantern was still putting out a little light as he reached the bottom of the stairs. Checking for his lighter, he opened the gas can and walked up the stairs. As he walked into the room he was surprised to see Alexia had once again toppled over on the mattress. This time it appeared as if she was in a prayer position next to the wheelchair. The blanket was still draped over her, but it looked like she was kneeling next to the wheelchair with her hands held together in prayer. He certainly wasn't going to deny her that last rite in the remaining minutes of her life. The older agent calmly walked past her and started dousing the interior floors and walls of the small room with gas. He poured a heavy line of fuel directly into the middle of the room and started soaking Alexia in gas. There was more than enough to do the job now. He stood in front of her and pulled out his disposable lighter.

"Sorry Lady, I just do what they tell me."

The older agent flicked the lighter two or three times until he had a flame. At that moment he watched in amazement as she lifted up her head and neck brace together and stared straight at him. With her mouth half open and her face strained and contorted she struggled to speak in a raspy, deliberate and almost alien voice.

"Ivan's waiting for you" said Alexia just as six deafening blasts rang out from the revolver under her blanket. At point blank range, the bullets went clean through the older agent's upper chest and neck. Almost immediately he fell over backwards clutching his neck with both hands as his lighter went out and dropped to the floor.

James stepped out of the cab and pushed the intercom buzzer. He knew Jen was expecting a call to fly out and pick him up tonight, but it was getting so late he decided to call a cab instead. After several more tries without receiving an answer he began searching through his keys for the gate's over-ride key.

After pulling apart some overgrown ivy, he located the small electrical console and inserted and turned the small key. The gates slowly started rolling apart. He was almost surprised it still worked as it had been ages since the last time he'd used it.

While he was sitting inside the cab waiting to drive through the gates, the light from the headlights occasionally reflected from the Beaucerons' eyes as they lurked around inside the gates. As the driver started driving up towards the house, he watched them as they started their usual pursuit of any vehicle entering the property.

It was a little unusual that Lisa didn't answer the intercom, but there were also hundreds of legitimate reasons why she couldn't, especially now when he had just showed up without warning.

"Just park right in front of the main door and whatever you do, don't get out of the taxi."

"Sure Doctor Clayton, no problem," said the driver. "There we are. Tonight's damage is one hundred and five dollars," said the driver.

"Here's my card. Add twenty for yourself."

"Thank you very much. I'll get it ready for your signature. There, here you are. Just sign at the bottom."

The driver handed his credit card back to James and watched with concern as James stepped outside into the midst of the three Beaucerons.

"Thanks for the ride. I'll open the gate when you reach the bottom. Don't step outside the car under any circumstances."

"Times! Times! Time's up! Start slowing down now and look for the bumpy road on the left," yelled Sarah forcefully.

"Okay, okay dear. I'm looking, but I don't see anything yet. No sign of any bumpy road around here. Wait. I just saw a car turn on to the highway from that side."

"What kind of car? A Caddy car? Tell me!" yelled Sarah.

"I can't tell honey, it's much too far away. I can barely see the lights."

"What color was it?"

"I can't tell Sarah, it's too far away. Do you want to go after the car or turn and go up the road?"

"Sally's waiting and she gets really angry when people abandon her."

"Okay honey, let's go and look for Sally here first. This must be the bumpy road right up here."

"Turn! Turn! Turn left! Right now—hurry!"

James walked upstairs still looking for any sign of Lisa.

"Lisa? Lisa? Are you around here somewhere?" said James as he continued to grow more and more perplexed.

As he walked down the hall he arrived at her bedroom; the door was wide open and the lights were on. James felt an uneasy sensation rush through his body. Normally this wouldn't be unusual, but Lisa's outstanding organizational habits would never have permitted even a trace of something as unkempt as this. Even the blankets and pillows had been removed from her bed.

James picked up the pace of his search. He wanted to know exactly who was here and where they were. He ran down the stairs and quickly made his way over to Alexia's living area. There wasn't any sign of her, or any of the regular nurses anywhere. James pulled out his cell phone and immediately called Jen. He knew for sure that she was expecting his call.

"The person you have called is away from the phone or temporally out of the service area".

He immediately tried Lisa's cell phone and got the same message. After making sure the house was definitely empty, James ran out the door and found one quad still parked outside. He started it up and drove up to Chalet Number Five faster than he'd ever done before.

After opening the heavy door he turned on the lights and quickly searched both floors of Chalet Number Five. The logs in the fire were still hot and he also found Kyle's bags lying upstairs. All the computers were still running and even the coffee pot in the kitchen was warm. James ran outside again and sped away up the trail to the helipad. They must be up there, all of them. They had to be.

James was feeling better once he noticed the lights were still on up at the hanger. They must have some reason for everyone to be up here. As the quad broke out from the trees he saw instantly that the hanger lights were on, but his helicopter was gone. Now he was genuinely concerned. They must have had an emergency. Maybe they had to fly Alexia to a hospital. There weren't too many other possibilities. James took out his phone again and made some calls to the local hospitals.

"This van sure wasn't built for roads like this," said Lisa as her head slammed into the ceiling of the van for the tenth time.

Sarah was screaming with all the thrill and enjoyment of a kid on a roller-coaster. Suddenly, she stopped quickly, composed herself, and became very serious.

"Wait! Wait! Stop! Stop! We're here! Be quiet and help me get out of the car."

Lisa was surprised to see that Sarah almost got out of the van on her own.

"Be very very, very, very quiet and follow me. I know exactly where Sally is."

Lisa and Sarah had parked the van about two hundred yards before the main farm house. They could see the Cadillac parked halfway between the old farmhouse and the other buildings further up the road. Sarah led the way as Lisa walked behind her. She was very uncomfortable with this entire situation and felt extremely vulnerable. There was no mistaking the dim light coming from the front room in the old farm house as they approached.

"Be quiet. Sally doesn't like you even a tiny, tiny, tiny little bit," said Sarah.

"I've never even met her," said Lisa.

"That's why you're still alive, she can be very very, very very bad when she wants to."

They both crouched down and waited silently outside for several minutes before quietly walking up to the front of the farm house. Sarah led the way as they slowly walked up the stairs and on to the porch.

"It smells like gas," Lisa whispered.

"Let's go inside," said Sarah quietly.

Lisa felt her foot sliding on the wet floor and screamed as she almost stepped on the older agent's head lying on the bloody floor. Alexia was clutching an old rag doll and suddenly lifted her head and pointed the gun directly at both of them and pulled the trigger. Three loud clicks broke the silence as the revolver failed to fire and Alexia dropped it on the mattress. Finding her sitting alone in the middle of a gas soaked room with a dead man on the floor wasn't what she was expecting.

"Where's Sally?" asked Lisa.

"Don't worry about her. I don't trust her anymore and besides—I think her and I need to have a little talk."

'Right Sally? You just tried to send Mom and me straight to burning hell! Didn't You?'

Lisa stepped over the obviously dead man and started untying the retaining straps attached to the wheelchair.

"We need to get her out of here. Help me get her back into the chair." Sarah snatched Sally from Alexia's iron grip and stuffed her back inside the duffel bag with several hard stomps of her foot.

'Double Cross Me! Double Dead You! Liar! Liar! Burn in Fire!'

"Sure Mom, good idea! Hold the chair and I'll lift her up."

Sarah picked her up like a bag of chips and set her down inside the wheelchair.

"Let's push her outside and I'll carry her down the stairs," said Sarah calmly.

Five minutes later they had moved Alexia out beside the road and wrapped her in a new warm blanket.

"Now what?" asked Sarah as they walked back to the van.

"I don't think we have room to take her, not in the wheelchair."

"So you're going to abandon her too?"

"No Sarah, I'll get some help for her, I promise. What about your friend Sally? Did you see her anywhere? Is she coming with us?"

"I think I might know where she's hiding, but she has somewhere else she needs to go. Stay here, I'll be back soon, don't try to follow me," said Sarah as she turned around and marched away into the night.

James knew right away after the first two calls that something was seriously wrong with this current situation. Everyone from the estate was missing, including his helicopter. Both the night shift hospital emergency flight dispatcher and Air Traffic Control Services had no record of any radio contact with them whatsoever. The Air Traffic Control Service had started a search on all the local radio frequencies, as well as continuous monitoring of all the designated channels, and also for any sign of any ELT signals in the area. At the same time they were retrieving and reviewing all radar data and searching for any confirmation of a flight. The distance from the airport to the estate would make any positive radar records unlikely unless they were flying close to the airport.

He was struggling to find an explanation for everyone's disappearance, and the fact that none of them could be reached or contacted in any way. There was nothing left to do at the heli-pad so he closed the hanger doors, but left the lights on in case they were just out on a local test flight. He did realize that Jen may have had a few new things to show Kyle after her recent training, but still he should have been able to contact her at any time. James started the quad again and began a slow ride back down to the house. He didn't want to think the unthinkable, but he knew that if something didn't break very soon, he was going to have to call Al Anderson.

James slowed down and stopped as he rode between the two garage buildings. He shut off the quad and opened the door to the first building. He needed to know exactly what vehicles were still here on the estate. He hadn't noticed any other vehicles parked anywhere when he arrived in the taxi. In less than five minutes he had his answer; only the van was missing. Lisa often drove that as well, so a rational explanation was still possible. They could have gone to town to pick up something, or even driven Alexia to the hospital. James locked the doors to both buildings and rode back down to the house.

Sarah reached down and picked up the lighter from the pool of blood on the floor. She tried to dry it off and then flicked it several times until she got a flame. Knowing that it still worked she stuffed it deep inside her coat pocket. Her duffel bag was still lying on the mattress and the gun was lying beside it. She picked up the gun and held in both hands. She liked the feel of it as she pointed it at Sally and then the dead agent.

'Bang! Bang! Bang!'

She practiced holding it in her hands and pointing it at different objects around the room.

'Bang! Bang! Bang!'

Finally she put it inside her duffel bag and closed the zipper tight. She bent over, lifted the gas can, and slowly tipped it over. It was still about half full and she started sloshing out the fuel; slowly at first, and then she was almost in a state of frenzy as she started pouring gas over the agent, her bag, and the mattress. Then she walked backwards to the top of the stairs pouring a steady stream of fuel as she went. Setting the fuel can down Sarah walked back inside to get her duffel bag.

'I knew you come back to save me!'

With her duffel bag in one hand she picked up the gas can with the other and walked back outside and up towards the Cadillac.

'I knew you wouldn't abandon me like your real mother did!'

Sarah reached the black Cadillac and tried several doors before the back door opened. She stuffed the duffel bag on the floor behind the front seat and drenched the back seats with fuel. Once again she walked away backwards pouring a line of gas on the ground before tossing the gas container back inside the car.

'I didn't tell her to shoot you Sarah—I was trying to stop her. I won't ever tell anybody about what you did in the car, I promise Sarah. Wrong Sally! Cross your heart and hope to die!'

Sarah bent down to the grass and flicked the lighter twice. The flames ripped across the ground and into the Cadillac. Moments later the interior was engulfed in a raging inferno. Sarah stared into the flames and finally kicked the back door shut and started walking back down towards the house. She walked up the steps to the house and lit the fuel on the front porch, then tossed the lighter inside. The blast from the fuel igniting almost knocked her over as she ran away. Both fires were burning strong as she kept running down the road past Alexia and back towards the van.

There was enough of a breeze that the house was quickly engulfed in flames.

"Oh-my-God, what have you done? Did you find your friend Sally?" yelled Lisa in a state of panic.

"No, she's gone! She had to go somewhere else. Let's get going Mom. I fixed everything for us. She can't hurt you now. Let's just get as far away as we can."

Just then several large explosions rocked the Cadillac and one of the buildings behind the car started burning.

"Okay, Sarah, get in the car, we're leaving right now."

"What about that one?" asked Sarah as she pointed her finger at Alexia.

"She's safe where she is. We'll call for help as soon as we're a long way away from here."

When they reached the highway Lisa stopped and turned on her phone. She told Sarah exactly what to say then dialled the number to the estate. Sarah left a short message on the machine before throwing the phone out the window.

"We're finally free Mom. I feel so much better now, but I'm really very very, very tired and very very, very hungry."

"We'll find something to eat soon, I promise."

James sat down on the exterior porch of the main house. There wasn't any point in waiting any longer. He opened his cell phone and placed a call to Al Anderson.

"Hi James, What can I do for you? I've got you programmed in my phone. I'm sure you were glad to see Kyle back home again tonight. I really have to apologise for keeping him working at CFRC-8 so long. They love him down there you know."

"Al, the reason I'm calling is there is nobody around here anywhere. Just when did Kyle return anyway?" The pause was long and silent.

"You weren't home when the Black Hawk arrived at your estate?"

"No, I was on shift at the hospital. Even my helicopter is gone now."

"Have you alerted Air Traffic Control and the FAA?"

"Yes, they're conducting a preliminary search right now."

"Listen James, let me make a few calls and I'll see if I can get some information. I'm going to have the Black

Hawk redirected back to your area to assist in a search, or any way possible. Keep your phone turned on and I'll call you back soon."

"Okay, thanks. I'll be waiting for your call."

James could tell the Beaucerons were much more active than usual. After searching around the kitchen he found some food for them and put it outside in case they had missed a meal. All three dogs devoured their food in no time. James kept trying to come to grips with the situation. It was highly unusual for Kyle or Jen to fly anywhere without a flight plan. They must have told somebody where they were going, unless maybe his helicopter was stolen by someone. Anything was possible at this point. Still, he felt confident that Al Anderson and his endless supply of resources would come up with some answers soon.

Within minutes of the call from James, Al Anderson had ordered the same Black Hawk helicopter diverted back up to the north, plus two additional machines were being dispatched to provide any assistance required. The Black Hawk crew had confirmed that Doctor Clayton's Bell 407 was on the helipad when they dropped off Kyle, and that Jennifer Lamar was there and unloaded him when they arrived. After that, he didn't really have any new information. A search coordinator had been called in to set up an initial search operation once all the helicopters arrived in the area.

James walked down the hall towards his office. There was a remote chance that Kyle had used it to do some flight planning, but so far he had no proof he was ever even inside the main house. When he sat down at his desk he immediately noticed that Alexia's portrait was ajar on one side. He jumped up and raced across the room to his safe. After a few spins of the dial his Murphy wall-safe was open and he knew instantly that he'd been robbed. He didn't remember exactly how much cash he had in the safe, but his firearm, cash and some ammunition were definitely missing. All his documents seemed to be in order, including Kyle's internment schedule. James didn't touch a thing and walked back to his desk to call Al Anderson. When he reached over to pick up the phone, the blinking number on the adjacent answering machine caught his eye.

Jen could feel her eyes opening and closing, but nothing else. Her senses were detecting motion, but her equilibrium was completely askew. It didn't matter what appendage she tried to move, she couldn't. She could blink, but nothing changed. It was beyond pitch black. Still, she couldn't stop her inquisitive mind from running on overdrive. Was she dead? Had she passed the sign in the subconscious corridor that connected the living with the dead? 'Sorry. No Returns.' How would she know? If you know, does that mean you are? It happened. It's over. You're done. You are not going back, ever.

Jen forced herself to swallow. She couldn't. She tried to scream, but she couldn't. It felt like her mouth and throat were being invaded by hungry, alien snakes. She tried to scream, but there wasn't any sound. All she could hear was a steady distant tone. She could feel panic pounding relentlessly at the door. Her worst enemy was trying to get in at all costs. She had to keep focused and fight to remain calm. It was simply her only chance if she was, in fact, still alive. She was completely disoriented and had absolutely no idea if she was horizontal or vertical, facing up or down, stable or spinning.

There were only two choices; she was either alive or she wasn't and there was something after death. Some form of cognition was definitely going on, despite the complete disconnect with her body. Then she realized it; her lungs were expanding and contracting. She was breathing. She had to be alive.

James reached across the desk and struck the 'play' button hard with his middle finger.

"Find this phone and find the wheelchair lady. Very, very, very, very big hot fires, burning on the mountains!"

James replayed the message over and over. It was a female voice that he didn't recognize calling from Lisa's cell phone. He had no way to trace the call or start any search without his helicopter, so he called Al Anderson. After a ten minute conversation, he had told him everything about the message and the robbery. Al informed him of the incoming search helicopters and a special internal forensic investigation team he would be bringing in.

The search for the cell phone transmission had just begun, and with the current technologies they could identify the cell phone tower and calculate the direction and distance to the mobile device. The results wouldn't take long and the machines would then be directed to the location of the phone call. He also advised James not to touch anything in his office and stand by for further developments.

James got up and looked around once more before walking away and locking the door on the way out. Lots of people could be coming over so he needed to try and secure the Beaucerons for their safety. They were still close by after being fed and surprisingly co-operative. James knew he desperately needed to get some sleep, but a few moments later the phone was ringing again.

"Hello?"

"Hi James, One of our helicopters has spotted several fires about twenty miles south of the estate. They're inbound now and I expect a report soon. I'll send a Black Hawk over to pick you up if you want to go as well."

"What kind of fires? Was it a fire from a helicopter crash?"

"Sorry, I don't have any details yet. Do you want to go? So far we've managed to keep everything internal, but if a forest fire breaks out during the night that could change quickly."

"I understand, sure send a machine over. I'll be up at the heli-pad in ten minutes and ready to go."

The pilots flying the first Black Hawk didn't need any coordinates to know where they were going. The night time fire was visible from twenty to thirty miles out, and as they got closer they could see at least two separate fires were burning.

"Are we landing right away?" asked the co-pilot.

"No, let's do an initial assessment from the air and we'll wait for instructions."

"Okay, copy that," said the co-pilot.

Doing a wind direction check doesn't get any easier for pilots than when they can see the smoke trail of a fire. The pilot in command descended over the fires and started a slow orbit around the area while staying just high enough not to aggravate the flames with his down-wash. The co-pilot manually operated the powerful Night-Sun lamp underneath the helicopter as they studied the area below for landing sites, wires and a current fire situation report.

Two buildings and possibly a vehicle appeared to be almost completely destroyed by the three fires. If the winds had been blowing from a slightly different direction that barn would have gone up in flames as well.

"Hey, bring her around to my side and air taxi down the side of the road. Hold it. There's someone out in the field over there" said the co-pilot as he focused the beam of the Night-Sun on the ground.

"Yes you're right. It looks like someone sitting in a chair," said the pilot in command.

"Looks like it might be a wheelchair from here," said the co-pilot as he adjusted the beam of light.

"Okay, let's make a radio call and let them know what we've got up here," said the pilot in command.

"Roger that."

The approaching drone from the helicopter's engines was getting louder and louder. James could barely keep his eyes open and he just wanted this nightmare to end. Where was everyone? What exactly was going on around here and why? He desperately wanted some answers. He put on a spare helicopter headset and watched the silhouette of the large helicopter appear above the tree-line before walking around to the side of the hanger for shelter.

The machine dropped down with impressive precision on top of his heli-pad and then rolled the throttles down to flight idle. James walked out towards the aircraft and waited for the pilot's signal before walking under the spinning rotors overhead and climbing in through the rear sliding door.

The turbine engines spooled back up to flight RPM as he adjusted his seat-belts and plugged into the intercom.

"Good evening Doctor Clayton, we've got some news for you. Regarding the tip we received. It looks like at least one person is alive up at the fire location. Al Anderson has diverted the third helicopter to pick up a team of forensic investigators."

"Has anybody landed up there yet?" asked James.

"No, we'll be the first machine touching down and we should be there soon."

After five or ten minutes James could see the faint lights from the fire through the Plexiglas windows. He was preparing himself for the worst. He didn't want anyone to discover the remains of Kyle and Jen amongst the ashes of a burned out helicopter. Nothing could prepare him for that.

James peered out of his window as the Black Hawk pilot stretched out his orbit and eased the machine into the landing area. The illumination from their lighting systems was far superior to his own as he saw how it lit up the entire area below. As they repositioned in the hover he could see Alexia was sitting out in the field. He still had absolutely no idea what she was doing out here at night.

He was the first one out the door the moment they landed and he immediately ran straight over to Alexia. She had no reaction at all, which was normal, and she didn't appear to be injured in any way.

James could smell the fuel immediately and started pulling back her blanket. The steady breeze had helped to evaporate some of the fuel on her clothes, but any prolonged contact with the fuel could also burn her skin. James examined her carefully, and apart from several random pink areas on her skin it appeared most of the fuel had been soaked up in all the layers of her blankets and clothing.

The other crew members had gone in the opposite direction to examine the aftermath of the fires. Both wooden structures were almost completely burned to the ground and a smoking charred metal hulk was all that remained of some type of vehicle.

"Are you alright Alexia? I'm so glad we found you. What's going on Alexia? What exactly happened out here anyway? Have you seen Kyle or Jen? Have you seen Lisa?"

James couldn't stop asking her questions even though he knew she couldn't respond. Alexia, as always, had no response at all. She just stared into the night with her usual blank expression.

"Doctor, Doctor Clayton!"

James turned to see one of the crew members jogging down the slope towards him.

"Yes, yes I'm Doctor Clayton."

"I wanted to let you know that we've just found your helicopter," said the crew member as he slowed to a stop.

"Oh no, I don't believe it!" screamed James unable to control himself.

"Your helicopter is fine Doctor. It's inside that barn up on the hill."

"I thought you found the wreckage in the fire—my helicopter is here, inside a barn?"

"Yes."

"Any sign of my son or anyone else up here?"

"No. Not a thing. We're waiting to hear back from Al Anderson regarding the helicopter."

"What are you talking about?"

"Well, he's in charge of everything now so they're deciding whether to keep your machine here for the forensic team, fly it back to the estate, or move it to another location."

"Okay, that's fair enough. I'm really too tired to be flying tonight anyway."

"I understand, we're making some arrangements to get you and your wife home shortly."

"Okay, thanks," said James.

"That's the least we can do for you," said the crew member as he walked away up the hill.

The smell of burnt charred wood was everywhere, inescapable. James sat down next to the wheelchair and moments later his phone was ringing.

"Hello."

"Hi James, it's Al again."

"Yes—"

"I'm glad to hear your wife's okay."

"Where's my son? Where's Jen? It was ultimately your responsibility to protect them," yelled James as he vented his frustration.

"I'm sorry, but I can't answer that yet, and I'm sure it's just a matter of time. We are going to have to leave your helicopter here for at least one night, and possibly two, so the forensic team can start collecting evidence."

"What type of evidence?"

"Well, apparently they found a bloody stretcher in the rear seating compartment."

"What? You said they found a stretcher."

"Yes, just like I said. Anyway the team will be on location shortly and hopefully we'll have some answers soon. I've sent a vehicle out there to pick you both up and take you home to the estate."

"Okay—thanks."

"No problem. We'll drop you both off at the front door. I'll send some forensic investigators over tomorrow to examine the safe if you don't mind."

"Call me if you have any news about Kyle or Jen."

"Don't worry. I'll call you right away if we have some new information."

"I'll be waiting."

"Take care, James."

James opened up Alexia's clothing to help dry out the fabric while they waited for their ride. Even though the dogs were locked up James took a moment to verify that Alexia was wearing a valid pair of scentlets before they went home. There were just too many pieces to put it all back together. What exactly had transpired in this remote location? It would be almost impossible to fit a stretcher and a wheelchair in the back of his helicopter at the same time. New unanswered questions continued to cascade into his mind.

He turned to see the approaching headlights of a vehicle driving up the road. James stood up, rearranged Alexia's blanket and pushed her closer to the side of the road. He waved his hand at the silver crew van as it slowed down and pulled over.

'Doctor Clayton?"

"Yes, that's me."

"I guess I'm your ride back home tonight. I hope you don't mind the van. At least it's got a power loading ramp."

"No, not at all. That's fine with me."

"Just give me a minute and we'll get her loaded inside."

"Sure, sounds good."

James strapped himself in the front seat after Alexia was secured in the back.

"Did you have any trouble finding this place?" asked James.

"No, Al Anderson gave me the coordinates and I programmed them into my new GPS with an on-board map display."

"Well those units have certainly made navigation easier for everyone."

"Al Anderson mentioned he would try to send one or two of your wife's medical assistants out to your estate shortly after you arrived. I think he had some type of safety concern or something like that."

"Thanks for letting me know. We usually always have somebody there looking after her. I don't know what happened to everyone tonight. How long will it be until we arrive at my estate?"

"It won't be that long, about twenty minutes according to my GPS," said the driver as he fidgeted with the controls.

"Great, I appreciate the ride."

"No problem at all," he said as he prepared to leave.

James had to shake his head to stay awake. Finally they reached the main gate and James again opened it with his manual key. They drove up to the house and the driver watched as James unloaded Alexia from the van. Within half an hour her assistants had arrived and Alexia was soaking in her custom bath while they treated her various minor fuel burns.

James wandered around through the house looking for clues as to what had happened before finally returning to his bedroom. He'd planned to lie down on his bed for just for a few minutes, but this time he fell asleep seconds after his head touched the pillows.

Jen was enduring one of the most intense mental ordeals of her life. She was trapped inside her own immobilized body, deprived of virtually all her senses. Where was she? It didn't matter what she tried, nothing happened. She felt like a brain in a jar with all of her physical commands to her body going unanswered. It was becoming unbearable and she could feel the onset of total despair and panic.

Sinzar slowed down as he approached the small town business strip. He could have blinked twice at his cruising speed and missed the entire town all together. Motel row. He checked his watch and kept his eye on the passing hotel signs. Most of the signs were dirty from the constant highway dust and missing any number of internal bulbs. He had seen a couple of vacancy signs already but this old motel looked nice and quiet as Sinzar eased the black hearse slowly into the parking lot.

He quickly checked all his new paperwork with a flashlight before parking and walking over to the office. An elderly lady answered the bell and she was more than happy to have another customer check in this evening. He knew it was very unlikely she would be turning on the No Vacancy sign anytime tonight. Sinzar asked for one room in particular and paid extra for the deluxe HD television package. He was already looking forward to relaxing and getting caught up on his favourite soap operas. Sinzar walked over to the hearse, started it up and then backed it up nice and close to his motel room door.

At least three rooms on either side looked empty. After getting what he needed from the hearse Sinzar grabbed his flashlight and opened up the back doors. He climbed inside and opened the connection console to check the current flows and pressures. Almost everything appeared normal except for one function; the intravenous sedation drip. Sinzar could see that Jen's intravenous sedation tube wasn't flowing at all. The lines to her forearms were tightly wrapped, and being that it wasn't a life or death issue, and she wasn't going anywhere, he wasn't going to spend any time worrying about it. As he lifted the cluster of tubes with one hand he noticed a tiny in-line cut-off valve was now in the closed position. He wasn't sure if they overlooked it earlier or if it was bumped to the closed position when they fitted everything back inside the connection box. In any case, it wasn't critical so Sinzar flipped the tiny valve open, closed up the console and climbed out of the back. He shut the heavy back doors of the hearse and made sure everything was locked up.

The steady noise Jen had become used to, had stopped. A single bang and a tiny vibration had signalled another change to her world. The pitch dark oblivion was getting darker. She was passing, she could see the sign clearly, 'Sorry, No Returns'. This time she knew it for sure, one hundred percent, she wasn't coming back.

Chapter 23

James had no choice but to book off work for personal reasons. Almost forty-eight hours had passed by since that night at the farm and despite an intensive investigation by Al Anderson's forensic investigation team there were still very few leads or answers. The partial remains of an unknown person had been discovered amongst the ashes of the house fire. The only thing that could be positively ascertained was the approximate size of the individual. It was most likely an adult, and definitely much too large to have been Kyle. They had hoped for a DNA match from the blood on the stretcher, but that had turned out to be nothing more than red dye mixed with olive oil.

They were unable to make any positive identification about the year or exact model of the car, but it was positively identified as a Cadillac by the dimensional information collected from the frame of the vehicle. Numerous trace elements of various explosives were found using spectrometer tests and that certainly would have contributed to such a complete incineration of the vehicle.

The old barn housing the helicopter had miraculously escaped the fire despite the adjacent structure burning to the ground. The helicopter was flown back to the estate earlier that afternoon, and James spent several hours going over the machine himself. The investigators had stripped and removed all of the seat covers and re-stowed the stretcher in the baggage compartment. Nothing else appeared to be out of place and both GPS units had also been removed for further analysis by the forensics team. They were hoping to retrieve the trip log data depending on how long the units were powered up. That might explain or help to locate exactly where they had picked up a patient that required a stretcher in the first place. He was becoming increasingly frustrated and it was taking all his efforts just to remain calm—two full days and still nothing. He had expected more from Al Anderson, much more.

Sinzar had been making good time on this run due to the long hours he had spent on the road. Nobody would be happy if he was wasting time transporting dead employees. Finally he turned down the dusty service road running behind a row of shanty-looking hangers at a small overgrown airfield.

Years ago this had been an important facility during the war efforts, but time and neglect had taken its toll. Sinzar unlocked a chain-link gate and pulled the hearse up behind an old metal hanger. The heat of the day was over now and he opened the side-man door first and then opened the rear garage door of the hanger. Within five minutes he had backed the dirty hearse inside and closed the overhead door. The main hanger doors facing the airstrip were closed and had likely been that way since the last time he had used this building.

It was a well-oiled system, a necessary evil, that of repatriating dead bodies back to Iraq; another unfortunate tragedy in the United States; a father and son killed in an auto accident while traveling abroad to attend his sister's wedding in the United States. The business of shipping their bodies back to the grieving families at home was alive and well. Somebody had to do it. Professor Akkaim and his team knew exactly what documents were necessary to operate this shell game of a business entirely for their own requirements.

This was the final pit stop before the crates were loaded onto a small feeder airline and then to a larger cargo aircraft for the flight back to the middle east. Sinzar would need an hour for each coffin to replace all the supply bottles and load the coffins inside the wooden shipping crates. All the paperwork for the customs declarations and the other false documents were waiting in a locked file cabinet inside the hanger office. They had done this a few times before and it was now becoming routine.

Sinzar rolled a large utility table up to the back of the hearse. After making all the disconnections he slid the first coffin onto the table and rolled it over to the side workbench. He walked across the hangar floor and grabbed the electric hoist control hanging from the I-beams installed in the top of the hanger. He then fitted a nylon lanyard onto each end of the coffin and hooked both loops through the hoist hook. After a few clicks on the 'up' button, the coffin was coming off the table and he balanced it between the lanyards until it was about a meter above the table.

Sinzar slid an empty shipping crate over to the utility table and slowly started to lower the coffin into the crate with the electric hoist. The over-sized crates were designed to easily facilitate the connections of the required lines and bottles between the coffin and the interior sides of the crate. He checked the vitals monitor and was satisfied after detecting a slow but positive pulse indication. When he was sure that all the systems were functioning properly he closed the crate and began screwing the lid down tight with a cordless screwdriver. After he'd finished preparing both crates all that was left to do was attach all the standard documents required for international shipping.

A few hours from now and Sinzar could blend back into his own reclusive oblivion. Once again he just couldn't stop himself from daydreaming about all the various possibilities. Money wasn't an object as long as he could keep filling all these RA-9 requisitions on time. Anywhere in the world could soon become his personal, private playground. After finishing so early this month he would have all kinds of time to enjoy himself before he needed to pick up his next assignment package.

James paused at the fork on the path to Chalet Number Five. He made a note to himself to come back here again and go over everything with a fine tooth comb. Al's team had now finished collecting evidence and things at the estate were slowly getting back to normal. Alexia's personal attendants were helping out with things that Lisa normally took care of, but it was still much too early to hire a replacement for her.

James walked up to the house and could tell right away that the Beaucerons were getting restless. They were usually never locked up for such a long period of time. James decided to open the kennel door and let them out. He walked around the side to retrieve a steel garden rake and a galvanized bucket to clean out the sand floors of the kennel.

Just as he was almost finished, he felt something hard in the sand and pulled back with the rake. He quickly realised he had unearthed the remnants of a chewed up leather work boot. He rolled it back and forth slowly with the rake to see if he could recognize it, because he certainly knew it wasn't his. Even though he felt it was a strange discovery he tossed the heavy boot in the bucket and finished cleaning out the kennels.

It was probably just packed with wet sand and could have come from anywhere, or anytime for that matter. Nothing else was pressing at this point. Everything was just a wait and see game right now, or at least until he heard about any new developments from Al Anderson. Just at that very moment his cell phone started ringing.

"Hello."

"Hi James, it's Al again. How's your wife doing?"

"She's okay. She had a few minor skin burns from the fuel, but she's almost her same old self now."

"Well that's good to hear. I have a little information for you, but it's nothing too exciting."

"What?"

"They were able to retrieve some information from one of the GPS units."

"And?" said James, growing impatient with Al's pacifying tone.

"Well we only have data from the first portion of the flight. We know the departure time and flight path. Shortly into the flight they diverted from their flight path to the hospital for reasons unknown and landed out on a rural highway. They stopped on a bridge for ten minutes and then departed to the south. Shortly after that the units stopped recording."

"Well obviously they must have seen something going on and maybe they landed to pick someone up. Did you check the bridge location?"

"Yes of course, but there was nothing out of the ordinary, just lots of broken glass and it's difficult to verify how long that had even been there."

"Well that's interesting. How long do you think they were at the farm?"

"It looks they could have been up there for three or four hours before we arrived."

"Anything else?"

"We also confirmed evidence that a sizable cache of munitions and various small arms were inside the burned out vehicle which was a late model Cadillac. Right now we're still trying to piece everything together. I'll let you know as soon as we have any new information."

"Okay thanks, keep me posted."

Professor Akkaim had watched the small flurries of activity outside the main gates to the estate; cars coming and going at various times during the day and night. The batteries for his surveillance system were growing weaker by the day and it was unlikely he would have the batteries replaced. A work order to retrieve the surveillance system would be a routine assignment that his agents could handle anytime.

Sinzar had sent in a current report and the professor now knew he had everything he wanted. The boy was well on his way over to the RA-9 facility, along with an extra additional back up motivator. The most important thing was that the boy knew his mother had been captured and that he'd seen her alive. He would almost certainly become a dedicated asset to RA-9 for years to come knowing his mother's life depended on it.

The professor was still waiting for an updated progress report from his agent in charge of the various surveillance activities back on the farm. Returning a live motivator overseas in a wheelchair just wasn't practical and the professor was sure most of people knew that as well. The order to dispose of the boy's mother was somewhat of a formality. Sinzar had assured him everything was going according to plan when he drove away with the hearse and that the agent had done an outstanding job with everything else. He was an experienced and competent agent who had proved his dedication to the organization many times over. A small delay in transmitting a progress report was certainly nothing to be overly worried about at this point. The professor shut off the monitor and went to check on the daily construction progress.

Most of the basic laser systems were now in place and work was ongoing in many areas. Hundreds of people were now involved on the underground construction project and he was very relieved to see that they were finally beginning to receive shipments of the DPK crystals. The fact that they had to build a new manufacturing plant to grow the crystals was a huge set back as the production was so limited. Each batch of thirty crystals took about eight weeks to grow and prepare for their laser fusion facility. They would require close to a dozen production runs to grow all the crystals they required. Every laser beam had to pass through the large crystals to convert infrared light to ultra violet light. Earlier on he had wished they had built two manufacturing plants for growing DPK crystals, but with all the other unexpected construction delays it probably wouldn't have made that much of a difference. He was certainly looking forward to working with the young boy who now had firsthand experience working inside the Central Fusion Research Complex 8 in California.

Sinzar backed the hearse out from the hanger and parked it in the tall grass beside the west wall. He opened a new drum of fuel and used a nearby hand pump to refill the hearse. He had about a two hour drive to reach a remote storage compound and then the hearse would be locked inside an old rusty shipping container until the next time it was required.

The pilots of the small cargo airline had stopped here several times before. They knew they had two crates waiting for them and no questions were ever asked. As a small carrier they were required to observe certain temperature and altitude restrictions and stay below altitudes that required pressurization.

The overseas cargo aircraft they were connecting with was essentially a large private jet. This cargo had to be flown in a pressurized temperature-controlled section of the aircraft. Requesting such conditions to ship dead bodies on any commercial airline would immediately arouse suspicions. Sinzar tightened up the cap on the fuel drum with a bung wrench and rolled the drum back against the wall. He cleaned his hands with a rag and climbed back inside the hearse. Two more hours of driving and a short cab ride from now and he'd be a free man for the rest of the month.

James tossed his pillows hard against the wall and sat up on the edge of his bed. He just couldn't sleep. He almost never suffered from insomnia, but lately everything was falling apart and his personal levels of stress and anxiety just continued to build. Although he just wanted to forget about finding the boot he knew he couldn't. James got up, got dressed again, and went downstairs to the small bar in the lounge area. Lisa always kept a special cache of cigarettes for any guests that would manage to run out. She could always save the day. James lifted the lid from an old artistically glazed clay pot sitting behind the bar and felt several packs stored inside. He found an unopened pack and a lighter and put them both in his inside jacket pocket. He didn't really have any intention of actually smoking the cigarettes, it just felt good to have them in his pocket. On the way out he picked up a flash light, some garden gloves, a container of paint thinner and a long screwdriver.

He closed the kitchen door behind him and found a short shovel out behind the kennels. James put on his gloves, picked up the bucket and his shovel and started walking away from the house. The Beaucerons were nowhere to be seen at the moment, which for now was just as well.

After walking several hundred yards out into the forest James stopped, put down the bucket and started digging a deep hole in the ground. He could just barely see what he was doing, but when the hole was deep enough he took out his screw driver and crouched down next to the bucket.

With his flashlight in one hand and the screwdriver in the other he began to probe the boot. He didn't need to be an orthopaedic surgeon to know what he was looking at. He had just confirmed exactly what he had expected. The crushed bones of an ankle were protruding from the dark red sand inside the boot. James lifted the bucket by the handle and dumped its contents in the bottom of pit. He then removed the lid from the paint thinner and poured the entire plastic container on top of the boot. He picked up his shovel and refilled the trench and packed it tight with his boots before covering everything up with the surrounding ground cover.

James made his way back to the house and hosed off the tools, put things away and started walking up towards Chalet Number Five. He was already trying to forget about what he had discovered tonight. He had more than enough things to worry about as it was. Out of sight, out of mind.

Sinzar waited at a highway lookout in the surrounding hills about five miles west of the airport. The rolling hills really only provided two choices for approaching and departing aircraft. He had watched as the small twin engine plane first appeared in the east and flew one circuit before making an approach and landed on the gravel strip. They taxied the aircraft up to the hangar and shut down directly in front of the doors.

It hadn't taken the two pilots more than ten minutes to open the hangar doors and roll the crates out beside their aircraft. The mobile wheel-equipped tables were almost the perfect height to facilitate loading cargo directly through the side door of the small plane. The pickup couldn't have been more efficient. One man locked up the hangar doors while the other restarted the engines.

They were probably one of the only flights to actually land on this strip within the last month. Sinzar watched through his binoculars as they slowly back tracked down to the far end of the runway, turned around and took off towards him. Minutes later he heard the sound of the engines passing over head as they climbed out of the small valley and continued on their way.

"What do you mean he hasn't checked in yet?" said the professor as he tried to control his frustration.

"Sorry Professor, we still haven't had any contact from him whatsoever. Should we dispatch some more agents out there?"

"No! Not yet anyway. Besides, what the hell would he be doing up there anyway? I'm sure they've got investigators combing every square inch of that place by now. That place would have turned into a full-scale major crime scene the minute they discovered Mrs. Clayton's body."

"Yes, you always raise such exceedingly excellent points Professor. There have also been reports of forest fires in that area."

"Did you say forest fires? On the same night?" asked the professor with a renewed interest.

"Yes, that's what we heard on the scanners."

"I'm sure our agent probably started them. What an excellent idea. I'm positive he has a good reason for being late. He's one of the most dedicated field agents we have."

The professor abruptly shifted his clip-board to its habitual home, tucked under his right arm.

"I've got some inspection reports to complete on several laser amplification units."

"Thank you so greatly Professor. I'll give you a situational update soon."

The professor was on his way without any delay.

"Goodbye from this moment in time Professor."

The assistant was becoming well practised at speaking to the back of the professor's head."

James once again admired Jen's door repairs as he let himself into Chalet Number Five. The Tulikivi and fireplace had both long since burned out and James immediately started rolling up some newspapers and stacking some thin dry kindling on top of it. Kneeling down in front of the fireplace he fished out the disposable lighter from his jacket pocket and lit the newspaper in several different places. The dry kindling made it easy to start and several minutes later he was carefully positioning larger and larger pieces of firewood. He watched as the fire instantly melted the plastic wrapping from the cigarette package. He certainly had no intention of smoking, but he had always been impressed with the design of the plastic wrap on those packages and just how easily they came off.

James reached over for a poker and adjusted a few logs in the fire. It was getting too hot to keep sitting next to the fire so he got up and found a comfortable position on the couch. He realized it had been a long time since he'd been sitting here alone in front of a fire. His life as a trauma surgeon was so consuming that he was always either working or sleeping.

When he was a young student they often made bets about how far they could flick the small ball of tin foil from the top of cigarette pack. He remembered winning more than a few bets in his student days as he watched the ball of foil fly across the living-room and into the back of the huge fireplace. Incredibly, it still felt really good just putting that full package back inside his jacket pocket.

What could have possibly happened to Kyle and Jen and Lisa? All he really knew for sure was that they had all completely disappeared without a trace. He didn't want to make the connection between Alexia's shooting and Kyle's disappearance, but it was getting more and more difficult to avoid that conclusion any longer. Maybe the first time was a random drive-by shooting, but two random events like this just had to be connected. Somebody wanted his son for reasons that he wasn't aware of.

James jumped off the couch as he remembered Jen's new laptop. Al Anderson hadn't mentioned anything about finding it in the helicopter. It had to be around here somewhere or else they had it with them. James started searching around, but couldn't find it anywhere. He began looking even harder and after twenty minutes he found it under her mattress.

It didn't take long to realise it was locked shut and he had no way of opening it himself. He took it with him back to the couch and sat down in front of the fire. With a standard screwdriver he began probing the sides of the computer, but decided against breaking it open. Somebody would have the know-how to open her laptop and access whatever information she had inside.

He stared into the flames as he tried to imagine where they could possibly be right now, this minute, and secretly began praying for their safety. He wasn't a religious man, but he just couldn't help feeling completely responsible for them, especially Kyle and Jen. As James was thinking about Jen's laptop he remembered that Kyle had been trying to track the people responsible for the GhostNet intrusions on his personal computer. James could hear the quiet hum from the bank of computers running above him as he placed two logs on the fire and walked upstairs to Kyle's room.

The professor walked back into his office, sat down and immediately placed another call to the shift supervisor.

"Well! Have we heard back from our missing agent yet?"

"No. Not a thing Professor. We haven't heard a word. Everyone expected he might stop by in Portland, but none of the other agents have heard from him."

"I want you to locate some current satellite photos of the area and see if you can find any new information. What about our two newest recruits? Do you have any updates from Sinzar?"

"Yes, we've just received his time-coded phone call."

"What was the time code message?"

"That they were both shipped out alive and on schedule which means they were shipped a few hours ago. We should be receiving them in the underground revival chambers sometime tomorrow evening."

"Well let's hope we can revive them after their trip. We've lost a few too many candidates during the overseas shipping process lately."

"Yes, well as you know, we're constantly trying to improve our system. Do you want them quarantined for the standard three day period?"

"Yes, that should be fine."

"What should we do about the woman? Do you have any special instructions concerning her future function here in the facility?"

"Not yet. Revive them slowly and keep them secured over in the quarantine chambers until further notice."

"Certainly, as you wish Professor."

James pressed the hot glowing butt deep into the fresh tobacco at the end of his third cigarette. He'd felt the initial nicotine rush course through his limbs to the very tips of his fingers and toes. Trying to decipher Kyle's files was like working in a foreign language. His numerically encrypted files were virtual roadblocks for anyone else trying to determine what exactly he might be working on with his small home-based supercomputer. James kept trying to remember the things that Kyle had talked about regarding his GhostNet search programs.

He was used to the fact that Kyle often discussed topics beyond the full comprehension of the people he was talking with which often resulted in a certain mental complacency on the part of the listener. Right now he was wishing he had paid a lot more attention to every detail his son had told him about. James sucked the last remaining smoke from the third cigarette and dropped it in his cola can. He decided to try and check his e-mail on Kyle's super computer. Several minutes later he was in his inbox and he immediately noticed one e-mail from Kyle titled 'Casper'. He opened the e-mail and found one hyperlink. With a click of the mouse he was in.

An elaborate program of cascading maps and chronological real-time search history was displayed in front of him in spectacular color graphics. He had hit the jackpot and found exactly what he was looking for. James sat back and stared at the monitor in a stunned silence. Iraq—someone inside of Iraq had an interest in a doctor's home computer system in Portland, Oregon?

There had to be mistakes or problems with his son's program. This just couldn't be possible. James studied the program's search history and the steady methodical elimination of various continents and countries. The program had clearly completed its search and was providing a set of GPS coordinates as the final end result.

As James gradually became more familiar with Kyle's program he started to learn how to use different features including the real-time satellite image overlays. Judging from the most recent image overlay the final coordinates from this program were situated smack in the middle of an old desert oilfield, possibly just inside Iraq. Something was wrong; it had to be.

James pulled out another cigarette and rolled the steel wheel of the lighter with his thumb. Just one thing kept troubling him as he inhaled the smoke deep into his lungs. He honestly couldn't remember Kyle ever being wrong. To do nothing because he thought his missing son was wrong wasn't an option. He had to do something and it boiled down to either disclosing this information to Al Anderson, or asking Bill Riker if he might be available. James decided to try Bill Riker first. He was already doing some type of work in that general area and had years of experience operating in other parts of the world.

James wrote down the coordinates from Kyle's program and checked his watch. He felt dizzy when he stood up and reached over to grab the handrail before going down the stairs. He locked up Chalet Number Five and started making his way back to the house. All of Bill Riker's contact information was on his résumé and James could only hope it was still up to date.

Half an hour later James was sitting on an outdoor deck of the house skimming over Bill's résumé again. He was already trying to gauge his reaction as he had virtually no information to give him. In any case he had to start somewhere so he sat back and punched in Bill's number on his cell phone. After an unusually long delay he finally heard the words, 'B. Riker, leave a message.'

"Hello Bill, its James. Doctor James Clayton. I'm calling from Portland, Oregon. I'm not sure if you're still working out of the country at the moment, but could you please return my call as soon as possible. It's regarding a most urgent matter concerning my son and I'm in desperate need of your services if you're available. Thanks Bill. I'll be awaiting your call."

The professor leaned over his desk and picked up the phone. "What is it?"

"Well Professor, we've been reviewing recent satellite images, as you requested, and we've also put some local surveillance in place."

"And?" yelled the professor.

"All we can say for certain is that there were several large fires at that location. We don't have any other details about exactly what happened up there."

The professor slammed down the phone and turned on his monitor filming the Claytons' estate. There wasn't any doubt about it now, the camera batteries were dying and he needed to decide if he should have them replaced or have the system removed completely. He was starting to accept the possibility that everything may not have gone according to plan up at the farm. His agent was rarely out of touch for this long without a serious problem. Nevertheless, he was a loose end, a possible link to the operation, and many questions remained unanswered. Overall though, they had met most of their objectives, and with some luck the young boy would soon be contributing to the success of the laser fusion project, providing he and his companion survived their journey.

James was driving home from the store when his cell phone started ringing. "Hello, James speaking."

"Hello James. Bill Riker here, returning your call."

"Hi Bill, just a moment I'm pulling off the road. Bill, I'm so glad to hear back from you."

"Well, let me guess. The other applicant didn't work out and you're offering me a job."

"Yes and no. First of all, are you working in the US now?"

"No, I've been on a protection contract in Iraq since the last time I spoke with you. Why do you ask?"

"Can I speak confidentially with you?"

"Of course, go ahead."

"Well it's a very long story, but to cut to the chase, my son Kyle is missing and so is the woman that I hired to protect him."

"Missing? How? Missing from where? What type of information do you have so far?"

"I think they may have been abducted and I don't know why, but I suspect it may be linked to another previous abduction attempt."

"Well James, I'm sorry to hear about your troubles, but why are you calling me? I'm not even in the United States right now. How could I be of any help to you?"

"We recently had some unknown people trying to hack into my computer system at home and my son designed a diagnostic tracking program to try and locate them."

"What is he, some kind of computer whiz?"

"Well for starters, he's a childhood physics genius with a photographic memory and currently being paid by the US government. He's just completed an internship at the CFRC-8 in California."

"That's the laser fusion place isn't it?"

"Yes, you've heard about it?"

"Well as a matter of fact yes, we have been doing some related work over here, but I don't really have all the details. I just try to keep people alive. Anyway, back to the first question. Why are you calling me?"

James opened one of the two new packs of cigarettes and lit one up. "Bill, my son's tracking program has provided some coordinates for where these hacking attempts may have originated and the location is inside Iraq."

"Are you sure they originated from this area?"

"All I know is what I've told you. My son designed a tracking program on a small supercomputer and these coordinates are the result of that program."

"Can you give me the coordinates?"

"Yes, call me back in fifteen minutes and I'll give them to you. I'm just driving home from the store."

"Okay, will do. I don't really know what to say at this point, but I'll see what I can find out for you. I can't promise you a thing at this point."

"Understood Bill, one thousand US a day starting now and a fifty thousand dollar bonus if you manage to locate them, and double that if you're able to return them safely. The offer's good no matter where you might find them."

"That's a very generous, but we don't even know if they've left the US."

"I know, but right now this is the only thing I've got to go on. Kyle's my son and I want him back. The woman's name is Jen, Jennifer Lamar."

"I'll try to see what I can learn about the location after I get the coordinates from you."

"Thanks Bill. Thanks so much for returning my call."

"You're welcome, talk to you shortly."

James flicked the butt out his window and lit another before starting his car, turning up the music and driving back home. He hadn't realized just how few cigarettes were up at the house, but he knew he'd feel better after replacing the ones he'd accidentally used.

Chapter 24

Bill had immediately programmed the coordinates from James into his hand-held GPS. After selecting the 'Go To' navigation mode he was stunned to see it was less than fifty miles from his current position; he was still inside the guarded compound where he'd been living since he started his assignment in Iraq.

He found a detailed area map and plotted the exact coordinates on his map. He sat down at a table and studied the map in a bewildered amazement. There was almost nothing of any importance going on in this area; mostly just old oil wells and an extensive array of pipelines criss-crossing the dessert in a myriad of different directions. There had to be a mistake, but he didn't have the heart to tell James.

The closest town to the coordinates was a small village called Blakivik and there wasn't much in that area, other than a few clusters of storage buildings supporting an uncontrolled airport facility. He had passed through the area before and could remember the layout clearly; mostly warehouses and a mix of office buildings and several compounds. For the most part it was an out of the way town that had only existed due to cheap oil and an airstrip.

Bill stocked up on some surveillance optics, cameras, and weapons, and decided to take a drive out to the area. The coordinates themselves were clearly in the middle of nowhere, but nevertheless, he was being paid handsomely and intended to do what he could to earn it.

He certainly had several close working associates that would likely give their lives defending him as he would for them, but tonight he would work on his own. Leaving the compound at night was a little unusual, but nobody here dared to scrutinize or question his activities. If he wanted to risk leaving the compound at night, that was entirely his own business. The people running these armed compounds did their best to provide security to the paying tenants within. What they did outside of the compound walls didn't matter to them in the slightest.

Bill pulled out of the gates and started driving towards Blakivik. It was another hot and dry night as usual, and very, very dark. Burning flares dotted the horizon in almost every direction and the smell of petroleum permeated the hot desert air. The main road was in surprisingly good condition and Bill was making good time even driving at night. He was starting to get the occasional glimpse of the town lights in the distance as he continued driving closer. Blowing sand was a common problem affecting road conditions in this area and fortunately the winds weren't that strong. The road started winding through the dunes as he approached Blakivik and Bill slowed down at a high point with a clear, but somewhat distant, view of the small settlement.

The traffic in this area should have been almost nonexistent at this time of night. Surprisingly, a steady stream of trucks was still moving through the area in both directions. Years ago, when these fields were operating at their peak production output, that would have been a normal sight, but not now. Most of the local oil reserves had been extracted years ago. It just didn't make any sense; there was nothing going on that he knew of that could justify this level of activity around Blakivik.

Bill rolled down a window and clamped a small bi-pod to the base of the glass. The windows were now so dirty they could have been tinted black. He sat in the backseat and started a more-detailed surveillance of the area. He could quickly mount and change several pieces of surveillance equipment to the unit for long distance viewing with a spotting scope, or filming, or even NVG work. It didn't take long to realize that the ghost town he was expecting was also surprisingly active. Several large warehouses that he thought would be locked up and shut down were all brightly illuminated inside and out, with several of their bay doors wide open. Even from this distance he could see several forklifts operating inside the warehouses. Several large hangers appeared occupied near the airport and the lights from moving cars showed this small community was anything but a ghost town.

He remained at his vantage point for several hours and continued to acquire all the base line data he could. There didn't appear to be a lot of commercial development inside the village, and most of the activity was in the general vicinity of the airport. Even from this distance he could see an extensive maze of hydro installations and a rail system passing through the town. An old graveyard was located beside the largest hangar at the airport. Nothing fancy, just a large area with random crosses and other assorted burial markers, stone statues, and a few neglected mausoleums. Several different aircraft, including a few helicopters, were parked farther away near the airstrip.

Bill locked a high-power zoom lens on his digital camera and started to methodically film everything there was to see. He realized that almost everyone he was filming was dressed in orange coveralls. Something unusual was going on here, it had to be.

After pausing to change the batteries in his camera he noticed two rows of amber runway lights blink on and off twice. He quickly finished installing the fresh batteries and locked the camera in the mounting bracket on the tri-pod. Bill started to scan the dark skies, but he couldn't see or hear any sign of an aircraft. Once again the runway lights blinked on and off twice. This time he noticed a couple of small vehicles driving out and coming to a stop in front of the largest hanger.

Bill kept his camera trained on the vehicles and was about to stop filming when once again the amber runway lights turned on, but this time they flickered once and stayed on. Finally after several minutes he could hear the faint sound of a jet, but he still couldn't see anything flying. Wherever it was, it seemed to be moving with remarkable speed when it crossed overhead, but now the sound was beginning to fade out. Then, without having heard any noise at all, he noticed the silhouette of a small jet turn off on a taxi-way and on to the apron. It was flying with all the navigation and landing lights turned off. Bill looked through the night vision scope and the only thing visible from this distance was a dim glow coming from the heat of the engine exhaust.

He kept the camera rolling as he watched the small jet taxi up in front of the large hanger. Both ground support vehicles began moving in quickly as soon as the jet came to a halt. Bill checked the focus on the camera's zoom lens and locked it in position. He took out his spotting scope and NVG scope and walked out the other door and around the side of the vehicle. He dropped to the ground below the other camera and extended his legs underneath the vehicle. Moments later he had a small tripod set up on the ground and carefully scanned the people working around the jet.

He could tell from the swirling sand that the engines were still running and it appeared they were also hot-fuelling the aircraft; certainly an uncommon practice at most airports. Once he was focused in properly he confirmed they were in fact hot-fuelling and he watched them as they offloaded two crates. Whatever is was it must have been important to be transported on a private jet. The two crates were stacked on a flat-deck trailer that was towed behind an airport baggage tractor. Bill watched

498

everything and knew that the pilots weren't getting out and that they had no intention of shutting the engines down.

Almost as soon as the fuel hose was disconnected, the jet started to power up and taxi back out towards the runway. Without any delay it back-tracked down the runway, turned around and began its take-off roll. The aircraft was still operating without any lights and the moment it left the ground the runway lights went out.

Bill needed to escort his clients in the morning and couldn't stay here all night. He pulled himself out from under the car and started collecting his gear. He had become used to the steady truck traffic on the road tonight. Nobody could see what he was doing, working from the far side of his parked car, but there certainly was an unusual number of vehicles using this road, and especially at this time of night.

He sat down in the front seat for a while to study the traffic pattern. The trucks where moving in both directions with equal frequency. Almost all of them were semi-trailers hauling closed containers in both directions. It was impossible to say for certain if they were loaded going in, or going out, or both.

Bill walked around to the back door and started packing up his filming equipment. He wouldn't get much sleep tonight by the time he was back inside the compound. Just before he was ready to leave he picked up his scope and panned around for one last look.

Immediately he noticed the baggage tractor parked in front of the hanger now had an empty flat deck trailer. Both of the crates from the jet were nowhere to be seen. He was surprised they'd been unloaded so soon and cursed himself for not paying closer attention to that shipment. Overall though, it was still a good start on his first night working for James Clayton even though he knew the mission was of the 'needle in the haystack' variety. He decided to call James with an update after he got back to the compound. There wasn't any doubt that something out of the ordinary was going on in this part of the desert.

James flipped the cigarette butt in the fireplace as he opened his cell phone. "Hello, James speaking."

"Hi James, it's me, Bill Riker," he said, after a short pause.

"Bill, I was hoping to hear from you. Do you have any new information?" James said, knowing he had to wait for an answer.

"All I can say so far is that I just got back from the area in question and there's a lot of activity going on around there. I'm still not sure exactly why."

"That's interesting. Is that unusual for any reason? Aren't they just sucking more oil out of the ground?" asked James with a degree of disrespect.

"Possibly, it's just that my understanding was that this area had been mostly depleted of known reserves several years ago."

"Well maybe they're just drilling deeper or using some new extraction techniques."

"Anything's possible, but I'm planning to investigate this area further over the next few days. Did you have any new information?"

"No Bill, nothing's really new from this end. I spoke with a friend of mine, Al Anderson. He works for the government and is the person who's responsible for the activities of my son Kyle. They're still conducting an investigation into their disappearance, but they don't have any solid leads yet."

"Let me know if they come up with any information James. Do they know I'm working for you?"

"No, I haven't said a word to them."

"I think it's best to keep it that way for now. I usually prefer to work alone."

"Sure Bill, let me know if you change your mind. I'm sure Al would help you out if you ever needed anything."

"That's good to know, I'll keep that in mind. What about your son Kyle or Jennifer Lamar? Can you tell me something that only you and your son would know about?"

"What do you mean?"

"What I mean, is there something that would demonstrate that I really am a friend of yours?"

"Oh sure, let's see. Okay, for Kyle you could mention LDR and for Jen you could use the name of the only restaurant where we had lunch; The Angry Horse Cafe."

"That should work. What does LDR stand for?"

"Life Death Ratio—I won't bother explaining it to you other than to say it's something only my son and I use concerning my work."

"Okay, I'll let you know if I have any new information and be sure to contact me if you get any as well."

"I will, you can count on it."

Professor Akkaim had been working in the main supercomputer complex when his pager went off. He walked over to the nearest phone and called his assistant. "This had better be important!" he growled into the phone.

"Please accept my most sincere of all possible apologies for the interruption Professor. I am positively certain that you would wish to be informed that the boy and the woman from the United States are now inside the revival chambers. All their vital signs appear weak but still normal, and it looks like they've both survived the journey. They should be out of quarantine in three days from now."

"Excellent! That's what I've been waiting to hear. I'll meet up with them later," said the professor as he slammed the phone down. He needed some help with a host of different technical problems and couldn't wait to see exactly what the boy had learned during his internship in California.

The underground revival chambers were a long way from the laser fusion labs. Most new recruits spent a considerable amount of time in that area of the complex, both during their revival and the standard quarantine period, as they eventually became acclimatized to the underground environment. The support side of the facility was much larger now, due to the constant influx of construction teams and specialists needed to build such a massive project. The larger it got, the greater the requirement for expanded infrastructure to house and feed all the people working underground on the project. Small-scale rail lines connected various underground areas and also provided for an efficient means of moving personal and equipment throughout the massive facility.

Galjinder Malsett was now personally in charge of the revival chambers. It had started out as just another one of his duties within the project, but the steady flow of people being abducted word-wide kept increasing and it was now his own department. Although it wasn't his fault when people didn't survive their journey, it was becoming his area of expertise to make sure they survived the transition.

After speaking with the professor earlier on, he had been directed to stagger the revival of the last two recruits, as he was still waiting for a final decision regarding the new female. This was a typical ruse used between the required professional just abducted and their motivator. Anything was possible however he didn't expect she would be required for anything after the first few days. He'd seen it all before many times. A partial revival and then an induced coma followed by death. Galjinder wasn't the one making decisions and it was never personal as the motivators were generally indistinguishable beneath the oxygen mask, hoses and shrink-wrap.

The boy was a different story. His crate had been opened as soon as it rolled into the chambers. His vitals were checked and his oxygen tank replaced without delay. The drugs that kept him sedated would be gradually reduced over several hours, and then later switched over to a new drug to reverse the effects of the sedation and start the revival process.

After ten hours Galjinder carefully removed the boy's mask and supply tubes with the exception of the intravenous drugs still being administered. The oxygen levels within the revival chamber were always kept higher than normal to help ease them through the revival process.

Although he wasn't a medical doctor, he did have access to all the drugs he was likely to need when working in the revival chambers. He had replaced the oxygen tank for the female and partially un-wrapped her head to remove the feeding tubes. Galjinder rolled an intravenous gurney next to the girl's coffin and replaced the sedation drugs with an IV bag and hooked it up to an automated pump monitor. After several small flow adjustments to compensate for her size he was satisfied she would remain in the same state as she was during her shipment. Soon the boy would be transferred to a solitary quarantine room for at least a few days. Galjinder went to check on the boy's quarantine room to make sure it had everything he might need as he wouldn't be allowed to leave during the quarantine period.

Kyle's eyelids fluttered and suddenly opened wide at the sound of the closing door. What may have taken most people several minutes to adjust to the surrounding sights and situation, Kyle had done in seconds and was instantly evaluating his immediate surroundings and available options. He sat up slowly from the coffin, taking care not to spill any of the Stacrofoam packing pellets. Jen's coffin was next to his and he studied her for several seconds. He confirmed she was still breathing and quickly examined and calculated the settings on the intravenous pump.

Kyle was still partially wrapped in shrink-wrap, but managed to sit up and lean over Jen's body. He pulled the slack tubing out from within her casket, placed it in his mouth and pierced a hole in the soft tubing with his teeth. He could taste the drug leaking out of her intravenous supply line, but it wasn't anything he could identify. He was upset with himself that he wasn't able to determine the drug, or class of drugs just by taste or smell alone. The most important thing was that Jen would no longer be receiving the drugs being pumped into her by the electric pump. Kyle carefully concealed her tube then submerged the back of his head and upper body below the small Stacrofoam pellets to his original position and closed his eyes.

Bill Riker continued to make a few casual inquiries whenever he had the chance. A few friends and acquaintances had agreed that there was a lot of activity going on in that area, but nobody seemed to know any specifics. He had never really paid that much attention to just exactly what the people he had been hired to protect were involved with. Generally speaking, the less you knew about some people, and their affairs, the safer you were. It was obviously something sensitive or he wouldn't be getting paid such good money. His only objective was to provide security and protection services to several people who worked long hours at a small manufacturing facility.

He decided to make an attempt to befriend them more than he had in the past. He had the impression they knew more than they let on, judging by their general avoidance of any social conversations. He still had a couple of hours left until he had to escort them back to the compound so he started to make plans for another trip out to Blakivik that evening. The more information he could gather the better.

He realized just how strange and extraordinary it was that James Clayton's missing son had somehow supplied the coordinates to a location so close to this particular area. There was clearly some type of activity going on other than extracting or refining oil, and he needed to know exactly what it was.

Galjinder returned from preparing the boy's quarantine room. It wasn't anything luxurious, but it wasn't exactly a prison cell either; just a small modest room, quite similar to a secure private hospital room. The boy's revival would be accelerated and it wouldn't be long until he was completely off the drugs and supplements and back on solid foods. He knew the professor was anxious to have him integrated into the development team working on the laser fusion complex. Galjinder took some sharp scissors and started partially cutting the shrink-wrap farther down one side of the boy's body then rolled him over and did the same to the other. He could work his way out on his own time, like a moth emerging from a chrysalis.

Galjinder unlocked the wheels and pushed the boy over to his room and placed him on the bed. He turned him over, loosened the rest of the plastic and placed a blanket over him. With one sharp pull, he lifted the security fence on the bed and locked it in position. He quietly turned down the lights and locked the door as he walked out of the room. Kyle instantly folded the intravenous tube in half and once again stopped the flow of the drugs into his arm. He knew he was very fortunate he had never been properly searched. Kyle continued to carefully study the room as his eyes adjusted to the limited light.

He needed somewhere to conceal some, or all, of the bullets his mother had given him. The room was sparsely furnished and had a built-in sink and toilet. Kyle reached down under the blanket and quickly removed the loose bullets from his socks. After realizing his limited options, he freed himself from the shrink-wrap and hopped out of bed. He then lifted the top from the toilet tank and removed the large black float. He took off the mounting arm and used it to puncture a small hole in the back of the float, just large enough to slip the bullets inside.

Moments later, everything was reassembled and the toilet was operating normally. At the very least it was a temporary solution, and they might yet be of some use in the very near future. Kyle climbed back into bed and closed his eyes. He realized the room was almost completely dark and he had hidden the bullets with almost no light at all. Eyes open or eyes closed, it made no difference. Once he knew the layout of the room it was permanently committed to his extraordinary memory. Kyle closed his eyes and surrendered immediately to an overpowering desire for sleep.

Bill had tried his best to befriend the men working at the manufacturing plant. They had told him the strangest thing. They were growing crystals, large crystals. He still wasn't sure if they were joking or not. He had never heard of anything like that and when he asked them what they were for they said they couldn't say, for security reasons. Some information was better than none, and if they were telling the truth, it might be another small piece of the puzzle. After returning them to the compound Bill packed some extra film, data sticks and batteries, then left for another late night drive out to Blakivik.

Jen's confused thoughts played in her head like a surreal movie. Everything was blurry and she could hear the constant hum of some type of equipment. Her mind was slowly beginning to function, but any commands to move her body went unanswered. She was either securely restrained or paralyzed. She tried desperately to recall what had happened to her without any success. One thing was sure, she had a heartbeat, she could feel it, and as far as she knew—dead people didn't have a heartbeat. So what had happened to her and where was she? Slowly she could feel her cognitive powers starting to return. She felt like a brain in a jar, completely separated from her own body.

Bill Riker had set up his surveillance in the same location as before. Although he could have moved in closer, this location provided a good overall vantage point to observe the small town and also the airport. The more time he had to analyze the information from the first night, the more his instincts told him something very unusual was going on. Once again he set up his recording devices next to the car in hopes of recording additional information. Like trusted assistants, the cameras quietly recorded anything they were focused on. Bill started to mark and count vehicles passing in both directions on the road into town. The winds were stronger tonight and the sand drifted easily across the dunes and over the road.

After almost an hour he had a long list of the different vehicles that had passed him in both directions. It quickly became clear that very few were carrying petroleum products, which should be the most common load here and surrounding areas. He needed to inspect the contents of one of these containers so he could quickly gain some new knowledge. It wasn't that complicated, he just needed to decide whether to take out a moving vehicle or find a parked one. Both scenarios had a small degree of risk, but he knew it would be much easier just to stage an unfortunate vehicle accident. He could choose the best location for an accident that would allow him more time to properly search a truck before anyone else detected the wreck.

Bill was tallying up his ongoing count of vehicles when once again he noticed the quick flicker of the runway lights. He picked up his infra-red binoculars and sat down outside the truck. He made a small adjustment to the tripod that was recording the area and focused it carefully on the airstrip. Just at that moment he heard the unmistakable noise of a small jet passing high overhead. Last night's scenario was starting to unfold in almost the same manner.

Right on cue the runway lights flickered again and remained on. This time he was picking up the heat signature in his infra-red binoculars slightly before he heard the sound of the engines. The jet was again flying without any navigation lights at all. It was like watching a movie for the second time. A small ramp tractor was hitched to a cargo wagon and was moving into the same position, again waiting for the jet to come to a halt.

Bill checked his watch and wrote down the time. It would be interesting to see what level of scheduling precision was going on here. Was he watching a daily scheduled flight, or one of many? Really it was impossible to know without a twenty-four hour surveillance operation. He waited to watch them unload, and he also wanted to see if they would be fuelling up again.

Almost every small detail was occurring in exactly the same manner, except that tonight there were two tractors and two freight wagons. One freight wagon was loaded with two crates and the other was empty. He wasn't taking his eyes off that shipment tonight; it would have his complete and undivided attention this time. The jet kept its engines running while it unloaded a single crate and workers loaded the other two crates inside the jet. No fuel was taken this time, and after they had finished the aircraft started increasing power and taxied back out towards the runway. This time Bill ignored the departing jet and concentrated on its special cargo. The small tractor with the empty freight wagon drove back towards the warehouse complex and the other one started slowly driving away from the buildings.

He adjusted the focus in his binoculars while he watched the tractor tow the freight wagon towards the old graveyard. Still, he couldn't see anything else in the area other than the graveyard. The driver came to a stop and then started backing around in a sharp turn. He backed the freight wagon up to the front of a large stone crypt and got off the tractor. He glanced around before opening two large doors and then activated a hydraulic lift on the freight wagon.

When the front deck of the wagon was almost forty five degrees the crate, or coffin, simply slid out of sight into the stone crypt. The driver lowered the lift, closed the doors and started driving back towards the warehouse. Just like dumping the trash. Bill had never seen anything quite like it. Were they filling a mass grave or secretly disposing of bodies in this remote location? He knew there would certainly be a market for such types of disposal services in this part of the world. Why were they flying them here for burials? And where were they all coming from? He had never witnessed such an efficient system anywhere in the world. He hadn't had a chance to review the tapes from last night, but he was definitely going to watch them later when he got back to the compound. Every instinct he had in his mind and body kept telling him that there really was something strange going on here in the desert.

Jen was starting to make out the sound of nearby activity and voices. Where she was remained a complete mystery, but the metallic sound of wheels or rollers was getting louder and louder. After the sound of one very loud impact it quickly became very quiet. Jen continued trying to retrace her recent memories. Suddenly it hit her, the helicopter, the accident, the victim, the struggle. Kyle! She began to recollect and replay those last events over and over, trying to remember anything after that. She just couldn't remember anything after that, absolutely nothing.

Once again she concentrated intently enough to hear and count her own heartbeats. She continued to need further reassurances just to tell herself that she was alive, or that she *could* be alive. Every time she tried to move nothing happened, and then she felt it. She was scratching her thumb with her fingernail. It was a tiny subtle movement, but after digging her nail into her thumb, she knew it was unmistakable. She was regaining her mental abilities despite being confined in some way. Her vision was completely blurred, but occasionally something, or someone, passed by close enough to dim the grey opaque light.

She was surprised at how calm she was becoming, despite her complete inability to rationalize or understand her alien surroundings. She tried to concentrate on the sounds she was hearing. The sound was familiar; it sounded like a power drill or screwdriver. Somebody was using something like that, and they were quite close to her. Then she heard the sound of a door or doors opening up.

"Good evening Professor Akkaim. How are you?"

"Never-mind that! Who was it that just arrived?"

"Well I'm opening the crate right now. I believe it's a female scientist from East Germany."

"Excellent! I was hoping she would be joining us soon. Did she survive?"

"Give me a minute Professor and I'll check her vital signs."

Galjinder finished unscrewing the lid from the crate and removed the top. The vitals console was situated outside the coffin and with a quick glance he knew that she had survived the journey. "Yes Professor, it appears she still has some life left in her. I'll revive her slowly to make sure we don't lose her."

"Good. What about the boy? When can he be moved to the main facility?"

"A couple of days from now and he should be ready for a transfer. What about the woman that came with the boy?"

"Let me think about her a little longer," said the professor.

"Yes, of course. She is on continuous sedation and won't be revived under those conditions. Let me know when you have minded you're made up."

"That is not how that expression is spoken Galjinder. It's made up your mind."

"Thank you so very kindly. When you 'it's made up your mind' you can let me know. Good bye Professor."

"I'll advise you of my decision tomorrow," said the professor as he walked away.

Jen had heard every word. Professor Akkaim? Who was Galjinder? What kind of continuous sedation? Where was she? And where was Kyle? Who was the female scientist from East Germany? Jen continued flexing her fingers and toes as she probed the unknown extent of the bonds that were immobilizing her.

She had finally realized that her face was inside some type of full-facial oxygen mask. The steady rhythmic sound of the air being pumped in was now unmistakable. She was without a doubt waking up inside her undefined prison. If they thought she was under a continuous sedation, they were wrong. She was becoming more and more alert with every passing breath. She needed time to recover and rebuild her strength.

Bill walked into his room at the compound and dropped his pack on the bed. It was getting very late, but he needed to see the surveillance tapes from the night before. He plugged in his laptop and transferred the files he had recorded with his camera. He began playing the footage on his laptop as he sat back on his bed, studying it intently.

Nothing out of the ordinary was being shown and the picture quality was generally poor with insufficient lighting. He began to fast-forward the footage, because it was getting so late. The camera was locked on the tripod and filming a large general area close to the airport ramp. He slowed the film down when he started to hear the sound of the jet engines being picked up on the sound track.

Struggling to stay awake, he fast-forwarded it once again and there it was; two shipping crates sitting on the freight wagon. It happened exactly the same way as he had just seen it tonight. The tractor drove out to the graveyard, backed up to the doors of the crypt, and both shipping crates slid off the freight wagon and disappeared inside the old stone structure.

Several minutes passed, and then to his astonishment he watched as another shipping crate emerged at the same angle and dropped down on the deck of the freight wagon. If he hadn't seen it with his own eyes he wouldn't have believed it. He scanned the area for chimney stacks or something that may have indicated an underground crematorium operation of some kind, but couldn't see anything like that. One thing was for sure, he needed to get a closer look and find out what was going on behind those two steel doors. Crates going in were one thing, but crates coming out meant there was something far more complex going on underneath the town of Blakivik.

Galjinder leaned over Jen and checked the fit of her oxygen mask. Realistically it was no longer required, but he would leave it in place until the professor decided what he planned to do with her. The administration of any other types of gas that may be necessary was always simplified when a full face mask was already securely in place. The sedation drugs were still flowing into her as they should be, so he returned his attention to the latest arrival. She would also be going into a quarantine room once she had been properly prepared after her trip to the RA-9 complex.

She had been led to believe that her husband would be employed in a sister facility and they would both be allowed annual visitation privileges if both their personal contributions to the success of the project was deemed to be in the top ten percent of all working employees. Many people would continue to work tirelessly for endless periods under this fabricated arrangement, as of course nobody was ever deemed to be in the top ten percent of employees.

As Galjinder began to remove her face mask and change over her intravenous lines for the revival procedure he could see she had a completely shaved head. It was unclear if she was like that prior to being shipped or not. He continued to cut the shrink-wrap open as she had been kept in the crate for longer than usual. Her eyes were soundly closed, but she was still breathing with broken shallow breaths. He knew from experience that she had almost become another unfortunate shipping statistic.

Kyle's mind was racing as he rapidly analyzed the range of possible options available to him. He knew it was his turn to watch Jen's back, but he was now dealing with minimal solid information and a high degree of speculation as to the exact nature of their present situation. That they had been abducted was clear. Who had taken them, to where, and for what reason, was not.

Kyle quickly slipped out of bed and checked to see the status of his door. It was locked from the outside so he hopped back into bed to consider his choices. He had several available options for opening the door. A bullet would blow out the center cylinder of the lock, but picking it would be far more advantageous if he could find or fashion a tool that would do it. Rigging the locking mechanism in such a way that it would fail to properly lock the next time it was used was another possibility. So was incapacitating the next person to walk through the door. He lay back in bed, closed his eyes and weighed out the risks and consequences of each option.

Al Anderson leaned back in his chair after reading all of the final forensic reports for the second time. It was more than a major setback to have lost Doctor Clayton's son and his female guardian in such a brazen abduction. Although they did have the make and model of the burnt out vehicle, all the Vehicle Identification Numbers had been completely removed with a grinder. The skeletal and DNA results from the body in the house had failed to match anyone in the AFIS or DNA data systems. Whoever was behind this was either very organized, very lucky, or both.

He had virtually limitless resources at his fingertips, but without a solid lead it was difficult to know where to continue their search. Repeated questioning of Doctor Clayton's wife, Alexia, quickly became a futile exercise. The ongoing search for his former house keeper had also failed to provide any new information. The blood found inside the back of the helicopter had been tested in a lab and conclusively ruled out as human blood. It seemed that wherever they turned in this investigation they ran into a brick wall. Al could only hope something would change, and soon. He desperately needed some kind of a new breakthrough in this case.

Jen tried to remain completely still as the blurry shape of a person kept hovering around close to her. She had overheard most of the last conversation between two people, but everything was now quiet again. Someone had briefly held her face mask and also checked the needles in her forearms. She didn't know why she was regaining her consciousness so quickly, but she was starting to feel more and more awake. She pressed her fingernail deep into her thumb one more time to confirm she wasn't dreaming, or worse.

Moments later she heard the sound of a door opening. The room then turned pitch black and again she heard the definite sound of a door closing. Had her captors left her here for a few minutes? Or had they left her here to die? She felt like she possessed super-human hearing powers as she lay frozen in total darkness and silence, searching for any possible sound that might yield a clue about her present location

Kyle had picked the simple door lock in less than forty seconds. He easily fashioned two lock picks from the thin wire clip in the toilet tank that held the chain to the back of the flush handle. He got down and looked underneath the narrow space under the door only to find more darkness. This area must have been shut down for the night, or longer; it was impossible to know for sure.

Kyle turned the door handle ever so slowly as he proceeded to open the door. At first he really had no sense of direction, just time. It had taken just over two minutes for somebody to move him from the lab or office, from where they were, to this new room.

They had taken him down a hallway. Had they turned left or right? Kyle closed his eyes and concentrated. He needed to focus on the sensations in his mind when they rolled him on the stretcher into the new room. Was it a right turn or a left turn? He relived the short trip again in his mind, lying on his back and listening to the wheels rolling on the uneven concrete floor. Slowing down and waiting for the door to be opened.

It was a right turn. No, two right turns. He was one hundred percent sure. He had been travelling head first on the stretcher, right turn out the door, just over two minutes and then another right turn and into the solitary room. It wouldn't be hard for him to retrace his steps now, even in total darkness.

Kyle kept his fingertips lightly touching the wall as he walked down the hall. It had only taken seconds to know these weren't any normal building walls. They were cold, stone cold and damp. Not like any hospital or building he had ever been in before. He had felt two doorways pass him by. He felt one at forty seconds down the hall, and another one, a minute and twenty seconds later. Forty seconds apart. The smell of unrefined petroleum was everywhere and he could hear a constant faint drone of engines running in the distance. It was just speculation, but Kyle concluded they were most likely large diesel generators.

Kyle started slowing down as he reached the two minute mark, his out-stretched left hand waiting for the third door opening. Almost to the second, his hand found a wet stone door jamb and the metal door installed within. This door had an unusual lock configuration with an ordinary door handle, but it also had an exterior deadbolt, obviously designed to lock something, or someone, inside. Kyle dropped down again and glanced under the door. This room was also pitch dark. So far he hadn't seen any sign of any interior lighting anywhere, just total darkness.

Galjinder finally found Professor Akkaim recalibrating the precise alignment of one of the recently installed KDP crystals.

"What are you doing out here in the main laser cavern? Don't you have enough duties to keep yourself fully occupied within the confines of the revival chambers?"

"Yes of course Professor, but there remains the small matter of the woman who arrived with the boy. Have you reached a decision regarding the fate of the woman?"

"I reached a decision the last time I spoke to you. I decided that I would let you know as soon as I made a decision."

"Very well then. I shall return at once to the revival chambers and await your respected guidance in this matter."

"Wait! Are they still separated from each other?"

"Yes, the boy is alone in a quarantine room."

"Did he see that she was alive?"

"Well I believe he knows she was beside him, but I don't know if he knew for sure that she was alive."

"You know full well that we can't dispose of her unless he knows she is alive and well."

"Yes of course Professor, but I have been awaiting your decision in this matter."

"Don't waste your time waiting for that. I've made my decision. Dispose of her and get her out of the complex while the boy is still in quarantine. If he has already seen her inside the facility, then he will have sufficient motivation to work for us."

"Very well Professor. I'll see to it at once."

Kyle turned the deadbolt slowly and unlatched the door. He opened the door and stood still as he tried to remember the exact layout of the room.

"Jen—Jen can you hear me?"

All Kyle could hear was the steady hum of electric intravenous pumps and the sound of oxygen being administered from the tanks. Kyle felt his way over across the dark room to Jen's coffin.

"Jen—Jen can you hear me? Wake up?"

His small hands began to probe around the Stacrofoam pellets and he quickly realized she was gone. Her face-mask, tubes and plastic wrapping were still inside the casket, but she was definitely gone. Kyle suddenly noticed the new sliver of light coming from under the door. Someone had turned on the lights in the hall, and moments later he could hear the unmistakable sound of approaching footsteps.

Instantly he pulled himself up and into the casket. He struggled frantically to submerse himself under the Stacrofoam pellets and covered his face with the mask, and concealed himself with the remaining pieces of shrink-wrap. He located the intravenous lines and clutched the ends tightly in his small hand. Kyle's entire body instinctively froze as the heard the door swing open and saw the bright blurry lights shining through his thick plastic face-mask. The oxygen was still flowing into the face-mask and Kyle did his best to breath with absolute minimal movement.

"I could have sworn I locked that door" said Galjinder out-loud to himself.

"My oh my, time to die."

"I could have sworn I locked that door" said Galjinder for the second time. Both of Galjinder's parents had been diagnosed with Alzheimer's at a fairly early age, so these occasional errant disruptions of his regular thoughts were not overly surprising to him. In fact it was becoming somewhat normal. He walked purposely over to the large wall-mounted drug cabinets, unlocked the doors and reached inside.

This drug would always stop the heart in under a minute. Galjinder extracted the required adult dosage into a large syringe and located the intravenous lines coming out from the intravenous pump.

"My oh my, time to die. May the good Allah have mercy on your soul," said Galjinder as he watched the new amber drug race through the clear tubes towards Jen's casket. "Such haste, such waste."

He didn't always like complying with these types of orders from the professor, but he knew the consequences of questioning his authority. Just do what you're told. That always worked best in this facility. People that didn't follow that basic rule, never lasted long. He was often called on to make sure of exactly that. He was usually the first person to see you on the way in, and often the last person to see you on the way out.

Galjinder replaced the intravenous bag flowing into the latest recruit. Her vital signs had shown a slight improvement, but only that; she was still in the very early stages of her revival, but not yet stable.

Galjinder disconnected the lines from Jen's oxygen tank and set it down next to the others. As he walked back between the caskets he shut the lid and then picked up the top of the crate with both hands. Moments later he was driving screws into the top of the crate with his cordless screw driver; getting her body ready for removal. With a quick push and turn he had switched both crates around and the German lady was now on the table and Jen's crate was back on the conveyor.

One thing Galjinder never forgot was not to leave a decomposing body in his lab. He reached up, selected the belt direction and started the conveyor. Slowly her shipping crate began the slow bumpy trip back up the long narrow tunnel towards the surface.

Galjinder walked over to a small fold-down bunk in his lab. Everything was under control so he decided to have a quick nap. Nobody would miss him for the next little while and he wasn't expecting anybody new to arrive, including the professor. He needed to take his mind off what he had just done. Within minutes after lying down he was fast asleep.

If Galjinder hadn't casually sliced into one side of her shrink-wrap earlier on, Jen would never have managed to escape from her plastic prison. He wasn't at all concerned as he believed she was still connected to the steady stream of drugs flowing into her dying body. She had fumbled blindly around the room and eventually found the locked door, despite the total darkness.

She knew that without her lock picks, she had no quick way of opening the door. She was awake, but still weak from her period of extreme confinement. Jen had continued to explore her surroundings with her hands and soon located a second coffin. Her hopes suddenly soared, thinking she was about to discover Kyle inside. Just as quickly she knew the mummified person she felt inside was far too large to be Kyle.

Once again she continued to follow the perimeter of the room and returned to the locked door. She then realized there was only one possible exit and that was crawling back up the conveyor belt. She may as well have been completely blind. Normally, in almost any dark environment, eventually your eye picks up some small degree of light. Not here; it didn't matter how long you waited, nothing had changed. Her sense of touch, hearing, and smell, plus most importantly, memory, was her only guide. She had the sensation that she was going up an incline, but she knew the darkness and vertigo could play tricks on anyone's mind.

All she really knew for sure was that she was moving forward on her hands and knees within a narrow tunnel. It was impossible to tell. She had been making slow but steady progress into the void, and then had to fight her sense of sheer panic as the belt underneath her shuddered suddenly and started to move.

The professor was continually getting closer and closer to the end of his rope with the mounting difficulties and problems of building this underground laser fusion facility. Everything was always delayed and nothing ever seemed to happen according to plan. He knew now that one of the biggest mistakes they had made was only building one factory for growing all the KDP crystals. It often felt like he had the whole world on his shoulders. He was looking forward to discussing numerous issues with the young genius that had been working at CFRC-8. If he truly had a photographic memory he might turn out to be one of the most valuable procurements RA-9 had ever acquired. Just thinking about the boy and the problems he needed answered spurred him to act.

He had waited long enough! Galjinder should have completed his little task by now. It was time to harvest the boy from the revival chambers. The professor looked through several pages in his thick clipboard before positioning it under his arm and walking away. He decided he had just enough free time in his schedule to personally take care of Kyle's initial introduction to the RA-9 Project.

Jen felt like she was riding a roller coaster blindfolded, her speed and destination unknown. She couldn't turn around and she couldn't back up. All she could do was ride it out on all fours. Minutes later, and without any warning whatsoever, her head and shoulders slammed into a pair of metal swing doors and she was pushed outside into a dark night. A few seconds later the conveyor deposited her onto a roller table of some kind. She quickly jumped off and crouched down below as she carefully scanned and studied her new surroundings. She couldn't believe her eyes; she was in the middle of an old graveyard of all places, not too far from an industrialized area.

Where was she? Jen just couldn't get that question out of her mind. She felt like she was awakening from a long period of amnesia. She immediately spotted several parked aircraft off in the distance so they had to be in the vicinity of an airport. She had no idea what country she was in, and more importantly, where Kyle was. She could hear the steady noise coming from the conveyor system and knew it would have to stop or change direction before she could go back inside. She may have found a way out, but she also knew she would have to return and find Kyle herself.

She jumped around when she heard the crash of the steel doors as they suddenly burst wide open. She froze in disbelief as the large crate moved towards her and dropped down on the roller table. Seconds later the doors slammed shut and the conveyor system ground to a stop.

521

The professor waited for the old mechanical lift to climb up to his level. The designs of these small mining shaft elevators hadn't changed much through the years. He watched as the lift slowed to a halt and then unlocked the iron lattice safety cage and stepped inside. The revival chambers were farther down below the main level and needed to be secure and isolated from the rest of the complex.

He glanced up at the small green light on the camera systems. Anyone using the lifts to descend to the revival chambers was always recorded on live-streaming video. This was just one of the many top secret areas within the laser fusion facility. Galjinder would often remain down on this level for days at a time, and only emerge when he needed new provisions. The lift jerked to a stop and the professor opened the cage, stepped off and started walking down the damp underground corridor. It was hot as always, and a string of bare light bulbs were wired along the shotcrete walls.

Jen casually turned around and noticed a small tractor or backhoe that seemed to be driving over in her direction. She quickly dove down below the roller tables and started crawling away in the opposite direction. She was lucky she had a head start and the element of darkness on her side. All the various grave stones and burial ornaments provided some degree of cover for her escape. She had managed to move away several hundred yards before the tractor reached her last location. The driver was dressed in orange coveralls and stepped off the idling tractor. She wished she had her usual assortment of weapons with her, but this time her choices were limited to close-range combat tactics.

Lying in the sand behind a stone grave marker, Jen watched with intense curiosity as the driver walked over and examined the crate. He turned around, walked back to the tractor, and then returned carrying some chains and straps. In no time at all he had two large nylon straps rigged at each end of the crate and then connected it to a two-point chain lanyard. The driver repositioned the front plough bucket above the casket and then hooked up the lanyard. With a few quick control movements the front bucket rose into the air with the load suspended below. Jen could see it was just a general tractor with a bucket on the front and a back hoe on the rear.

She watched from her graveyard vantage point as it slowly drove over to the other side of the graveyard with the crate swinging slowly from side to side. If she had been on her own it would have been a perfect opportunity to flee. She decided to wait until the tractor had left the area before checking to see if the doors to the conveyor were open. She crawled back a little closer using the gravestones for cover.

The tractor was now dimly silhouetted in front of a far-off exterior building light. The driver still had the crate suspended in the air, but was now operating the rear back hoe attachment. He was digging a hole or trench. The main thing was that she hadn't been seen and she needed to get back inside those steel doors, and soon. She definitely had to make a move while she still had darkness on her side. Walking around here unarmed in the daylight just wasn't an option.

Jen glanced back over to the silhouette and watched patiently as the driver lowered the crate into the pit. Suddenly the obvious struck her; he was just a gravedigger adding another guest to his collection. Jen decided to wait until he was done before going back to check on the entrance to the underworld. She would have the element of surprise going for her as she made it down the conveyor belt, but if it was turned on she would be forced to ride it back to the top. No speculation was required. She knew exactly how impossible it was to descend against the conveyor system. It would also be dangerous to go down the conveyor if it was running towards the underworld. She would have lost all of her chances for any element of a surprise entry. She really only had one choice; she needed it stopped; she needed to disable that conveyor system.

"Galjinder!" yelled the professor as he pushed the first door wide open and walked inside. "Where are you? Are you in here?"

"Hello, yes—yes—I'm here. I wasn't expecting anyone. I was just having a little rest. You know how easy it is to lose your sense of day or night down here."

"Yes I do. Listen, I've decided there isn't any point in keeping the boy here any longer. I have so many questions for the boy and I've come to show him everything we've accomplished so far. I am anxious to probe the boy's mental abilities in the area of computers and laser fusion."

"Yes, of course. Let's hope he is of the greatest of service to our cause."

"Is this the new woman from Germany?" asked the professor as he walked over to examine the lady. "Look! She's bald!" exclaimed the professor.

"Well yes she is. She arrived like that."

"And what about the child's female guardian? Is she in the hands of God?"

"Yes Professor, she's dead and buried by now."

"Excellent! Come along and introduce me to the boy."

"Yes at once Professor. He may still be sleeping."

"Well then we'll just have to wake him up. Won't we?"

"Yes of course, follow me."

Galjinder rubbed the sleep out of his eyes as he led the way down the corridor. "Just up here Professor, I'm sure he will be ready and hungry for some regular meals soon. What are we going to say if he asks about his friend?"

"Don't say anything. I'll handle that. If you have to you can say your only concern is the health and welfare of new arrivals. What goes on inside this complex or where people are posted is something that you simply have no information about. Are we clear on that Galjinder?"

"Yes, clear as the ball of crystal. Here we are."

Once again Galjinder had a shock when the door opened up without a key, but he didn't say a word. "He's in here Professor," said Galjinder nervously as he opened the interior door and turned on the light.

"I don't see anybody in here, where is he?" yelled the professor as he felt himself being overcome with rage.

Galjinder frantically looked under the covers and under the small bed. "He was here Professor. I brought him here myself and personally locked him inside this room."

"Begin a detailed search of every inch of every room in the revival chambers immediately. I'm going to alert our security teams. There are only so many places he could hide in this facility. You had better hope and pray that he is found Galjinder. That's all I can say, hope and pray."

Galjinder couldn't stop shaking as he checked through the other rooms. He had to find the boy.

Fifteen minutes later he started the search over again. Once more, he searched every closet, every cabinet and cupboard. He wished he had never left the revival chambers. He couldn't even remember if he had locked the elevator when he went away to find the professor. Suddenly he could see it was possible; the boy could have summoned the elevator with a press of a button, climbed inside and rode it back up to another level, except that the elevator was there when he came back.

He was feeling so stressed now that he wasn't even sure about that. His knew his memory was slowly getting worse and worse and he now wished he was far, far away from this place. Suddenly he turned and walked over across the room to the conveyor. He paused for a moment before he turned on the switch, then hopped up and lay down on the moving belt. Either way he had no choice; if the boy had escaped under his supervision he was finished.

Jen had briefly searched around the gravestones for something to immobilize or prevent the conveyor system from operating. There was nothing at all to be found except sand and gravestones so she had decided to take her chances and try to get inside. She opened the doors and then crawled for about ten meters, head first down the incline—when the conveyor system once again started up with a jolt. She tried to remember how long it had taken to ride it out the first time up, but she had no real recollection of time. She lifted the heels of her feet up to meet the approaching doors and it was apparent that it would be impossible to get inside if the conveyor was running in this direction.

This time she was a little more prepared as she was forced out through the doors and dropped on the roller table. She needed to get closer to the warehouse or buildings to find something to block the conveyor. Jen climbed off the table and stayed close to the ground as she made her way out through the maze of head stones and monuments. Just a wooden two by four or a length of pipe would work to jam the conveyor belt. She had to find something she could work with and then get back inside and try to find Kyle.

The professor had immediately called several security team leaders, who in turn summoned every available person to assist in the search. He sat down at his desk and started reviewing streaming video history from the main floor elevator shaft. He could see Galjinder as he was stepping off of the mine elevator and also saw him later when he returned to the revival chambers.

So far, there was no direct evidence that boy had used the lift to change levels. The professor continued to provide any updates to the security teams with radio communications and also alerted ground level security personnel operating outside the facility. If the boy was still in the revival chambers he would find him personally. He left his office and struggled to contain his fury as he quickly made his way back to the lift. The fact that Galjinder would soon be paying for his incompetence was a given.

Jen could see the heightened activity everywhere. Everyone she could see looked like they were wearing the same orange coveralls. It was as if something had disturbed a hornets' nest. She was still in the graveyard and managed to dig herself partially under the sand next to an old stone crypt. Vehicles with overhead spotting lamps were driving back and forth throughout the area. She curled herself up as much she could and watched all the activity from her small sand burrow. Being only partially buried she was still in a very vulnerable position, but safe for the moment.

Reviewing the video surveillance tapes wasn't the only reason the professor had gone to his office. He had also picked up his personal small semi-automatic handgun. His growing rage over the disappearance of the boy from inside his own facility seemed to have no end. He felt inside his lab jacket pocket and gripped the gun in his hand. If he was going to have to dispose of Galjinder, the revival chambers would be the best place to do it.

The lift jerked to a halt and the professor opened the cage door and stepped outside. He had a master key to the lift and locked the cage and disabled the lift. Slowly he started walking down the corridor to the first set of the doors and then changed his mind, walking to the very end.

Nobody else was coming down to the revival chambers now so he decided to do his own personal search. There simply weren't many places to hide down here, and before long he was back at the first door. The professor cautiously pushed the door open and immediately noticed the steady sound of the running conveyor. Minutes later he had searched every last inch of the room.

The only person here was the new woman from Germany. The professor immediately updated the exterior security teams with the latest discovery of Galjinder's absence along with a shoot-to-kill command. Personnel would be directed to the upper conveyor entrance at once.

Jen watched as one of two small trucks started to accelerate towards the graveyard. Just then her peripheral vision noticed the conveyor access doors burst open and a man rolling off the belt. He was a taller man with a beard and was wearing what looked like a white lab jacket.

He jumped off the table at the sight of the approaching vehicle and started running as fast as he could. Jen kept watching as the vehicle changed directions and appeared to be in pursuit of this man. She had no idea if he was an employee or who he was. Maybe he was trying to escape from the same area that she had just escaped from. In any case it just didn't make any sense that an employee was being pursued like this. Then without warning she could hear and see shots being fired. The man was being hunted like wolves from a helicopter. He had few options; the terrain wasn't in his favour as the vehicle could travel in any direction. Suddenly he started running directly at her. She had been seen and he was screaming at her to help him.

Jen jumped up on her feet and prepared to make a run for it. In what seemed like a slow motion movie, the man in the lab coat ran straight into a headstone and flew through the air. When his body hit the sand it was completely still. It was obvious to Jen that the man he had just been hit with a lethal shot.

With nowhere to run, she put her hands up as the vehicle skidded to a stop in the sand and she was flooded with the glare from the powerful overhead searchlights. Two men jumped out and one ran up to her with his handgun drawn and the other went to check on the technician.

"What's your name?" demanded the man closest to her.

"Jennifer Lamar" was all she could say.

"Lie down on the ground, now! Face first and don't move."

Jen had a bad feeling about this situation. She didn't have any advantages at the moment. Well maybe one; she was still alive.

The professor sat down as he held the radio in front of his face. He listened to the details of Galjinder's brief escape attempt and subsequent pursuit and execution. For a few minutes he regretted giving the order, but if it wasn't for his incompetence the child wouldn't be missing right now. He needed to take the appropriate disciplinary action. It was simply expected of him. He knew it and so did every other person working around here. Leniency was a sign of weakness. The professor pressed the radio to his ear.

"What woman? Jennifer Lamar? There has to be some mistake! Are you positive? She should have been dead already."

"Bring her back down to see me in the revival chambers and I'll see to it myself. No, I don't want you to send her down on the conveyor. Drive around and escort her down here personally. I'll unlock the elevator. Don't forget, she could still be dangerous. Okay, I'll be waiting for you down here."

The professor took a deep breath and turned off his radio. He was already regretting that he had just volunteered for this task.

"Should we hood her?" asked the driver.

"Yes, I think that's probably a good idea."

The other man went to the back of the vehicle and dumped a few assorted tools and gear out from a smaller black duffel bag.

"Keep your face in the sand and don't move" instructed the driver as he pulled up the back of her head and fitted it inside the open bag. Two wraps of grey duct tape sealed the black duffel bag around her head and the man dropped down and placed a large tie wrap around her wrists.

"Even the great Houdini couldn't get out of that" said the man proudly as he stood her up and walked her back to the truck.

"Get in Miss Lamar. You have a blind date with the professor and he doesn't like to be kept waiting."

They assisted her into the back of the convertible truck as another truck approached quickly and skidded to a halt next to them.

"Looks like you two have everything under control here. Did you see any sign of Kyle Clayton around here? Or get a chance to look for smaller tracks around the conveyor?"

"No, not yet, but that's a good idea. We have to take her in. The big boss is waiting."

"Sure, I heard that on the radio. I'll have a look around here for tracks anyway," he said as he stepped out of his vehicle holding a large flashlight in one hand.

With lightning speed and efficiency he drew a hand gun equipped with a sophisticated silencer and shot both men in the forehead in less than two seconds. He calmly walked over, stepped up into the backseat and fired another round directly into the top of each man's head, with a trajectory going straight down through their heads and into their bodies. He propped both men up in their truck seats and leaned forward and shut off the engine and head lights.

Without a word he walked Jen over to his vehicle and placed her in the back seat of his truck.

"Who are you? Where are we? Where are we going? I heard shots fired."

"I'm a friend of James Clayton. Do you know Kyle's exact location right now?"

"No. No I don't. Did he escape or something?"

"I'm not sure, but he's missing and they're searching everywhere for him."

"Oh my God!" said Jen feeling completely powerless to help. "What's your name?"

"Bill, Bill Riker."

"Untie me then Bill."

"I will as soon as we get farther away from here. Right now it may be useful if you look like my prisoner. There's a good chance of running into a roadblock or checkpoint on the way out of here."

"Where is here and how did you find us?"

"We're in a town called Blakivik close to the Iraq border."

"Iraq! That can't be possible."

"That's where we are, believe me. I got a call from James and he wanted me to check out some coordinates he had from some type of program his son had been working on. I never really believed you were here until I set up a radio scanner and started to monitor the local radio communications. Up until tonight I've only been doing preliminary surveillance when I had the time."

"How do you know James Clayton?"

"He almost hired me."

"He almost hired you for what?"

"He almost hired me to look after his son."

Jen couldn't bring herself to say that was her job. The words were stuck in her throat. "What are you doing here in Iraq?"

"I often do contract work in this part of the world."

"What type of work?"

"The type most people don't want to do. Private protection work mostly. Who is the professor?" asked Bill as he continued driving around the far side of the airfield.

"The professor—I don't know. I just woke up inside a crate wrapped in plastic and finally managed to free myself and climb out through an underground conveyor system."

"What else was in there, where you woke up?" asked Bill.

"I don't know really, just another crate with a person inside. That other person was wrapped up in plastic too with a mask on their face. I couldn't see anything, but that's what I felt."

"Was it a crate that looked like a coffin?"

"Well yes, I didn't think about that, but sure, similar dimensions."

"What about the dead man?" asked Bill as he was getting further away from town and still unchallenged.

"What dead man?" asked Jen.

"The man wearing the white jacket—the one that was chasing you."

"I have no idea who he was. I didn't think he was chasing me. I thought he was trying to escape."

"Escape—I didn't even consider that. Well one thing's for sure."

"What's that?"

"You're friend, the professor, was quite surprised you were still alive."

"You heard him say that?"

"Yes, he said it on the radio and he wanted the two men who caught you to deliver you to him personally. He said something about taking care of matters personally."

"Do you think he wants to kill me?"

"That's what it sounded like."

Jen's mind raced through all this new information as she tried to piece together all the known, and unknowns, of everything that had just transpired.

"Bill! Bill! You have to pull over and untie me right now. I think I know where Kyle is and we have to move fast. His life may depend on it!" pleaded Jen in desperation.

"Sorry, it's just too dangerous to go back there now."

"Then stop and let me out, because I have to take that chance, it's my job."

Bill kept driving for another minute before slowing down and pulling over.

"Alright then, let's do it," said Bill as he turned around stopped the truck.

Chapter 25

Bill's razor-sharp knife had sliced through Jen's wide tie wrap with ease. He turned her head away as he removed the tape from around her neck and pulled the dirty duffel bag away from her head. Despite the low lighting inside the vehicle he was instantly struck by her beautiful skin and exotic facial features. Her face was covered in dust and grime and her hair was matted and dirty, but she was fit and stunning. She was a few levels above any woman that had ever thrown him a second glance.

"Let's make it official, shall we? I'm Bill Riker, pleasure to meet you," he said as he extended his hand out to her.

"Jennifer Lamar, it's a pleasure to meet you too Mr. Riker, and thank you so much for saving my life."

"Save your gratitude for now. We've got a long way to go until we're safely out of this place, and please call me Bill."

"Okay Bill, then thanks for stopping and also going back with me."

Jen had kept her eyes on this man ever since he removed her makeshift hood. He wasn't a huge bodybuilder type, just a man of normal stature with a lean physique. He had a certain steady seriousness about his manner and a voice that exuded a high degree of personal confidence in his abilities. Jen snugged up her seat belt as she watched him turn around and start driving back.

"Can you show me the silencer you were using on your handgun? It sounded so much quieter than any models I've ever used before."

Bill paused for a second before drawing his weapon, flipping it around in his hand and passing the handle to Jen.

"So then, where exactly is our friend Kyle?"

Jen admired the feel and balance of the weapon then casually opened the clip to check for bullets.

"This is really nice. What about the silencer? I don't see any information on it."

"You won't. It's my own personal design and its custom made by a private gunsmith in the US."

"Well it's a beautiful weapon," said Jen as she leaned against the door and pointed it at Bill's head.

"Oh you don't have to do that, really you don't."

"Sorry Bill, but I do, just a few questions."

Bill knew he had at least a fifty-fifty chance of knocking his gun clean out of her hand before she could fire, especially with the silencer still attached. He was born with extraordinary reaction speed compared to almost anyone who had ever cared to test it.

"Why would you kill two men to help me, a person you had never met?"

"That's easy Jen, a simple one word answer; money."

"Money—who is paying money for us?"

"Well, James Clayton of course."

"So there's a reward for finding us?"

"Yes, for the safe return of both of you."

"How do I know you aren't using me to find Kyle? You're almost certainly exposing yourself to increasing risk by going back with me now."

"Same answer Jen."

"Is that the one word answer?"

"Are we worth money dead or alive?"

"You are worth exactly twice as much alive, both of you. Listen to me, if you help me find Kyle alive, I'll pay you a twenty five percent finder's fee."

"I don't need any extra money to motivate me to find Kyle, and I don't care what financial arrangements you have, as long as we get away from here safely. Tell me this, what color is Doctor Clayton's helicopter?"

"I don't know. I've never seen it, but he told me something about you."

"What's that?"

"He told me where you both had a lunch together, an interview I believe."

"Yes, and where was that?"

"It was a place called the Angry Wolf or the Angry Horse, something like that. Are you happy now?"

"Here's your gun Bill, it's a beauty. Do you have any more?" ask Jen, satisfied with her quick interrogation.

Bill hit the brakes and pulled over. "So Jen tell me, where do you think Kyle is right now?"

"Underground."

"Are you telling me we're going down through those doors in the graveyard?"

"No. Bill, try to drive a little faster if you can. I'm getting worried sick about Kyle."

"Just where do you think he is Jen?"

"I think he's buried in the graveyard. That's my theory," said Jen as she clasped her head with both hands.

"You think he's dead?"

"I hope not, but we have to hurry!" yelled Jen, upset that she was losing control of her composure.

"I hate to tell you this, Jen, but the survival time for a person buried alive isn't long. Unless he was just buried, we are probably too late already."

"I think he's in a coffin, that's what I think."

"What's the basis for your theory?" asked Bill.

"Look, it may be a long shot, but I have a strong gut instinct here. Remember the man in the white jacket?"

"Yes, but I have no idea who he was."

"Well he saw me just before he was shot," said Jen.

"So, what does that have to do with anything?"

"Well, he looked like he was shocked to see me."

"What did he say?"

"Nothing, he didn't get a chance, but I could read it on his face. I could see it in his eyes."

"That doesn't mean anything," said Bill.

"That's not all. I escaped from one of those coffins when I was underground and not long after that I saw one come up the conveyor, and then I watched while a tractor buried it."

"You saw that? Do you think they buried an empty coffin?"

"People don't usually bury empty coffins. Somebody must have been in it."

"So you think Kyle is inside the coffin, buried alive?"

"I don't know. He hasn't been found yet, has he? He escaped, didn't he? I know it's a long-shot, but I have to check it out."

"And what if he isn't?"

"If he isn't, then I'm going back inside, with or without you."

"Okay, I guess we better get moving. I'll take the same route around the airfield when we come back into town."

"Airfield, did you see an airfield here?"

"Yes just a single lighted strip. I've had this place under surveillance for a few nights. I've noticed an unmarked jet coming in at night and dropping off those crates. Sometimes they pick them up as well."

"Do they have people inside?" asked Jen.

"I don't know, but I've watched as they unload them from the jet and drive them to the graveyard."

"Then what happens?"

"They push them right through those two doors. That's what happens to them," said Bill.

"Well something really strange is going on around here."

"You can say that again. Reach under your seat and you'll find a handgun in a flex Kevlar case. There should be fifty rounds in the side pouches."

"Do you have another silencer?"

"Sorry I don't. I'll take care of anything in that department. Use yours only if you have too."

"Okay I will, thanks."

Jen studied her surroundings intently as she loaded her new weapon. She could see a few aircraft parked in the distance, but they were still too far away to make a positive identification.

"How long could he last buried underground?"

"If he was buried in a coffin underground without oxygen, twenty minutes maybe. That depends on the fit and the size of the coffin."

Bill leaned over and turned up the volume on the radio scanner as they were entering Blakivik. It was clear there was a lot more verbal traffic on the radios now.

"Do you think they found the dead men?"

"I don't know, it's possible. If I had known we were coming back here, I would've taken a set of coveralls from one of those men for you to wear."

"What's our plan Bill? We can't just drive back into the middle of the graveyard. Can you let me out close to the buildings? I can try to make my way in on foot."

"I don't like the idea of getting separated," said Bill as he slowed the truck down.

"We're going to need that backhoe to dig him up or else it will take too long."

"Can you operate a backhoe Jen?"

"Well, no I haven't tried, but I'm sure I can figure it out."

"It might not be that easy. Let's try to find a place to park behind one of these large warehouses."

Bill turned off the headlights as he neared one of the industrial zones spread throughout the town. As they approached the largest of the warehouses he turned into a huge storage facility with rows and rows of containers.

Most were stacked between three and six containers high. Bill concealed his vehicle as much as possible on the darkest side of the yard in between a row of containers.

"Do you know exactly where they buried him?"

"I'm not sure, but if I returned to the same spot I think I could tell. It should be possible to tell where a fresh grave was just dug, don't you think?"

"Maybe, we'll see. Take the scanner with you and turn the volume right down."

"Okay, anything else?"

"Take that flashlight out from the glove compartment. We might need it."

"Okay, let's go."

The professor was lost in a daydreaming spell when he suddenly realized his radio was turned off and that they should have delivered the woman to him by now. He sat up and turned the radio back on and immediately heard the frantic voices on the radio. Two dead bodies had been discovered. Not just any two, but the two men charged with the simple task of bringing one unarmed captive woman back to the revival chambers.

The professor was just too angry to speak. He pulled his handgun out from his pocket and placed the end of the barrel under his chin. He needed a little time to think. He needed a little rest, a little escape from the strain of working under such stressful conditions. He knew just how close he was to crossing the line; the line between reality and the human breaking point. He closed his eyes, and squeezed the transmit button. "This is the professor speaking. If anyone finds the missing boy—I want him returned to the revival chambers unharmed. The woman he was with has also escaped and just murdered two of our own. If anyone sees her, they are free to shoot her on sight, and I'll provide a handsome financial reward for anyone who does exactly that. Keep me informed of any new developments," commanded the professor.

"Did you hear that?" asked Jen in disbelief.

"Yes, every word."

"Lucky he didn't say just exactly how much that reward was."

"Yes, very lucky," said Bill with a grin. "It might be a little hard to collect after just killing two of his men."

"Hold it, get down and take a look over in that direction Bill. I think I can see that tractor again."

"Yes, I can see it too. It looks like it's working down by the edge of the graveyard."

"Stay low and let's keep moving forward," said Jen with a real sense of urgency.

There wasn't much for cover other than darkness and the warehouse walls. They still had to cross a wide open area to get to the graveyard. Bill started to scour through the industrial waste littered around the side of the buildings. A huge assortment of old pipes and barrels, various tanks and pieces of scrap metal were lying everywhere. It was obvious that nobody had spent any time organizing this area for years. Bill started looking through some smaller five gallon drums and found one drum containing old used oil.

"Put some of this on you Jen. All over your skin and on any light clothing. We need to be as dark as possible to cross over to the graveyard. Keep it out of your mouth, ears and eyes."

Several minutes later they looked like a pair of wet coal miners with bright white eyes.

"Okay, let's keep going along this way first. Can you see the man operating the tractor?"

"Yes, he looks like he's digging another grave," said Jen.

"Yes I think you're right. He's definitely sitting in the backhoe seat now and I want to get his back to us before we cross over."

They kept moving further along the side of the warehouse to find the best possible position. Once they were ready they bent over and made a sprint for the closest cluster of grave stones. They finished their dash and dove behind the largest headstone in front of them. The sand stuck to their oily skin like feathers to tar, but all in all it just kept improving their camouflage. They could see the other vehicle was still sitting in the graveyard some distance away, but there wasn't any sign of the dead men Bill had left propped up in their seats. They both kept moving closer and closer to the tractor and stopped about fifty yards away.

"What do you think Bill, should we try and capture him and have him operate the machine?"

Jen heard two quiet shots and looked up to see the backhoe operator fall forward on top the controls as Bill put his handgun away. "I see you didn't like that idea."

"Sorry, don't forget you're a shoot-on-sight target around here. Let's go!"

They both sprinted to the tractor and Billed pulled the man out of the seat. Right beside the machine was a macabre-looking pile of three bloody bodies awaiting admission to their eternal group home. The operator had excavated a larger than normal pit, and obviously wasn't planning any individual services.

"Jen, try to remove at least two pairs of coveralls before you roll them into the pit."

"Where's Kyle? We have to find him first!"

Jen couldn't speak after hearing what Bill had asked her to do.

"Uh—just wait a minute Bill."

Jen frantically tried to get her bearings as she took a quick look around the general area. She could see where she was positioned earlier; beside the men's parked vehicle. She tried to line up the same building light. She could feel a sense of panic as she scrambled amongst the headstones searching the ground.

"I don't know where to dig, it's so dark."

"Use the flashlight if you have to. Cover it with your shirt. Keep it close to the ground and pointing away from the buildings."

Jen quickly looked around in many of larger spaces without marked graves.

"Okay wait, I think I've found it. It looks like lots of fresh tractor tracks and a recent excavation.

"It's your call Jen. I'll dig there if you want, but we have to hurry."

"Yes, yes I don't see anywhere else it could be around here. Let's try."

"Okay, take my gun and cover me after you get the coveralls. You had better watch yourself around this machine as well. I'm just learning to drive it myself."

Jen did everything she could to will her mind into another place; resting on a tropical beach with the smell of a warm ocean breeze filling her lungs. Not wrestling the bloody coveralls from two dead bodies and dumping them all into a pit. She worked as fast as possible and seemed to return to the present situation as she pushed the last man into the pile with her foot. She kept a careful watch around the area as she continued to kick sand and dirt on the four men piled in the grave.

Bill had made numerous short awkward movements with the machine before he finally managed to reposition the machine and figure out the functions of the various controls. He needed a crash-course because of the dual functions, but he was now in the backhoe seat and learning how to dig. It didn't take him long until he could operate the machine. Jen finished covering up the men, rolled up the dirty coveralls and ran over next to the backhoe. Bill was making amazing progress, but Jen felt all the fears she ever had coming to the surface. She was fighting to suppress one of the most severe onsets of an anxiety attack that she had ever experienced in her life. Her eyes were glued to the hole Bill was digging and also scanning the area. She had been reaching her hand in the hole and turning on the flash light after every load of sand. With the next pass of the bucket several pieces of wood shot up through the sand.

"Careful," motioned Jen silently with her waving hand as she stretched lower and turned on the flashlight.

Bill moved the bucket farther forward and tried to hook onto the top of the crate. Finally he was lifting it from the far end and then the top started to break away from the shipping crate.

They could both see the tanks and tubes surrounding the coffin inside. Jen jumped into the grave and ripped the few remaining pieces of wood away and pulled up hard on the lid of the coffin. She almost died when Kyle's hand lifted up from inside. Jen held his hand as she pulled away is face mask.

"Oh My God Kyle—Kyle—you're alive."

He squeezed her hand, but he was very pale and weak. Jen pulled away the tubes, shrink-wrap and Stacrofoam as she helped him out of the coffin.

"Jen—"

"Yes Kyle? Sorry I'm late, just trying to cover your back. We're in serious danger and we need to get away from here."

"This is Bill. He's a friend of your dad's and he's trying to help us."

"Is that Bill Riker under all that oil and sand?" asked Kyle knowingly. "So does that mean we're in the Middle East?"

"Yes we are, but let's just concentrate on trying to get away from here right now. Jen, can you and Kyle get those coveralls on?"

Bill dumped a few buckets of fill in the pit and partially buried Kyle's coffin. He jumped off the tractor, rolled up the sleeves and cuffs on Kyle's legs and rubbed some oil from his face on to Kyle's.

"Sorry, doctor's orders," said Bill with a slight grin. "Jen, can you pass my gun back over please."

Jen could see that the silencer on Bill's gun hadn't escaped Kyle's watchful eye. "It's quiet Kyle, really quiet."

"Nice. What now?" asked Kyle."

"We need to get back to my vehicle, fast, that's what."

Bill climbed up on the tractor, turned the key and shut it off. "How are you doing Kyle? Can you run if you have to?"

"I'll try," said Kyle as he stood up in the filthy over-sized coveralls.

"Okay, let's get moving. We need to get back over to the far side of that warehouse."

Jen took the lead and Kyle followed her away from the graveyard. Bill paused for a minute before following them. When they reached the cover of the high exterior wall, they made their way towards the back of the huge building.

"Stop, hold it for a minute," said Bill. "Pass me the scanner Jen."

They paused to catch their breath as Bill slowly turned up the volume on the scanner.

"Somebody sounds a little excited, but he isn't talking in English. Okay, let's keep moving."

As they made their way around to the back side of the warehouse they could see what all the commotion was about. Three vehicles and numerous armed men had located and pinned Bill's truck in between the rows of containers. Bill crouched down low, turned down the scanner volume and studied the situation for a minute.

"Way too many intangibles," whispered Kyle into Bill's ear.

Bill turned and whispered in Kyle's ear, "You're absolutely right Kyle, let's get the hell out of here."

The professor perked up in his chair after hearing about the new developments. Finding an unidentified vehicle within the storage compounds was an interesting discovery, however so far there was no positive connection between the missing pair and the vehicle. The odds were much higher that this was an unrelated coincidence, rather than part of an elaborate escape plan. Nobody from the outside could have known about their location, or have possibly found them here, the professor was confident about that.

"This is the professor speaking. I want you to search every single inch of that vehicle and bring the Vehicle Identification Numbers to the cyber computing supervisor at once."

"So sorry to inform you of this Professor, but regrettably all of those numbers appear to have been permanently removed."

The professor couldn't bring himself to respond.

"Professor—"

"Yes, I heard you! Assemble a team of the best forensics people we have and bring them over there at once. Have them collect fingerprints, footprints and anything else they can find. Should I spell everything out for you? Keep searching and investigating that vehicle until you find out who was driving it and what it's doing here! Understood?"

"Yes of course, right away Professor."

"Stop—we can't keep moving into the lighted area. If we keep moving along this wall we'll be in front of the open doors of the main warehouse. Let's cross back over to the graveyard. At least we have two potential vehicles over there, and that area has already been searched."

"Okay with me, let's go" said Jen.

Soon they were back amongst the assorted graves and headstones. Many were just blank and devoid of epitaphs or names. Bill moved over to check the vehicle where he shot the two men. It had been shut down and the key had also been removed.

"How did that vehicle look Bill?"

"It's possible we could use it, but they took the keys so it will take a little extra time to hot-wire it."

"Can you hot-wire it Kyle?"

"Sure, but it will take longer without tools."

"Bill has a knife, if that helps."

"Thanks! That should help. I can see some vehicles moving around in front of the warehouses so we better get started."

"Wait, wait a minute Kyle," said Bill as he jumped up and started up the tractor. He sat in the backhoe seat and manipulated the digging arm and bucket back to the stowed travelling position. He jumped back to the driver's seat and started trying the different levers until he had a basic grasp of their fundamental operation. He dropped the front loader bucket to the ground and then tilted it all the way back.

"Get inside."

"Are you sure Bill?" asked Jen apprehensively.

Bill turned the key and shut off the engine. "Yes, the tractor is supposed to be working out here. Nobody is supposed to be driving that other truck right now, and if anyone sees it's been moved or just driving around, it will only attract attention. Besides, the two of you will be in a virtually bullet-proof container."

"I like your idea Bill. That's definitely the better of those two options. Let's do it," said Kyle as he stepped inside the dirty steel bucket. "Come on Jen, I don't think we should be staying here in this graveyard any longer," said Kyle.

Jen walked over and got inside next to Kyle.

"Jet," said Kyle.

"What did you say?" asked Bill.

"I said—jet. I can hear the sound an approaching aircraft."

"Well, maybe we could convince them fly us out of here," said Bill.

"Kyle could fly it out," said Jen.

"Please Jen, this isn't a time for jokes," said Bill.

"It's no joke. We both fly helicopters and Kyle could fly it. Believe me, I'm not kidding!"

"Okay, well let's get going and see if we can possibly commandeer that aircraft. Be ready with your handgun Jen, our lives might depend on them. Wait a minute, Jen, come and give me a hand over here. I have an idea."

"Sure. What do you want to do?"

"I want to get Kyle's shipping casket up on the front loader."

"Okay. What for?" asked Jen.

"It will give you some additional head room in the bucket and should allow us to get closer to the aircraft. These caskets seem to be regular freight on this aircraft from everything I've seen. Let's empty everything from Kyle's casket and tear the top off."

Bill started up the tractor and began to manipulate the front bucket. He placed the open casket on its side and punctured the front teeth of the bucket through the side in several places. He set the bucket back on the ground and together they placed the inverted casket on top of the large front bucket.

"Here Jen, I'll trade you guns again. If I get you in close enough, then try to take the aircraft. We might only get one chance and we have to be committed to it. Okay, get in and I'll slide the casket over you."

Bill needed to get a little smoother on the controls or he could easily drop the casket. After several attempts he raised the front bucket about half as high as it would go, while balancing the casket on top. Even someone driving around in a truck shouldn't think this was too out of the ordinary, or have any idea of what was inside.

After several uncoordinated turns and knocking several stones from an aging crypt, Bill was finally moving along slowly in second gear towards the front of the warehouse. When they were halfway there he saw exactly what he was looking for; the flashing of the crude runway lighting system.

Bill downshifted to first gear, almost dropping the casket, and continued advancing slowly. The ground was very uneven, but Bill could tell that Kyle and Jen were holding and repositioning the casket from inside or it would have certainly fallen off by now. He could see what looked like a small tractor with one empty baggage trailer, waiting for the jet.

A small tanker truck was also waiting on the edge of the apron in front of the warehouse. Bill slowed to a stop a hundred and fifty yards away. He gently touched the controls to review their functions and knew Jen and Kyle would be looking out from their high perch. Bill waited until he saw the dark outline of the small jet taxing towards the ramp. As soon as he saw the baggage tractor begin to move Bill put it in gear and started moving forward.

"Lie down Kyle, and whatever you do, don't put your head up until I tell you."

"Jen, there isn't any danger yet. Besides, four eyes are better than two for surveillance purposes."

"Okay Kyle, but first sign of any trouble or gunfire I want you in the bottom of the bucket."

"I will, don't worry about that."

The front teeth on the bucket had knocked six holes in the forward side of the casket. Just the right size to conceal them, yet still large enough to allow them to see outside and also fire their weapons. They were now rounding the corner of the warehouse and travelling across the lighted ramp out in front of the huge open doors. Jen watched as the small dark jet slowed to a halt and the small baggage tractor slowly pulled up alongside the jet.

Bill was slowly driving forward when he suddenly started a gradual right turn and proceeded directly towards the running jet. He approached with his outstretched offering of one more shipping crate for the waiting aircraft. As he neared the aircraft he turned again and started heading directly to the front of the jet. He began raising the bucket up to the same height as the side cockpit windows. Jen watched as a side window slid open and a handgun appeared which was now trying to target Bill as he drove the tractor straight at them.

"Get down, now!" screamed Jen in no uncertain terms. She didn't need any special instructions from Bill before she quickly fired several close range shots, each of them passing right through the glass and striking the two men in the cockpit.

Bill immediately began to lower the crate and manoeuvred it just inside the open side doors of the aircraft. Jen pushed the crate away to the side and onto the floor of the jet as they both jumped out from the loader. Bill could see the tractor operator running away, towards the tanker truck. As he backed up he turned the loader around and started to push the other small tractor and trailer away from the jet and towards the tanker. As soon as the two machines were clear Bill made a dash back to the aircraft.

"Let's go!" he screamed as he dove inside the open door.

Jen had pulled the men out of their seats and Kyle had climbed into the left seat and began increasing the throttles. Bill could see the headlights of the tanker truck turn on as it started racing over towards them.

"Jen, you'll need to use the foot-pedals from the other seat. I can't reach them without extensions," said Kyle calmly.

Bill started firing at the approaching truck while he pushed the two men out the side door.

"Jen, no delay please," said Kyle as she jumped in the other seat. "Full left pedal please and keep your head low. I see other vehicles approaching." said Kyle.

They both felt another shot hit the edge of the broken glass window as Kyle accelerated down the taxiway and out onto the runway.

"Use the pedals to keep us centered between the runway lights, and don't push your toes forward and apply the brakes," said Kyle as he pushed both throttles forward. "No time for a run up."

Bill fired several more shots before he finally managed to close and lock the side door. Kyle checked the heading for his departure roll and watched and waited as they neared their take-off airspeed. Just at that moment the runway lights went out.

"Maintain your pedal position Jen," said Kyle calmly and several seconds later the jet pulled up at a sharp angle and accelerated into the dark sky.

"Where too?" asked Kyle.

The professor couldn't believe the reports that were coming in over the radio. He still didn't have any positive information, but all the circumstantial evidence was clearly mounting. Somebody had successfully commandeered an aircraft and flown it out from the airstrip at Blakivik.

Fortunately the aircraft was outfitted with an on-board tracking system, so at least he could monitor their progress. The professor continued to massage the underside of his chin with the barrel of his handgun. He was being plagued by setback after setback. Once again he turned his radio off and redirected his thoughts to more pressing technical issues that he had hoped to solve with the young boy's help. Deep down he knew it was just another of many delays.

Bill climbed forward and crouched down behind the two front seats. The rest of the seats had been removed to accommodate the current cargo configuration. They also couldn't talk to each other over the noise due to the wind rushing in through the holes on the glass. Kyle and Jen were wearing the only two headsets on the aircraft and Kyle asked Jen to pass hers to Bill.

"Do you want the good news or bad news first?" asked Kyle.

"Let's start with the good news," said Bill.

"Well, we're flying away from that place."

"And what's the bad news?"

"We have no pressurization and we're flying on reserve fuel."

"Reserve fuel—"

"Yes Bill, we have about fifteen minutes remaining. They must have been planning to take on fuel at their last stop."

"Yes, well there was a fuel truck waiting. How far is the nearest airport?"

"I just checked the GPS 'nearest' function."

"What did that tell you?"

"That the nearest airport from this position is near the US embassy in Baghdad."

"How far away is that?"

"It's not the distance Bill, it's the time. It's forty-five minutes away."

"So you are saying we are going to run out of fuel before reaching the next airport?"

"Yes," said Kyle calmly.

"So, what do you suggest?" asked Bill.

Kyle increased the resolution on the GPS maps and studied the area for a moment. "We'll have to make a highway landing prior to fuel starvation."

"That's it? That's our only option?" said Bill, his disappointment obvious.

"It's our only logical option Bill. Can you take your handgun, point it at this box and wait for my trajectory adjustments?" said Kyle as he pointed at a box mounted in the center console.

"You want me to shoot this box? Right here and now?"

"Yes, at a precise angle. Point it just a little lower down and farther over to the left side. Good, fire once."

"Like that?" said Bill after firing a shot.

Kyle quickly checked the operation of the flight controls.

"Good shot Bill. You've disabled the on-board tracking system. Do you have anyone you wish to speak with on the aircraft radios?"

"No Kyle, we may very well be a wanted aircraft right now and I think it's best to stay under the radar."

"I agree. The highway is our only option right now and I'm going to need Jen's help on the pedals. If you don't mind maybe you could pass Jen your headset and I'll update her on the situation."

"Sure, good luck putting this thing down."

"Thanks Bill."

Jen listened carefully to the details of Kyle's new information as he adjusted both engines for maximum fuel endurance. She knew something was wrong because Kyle lowered the landing gear, and she knew enough about flying to know that a night-time highway landing had plenty of potential hazards.

"How far is it to the highway Kyle?"

"It's six miles. It appears mostly straight from the GPS map, but we'll have to access it from a lower altitude."

Kyle kept the jet flying on a low speed, low level intercept course.

"Do you think its paved Kyle?"

"I don't know yet Jen. I've calculated the wind using an air-speed to ground-speed comparison. Please prepare to enter a string of user way-points into the GPS when we reach the highway. Identify them in a numerical sequence, about ten seconds apart. I'll be setting up a low-level flight directly over the highway first and then we'll decide on the most favourable terrain for a landing. I'll calculate the slope from the information on the Radar Altimeter."

"Okay, I'm ready to start programming the user way-points when you're ready."

"Standby Jen, I have a visual on some vehicle traffic now and commencing a left turn over the highway. Wait until I'm perfectly centered. Okay Jen, start now. Program an automatic position waypoint every ten seconds."

Jen concentrated intently as she created a string of numerical way-points above the highway.

"High tension wire crossing at way-point five," said Kyle.

"Should I mark it?"

"No, I have it memorized."

"High tension wire crossing way-point nine," said Kyle as he pulled the nose up and started to circle around and turn towards the highway.

"How's the slope Kyle?" asked Jen.

"Average slope calculation of three degrees down slope."

"So Kyle, into wind down-slope or downwind up-slope?" asked Jen like a seasoned flight instructor.

"Right engine deceleration—left engine deceleration. In to wind down-slope landing—imminent. Right engine flame-out. Dual engine flame-out. Insufficient altitude for an air-start. Critical in-flight emergency now in progress—I need the 'Go To' Nav function set to the nearest way-point. Stand-by on pedals."

"Nearest waypoint is waypoint four," yelled Jen as she frantically worked the keys on the GPS.

"Start calling the Rad-Alt numbers, fifty foot increments, starting now," said Kyle as he dropped the nose and started a series of tight S turns.

"Six hundred feet!" yelled Jen over the eerie sound of nothing but air, rushing in through the broken windshield of the dark cockpit. Kyle switched on the forward landing lights.

"Five hundred—four hundred—three hundred," yelled Jen as they were dropping too fast for her to call fifty foot increments.

Kyle nosed it over again for a split second to miss the overhead power lines on way-point nine.

"One hundred," screamed Jen as Kyle quickly adjusted the aircraft's attitude for landing.

"Ready on the pedals, stand by for braking," said Kyle as the aircraft's main gear struck the road hard and almost instantly followed by the nose wheel. A strong violent shuddering vibration in the nose gear left everyone momentarily speechless.

"Landing gear's stable. Keep us centered on the road and start to gently apply the brakes," said Kyle as he climbed up on his seat to look over the main instrument console.

The deceleration on the rough hard-packed road seemed to take forever and Jen eased it slightly off to the side of highway before they came to a complete silent stop.

"Nice job Kyle!" said Bill as he patted Kyle on the back of his shoulder.

Kyle left the battery and landing lights on and started getting out of his seat. "Hurry, let's get out of here! We have approaching vehicle traffic."

Bill had the side door open before Kyle had even finished talking.

"Good job! Both of you! That was awesome!" said Bill as he helped them both out from the side of the aircraft.

"Do you have any idea where we are Bill?" asked Jen still feeling embarrassed about her loss of composure in the cockpit.

"Yes, I think so. I was studying the GPS map display over your shoulders as we were flying over here. I might even be able to make it back to work tonight, with a little luck."

"Are you close to where you're working Bill?" asked Jen.

"Well, reasonably I guess, maybe a hundred miles or so. We're going to need to acquire another vehicle or ride to get away from here."

Bill pulled out his cell phone and checked for a signal.

"We don't have any signal coverage yet, and I don't want to use the sat phone in the aircraft as it might expose our position. Jen, I'll trade you guns again if you don't mind. That was some nice shooting back at the airport. Good reaction time."

"Thanks Bill? What's your plan now?"

"I have some friends that can help us if I'm able to contact them. Anyone driving by here will have to slow down in order to pass by this roadblock. Let's move away from the road and see if anyone stops to investigate. It's not every day that you see a jet sitting on a highway, and the battery should keep the landing lights on for a while."

"Maybe we should wait in the jet?" suggested Jen.

"That's not a bad idea, unless the people that are looking for us find us inside. Better to stay back and see who stops first."

"Okay, let's move it! I can see a truck coming in the distance."

All three of them sprinted away across the open sand as far as they could before dropping down behind a gentle rise in the terrain.

"It looks like a large flatbed truck, and it looks like its empty," said Kyle.

They all lay down as low as they possibly could and watched as the truck started gearing down as it approached the aircraft.

"It's got a sleeper cab, but I can only see one driver from here. He's stopping. He's getting out and the engine is still running."

"Now! Fast as you can!" said Bill in a loud whisper as he jumped up and started sprinting towards the rear of truck.

Bill stopped outside the driver's door and waited for Jen and Kyle to climb inside before going after the driver. Bill came up from behind him as he was climbing inside the jet. He held his gun to the back of his head while he forced him into the shipping crate. He rolled the crate over and secured the lid with a spare cargo strap before running back to the truck.

"Is he still breathing?" asked Kyle when Bill returned.

"Yes, he's fine. He's just a little tied up inside your old coffin for a while," said Bill as he climbed in the truck.

"Been there, done that," said Kyle with a grin.

The transmission let out several loud grinding shrieks before Bill started to get the rig moving. He needed to drive around the wing of the jet before getting the truck back on the highway.

"Lots of fuel in this machine," said Kyle as he surveyed the instruments on the dashboard.

"Well if we run out of fuel I think I can save us. You really did a fantastic job handling that aircraft, not to mention an emergency night landing after a multi-engine flame-out."

"Thanks Bill—I couldn't have done it without Jen. I'm sure we would both still be back there if it wasn't for you—right Jen?" said Kyle as he looked around. Jen was lying on the bed in the sleeper, sleeping like a log.

"There's lots of room up there for you too Kyle. Why don't you have a quick rest and I'll wake you both at the next stop? We need to find a place to get you two cleaned up, rested, and ready to leave the country."

"I think I like the sound of that," said Kyle as he climbed up from the passenger seat to soft upper mattress.

"Maybe I'll just close my eyes for a couple of minutes," said Kyle as he laid his head down on a pillow and immediately fell asleep.

After a lucky break during their extensive search, the second abduction of Lisa and her daughter had been carried out with swift efficiency by four armed agents. They were forcefully separated almost immediately during broad daylight inside a large outdoor parking complex and whisked away in separate vehicles.

The professor needed Lisa back working at the Claytons' estate as soon as possible. The daughter could once again serve as Lisa's motivator and of course the opportunity existed for a reciprocal motivator arrangement between the two of them. It had been used in the past to keep two people working when they both thought their continued compliance and support of RA-9 activities would save their partner's life. At this point, it just wasn't known if Lisa's daughter could be used for anything whatsoever.

Chapter 26

James Clayton had to book off work for the entire week. He had been virtually married to his cell phone since Bill's last message and couldn't understand why it was taking so long to hear back from him. Bill had previously sent a second text message requesting a direct transfer of US Funds to a numbered bank account in Kuwait for expenses incurred. James had transferred the funds exactly as Bill had requested and was still unable to reach him by phone despite numerous efforts.

He had to go into town earlier on, to pick up a couple of cartons of cigarettes, and also decided to buy a two week supply of the strongest nicotine patch available. He was rather surprised at just how easily he had slipped back into his old college habits. James put his feet up on the table and lit another cigarette and watched as Lisa came in from the kitchen with another bottle of wine. James jumped when he heard his ring-tone and lunged for his phone on the first ring.

"Hello. Bill! Bill Riker! There you are. You have no idea how happy I am to hear your voice. Please tell me how everything is going? When will I see Kyle and Jen? Port of Latakia—where's that? Okay good. So you'll be talking with them tomorrow. Did I tell you they've invited Kyle to attend some leading-edge experiments for a week at the Mass Hadron Collider in Switzerland? They want to start early next month. Geneva. You won't stand a chance of holding him back from that place. He talks about it all the time. It's the largest collider ever built in the world. Sure, that would be fantastic. We can make the arrangements to get them home after that. Send me an invoice with all your expenses and I'll pay your day rate until they arrive in Geneva airport. Twenty-five percent—are you sure? She's well paid you know. Okay, I'll take care of it Bill. No, I won't tell a soul. Say 'Hi' to both of them for me and I'll talk with them later on. Excellent, make sure you come over for a visit after you get back. Okay, I'll watch for that Bill. Thanks again, Bye for now."

James tossed his phone on the coffee table and leaned back into the soft couch. That was the call he had been waiting for; Kyle and Jen were now getting closer to home by the minute. James knew he could never face Kyle, or any of his surgical colleagues, with a cigarette in his hand. He made up his mind, stood up and emptied the ashtray into the fire and then tossed the rest of his cigarettes in the fire. He sat back and watched as the plastic melted, then finally started to smoulder and burn. He opened up a box of patches and fidgeted around with a patch trying to remove the cover.

"Hey Lisa, have you got a pair of scissors hiding in the kitchen?"

"Yes, they're in the second drawer down, on the left side of the cutting board."

James stood up and looked over as Lisa stood behind Alexia's wheelchair, brushing her hair.

"It's so good to have you back Lisa. Was she difficult to feed tonight?"

"Yes James, very difficult for some reason."

"That's too bad. Sorry to hear that," said James as he walked towards the kitchen to get the scissors.

"Can you smell it Kyle?" asked Jen.

"The excessively rich exhaust from a poorly tuned engine billowing out from the end of a rusted tailpipe?"

answered Kyle, as they lay amongst the rolls of carpet in the back of the truck.

"No, the ocean," said Jen from under the black veil of her burka.

"There aren't any oceans anywhere near here. You must be referring to the sea. The Mediterranean Sea, from the looks of the celestial map I was watching a few hours ago on the night sky."

"I'll take your word for that Kyle. Where do you think we are on the Mediterranean?"

"I'm not sure exactly, as we haven't arrived yet, but possibly the Port of Latakia."

"The Port of Latakia—I remember my father telling me about that place when I was a child. It's got a lot of history."

"Was your dad here before?" asked Kyle.

"Yes, when he was much younger. By the way, have you noticed that there seems to be more and more traffic and people around here now?" asked Jen.

"Yes I was thinking the same thing. I can see boats, more and more of them," said Kyle.

"I don't know about you, but getting on a boat sure sounds good to me right about now."

"Yes, it sure does. Jumping into the water sounds even better. Remember the golden rule, ladies first!"

"We'll see about that. It looks like we're driving away from the water now," said Jen.

After another thirty minutes they pulled into a dry-land shipyard and watched as the driver manoeuvred them through some very expensive looking boats supported on blocks. They pulled up next to a sleek white yacht that was loaded on a large trailer behind a commercial truck cab.

The driver stopped the truck and escorted Kyle and Jen up onto the yacht and over to a shallow concealed room beneath the deck boards. There were two narrow beds and a cooler inside. Kyle and Jen climbed down inside and watched as the doors closed above them. All in all, it was probably the best accommodations they had seen on the trip. There was a small light in this stow-away compartment and they both quickly removed their heavy black headgear. Jen opened the cooler and quickly pulled out two cold drinks from the ice.

"Thirsty?" asked Jen as she passed one to Kyle.

Moments later they heard the sound of the commercial truck starting its diesel engine and they felt the trailer starting to move. They were both hoping it wouldn't be long until they heard waves lapping at the sides of the hull.

James had decided he needed a steady supply of nicotine gum to supplement the patch. Although this was clearly not the recommended procedure, he was confident it was better than buying another carton of cigarettes. James had been up at the heli-pad washing his machine to keep his mind off his troubles and hadn't noticed that he'd received a new voice mail from a restricted caller. He walked into the hanger and pulled a stool over beside the workbench. The message was a long one, from Bill Riker.

He carefully listened to Bill's message, twice. Kyle and Jen had departed the Port of Latakia for Monaco on the famous Cote d' Azure. Their boat trip would take three days and Bill had made all the necessary arrangements to get them to Geneva by the fifth of the month. He would be arriving in Monaco ahead of them, but required the remaining outstanding funds transferred to his existing bank account in Monaco. Along with being the second smallest country in the world, and having the highest density and per ca-pita income, it was also an income tax free country; a perfect place for Bill Riker to collect his fees.

He also required the assistance of the government contact James had suggested earlier. He needed them to process and deliver new identification papers, bank cards and passports to his hotel in Monaco before Kyle and Jen's arrival. Bill would make sure they were both onboard the afternoon flight to Geneva on the fifth day of the month; however, he couldn't assist them any further after that due to previous commitments. They had a scheduled ground transportation service from the Geneva Airport to the Mass Hadron Collider and they'd be arriving before the new experiments were scheduled to start.

He had also mandated that no investigative or retaliatory actions should be undertaken against the people responsible for the abductions for the time being. People had been killed during their escape and Bill didn't want all those details released to authorities at this time. They had all managed to escape unharmed which was the main primary objective of his mission. Investigating and prosecuting those responsible was secondary in nature, and they could make those decisions later on.

James set the phone down and briefly considered the rapidly escalating costs of getting Kyle and Jen back home. He needed to have some clear figures in his mind before he called Al Anderson. He didn't doubt that Al would cover or reimburse him for all of these related expenses as Kyle was indirectly under the government's employ, and they were still contractually responsible for him.

He found a pad of paper and started making detailed notes before calling Al Anderson with his wish list. He was also aware that Al would be full of questions as well, but Bill still wanted all the details of his work kept under wraps. He knew that was something Al Anderson should understand, although in fact he didn't really have much information himself. With his wish-list in hand, and a fresh nicotine patch on his shoulder, James placed a call to Al Anderson to try and get the wheels in motion.

Just when Kyle thought he was about to lose what little he had in his stomach, the overhead doors slowly opened upward.

"Bonjour, you can come out of there now," said the older darkly tanned captain with his strong French accent.

They both climbed awkwardly out of their cupboard under the floor boards and took a few extra steps to adjust to the slow swaying deck of the vessel. They were completely out of sight of land and the sky was one of the most spectacular sunsets either one of them had ever seen.

"We're now safely outside of Syria's maritime boundary. You two can use the second state room on the right, and you'll find a small selection of woman's and children's clothing in the dresser and the closet. Wear what you like and make yourselves comfortable onboard our vessel. The steward will bring you both some dinner a little later on. Welcome aboard!"

"Thank you very much," they both said at the same time.

Kyle and Jen quickly walked to the state room anxious to shed the dirty black robes they had lived in for far too long. They were both surprised at the opulence inside the large luxurious state room. Lush linens and carpets, gold plumbing fixtures and expensive furnishings were chosen with an obvious touch of an interior designer. It didn't take long for each of them to find some suitable clothing to wear.

"Ladies first," said Kyle as he motioned his hand towards the entrance to the luxurious washroom.

"I might just take you up on that," said Jen with a smile as she walked inside and closed the door.

Al surveyed his notes after his lengthy conversation with James Clayton. He wasn't too happy that he hadn't been the first one to locate the missing pair, but nevertheless they were on their way back home and that was the main thing. Fortunately the passport photographs that were taken earlier on would simplify processing any new documents for the both of them. Money wasn't really an object in this case and he was certainly aware of the associated costs of moving people around undetected in certain countries. As far as transferring funds to the account James had requested, there were few countries in the world that were easier than Monaco.

Al considered the most likely reason for their abduction was kidnapping for ransom, in which case the money he was paying now would be nothing compared to what they could have demanded. And as he knew from many other such intercontinental abduction attempts, the chances of getting the victims back alive were remote at best. No, overall he'd have to be satisfied about finally locating the missing house keeper sleeping in her minivan in the Disneyland public parking area in California.

Her claim of accidentally discovering Alexia's prescription drugs in her bag instead of her own, and the resulting case of temporary amnesia was unusual, but not unheard of. She was continually unable to provide any information at all about how she had possibly arrived there. James also thought it was strange, but not enough to prevent her from returning home to her previous place of employment. In fact he was more than happy just to have her back home.

The requests from James had been reasonable and Al Anderson had the available resources to take care of them with relative ease. Even the timing of the Mass Hadron Collider visit was fortunate. Kyle would be back in time to start his second internship at the Central Fusion Research Complex 8 with about one week at home before he got started. He would have everything that James requested sent to the Hotel Monaco with time to spare. This file was as good as closed; just the way Al Anderson liked it.

Kyle and Jen were finally starting to feel like human beings again. The French captain of the yacht was hospitable and going out of his way to accommodate any of their needs. They had considered asking him for a swim in the ocean, but decided not to. It was still a real mystery about where they had been and why they were there. They both had numerous topics to discuss between them. Jen didn't know about Kyle cutting into her intravenous tubes, or the hidden bullets, or the man back at the farm. She couldn't believe it when Kyle told her it was the same man who killed his last bodyguard and shot his mother. In any case they both knew their discovery by Bill Riker was based solely on the coordinates from Kyle's program. Why they were there, was another unexplained mystery.

Travelling offshore on this yacht was now becoming a real treat for both of them, and the weather was still warm and beautiful. They couldn't have picked a nicer place to be even if they'd tried. The only information the captain had been willing to divulge was that Bill Riker would be there to meet them when they reached the marina. After everything they had just been through that was enough information for both of them.

Bill had flown in the night before and rented a car to drive from Nice to Monaco. Generally speaking, it was just as easy to get around with a taxi, but Bill wanted to keep a closer eye on his precious human cargo from the minute they arrived.

He had checked into the Hotel Monaco where he usually stayed when he conducted his own financial affairs in Monaco. As requested, his package was waiting inside the locked safe of the hotel. He thought about trying to improve his relationship with James Clayton, strictly to learn who was able to provide such perfect documents in such a short time span.

Bill finished examining the documents, cards, and airline tickets in his hotel room and checked the time. It would be daylight soon and he had time to catch a few hours' sleep before Kyle and Jen would be arriving at the marina. Bill placed the package under his mattress, locked the door and set the alarm. Right now five hours sleep seemed like ten. Bill pulled back the covers, slid his hand gun under the pillow and crawled into bed.

Kyle and Jen were both out on the main deck as they approached closer and closer to shore.

"It's Monaco, the second smallest country in the world." said Kyle.

"Monaco? How do you know that? And what are we doing here?" asked Jen already regretting the question.

"I've seen pictures in an encyclopaedia before. It looks like we're coming into dock at the marina and then most likely meeting up with Bill again."

They were both amazed at the sheer number of boats criss-crossing the water everywhere.

"You probably need a reservation just to berth here by the looks of things. I've never seen so many boats," said Jen as they drew closer to all the marine traffic.

"Well I don't think the captain needs our help docking. It will be nice to get our feet back on solid ground again."

"Yes, that's for sure!" said Kyle as he stretched up on his toes and peered over the railing.

"So, then what's the smallest country Kyle?"

"The Vatican City," said Kyle, matter-of-factly."

"I would never have guessed that one. That seems so strange," said Jen with a smile.

"Lots of helicopter activity around here as well," said Kyle.

"Yes, I was just thinking the same thing."

"Monaco is probably a good business location for a helicopter company with the absence of an airport and the highest per capita earnings in the world."

"They seem to be doing alright judging by all the activity," said Jen.

"That's true, but it's hard to say for certain without a detailed financial audit of the company's books."

"I'm sure you could handle that in the time a takes to have a coffee," said Jen with a grin.

"Have a look way up ahead, next to the empty berth on the dock. I'm pretty sure that's Bill Riker."

"Good eye Kyle! I think you're right," said Jen as she stretched her hand up and waved.

Bill stood patiently as the sleek yacht drew closer and closer. It was a warm beautiful afternoon with a nice breeze blowing in from the waters of the Cote d' Azure. Despite Bill's warmer than necessary clothing, and several days without shaving, he seemed to be blending in with the above-average looking cosmopolitan crowd lounging seductively around the yachts at the marina. Bill was summoned onboard by the captain of the yacht to clear up the final payments for services. He had been temporarily, but politely, disarmed by crew members prior to their brief closed-door meeting. Ten minutes later they returned his personal handgun, unloaded but still outfitted with his customized silencer.

Everyone was all smiles as the three of them departed the yacht and started walking way.

"I noticed they took your gun away," said Kyle.

"That's to be expected in these types of circumstances," said Bill.

"These people have a good reputation for doing this type of work and I'm sure they want to keep it that way," said Bill.

"Well I had a few bullets and no gun and now you have a gun and no bullets."

"Not for long. I'll be reloaded when we get to my car."

"Are you expecting any trouble Bill?" asked Jen, sensing his unease.

"I'm always expecting trouble Jen. That's my job. It's just amplified a little when I'm unarmed."

"Do your bullets fit my gun Kyle?"

"Did. No, I'm sorry, but I had to hide them in the underground Quarantine room."

"Quarantine room? What was that place anyway?" asked Bill.

"We don't really know, we didn't see much of anything," Kyle answered.

"What were you going to do with the bullets?" said Bill with a smile.

"I can think of dozens of possibilities, depending on available materials and supplies. Most likely I would try to devise a suitable apparatus in which to fire them. Simply pushing a bullet into a human ear and striking the primer with a suitable object could feasibly create a strategic advantage under certain close-quarter combat conditions."

"Well, you're absolutely right about that Kyle. They have lots of potential and I'd rather be with them, than without them. That's our car just over here."

"The black one?" asked Jen,

"Yes, the black one," said Bill as he unlocked the car from thirty feet away with the key-less remote in his pocket.

Minutes later they were locked inside and Bill turned on the air conditioner while he reloaded his handgun.

"I have some good news for you two, especially you Kyle," said Bill as he glanced back at them in the rear view mirror.

"What kind of news?" asked Jen with obvious concern for Kyle.

"Kyle has been selected to join a small group of people attending several new experiments at the Mass Hadron Collider."

"The Mass Hadron Collider—that's fantastic!" said Kyle obviously overjoyed. "When are we going? How long are we staying? What experiments are they planning? Do you have any details? I'm so excited about this you have no idea!"

"All I can tell you, is that you'll both be there by tonight, and in five days from now you will be landing back home in the Portland Airport. James will be waiting for you there."

"What about Jen? Is she invited this time?"

"Yes, as a matter of fact she is. Apparently James said that little stipulation was a deal-breaker, and if she wasn't going with you this time, then both of you were coming home immediately."

"James said that?" asked Jen.

"Yes, that's the information I have."

"What about you? Will you be able to join us?"

"No, I can't. Not this time. We have about one hour until I'll be putting you both on a helicopter flight to the Nice airport in France. I'll need most of that time to brief you on everything I have here for you. But I wish I was going. That collider place sounds interesting. I know it's a huge underground facility of some kind. I read that they were planning to make 'black holes' there or something."

Bill glanced back at Kyle knowing he was biting at the bit to enlighten them both on the inner workings of the world famous Mass Hadron Collider.

Bill felt like a kindergarten dropout after listening to Kyle talk about the Mass Hadron Collider; how the world's largest and highest-energy particle accelerator worked; and how they hoped to address some of the most basic fundamental questions and mysteries of physics. Even so, he was impressed. He could see right away just how extraordinary James Clayton's son really was.

"Maybe I should give you a couple of bullets for good luck," said Bill as he glanced back at Kyle.

"Are we flying to Geneva on a domestic flight?" asked Kyle.

"How did you know we were going to Geneva?"

"Well, it seems logical if we are going to be there this afternoon."

"Thanks Bill, it's something to think about. You never know when, or where, they might come in handy. Look, a casino!" said Kyle as he pointed it out with his hand.

"I have a feeling they might not like to see you walking into that place," said Bill as they all started laughing out-loud.

Bill pulled the car into the lot outside the hotel.

"Let's go inside for a little while—this shouldn't take us long. You can walk up front Jen, if you don't mind, and Kyle, I want you to stay in middle."

The three of them made their way through the lush lobby of the hotel with extensive water gardens and tropical plants everywhere. They stood briefly outside the ornate elevator before riding it up to the top level. Bill whisked them from the elevator and down to his room, and then locked the door behind him.

"Okay, have a seat you two and make yourselves comfortable."

The brief uneasy thought of his package not being there was quickly dismissed when he touched it and pulled it out from under the mattress. Kyle and Jen were seated in the two comfortable chairs in the hotel room as Bill began to show them the contents of the package. They included perfectly processed passports for each of them, travel visas, and bank and credit cards for Jen, complete with corresponding pin numbers.

"James said you're free to use the credit cards for any expenses you may incur, no pre-authorizations required. I have all the prepaid airline tickets and of course all the reservations have been made for you, including your helicopter flight from here to the Nice Airport in France. One flight to Geneva, and a short drive later they will be expecting you. I understand they have some deluxe accommodations for the chosen few that get to visit the Mass Hadron Collider. After listening to Kyle talk about it I'm starting to wish I was going too."

"Why don't you Bill? It's a chance of a lifetime," pleaded Kyle.

"I'm sure James can arrange it for you," added Jen.

"No, I have to get back to my other contract. It was hard enough just to get away for this little trip. After I drop you at the helipad I need to drive to Nice myself and catch a later flight, then back to the sand dunes. Here's a little extra cash for you if you need it. I can't get to the bank till later. I'm sure you can find a bank machine at the airport if you need it."

Bill checked his watch as he reorganized the contents of the package.

"Well, that's about it. We should get going. You have a helicopter waiting for you."

Bill could see Kyle's enthusiastic response to that as well.

"Thanks Bill! I saw a Sikorsky S-76 flying around earlier on. Do you know what type we'll be using?"

"No I'm not sure, but we need to get moving now."

"Okay thanks, we're ready to go," said Jen as she collected everything Bill had given her and put it inside her light tan jacket.

They all made their way back down through the lobby and out to the car. Bill told them both to sit in the back seat before navigating his way through the crowded tight streets and down to the heli-pads by the sea. It was a busy operation and they parked as close as possible before walking up to the small passenger terminal.

"I have a reservation for Jennifer Lamar and Kyle Clayton," said Bill to the attractive ticket agent.

"Yes, we've been expecting you for a flight to the Nice airport."

"That's great," he said while handing her the ticket confirmations.

"Still just the two of you flying today?" asked the attendant with a warm smile.

"Come on Bill, are you absolutely one-hundred percent sure? It's a chance of a lifetime," pleaded Kyle.

"Sorry Kyle. Maybe we can get together back at your dad's place sometime in the future and you can tell me all about it. Okay?"

"Okay, that's a deal then. Jen and I can take you out flying in my dad's helicopter."

"Now that sound's really good! I'll definitely take you up on that!"

"Your machine is ready to go when you are. This gentleman will assist you with loading," said the female passenger agent.

"What type of helicopter are we flying in?" asked Jen.

"We have a Sikorsky S-76 booked for your flight today," said the attendant.

"Nice!" said Kyle.

"Well that's about it then for now," said Bill, not sure whether to hug them or shake their hands.

Jen opened her arms and quickly solved that little problem.

"Thanks so much for everything," she said as they fell naturally into a longer than usual embrace.

"So I hope we'll see you to back in the US sometime later this year."

"Yes of course. I'm looking forward to that myself."

"Thanks again for everything," said Kyle, as he reached out his hand.

"You're welcome Kyle. It was really a pleasure to meet you," said Bill, as he pressed two bullets into Kyle's palm with a magician's touch.

"That's just in case you ever need them. I look forward to seeing you both again in the future," said Bill as he released his grip.

Kyle had a surprisingly strong grip for someone his size.

"Thanks again for everything," said Kyle as the bullets disappeared from sight with equal ease. Bill moved over to the main terminal window and watched as they were escorted out to the helicopter. Bill kept standing there while they were being loaded inside and both engines were started. Several minutes later the rotors began turning and they lifted off the pad on their way to Nice, France.

Kyle and Jen didn't have much time to spare by the time they were loaded aboard their flight to Geneva.

"I hope you didn't feel too pressured into this trip to the Collider. I can guarantee it will be one of the most interesting things you will ever see. I'm also going to try to get you into the Central Fusion Research Complex 8 back in California as soon as I get the chance. It's hard to say which place is more interesting. They're both on the leading edge in their respective fields."

"No Kyle, as a matter of fact I'm excited too. We might be watching history being made before our eyes. Look at the beautiful mountains over there. Swiss Alps I presume."

"I'd say that's a safe assumption."

They both looked up as the seat-belt chime sounded and they listened to the young captain's pre-landing announcement.

"The Mass Hadron Collider extends under the French Swiss border. They had some serious problems when they first started up, but most of them are resolved now. They could soon be making discoveries that may change the future of mankind."

"Are you sure about that Kyle?"

"Yes, it's very possible."

They both watched out the windows as the captain flew a precision approach into the Geneva Airport.

"I've never been to Switzerland before," said Jen as they watched the sun disappearing behind the mountains.

"The airport is shared between the two countries. I think you can land here and go to France without officially entering Switzerland." said Kyle.

"Interesting, that's the first time I've heard of that. He's on final. Let's see how smoothly he puts it down."

Seconds later the commercial jet landed a little harder than usual.

"Well I think 'Captain Crunch' needs a little more practice, don't you?" said Jen with a smile.

"Maybe a little, but it wasn't too bad considering the current crosswind conditions," said Kyle, returning her smile.

Travelling without any luggage was as easy as it gets. Kyle and Jen let most of the other passengers off the aircraft first and then walked casually out and into the main terminal building.

"Do you need anything at all before we go? They have few stores here at the terminal," said Jen as she approached a small line of automated bank machines. Jen inserted her bank card to withdraw some extra cash, at least enough to get them comfortably back to Portland next week.

"Are you sure there isn't anything you need?" asked Jen again as the machine started to dispense some cash.

"Not really Jen. I'm sure they'll have everything we need when we get to the Collider."

Jen was still staring at the printed bank receipt from her chequing account. "There must be some mistake," said Jen, still staring at the bank receipt.

Her mind was doing the quick math from her agreements with James, but she had far more funds in her account than she expected to have. With her card still in the machine, she requested a printed version of her 'recent transactions' and found a very large deposit posted on today's date. She knew she could verify it later on, but it was almost certainly from Bill Riker.

"Planet Earth to Mars—is everything okay Jen?" asked Kyle, obviously aware of her temporary distraction.

"Yes, I'm sorry, everything's fine. I think I know exactly what you need before we go. I'm going to buy you a real latte!"

"Triple sugar?"

"Triple sugar it is. Follow me. That little cafe over there will make them for sure."

They both had waited patiently as the two baristas prepared several different specialty coffees, including Kyle's large latte. Jen had ordered a passion fruit and mango green tea, medium with the bag on the side.

"Would you like something to snack on Kyle? They have some delicious looking things in the pastry cabinets here."

"No thanks," said Kyle as he stirred three heaping spoons of sugar into his latte. "Should we sit down and drink them here?" asked Jen.

"I'm anxious to get up to the Collider to be honest, but we can if you like."

"I like your idea. Why don't you take a lid for your latte and pass me one for my green tea?"

"There you go. No sugar for your tea?"

"No, I don't use it. I like it just the way it is. Ready?"

"Sure, let's go!"

The automated front doors opened as they approached and they both walked outside. The sun was starting to go down and there were still lots of people coming and going outside the terminal. A line of taxis extended back from the taxi sign and people were lined up and loading into the lead car.

"Up here Jen!" said Kyle with his excellent vision. The next sign post past the taxi sign said 'Mass Hadron Collider, Confirmed Guests Only' and they both walked up to the young, heavy-set woman waiting beside the sign.

She was dressed in an official looking full length dark blue coat and a matching hat, a gold MHC logo was sewn on her coat with a matching gold pin adorned the front of her hat.

"Your names please?" she asked politely.

"Jennifer Lamar and Kyle Clayton," said Jen.

"Do you have picture papers?" asked the young woman.

Jen pulled out their passports and showed them to her.

"I have you on our list," she said with a peculiar smile. "Please follow me."

Kyle and Jen followed her slow steps as she walked the short distance up to a black limousine parked by the curb.

"I hope you both enjoy your stay here at the Collider, you should be arriving in about forty minutes," said the woman as she opened the rear door for them.

Kyle got in first and then Jen. Both of them were grateful they had decided to take lids for their hot drinks.

"Thanks," said Jen as the woman was preparing to close the door.

"Oh, you're very, very, very welcome," said Sarah as she pushed the door shut with both hands.

The door closed tight and the auto locks engaged. They were both admiring the deluxe interior in the back of the limousine as it pulled away from the curb. Kyle was sipping his hot latte and wondering why all the rear-view mirrors were covered with black tape when Jen started giggling away in her seat. Kyle looked over and saw Jen swinging her teabag back and forth like a little kid, pointing to the silly gold tassels, hanging from Sinzar's strange purple hat.

15841610R00336

Made in the USA
Charleston, SC
23 November 2012